REQUIEM OF THE HUMAN SOUL

REQUIEM
of the
HUMAN SOUL

J E R E M Y   R.   L E N T

2009

PERMISSIONS

A Hard Rain's A-Gonna Fall
Words and music by BOB DYLAN
© 1963 by Warner Bros. Inc.
Copyright renewed 1991 by Special Rider Music.
All rights reserved. International copyright secured. Reprinted by permission.

Mind Games
Words and music by JOHN LENNON
© 1973 (Renewed 2001) LENONO.MUSIC.
All rights controlled and administered by EMI BLACKWOOD MUSIC INC.
All rights reserved. International copyright secured. Used by permission.

Big Yellow Taxi
Words and music by JONI MITCHELL
© 1970 (Renewed) CRAZY CROW MUSIC.
All rights administered by SONY/ATV MUSIC PUBLISHING,
8 Music Square West, Nashville, TN 37203.
All rights reserved. Used by permission of ALFRED PUBLISHING CO., INC.

The name **Foreign Affairs** is used by permission of the Council on Foreign Relations. The article published under the name *Foreign Affairs* is an entirely fictional creation and should in no way be viewed as representing the current or future views of *Foreign Affairs*.

Design and layout by Vancouver Desktop Publishing Centre.
Printed in Canada by Printorium Bookworks.

To Chief Joseph,
and to the countless, unnamed souls like him.

"History is the story told by the victors."

Contents

Timeline

1 Harry Shields

Oh, where have you been, my blue-eyed son?
And where have you been my darling young one?

I'm making my way down a corridor in the United Nations building in Manhattan. My heart pounding out of control. My temples beating so hard against my brain I can hear nothing else but their thud-thud. I'm carrying in my pocket a little metal object that will bring utter destruction to everybody around me in just a few moments. I am the bringer of doom. I am the savior of my human race. I am a confused, desperate man who knows what he needs to do. I find the right door. I enter. I am about to unleash a destruction on a greater scale than the world has ever seen. I am about to save my race. How did I get here? How did I get here?

"Now, Eusebio, do you happen to have an idea of how many tigers were freely roaming the wilds of Asia during the late nineteenth century, just three hundred years ago?"

I'm sitting in a comfortable conference room, with leather chairs and oak paneling, thick carpet and soft lights. I'm with two d-humans. At least, that's what we call them. They just think of themselves as humans. To them, we're the ones who don't fit. To them, we're Primals. Made from primal human DNA. Completely unenhanced.

One of the d-humans, a beautiful woman, looks like she's in her thirties. Then again, all d-human women look beautiful, so this doesn't distinguish her. Her name is Naomi Aramovich. She has strawberry blonde, slightly wavy hair, warm brown eyes overflowing with kindness. The other d-human is tall and muscular, with a strong face sporting a thick mustache. D-humans are all much taller than us but this one's real big—close to seven feet. His eyes blue. His face cold and steely. His name Harry Shields. He's the one asking the questions.

"No. No idea," I reply. How would I know the answer to a question like that? Sure, I'm a history teacher. But not that kind of history. I teach my tenth-graders about the American Indians, the Aboriginals. The people who roamed free on this earth before men like Harry Shields came and devastated them.

"Well, best estimates are there were over a hundred thousand of these magnificent creatures in the jungles of India and Southeast Asia."

"Uh huh." I have no idea where he's going with this.

"And do you know how many tigers existed in the wild a hundred years later, at the beginning of the third millennium?"

"No."

"Well, believe it or not, there were less than five thousand of these great creatures left in the wild by that time. Of course, by then, there were conservation projects under way to save the tiger from extinction. Sadly, they didn't work. Do you know the last time a tiger was seen in the wild?"

"No, I don't."

"The mid-twenty thirties, about a hundred and fifty years ago. Now, Eusebio, let me ask you this. Why did the tiger become extinct?"

"I don't know exactly," I respond. "I guess hunting . . . and no more jungle."

"Not bad. Now, who do you think was responsible for the hunting?"

"Well, I'm not sure. I guess probably the English colonialists . . . and then the local people."

"And who do you think was responsible for the loss of the jungle?"

"Probably a lot of people. The local developers, I guess, who cleared the jungles for farming . . . and the villagers."

"And what, Eusebio, is in common between all those people you just described?"

"I don't know what you mean," I answer.

"Think about the only thing that all these people have in common."

"I can't think of anything. They were all human beings," I reply.

"Wrong, Eusebio, not human beings. They were all Primals. It was the Primal race, your race, who colluded in the extinction of the tigers, wasn't it, Eusebio?"

There is nothing I can say. I nod.

"Please speak up, Eusebio." Harry Shields' tone is more haranguing, more prosecutorial. "Was the Primal race responsible, single-handedly, for the extinction of the tigers in the wild?"

"Yes. I guess it was." I have to tell the truth. I have no choice. I'm sitting in a neurographic chair. A special armchair, with another set of "arms" extending around the back and both sides of my head. These "arms" are a few inches away from my head. I can hear a slight hum around me, and I know that millions of scans each second are piercing through the neurons of my brain, creating neurographic images of my thoughts. It immediately detects if I lie and sets off an alarm. They call that a "neurographic event." I've already had one of those, and I don't want another.

"Now answer me this, Eusebio. Was there ever a commission held to identify the responsible parties? Was there ever an 'extinction crimes' tribunal? Did the Primal race even call it a crime?"

"Not that I know of," I was forced to reply.

"Now, Counsel Aramovich and the Primal Rights group have been arguing for years in this PEPS session that it's a crime, prima facie, to carry out the extinction of the Primal species. Please answer me this, Eusebio: why should we view it as a crime to implement the extinction of the Primals when the Primals themselves were prepared to drive countless other species to extinction without anyone being held accountable?"

I was stunned. How dare this d-human, who looked liked he wouldn't give a damn if every animal in the world disappeared . . . how dare he use this argument to extinguish the future of my race!

The PEPS session. That's what I was participating in. The Proposed Extinction of the Primal Species. A set of hearings at the United Nations, going on for years, about whether our race should be eliminated from this earth. There are seven billion d-humans in the world and just three billion of us. But that's three billion too many, from their point of view. And I'm the Primal witness, on the stand for my race. That's why I was abducted from my little community of Tuckers Corner. Because Naomi Aramovich and her fellow Primal Rights activists chose me to defend my race.

And I seemed to be doing a lousy job of it so far.

I tried to think quickly and logically.

"You can't use an argument like this, Harry, and get away with it," I responded angrily. "Whatever crimes were committed in the past, whatever wrongs were done, they were done by the ancestors of all of us—d-humans and Primals alike. You can't accuse Primals alone for what was done in the past."

"Eusebio," he responded, "by the time the tigers were completely extinct in the wild, there were no d-humans, as you call them, of voting age anywhere in the world. The earliest 'PNOs', as they used to be called, pre-natally optimized humans, were born in the late 2020s and would just have been learning to read and write when the last tiger died in the wild. How could you possibly accuse my race of involvement in a crime that your race alone committed? You know as well as I do, Eusebio, the first time a d-human was elected President of the United States was the end of the twenty-first century. Anything done to the world in that century was done by Primals, not d-humans. So, of course I can—and should—accuse the Primals of making the tigers extinct. Has anything changed in the nature of the Primal, that whatever led them to destroy the tigers is no longer true of you and the rest of your race? If so, please tell me about it."

I was so struck by this heartless prosecutor accusing me and my race of mercilessly destroying the tigers, that I couldn't think clearly for a few moments. I've always cared deeply for the animals around me. I thought of my cat, Jigger, how I would pull the ticks off her when she returned from her forays in the fields behind my house. Suddenly, I worried what would be happening to Jigger, now that I was gone from Tuckers Corner. Then, I thought of the Barlows, my neighbors, a warm and friendly elderly couple. They would look after her.

And then my mind was back to the present, to the PEPS session conference room, and Harry Shields' accusations.

"How can you condemn a whole race," I argued, "for the actions of just a few? It wasn't the whole Primal race that killed the tigers. Most people in the world had nothing to do with it." I felt I had him cornered.

"By the first half of the twenty-first century, this simply wasn't true," came Harry's response. "If you look at the record of the time, there was massive global awareness of the plight of the tiger. International treaties to prevent trade in tiger skins, global organizations telling the world how close the tiger was to extinction. Any literate person knew the tiger was disappearing. But all anyone accomplished was to delay it by a decade or two."

Harry continued his barrage. "Eusebio, you're a history teacher. You know that by the twenty-first century, when the world seriously wanted to accomplish something, they could do so. UN peacekeepers were sent to trouble spots. Were any peacekeepers sent to India to control poachers? Did the wealthy countries fund programs to persuade the villagers not to raze to the ground the last of the jungles where the tigers lived?" Harry paused for a moment. "No, Eusebio, none of these things were done. The whole global community of Primals was responsible for the tiger's extinction. They all colluded in their acceptance of the inevitable and assuaged their collective conscience by making noble, empty speeches, signing international treaties that did nothing."

"Tell me, Eusebio," Harry spoke to me now in a quieter voice. "Use your own knowledge of that time. If preventing the tiger's extinction had been a priority for the Primals, wouldn't they have achieved it?"

I knew I couldn't lie. "Yes," I whispered back. But I still couldn't accept how he was using the tiger's extinction to justify wiping out our race. I came up with another approach.

"There's a huge difference," I said, "between what happened to the tigers and your PEPS proposal. The people of the time never planned to eliminate the tigers. They never proposed a campaign to wipe them out. They just had other priorities."

Harry seemed to have been expecting this line of argument. He smiled, and without a moment's hesitation, answered me back.

"Eusebio, under international law, if you have the power to stop a crime, but do nothing about it, you're guilty of conspiracy." Harry turned to Naomi. "Counsel Aramovich, can you confirm this is true?"

"Yes, it is, Counsel Shields," Naomi responded. "I would point out that frequently, judges will give a more lenient sentence to someone who was not the key protagonist."

Thanks, Naomi, that was a big help, I thought to myself. You're supposed to be on my side.

Harry turned back to me with a satisfied smirk. "Now, Eusebio, I put it to you that the PEPS proposal is far more humane, far more legitimate and fair, than what your Primal race did to the tigers. Most of the tigers died from starvation, shot for their skins, or caught in traps, dying in agony from their wounds. Our PEPS proposal won't harm a single Primal. No Primal children will be watching their mother get shot in front of them and then starve to death because their mother's milk is gone."

Harry Shields looked up to the ceiling and let out his breath with a slow, whooshing sound, a phony expression of sorrow on his face. Then, he turned back to me, accusingly.

"That's how most tiger cubs died, Eusebio," he continued. "No Primal will be hurt and certainly no Primal will be killed as a result of our proposal. We're merely looking at a gradual reduction in the Primal race over generations, permitting all Primals to live out their lives to their natural conclusion. And our PEPS proposal is honest and legitimate. We're going through due process. We're not acting like the Primals of the twenty-first century, saying one thing in the UN while permitting the exact opposite to happen in the real world."

I was clearly getting nowhere. It was true what he said. They weren't going to kill any of us with their PEPS proposal. D-human society is too civilized for that. No ugly killings, no massacres, none of the horrific atrocities our Primal race has blotted all through its sordid history. It's a clean, humane extinction plan. A radioactive compound called Isotope 909. Once released, it will partially sterilize the ovaries of all Primal women around the world, but have no effect whatsoever on d-human women. Partially sterilize. Because any Primal woman who hasn't yet had a child will still be able to give birth once. Just once.

So the Primal species will just gradually fade away. It's a bland euthanasia, painless and victimless, that creates a final solution to what they call the "Primal Question." Once we're down to about twenty-five thousand, roughly twelve generations from now, they won't let us disappear entirely. They'll use cloning techniques to keep our population stable. And they'll keep the remaining Primals safely enclosed on reservations.

Yeah, a lot more civilized than what we did to the tigers. But I couldn't let him get away with this. It simply made no sense to me that the loss of a hundred thousand tigers could justify the extinction of three billion humans. That was utterly ridiculous. I realized this was the argument I'd missed—and I told him so.

"That's just absurd!" I added angrily. I did the math quickly in my head. "You're talking about an extinction thirty thousand times greater than the tigers."

Harry Shields sneered back at me. "Oh, so it's a numbers game," he replied sardonically. "The crime of extinction is a function of how many there were to begin with? Well, under that approach, I guess the worst crime of all would be the extinction of cockroaches and flies, because there are so many more of them. And so, the rarer a particular species is, the more acceptable it is to wipe it out. Is that what you're telling me, Eusebio?"

Harry's arguments were driving me to distraction. I just knew his logic was flawed, but I couldn't make any headway. Everything I tried made me look more ridiculous, but I knew it was *his* position which was absurd. I tried to calm myself and think carefully.

Why was I so angry? I realized we humans believe there's something special about us, something that makes us more important than other species. Was this really true or was it simply that we'd always been the ones in charge, so we could get away with believing it? If so, my race was in trouble, because the d-humans were now the ones in charge. If there really was something truly special about us—then I knew I'd better figure it out right now.

I leveled back my gaze to Harry Shields. "OK, Harry, it's not about numbers. There's something special about human beings— about Primals. Something that would make the PEPS proposal a far greater crime than the extinction of other species."

"So what's that, Eusebio?"

"Well, to begin with, there's language." Finally, I'd hit on something.

"So it's language, the ability to conceptualize thoughts and feelings and communicate it on different levels, which makes Primals special? And that's why we can't compare the extinction of other species to the PEPS proposal?" Harry said.

"Yes," I replied firmly. I felt I'd finally scored a major point.

Harry was silent for a few moments. He appeared blocked in his line of arguments. He seemed to be thinking. Then, very calmly, he spoke up again.

"Now, Eusebio, I'm going to play some sounds for you. Listen carefully and see if you can guess what they are."

Harry pushed a button on the console in front of him. I began to hear deep rumbling sounds. They seemed to tear through me. They started softly, wavered, became more intense. They seemed to have a melody, but this was no music I'd ever heard. What struck me was the range of feelings and, at the same time, an almost infinite complexity. I had no idea what I was hearing. But I knew this was something special. I was moved by the sounds, by their emotion, even though I didn't know what I was feeling. After a while, I realized I could sense a sadness, an anger, but there was a depth way beyond those feelings.

Harry hit the "stop" button. The sounds ended.

"Any idea, Eusebio?"

"None. No idea at all."

"Could you feel anything?"

"Yes, sadness. Anger. But something else . . . I don't know . . . "

"Would you say the sounds were simple or complex?"

"Very, very complex."

Harry betrayed a look of smug victory as he started speaking again.

"Those sounds, Eusebio, are recordings of elephants performing a ritual over the bones of one of their family. They are infra-sound—sound that travels at such low frequency that we can't hear it. At the end of the twentieth century, Eusebio, some of your Primal ancestors discovered the existence of elephants' infra-sound. That recording was speeded up about fifty times into a frequency we can hear. In case you're interested, Eusebio, what you heard was a family of elephants performing a ritual of ancestor worship, slowly passing to each other, with their trunks, the bones of a great bull elephant shot by an ivory poacher a few months earlier. The elephants spent two hours reminiscing in turn about their lost friend."

Harry turned to me with a conspiratorial expression. "You know, Eusebio, it took decades of research before they cracked the code of the elephants' language. It's lucky they took a lot of recordings during that time. Any idea why?"

I shook my head.

"I'll tell you why. Because by the time your Primal ancestors had finally cracked the code, there were no elephants left in the wild. All the herds had disappeared along with their habitat. No wild elephants in Africa. No wild elephants in Asia. Only 'slave elephants'—born into captivity. And, you know what, Eusebio?"

I was feeling sick in the pit of my stomach. I shook my head silently.

"The 'slave elephants' stopped speaking except for very basic communications. By the time your Primal ancestors had finally discovered the complexities and subtleties of the elephant language, there were no elephants left for them to talk to."

Suddenly, he changed his demeanor and raised his hand, pointing his finger at me. "Now, Eusebio, tell me again what you were saying about language, because it didn't seem to have saved the elephants."

I was dumbfounded. I looked across at Naomi Aramovich for help, but she seemed strangely distracted with a glazed expression on her face. She seemed to be doodling idly on her PDA. I was silent. I'd already been defeated by the PEPS session. And this was just my first day. Then, I realized I had one last, desperate argument I could make.

"OK, Harry, but there *is* a reason why you can't compare the extinctions of other species to your PEPS proposal. No matter what you say about the difference between Primals and d-humans, we're really the same species."

I was remembering, too late, how Naomi had told me yesterday they had already used this argument—and lost. I kept going anyway.

"Even if we accepted that you d-humans are better in some way, because you're genetically optimized—and I don't accept that—but even if it were true, you'd be committing a terrible crime with your PEPS proposal, because you'd be destroying your own species."

"How can you say we're the same species?" Harry responded. "What do you base that on?"

Now I'm not a technical person, but I thought this would be an easy one.

"On our DNA of course. We have essentially the same DNA, with the exception of the genes optimized for d-humans."

"In a recent study comparing a d-human," Harry responded,

"such as Counsel Aramovich or me, with a Primal such as you, it turns out that nearly one per cent of our functional DNA is different. I think the amount of identical functional DNA is approximately 99.3 per cent."

Yes! I'd finally scored a point. "So, you see, we're almost identical," I exclaimed with relief.

Harry ignored my comment, and continued talking. "Now, the Primals who first developed DNA sequencing, in the early twenty-first century, did the same type of analysis comparing the Primals' functional DNA with that of the chimpanzee. Do you know what per cent was identical?"

As usual, I shook my head with a sinking feeling.

"99.4 per cent. That's right, Eusebio, your DNA is closer to the chimpanzee than to us. Unfortunately, that didn't stop your Primal ancestors from killing off the chimpanzees in the wild, too. They survived longer than their close cousins, the other great apes. The mountain gorillas, bonobos, and orangutans all died out in the first half of the twenty-first century. The chimpanzees survived another few decades. And, to the credit of some of the Primals, they used to use the same arguments that you just used, that it would be a crime for the Primals to kill off their closest living relative. Sadly, not enough people listened to this argument. Or at least, if they listened, they didn't care."

"So, Eusebio, if your own Primal race couldn't be bothered to save its closest cousin, why should we listen to that argument now? It's the ultimate in hypocrisy."

I can't bear to describe the rest of the morning. Harry Shields went through the litany of extinct species, seemingly without end. The loyal African hunting dog. The gentle and peaceful sloth, once hanging down from the trees of the jungle that no longer existed. The shy okapi with its big ears, hidden deep in the African rainforest until there was no more rainforest to hide in.

It was torture to be blamed, one by one, for the crimes of my ancestors. Naomi Aramovich didn't raise a single finger to help me. By the end of the morning, I was hungry and tired and I just wanted the haranguing to end. I kept looking at the cold, hard eyes of Harry Shields, thinking to myself, if he'd lived two hundred years earlier, he would have been one of the very people he was now condemning—a cold, heartless bureaucrat making decisions to fund some development project that wiped out another ten thousand square miles of primeval rainforest. And if I'd lived two hundred years ago, I'd have been a schoolteacher, watching nature shows on TV and donating more than I could afford to the World Wildlife Fund.

And here was I, on the dock for my fellow human beings, being accused by this hypocritical prosecutor for these crimes, when he was the one trying to carry out the greatest extinction program in history.

Then, finally, as the morning drew to a close, I remembered the conversation I'd had with Naomi the day before, when she'd been describing the struggle of her Primal Rights group against the PEPS proposal. *"We lost the arguments about the ethics. We lost the argument on enlightened self-interest. We've retreated to one final argument . . . The Primal soul."*

After receiving yet another battering from Harry Shields about how eighty per cent of the globe's biodiversity had been destroyed by the brutal devastation conducted by our Primal race, I summoned up the last energy I had left, took a deep breath and blurted out:

"The human soul."

Harry Shields stopped in his tracks.

"The what?"

"The human soul. If you carry out your PEPS proposal you'll be committing a crime greater than all the devastation we caused. You'll be destroying the human soul."

Naomi's face suddenly lit up for the first time in hours. Harry looked like he'd received a body blow. In a second, he regained his composure, but something had changed. His prosecutorial tone had momentarily disappeared. He looked over at Naomi and said, in a quiet, matter-of-fact voice:

"Counsel Aramovich, the Primal witness has raised the question of the human soul. I'd like to propose that we adjourn now for lunch, and when we return, we'll take up this question."

I felt, for the first time since the beginning of the session, that I'd done something right.

Naomi smiled. "Sure, Counsel Shields, I think that makes sense." She looked over at me. "Eusebio, let's go for a moment to the Privileged Room next door."

With that, the morning session was over, and I got out of my neurographic chair, battered and exhausted. But I'd finally made a stand for humanity.

2 Naomi Aramovich

I heard the sound of a thunder, it roared out a warnin'
I heard the roar of a wave that could drown the whole world

I was standing in the Privileged Room with Naomi.

"How could you just sit there and watch me take all that abuse from Harry Shields?" I shot out my words at Naomi with anger pent-up from the hours of verbal pounding I'd just endured.

"Don't worry, Eusebio, you did just fine." Naomi was her usual unperturbed, cheery self.

"What do you mean—'I did just fine'? It was a slaughter. I don't see any point in even carrying on this hearing. Harry Shields ran circles around me."

At this point, Naomi actually chuckled. "No, Eusebio, that's not how it was at all. There was nothing you could say. There is simply no way to defend the past actions of the Primals from any moral or ethical perspective.

"But that's not the point of these hearings, Eusebio. I was just waiting for you to get to where you finally ended—the human soul. Remember what we talked about yesterday? That's our last legitimate defense. The only valid basis for stopping the PEPS proposal. That's why we brought you here to represent the Primal species, Eusebio—to talk about the human soul. Not to defend crimes of your ancestors which are simply indefensible."

It was true what Naomi said. I thought back to the day before. The first time I'd ever set eyes on Naomi Aramovich. Ever heard of the PEPS proposal. Ever saw New York City.

"It seemed like we were finished," Naomi had said to me yesterday.

Prepping me for Harry Shields. In a luxury hotel room in New York. My velvet prison. "They were steamrolling ahead with the PEPS proposal." Naomi had looked intently at me. "And then we came up with one final argument. It's a long shot. But we're desperate. There's nothing else between this argument and the implementation of PEPS."

"What's the argument?" I had asked.

"The Primal soul. We're trying to use the very argument that was the basis of your Humanist society founded by Dr. Schumacher."

Dr. Schumacher? I couldn't believe what I'd just heard. What was a d-human doing mentioning the ideas of our founder, Dr. Julius Schumacher, from a hundred years ago? Dr. Schumacher, the developer of neurography, a double Nobel Prize winner and one of the most respected men in the world—until he came up with the theory that manipulating the human genome might, just possibly, extinguish the human soul. The world didn't want to hear this. Dr. Schumacher became a prophet to a small number of people, and a pariah to the rest. His few followers, called Humanists, avoided any kind of genetic enhancement for their offspring because they didn't want to risk what might happen to their children's souls. Everyone else ignored him. But my great-grandparents were part of that small group of Humanists. And that's why I was born human. A Primal.

I had to ask Naomi more about this. What did she know about Dr. Schumacher's ideas? Why did that matter to her? But she didn't give me a chance. She was on a roll.

"It's not an easy argument to make," she continued. "We're trying to tell our own people we've lost something that many claim doesn't even exist."

And that was the first time I heard that the only thing that lay between my race and extinction was our soul. Something that couldn't be seen. Couldn't be measured. Couldn't even be proven to exist. And what the hell did that have to do with me, anyway?

So that's how it all began. Well, I guess, to be accurate, it began an hour or two earlier than that. When I first woke up in that hotel room.

A strange, luxurious hotel room. What had happened? Where the hell was I? I wracked my brain. The last thing I could remember was sitting at home in Tuckers Corner, alone, eating my dinner and researching for the history course I was giving to my tenth-graders. I heard a noise in my apartment and went to investigate. I was hit by something and passed out. I don't know how long ago. It felt like days, judging by my hunger.

Why was I here? Who? What? Where? The questions overwhelmed my brain but then my bodily needs trumped them all. I put on the freshly pressed, brand new bathrobe hanging next to the bed, walked into the spacious bathroom with marble floors and limestone walls, and took a piss into the grandest toilet bowl I'd ever seen in my life. Walked back into the bedroom, when a soft announcement-like tone chimed. A three-dimensional image of a d-human woman appeared.

"Welcome to New York, Eusebio Franklin," she said. "My name is Naomi Aramovich. I'm an attorney from a group fighting for Primal rights. You're our guest here, Eusebio. I hope you're comfortable. We have you staying in one of the best hotels in New York."

"Why am I here? What's happened to me?" I asked. Totally confused.

"I'll be at your hotel room within an hour, and then I'll answer all your questions. In the meantime you must be hungry. Push the button on the wall over there, and you can order automated room service."

The image of Naomi Aramovich disappeared. I walked to the door of the hotel room and found it was locked.

Guest? I thought to myself. I feel more like a prisoner.

I walked over to the window, stretching floor to ceiling. The curtains automatically drew themselves open, allowing me to see the spectacular sight below. I sucked in my breath. I was in a skyscraper high above New York—the City on the Water. Around and below me dozens of other skyscrapers, joined together by countless enclosed bridges, forming one gigantic three-dimensional grid. Far below, I could see the waters of the Atlantic Ocean, from which the skyscrapers rose.

I'd heard of the grandeur of the three-dimensional grid that was

New York. How the skyscrapers had all once been on dry land until the sea level rose, and how they'd built the skyways linking all the buildings to each other when the water overwhelmed the streets. But I'd never actually seen it. I was awe-struck.

Finally, breakfast ordered and eaten, the door opened and Naomi walked in. She was tall, with the classic features of a film star. Not surprising. She was, after all, a d-human. Her features were attractive, but not awe-inspiring, so I guessed she came from a well-to-do, middle-class family that decided to invest in her intelligence and personality and not just her good looks.

Her face was warm. Her manner engaging. But when she sat down to talk with me, a heavy, somber mood took over.

"I need to explain to you some very disturbing things, Eusebio. Please listen carefully, and understand very clearly—I'm on your side. I've been a Primal Rights activist for many years. I've spent most of my career fighting to give your race a voice in its own destiny. That's the reason you're here. It hasn't been easy, but we've finally gained agreement from UNAPS for you to speak at a special session of the PEPS hearing. You will be the voice of your race."

I'd heard of UNAPS—the United Nations Authority on the Primal Species. But at that point, I'd never heard of PEPS.

Naomi took me through the math. The magic number the demographic experts had come up with was 38 per cent. That is, each new generation of Primals would number about 38 per cent of the previous generation. That, Naomi explained, took into account all the demographic variables like infant mortality, life expectancy, etcetera, etcetera.

Right now, according to Naomi, there were about three billion Primals on the Earth. Eight generations from now—it'll be around a million. Another four generations, and we'll be at twenty-five thousand. Time for the reservations and cloning to keep the number constant.

People supported PEPS because of its humanity and decency. A genocide without killing a single creature. Naomi told me that she, along with a small group of Primal Rights activists, had been fighting against it for years. They'd been using—and losing—all the arguments they could muster.

The enormity of what she was saying began to pulse through me. I suddenly realized my body was trembling. Shuddering. The adrenaline was pulsing so quickly I was having difficulty controlling myself. Naomi kept rattling on. Clearly, this was a subject near and dear to her heart. I didn't want her to see how I was suffering. As if I had some pride to maintain in front of her.

"First," Naomi went on, "we made the legal arguments against genocide. That got blocked right away because they define Primals as a different species, so international law doesn't apply."

"So then," Naomi looked wistfully to the ceiling, "we worked on the ethical angle. Even if Primals are a different species, we have no right to pull the plug on them."

"Well, of course," I responded, trying to keep my voice calm. By now, my trembling was back under control. "So how did they deal with that?"

Naomi shook her head. "We got blown away. They just pointed to what the Primals had done to other species, tigers, polar bears, gorillas . . . the list just kept going. If the Primals wiped out these other species, why should they be treated any different?"

That's when she told me their argument about the human soul. Our last stand against extinction.

I was silent. I was looking at Naomi, trying to figure her out. How could she make an argument to save my race, by denying her own possession of a soul? I had a lot of figuring to do.

Naomi was shaking her head slowly. Then, suddenly, more animated, she gazed across at me.

"Finally, UNAPS agreed to our demands. A hearing where a representative of the Primal species could speak up for his own race. "

As she was talking, an unbearably heavy dread began weighing on me like a lead thundercloud. I began to realize that this "representative" of my race that she was talking about was none other than me. Why me? What was special about me? Nothing that I could think of. I knew immediately I wasn't up to the task. The dread infused every molecule of my being. I could hardly stand each moment. And she kept talking to me.

"We were given permission to select a Primal to speak at the PEPS hearing. This wasn't easy. On the one hand, we wanted somebody truly representative of the Primal race. On the other hand, a typical Primal is barely literate."

Naomi looked over at me with an expression of profound pity, as though I were suffering from an extreme form of disfiguring leprosy.

"You see, Eusebio, I'm terribly sorry to say it, but the vast majority of your fellow Primals live in dire conditions. They are the global underclass, Eusebio, who could never come close to affording even the most basic genetic enhancement. For the most part, they're illiterate, starving and diseased."

Naomi paused for a moment, looking thoughtful, then continued.

"And then there are the groups against genetic enhancement ideologically. Religious fundamentalists, conspiracy theorists . . . there's no end of groups like that. But they could hardly represent the whole Primal race."

Naomi looked intensely over to me and grabbed my hand, like we were close friends. Her fingers felt warm and vibrant.

"Eusebio, we decided to find someone from the Humanists, because they're educated, they understand their own history. And with the tradition of Dr. Schumacher, perhaps they could answer questions about the human soul."

I was finding this hard to comprehend. Out of the billions of people in this world, why would anyone think of us, the Humanists, as representative of anything? There are not much more than, perhaps, twenty thousand of us throughout the world.

By this time, Naomi was gazing intently at me. I didn't want to return her gaze. I didn't want to hear what she was saying. I felt I should be asking her all kind of intelligent questions. But I was in shock. Dumbstruck.

"We needed someone representative, genetically, of a broad spectrum of the Primal race. So, we took hair samples to check the genetic background of each of the possible candidates.

"There were five people, Eusebio, including you, who came back with DNA reasonably representative of the Primal race. In your case, your DNA turned out to be twelve per cent Negroid, fourteen per cent American Indian, eighteen per cent Semitic, eight per cent Asian and forty-eight per cent Caucasian. We're not crazy about the high percentage of Caucasian DNA, because so few Primals are Caucasian, but at least it's less than half."

"So you're saying you took a sample of my hair and analyzed it?"

"Yes. We entered your house one time when you weren't there and found some hair samples."

I felt violated. But Naomi kept going before I could respond.

"We then established certain suitability criteria," she continued. "We didn't want to take anyone who was part of a close-knit family structure. That eliminated two more candidates, leaving three of you."

She said it so dispassionately. "Certain suitability criteria . . . A close-knit family structure." For the millionth time in my life, I thought of Sarah. And our beautiful little daughter, Sally, who's no longer so little. Sarah, my love. But Sarah was no longer with me. Only deep within my soul. And Sally—well, she's across the ocean, living her own life. And so, I thought to myself, with a smoldering pain that never goes away, Naomi was right. No "close-knit family structure." Not anymore.

"So, finally, Eusebio, you were chosen as the representative of your Primal race. I was the one who made the final call, and in the end I used a special criterion. I liked you."

If she thought this would win me over, she was damn wrong. All I could feel was my anger. Anger at being kidnapped by these people. At their invasion of my privacy, my life. Anger at the notion that these d-humans were planning to put an end to our existence on this planet. Anger—mixed with dread—that for some bizarre reason, I should have been picked to defend my race.

"You can't do this to us! You can't do this to me! Who the hell do you think you are?" I finally found my voice and shouted out to Naomi.

Naomi remained unperturbed and earnest. "Remember, Eusebio— I'm on your side. I've been a Primal Rights campaigner for most of the forty years of my professional career. I've sacrificed far more prestigious opportunities in international law to keep up the campaign for your race."

In the middle of my rage, my mind stuck momentarily on something she had just said. Forty years! I looked at the woman across me who, in our society, I would have pegged as being in her mid to late thirties. I did some quick mental arithmetic and realized she was probably about seventy years old. It struck me like a body blow. The realization just made me angrier.

Naomi was still talking away. "When I was conceived, Eusebio, my parents prioritized my compassion gene set higher than the normal range. They were hoping I'd become somebody who would improve our society. They had no idea I'd focus my compassion on the Primal race, which they don't even view as part of our society. They hate what I've done with my life. It's not just my career that I've hurt by fighting for Primal rights."

My anger continued to overwhelm everything I was hearing. I spat out, derisively:

"So I'm supposed to feel bad for your career path while three billion of my race are headed for extinction!" As soon as I said it, I regretted it. I tried to remember it had been her choice to help us. Then I realized my comment had no more effect on her than a tame dog's snarl would have on its owner.

"No," Naomi replied. "You're supposed to feel the rage that you do feel about the plight of your race. That's one of the reasons you were chosen."

I looked at Naomi Aramovich. I saw her gazing back at me with her earnest, caring, beautiful face. For a moment, I hated her, sitting there sincerely telling me about the fate of my own people. I hated her for her perfection, for her good health, her beauty, her compassion. Then, I realized, it wasn't her, it was her society of d-humans that I hated for what they had allowed to happen to our race. I thought of the life of Julius Schumacher. Was this what he had foreseen and tried to prevent? Was there any way he could have managed to force back the tidal wave of technology?

Naomi was silent, looking at me. Was she wondering what I was thinking, how I would react? Or was she so sure of my reaction, after her analysis of everything about me, that she was merely being polite?

My life hadn't prepared me for this. That was one thing I was sure about.

"So what is it you want me to do?" I asked Naomi.

"To act as the representative of the Primal race in the PEPS hearing."

"What does that involve?"

"You just need to take part in a discussion with me and one other person. His name is Harry Shields. He'll ask you questions and you simply need to answer them. Truthfully and honestly. That's all."

"That's all?"

"Yes. We agreed with the PEPS authorities in advance to keep the hearing small and informal. You don't need to be intimidated by a big, formal affair."

Again, I felt my skin crawl. She talked about me the way I would talk about my pet cat, Jigger.

"Of course," she added, "Everything that's being said will be recorded for further analysis and posterity. Also, it's accepted procedure in any legal hearing for you to sit in a neurographic scanner. You won't notice anything; it's just a special type of chair with a frame around the head so you can be neurographically analyzed."

"Neurographically analyzed?"

"Yes, it identifies if you're not being truthful and analyzes what you're actually thinking. No legal hearing takes place without it. Nothing that's said outside a neurographic scanner could be legally binding."

I felt the anger welling up inside me again.

"Well, why the hell do you need to speak with me? Just wire me up, ask me questions, and you'll know what I think."

As usual, Naomi remained unperturbed.

"Because how you construct the thoughts in your head and transform them into syntax is an essential part of the process. The thoughts themselves mean very little without you turning them into what you say."

I had so many other questions, I didn't know where to begin.

"And what if I refuse to do this?"

For the first time, I saw a cloud pass over Naomi's shining eyes.

"Eusebio, part of our preparation is our analysis of your character. We know you won't refuse."

"But what if I do?"

"You'd be dooming your race to extinction without a fight. You wouldn't do that."

I knew she was right. I felt a sucking feeling deep within me, as if my insides were being vacuumed away.

"When does this hearing begin?"

"Tomorrow. Part of our agreement with UNAPS was that you shouldn't be corrupted by spending any time in d-human society. We wanted to make sure you were fresh from Tuckers Corner, pure and unadulterated."

Unadulterated? What were these people talking about? Again, I looked at Naomi Aramovich. I tried to see into her eyes. Who was this person? Did she have a soul? She seemed to be so caring for me and my fellow humans, and yet she was somebody so different. Something so different. Could I trust her? Did I have any choice?

I had no answers to these questions. I tried to look more deeply into those kind eyes, more piercingly. She kept smiling earnestly back at me. I tried, and I tried, but I couldn't get through behind the eyes. I couldn't make contact with something that would let me believe in her. All I knew was that I was caught up in something much larger than me. I had a part to play in a great, historical choreography but nobody had taught me any steps. And I had no choice but to dance.

At least, that's what I thought until Yusef appeared.

3 Yusef

I met a white man who walked a black dog

It was late in the evening. Naomi had left the hotel room. I was lying in bed. Naomi had pointed out a button next to the bed that would infuse the air with something called Monazepam to help me sleep.

I was lying in bed, thinking about the events that had pulled my life apart. I was about to push the Monazepam button when I heard a tone sound in the room. It was the same tone that had announced Naomi's 3-D image appearance earlier in the afternoon.

I turned the lights on and looked over at the 3-D imager. To my shock, I saw an image of a man staring at me.

"Who are you?" I barked out.

"Eusebio, have no fear. My name is Yusef. We need to talk with you. We've secretly re-wired your 3-D imager so I could visit you tonight."

I looked more closely at the man. He had neatly cropped black hair and slightly olive-colored skin. He was clean shaven with strong, attractive Semitic facial features. He had a slight guttural accent. He was wearing white clothing, which looked like something between a modern business suit and a robe.

"Who are you?" I repeated my question.

"Eusebio, I am a freedom fighter for our human race. I am speaking to you from somewhere in the Middle East. I can't tell you where."

"What do you want with me?"

"Eusebio, I'm here to tell you not to take part in the PEPS hearing."

I noticed that he kept beginning each answer with my name. It annoyed me. I realized, thinking back, that Naomi had done the same thing. They're all trying to build my trust, I thought to myself.

"How do you know about the PEPS hearing?" I asked Yusef.

"We know everything about the PEPS hearing. Much more than Naomi Aramovich would have told you this afternoon."

"Why don't you want me to take part in it? I don't understand." I responded.

"What do you know about the Rejectionists?" he asked me.

"The Rejectionists?" I was utterly clueless.

Yusef shook his head gently and smiled back at me.

"Eusebio, I've been sent to you by the Rejectionists. There are millions of humans like me who support them. We're the last refuge of free humanity in the world. The Rejectionists, Eusebio, are the d-humans who refuse to go along with the GALT treaty. They're waging a battle to save the human soul. And we help protect them."

I was stuck on something he'd said. What was the GALT treaty? I asked Yusef to explain.

"I'm sorry, Eusebio," Yusef answered me back softly. "We knew your community was isolated, but I just didn't realize how much. GALT was signed almost seventy years ago, Eusebio. For better or worse, it's the foundation of our modern world."

Yes, our little community of Tuckers Corner is completely isolated from the modern world. We have no access to the technologies the d-humans use to transmit their daily flow of information to each other. And, as the generations passed, we'd simply stopped caring.

"You need to know, Eusebio, as a fellow human being, what it is we're fighting for," Yusef continued.

He talked about the two decades of the Great Global Wars that finally ended in the early twenty-second century. Hundreds of millions dead—more deaths than all the combined previous wars in recorded history. How the wars arose from global climate change—people flooded out of their homes, looking for new places to live; famines from the severest droughts in history; deserts spreading throughout Africa, Asia, and South America. As these terrible events spun out of control, the poorest countries most vulnerable to disaster began to fight each other for access to water and arable land.

By the early twenty-second century, Yusef continued, the world had exhausted itself. The United Nations was given global policing power with a full-time army. Underlying this new peace was the Global Aggression Limitation Treaty.

Suddenly, Yusef became excited.

"Someone like Naomi Aramovich," he said, "will tell you that GALT was the greatest breakthrough in human history. An end to war. That it led to global prosperity, that it's the foundation for future progress. Nothing could be more wrong."

Yusef leaned forward and looked at me intently. For a moment, I completely forgot he was thousands of miles away, that I was just looking at a virtual reality image of him. He seemed right there in the flesh, next to me.

"GALT, Eusebio," Yusef almost whispered it to me, "was the beginning of our struggle for the human race."

As the world recovered from the destruction of the Great Global Wars, Yusef told me, the nations of the world vowed never to let such destruction occur again. They identified two sets of genes in human DNA—the "aggression" set and the "doctrinal belief" set. When both sets of genes were primary, it was a virtual certainty that the person would be violent or intolerant to others who didn't share his beliefs.

This, Yusef went on, formed the basis of GALT. All countries agreed that genetic optimization should only be allowed when it subordinated both the "aggression" and "doctrinal belief" gene sets in the embryo. The d-human society of the future would never again embark on the self-destruction that led to the Great Global Wars. Of course, every nation had to agree to this treaty, enforced by the UN. Otherwise, a rogue nation could secretly create a generation of warriors genetically equipped to conquer their less aggressive neighbors.

"It seemed like a worthy goal," Yusef explained, "but it came at a price that many could not accept—the ability to know God, the ability to remain human, to keep one's soul intact. It was, Eusebio, a Faustian bargain. You see, subordinating what they call the 'doctrinal belief' gene set does the most terrible thing to a human being—it prevents him or her from ever truly knowing God, from being in touch with the infinite."

Yusef could see he was reaching me. He leaned forward again, looking straight into my eyes.

"Eusebio, this is what led to the formation of the Rejectionists, people who believed there were alternative paths to peace than sacrificing man's contact with the infinite."

Yusef finally stopped and took a deep breath. "Did Naomi happen to tell you about Isotope 919?" he asked me.

"Isotope 919," I responded. "You mean what they plan to use to sterilize human women after they've had one birth?"

"No," he replied. "That's Isotope 909. Isotope 919 is much simpler. It immediately sterilizes human women. What Naomi didn't tell you is that the d-humans, those civilized, dispassionate officers of the UN, plan to use Isotope 909 on most of the humans in the world, but in the regions where Rejectionists are hiding out among humans—what they call the 'Believers' Belt'—they're going to use Isotope 919. Within a generation, the last free region of human beings will be completely eliminated, a deserted wasteland."

"Why?" I asked, although I had already guessed the answer.

Yusef sighed. "There's so much you don't know, Eusebio, and so little time to explain. The Rejectionists are the people the d-humans fear the most. They have access to Middle Eastern wealth that can buy weapons to fight GALT. They can mingle in d-human society and not be noticed. And with the support of millions of us humans, they have a potential army that could take power from the d-humans that rule our countries.

"In fact," Yusef continued, "some of us believe that destroying the Rejectionists is the real reason for the PEPS proposal. They want to dress it up with their sanitized long-term planning, gradually eliminating the so-called Primals, so they can win global support for what they're doing. Then, when nobody's looking, the military in the

Believers' Belt will substitute Isotope 919 for 909. No one will know for months. By then, it's too late."

I was beginning to wonder, at this point, if I wasn't hearing a paranoid fantasy.

"How am I meant to believe you?"

"By using your reason, Eusebio," Yusef answered. "You've been abducted from your society, against your will, by a d-human who's held you captive. Now, I'm a human, like you. I didn't kidnap you. A number of people had to risk their lives for me to speak with you tonight. Why should I be lying to you? Why should she be telling you the truth?"

He had a point. I was beginning to wonder about what I'd accepted unquestioningly from Naomi earlier in the day. I had, after all, looked into those kind eyes and found something missing deep down.

"So why would it make a difference whether or not I participate in this PEPS hearing?" I asked Yusef.

"You'll be legitimizing their process," he explained. "You will be their stooge."

"So are you telling me that Naomi is lying to me, that she's part of some evil conspiracy to destroy your people with this Isotope 919?" I asked Yusef.

"No, I'm not telling you that. They're using Naomi Aramovich too. I'm not even sure if Naomi knows about Isotope 919. She's the kind of person who would publicize it and argue against it if she knew. We think she's sincere, and the Primal Rights activists are well-meaning but misguided. Their very opposition gives validity to the legal process of the PEPS hearing. They're using her, just like they're about to use you, Eusebio."

By this time, my mind was a whirling mass of contradictions. After speaking with Naomi earlier, once I'd recovered from the initial dread, I'd felt a sense of purpose. At least there was something I could do to fight for my race. I could give it my best shot.

Now, Yusef had pulled my foundation from under me. It seemed that every choice I took would have dire consequences. Naomi had told me that refusing to take part in the PEPS hearing would doom my race. Now Yusef was telling me that taking part in the PEPS hearing would doom my race. I had nowhere to turn, no Julius Schumacher to give me guidance. I was, quite literally, clueless. And the future of my race depended on what I decided to do.

I looked at the 3-D image of Yusef. Directly into his eyes. I realized I was connecting deeper with him through his image than when I looked at Naomi earlier that afternoon, in the real flesh and blood. Did that mean I should believe Yusef instead of Naomi?

As I thought of refusing to attend the hearing, I was amazed by my own feelings. I realized I didn't want to disappoint Naomi. She and her fellow activists had spent years persuading UNAPS to have their hearing, and she'd chosen me to represent my race. I thought of the earnestness and kindness in her eyes.

I then realized, with a shock, that I didn't want to disappoint myself. Naomi, it seemed, had reached something in my ego that afternoon. I realized I'd been feeling proud that I would have this chance to defend my race. I was actually looking forward to the hearing tomorrow. I was going to kick some butt. Now, I had Yusef telling me I was their stooge, that the best thing I could do for my race was nothing, to walk away, not to take part in the great dance that had been arranged for me.

I spoke to Yusef's 3-D image:

"I need to think about this. About what you've told me. I'm not sure what I'm going to do."

I was lying. Deep down, I knew I wanted to defend my race in the hearing. I just didn't have the guts to tell Yusef the truth.

Yusef looked back at me. I knew he'd seen through me completely.

"Eusebio," he said, "I wish I could do a better job of explaining to you what you're getting yourself into. This is not a debating society. This is not a matter of pride, of how good you are at making your case. These are people who have no soul, people planning the extinction of our species. These people will stop at nothing to destroy us because we're inconvenient to their progress. Don't let them use you against your own race."

His voice took on a new tone of gravity.

"Eusebio, if you attend that PEPS hearing tomorrow, you will get yourself embroiled in something much greater and more disturbing than anything you can ever imagine. This is not what your life has been about. You will be completely out of your depth. For your own sake, don't do it."

I was beginning to get a little testy by now. "Yusef, please—enough. Leave me alone to think about it."

"OK, Eusebio. I'll leave you now. My brother, whatever you decide, we're with you. We are all brothers and sisters, we humans. We are fighting for our existence. We can't afford dissent among ourselves. I've told you what we believe and what we think is best for you. But whatever you do, we pray for your success, for your sake and for all our sakes. May God be with you."

With that, Yusef's image disappeared from my room.

Yusef's grace at his departure, in contrast with my abruptness, left me feeling rude and ashamed. In my society, integrity is our highest value. I'd just betrayed not only myself but everything I hold dear. I'd tried to get rid of Yusef because what he was saying disturbed me. And it disturbed me because it may have been true. I was overwhelmed. I thought about what Yusef had just said, *"you will be completely out of your depth."* I already felt that was too true.

I realized I had no way of getting in touch with Yusef. I couldn't continue the conversation with him even I wanted to. That was perhaps my one and only chance to discover the truth. I'd blown it.

But at the same time, I knew I was going to attend the PEPS hearing the next day. I wasn't going to boycott it. That was my destiny. I guess another way of putting it, less grandly, was that it was easier to keep going on the path set out for me, than to choose a different one.

Was I right? What could I possibly say to defend the human race against Harry Shields and UNAPS? I thought about the Great Global Wars and GALT. I thought about Dr. Julius Schumacher, how he'd fought so hard to prevent things from turning out the way they did. And why did Naomi mention him this afternoon? I hit the Monazepam button a couple of times—hard—and moments later, with images of Naomi, Yusef and Julius Schumacher flitting through my mind, I fell asleep.

4 Manhattan

I saw ten thousand takers whose tongues were all broken

An alarm chimed somewhere. I woke up. Morning. As I sat in bed and looked around at this hotel room, where the lights were gradually getting brighter, the thoughts of Naomi Aramovich, the PEPS hearing, and Yusef's visit flooded my mind. I gasped when I remembered where I was. And why.

The shower was the best I'd ever experienced. It was voice-activated, which took some getting used to. When I spoke "warmer," the water became warmer. When I yelled it, it suddenly became too hot. The towels were the softest I'd ever felt. Drying myself was like stroking a cat. A little card dropped out of the folded towel. *"Ultralux, genetically engineered for the finest in softness and absorbency."* They weren't kidding.

I found a gigantic closet in the room where—magically—my clothes from home had been taken, pressed, and renewed. They looked so good, I almost didn't recognize them. I hadn't seen my shoes, polished and gleaming like that, since I first bought them years ago.

The breakfast was exquisite. But I began to realize that the eggs were a little too "eggy," the bacon a little too "bacony." It didn't seem natural. Genetically engineered, I thought to myself, for the finest in egginess and baconicity.

I felt like I'd died and gone to hotel heaven. A heaven I had not chosen. A heaven where I was locked in. I thought of Yusef, last night, telling me: *"You will be their stooge."* I shuddered.

Naomi Aramovich arrived, cheery and condescending. She was

going to take me to the United Nations building, about twenty blocks from the hotel, where we would begin the PEPS proceeding. We walked out of the serene hotel room together, into the soft, calm hotel corridor. Then, up the elevator to a level called "Skywalk 4 Uptown," and as soon as the elevator doors opened, I was hit by a cacophony of noise and motion and people and lights and images and more noise roaring at me, like a series of slaps in the face.

As we stepped out of the elevator, I couldn't make sense of anything. Everywhere I looked, there were people moving. There were giant flat-screen panels everywhere, showing different images. Some looked like gigantic commercials, some looked like a sports game being played somewhere, some like news updates, some like business charts. The color of the lights kept changing, and after a few seconds I began to realize some of the noise was the soundtrack to each of the different massive images around me, over the roar of endless people moving and talking and laughing.

Naomi put her arm round me as though I were a scared rabbit. Which I was. "Don't worry," she yelled over the cacophony. "This is just Skywalk 4. It's one of the moving walkways that go uptown. We'll get on it and change in a few minutes to Skywalk G which goes cross-town to the UN building."

After a few more moments, I began to realize what I was looking at. I'd heard of the "moving walkways" of the world's great cities, but had never actually experienced one. They were strips of moving sidewalks with spaces either to sit or stand. Each strip was adjacent to another strip, which moved five miles per hour faster, until the tenth strip, which moved at fifty miles per hour. Then, there was a wall, and on the other side another ten strips going in the other direction. I saw people stepping nonstop between the strips.

"You time your movement on the different speed strips," Naomi shouted above the noise, "so you can get off at the right block. This way, you can get from downtown to uptown in just five minutes."

Naomi herded me onto the slowest strip. "We'll stay on this strip," she yelled, "so you won't have to maneuver." I stood with Naomi as the walkway moved us along at five miles per hour. I looked up and saw massive screens showing me images I couldn't understand. I started to pass under a screen showing a woman holding something that looked like a household appliance, and I heard a momentary sound bite:

"I couldn't live without my Robopad." I had no idea what this was. The next screen showed a graph with an upward moving line. It could have been a stock, or the price of electricity—I had no clue. I heard the voiceover say something like "Shawmucks shooting up," and then I was on to the next screen.

I turned my head from the screens and looked around me at the hordes of moving people. Many of them seemed to be talking to each other, laughing or in earnest conversation. Others were staring at the giant screens. Some seemed to be talking to variously shaped gadgets attached to them.

Every person I saw looked healthy. Every person looked attractive. Every person seemed engaged and happy. Every person I saw, I realized with a wave of nausea, was a d-human.

Suddenly, amid the noise and constant motion, I saw the most bizarre sight. Something that looked like a huge prehistoric pterodactyl appeared out of nowhere, flying high above everyone, and then swooped down on a man and woman talking together on the moving sidewalk. They just ignored it and a moment later it disappeared. Meanwhile, a group of teenagers close by burst out laughing.

I turned to Naomi in complete confusion. "What was that?" I could barely utter the words. Naomi laughed.

"Don't worry, Eusebio," she shouted back. "That's just an M3DI—a mobile 3-D imager. It's the newest gadget—the kids love them. After a while, you get used to it and it doesn't bother you."

A few moments later, Naomi pulled me off the moving walkway, into a continuously moving elevator, and down to another level, where the walkways were now perpendicular to the first set.

"Now we're going cross-town for a few blocks," she assured me.

Again, the cacophony was the same. A couple of minutes later, she led me off the walkway. As we started towards what seemed like an exit, I heard a loud siren piercing through all the other noise. Over to my right I saw a young woman, dressed casually, who had also stepped off the walkway. To my amazement, a series of white vertical laser beams appeared around her, extending from the ground to the roof, while the siren kept sounding. She was caught in a cage of laser beams. To my bewilderment, she seemed utterly unconcerned. She just stood there, in her laser cell, chewing gum with a bored expression on her face, while everybody kept walking around her, ignoring her.

Within a couple of seconds, an egg-shaped vehicle whizzed up to her, the words ROBOCOP written on it. An arm extended from the vehicle, moved to her right shoulder blade, and seemed to scan something there. Then the arm moved in front of her eyes and again seemed to scan something. A moment later, the laser beams disappeared, and the girl continued walking, now with a sour expression on her face.

"What just happened?" I turned to Naomi. I didn't know whether to feel panic or shock, but I seemed to feel both.

"Listen," Naomi replied. "We're about twenty minutes early, so let's stop at the Betelbar right here for a Betel juice."

With that, Naomi took my arm and led me into a brightly lit alcove away from the continuous motion and hubbub of the walkways. I noticed the dancing words "Betelbar" moving across the threshold as we walked in.

"What's a Betelbar?" I was getting tired of asking Naomi about every thing that was happening around me. For a moment, Yusef's words again passed through my mind: *"You will be completely out of your depth."* How many times would these words haunt me?

"Betelbars started in India about thirty years ago, and they've taken over the world," Naomi cheerfully replied. "Betel juice is like coffee, only better. It's a mild stimulant, but it also gets rid of headaches and indigestion."

Naomi ordered two Betel juices. For the first time, I became aware of everybody looking at me. They all had the same expression—a warped combination of surprise, curiosity, and pity. It was the kind of expression you'd have if you saw a paraplegic get out of his wheelchair and stagger forward by himself without assistance.

I realized this crazy cacophony of continuous motion, so strange and alien to me, was the norm for every one of them. For them, I was the thing that was strange and alien. I was so clearly a Primal and had no place in their society. I was much smaller than they were, but far more than that, I had all the quaint, strange idiosyncrasies of physique and expression that had been ironed out of the d-humans, which labeled me as unequivocally Primal.

We sat down at a table. As soon as we did so, a woman appeared out of nowhere, sat down next to us at our table and started talking.

"Hi, my name's Barbara. Would you like to know more about the new Robopad? It's amazing . . . "

Before she could say any more, I interrupted her with an irritated tone.

"Excuse me, but—"

At that moment, I noticed Naomi pushing a button at our table, and the woman instantly disappeared. Some people, at the table next to ours, started chuckling quietly among themselves.

Once again, I was bewildered beyond my imagination. What had just happened? Naomi tried to hide her own amusement as she explained:

"Eusebio, that was just another M3DI. The way Betelbars make so much money is not from selling Betel juice, but from the advertising. You can talk to the M3D avatar for hours, and never get bored. If you don't want the M3DI, you just push this button on the table, and they leave you alone."

Now, as I looked around the Betel bar, trying to ignore people's amused expressions looking at me, I noticed that about half the tables were occupied by people talking with avatars. I was beginning, slowly, to notice a slight flickering in the M3DI images, which enabled me to tell them apart from real people.

I tried to regain my composure. I turned to Naomi.

"So, what was happening to that girl caught in the laser beams?" I asked her with my sternest voice.

"She got off the walkway, Eusebio, at a place she wasn't authorized."

"What do you mean, 'not authorized'? And how would anyone know?"

"No one in the United States can go anywhere without prior authorization. You know you can't leave Tuckers Corner without authorization; but this also applies to d-humans. It's the basic Homeland Party platform."

"How can you put up with having to get authorized before you go anywhere?" I asked Naomi incredulously.

"It's not so bad," Naomi responded. "It's an automatic part of your life—you don't even think about it. Besides which, it's worked."

"It's worked?"

"Yes, we haven't had a terrorist attack in our country for over a hundred years."

I looked at her, thinking she must be joking, and then I saw in her eyes that she was dead serious. The chasm that existed between me and all the people I saw around me . . .

"How do they monitor whether you're authorized?" I asked her.

"They just scan your nanochip. Every few seconds, there's a satellite scan out there checking my nanochip and making sure I'm authorized to be wherever I am."

"What's your nanochip?" The question was too obvious. I felt annoyed at Naomi for forcing me to ask her. Or maybe she just assumed I knew.

"Every American has a nanochip," she answered nonchalantly. "Except for Primals, of course. It's basically a smart protein injected into your right shoulder."

A new thought slowly dawned on me.

"Naomi," I asked. "How is it that I've been able to come here without those laser beams going up around me?" As I asked the question, I knew what the answer would be, and my flesh crawled at what I was about to hear.

"When we took you, Eusebio, from Tuckers Corner, we injected a nanochip into your right shoulder. It's such a small injection that you can't even feel it, but you have a nanochip now. Of course, we had to do that so you could attend the PEPS hearing here. You can't even come into Manhattan without at least a Level 3 clearance. You've been given Level 2A, Eusebio, just like me. That's the only way you can enter the UN building."

By this time, I was already so accustomed to the feeling that everything in my life had been violated by the good intentions of Naomi Aramovich and her Primal Rights activists that I found myself shrugging off this new violation. Instinctively, I touched my right shoulder with my left hand but, as Naomi had said, I felt absolutely nothing.

"Well, let's go, Eusebio," Naomi continued with her cheerful nonchalance. "We don't want to be late for the hearing."

With that, we left the relative peace of the Betelbar, back into the bustle of the walkways, and then took an entrance into a building where another egg-shaped machine—this one called Roboguard—scanned Naomi's and my irises and waved us through some kind of metal detector.

I was in the United Nations building and on my way to the 146th floor to begin my attendance at the PEPS hearing.

New York Journal

September 29, 2044

Matterhorn Insurance plays genetic favorites
Announcement adds fuel to simmering controversy

Matterhorn, the nation's second largest health insurance company, broke new ground yesterday with its announcement that it would offer deep discounts in health insurance premiums to customers whose genes have been screened and optimized.

Matterhorn's announcement is taking clear aim at a market still in its infancy, but promising huge growth and profit margins. This market comprises people whose genes were optimized before they were born, in the Petri dishes of an in vitro fertilization (IVF) clinic. There are only three million pre-natally optimized people (PNOs) in the United States right now, and eighty per cent of these are under eighteen and therefore mostly insured by their parents. However, the market is growing at a dramatic rate. This year, approximately one million PNOs will be born, about ten per cent of new births in the nation. That percentage is increasing rapidly. Analysts predict that, as soon as 2050, twenty-five per cent of new births will be PNOs.

PNO technology first became publicly available about twenty years ago. When parents choose PNO they go to an IVF clinic, which analyzes the genetic make-up of different fertilized eggs. Then, having chosen the best egg, the clinic performs what is known as a digital panel, or d-panel, of tests on the egg. It looks for genes that are predictors of disease—this number has risen over the years from around twenty initially to several hundred nowadays. When genes are identified as a future threat to the embryo, they are either turned off through the application of an enzyme, or the healthy version of the gene is made dominant. In the early years, the cost and complexity, along with uncertainties about the long-term outcome, meant that only a small number of "early adopters" chose this approach for their offspring. However, as the technology has improved, and the long-term benefits are becoming more dramatic, the PNO market is rapidly becoming a mass market.

Matterhorn's announcement yesterday reflects this changing reality. Their proposed discounts, which range from twenty per cent to as much as sixty per cent off base premiums, are based on the anticipated increased health of the PNOs versus the rest of society. A Matterhorn spokesperson yesterday claimed that "even with these deep discounts, Matterhorn expects this market to be highly profitable, because of the low expected medical costs of the PNO segment."

The announcement didn't have much effect on Matterhorn's share price, which rose by 0.6 per cent yesterday. Industry analysts said that other insurers are likely to follow Matterhorn's lead with similar pricing plans. However, the announcement boosted bio-technology stocks in the genetic engineering index—up almost ten per cent on the news yesterday, because of expected increased consumer focus on the benefits of the d-panel.

Social benefit or social plague?

The use of the d-panel has been a forum for controversy from the outset. Christian fundamentalist groups were initially opposed, but some became supporters once they saw that the technology could reduce the number of abortions for medical reasons. Since then, the controversy has shifted to the question of how the d-panel is used in society. This has now become perhaps the biggest issue in the realm of bio-ethics.

The European Union took a decisive step in legitimizing widespread use of the d-panel two years ago, in 2042, when it issued a directive that all member countries had to make the d-panel available for free to its citizens. Member countries were given five years to comply, but six of the Western European nations have already done so. Last month, the British National Health Service came out with projections for the expected reduction in incidence and mortality from certain diseases which are part of the EU d-panel screening. (See Table 1.) Some industry observers speculated yesterday that the dramatic numbers in these projections may have been the catalyst for Matterhorn's announcement yesterday.

Consumer rights advocate groups were arguing yesterday, however, that

Matterhorn's premium discounting was the wrong lesson to draw from the European experience. Instead, they argue that the U.S. should follow Europe's lead and federally legislate to ensure wide availability of the panel. Dennis Prudhoe, spokesperson for Genetically Optimized America, a public advocate group, said yesterday that "Europe is creating a healthier population than America. Even China has announced plans to phase-in free d-panels for their population over the next ten years."

"Second step on the slippery slope"

Mr. Prudhoe and others argue that Matterhorn's approach—the market-based approach—will ultimately lead to two segments of society, the genetically optimized and those whose parents can't afford access to the d-panel. Matterhorn's announcement, Mr. Prudhoe stated, was the second step on the slippery slope to that scenario.

The first step, argues Mr. Prudhoe, was taken over twenty years ago, in early 2023, when the insurance industry introduced premium discounts for people who submitted to genetic screening as part of their health insurance application. Federal legislation had outlawed penalty pricing for people with "bad genes," but the insurance industry side-stepped this restriction by offering, instead, premium discounts for people with "healthy genes." According to Mr. Prudhoe, the premiums for customers who refused the genetic screening increased substantially, putting overwhelming pressure on new insurance applicants to do the screening. By 2031, they say, eighty-eight per cent of new insurance applicants did the genetic screening.

Mr. Prudhoe argued yesterday that the same thing will happen again, following Matterhorn's new pricing plan. Families will feel increasing pressure to undergo the d-panel for their offspring, otherwise their children won't be able to afford health insurance in the future. Those who can't afford the d-panel technology—or don't believe in it—will produce a next generation who will lose out on health insurance, which will only increase the gap between the "haves" and the "have-nots" in the U.S.

The "market approach" to public welfare

Already, some corporations are offering the d-panel to their employees as an additional medical benefit. Most Silicon Valley companies offer this

Table 1: British National Health Service projections for expected reduction in incidence and mortality of certain diseases for PNO humans:

Disease	Reduction in Incidence	Reduction in Mortality
ALS/Lou Gehrig's disease	*85%*	*97%*
Alzheimer's disease	*73%*	*77%*
Arthritis	*44%*	*N/A*
Breast cancer	*62%*	*78%*
Colon cancer	*43%*	*57%*
Congenital heart disease	*78%*	*92%*
Cystic fibrosis	*99%*	*99%*
Diabetes	*32%*	*N/A*
Hemochromatosis	*76%*	*82%*
Hemophilia	*93%*	*98%*
Huntington disease	*85%*	*88%*
Leukemia	*47%*	*43%*
Muscular dystrophy	*94%*	*96%*
Obesity	*25%*	*N/A*
Ovarian cancer	*72%*	*79%*
Prostate cancer	*33%*	*13%*
Sickle cell disease	*61%*	*82%*

benefit to employees, and even some of the largest corporations in the country are offering it to employees with five years' or greater tenure. Employee benefits experts say it will be only a few years before PNO becomes a core benefit. This, however, fails to satisfy Mr. Prudhoe and the Genetically Optimized America advocacy group. "Once again," said Mr. Prudhoe, "this development only exacerbates the divide between the haves and the have-nots."

The bio-ethical issues are not likely to go away any time soon. In fact, companies across the world, from California to China, have spent years developing techniques for inserting foreign "donor" genes into an embryo. While no one has yet claimed they have performed this procedure on a human embryo, it is becoming a standardized and reliable method for producing "designer" animals. This is already improving agricultural productivity, and many say it is only a matter of time until the same methods are used to produce "designer babies." A spokesman for the British National Health Service responded to this claim by saying that "such a development will never happen." According to the NHS, there is a profound ethical gap between screening for optimal genes naturally produced by two parents, and inserting "donor" genes foreign to the parents. However, Mr. Prudhoe and others fear that, if such a technology were ever to be applied to humans, it would create an even greater gulf between the "haves and the have-nots" than currently exists.

—New York Journal *analyst, Jerome Wickens*

5 The Betrayal

Where the executioner's face is always well hidden

So, here I am, I muse to myself. For a moment, all reality seems to go on hold, and I feel I'm removed from myself, watching myself as in a dream.

I'm sitting in a comfortable leather arm chair at a beautiful conference table—walnut and oak, I think, with a metallic trim that Naomi told me was titanium. Naomi is sitting at my left, with her usual expression of cheery optimism. In front of her is a flat-screen. Opposite me is Harry Shields—his physique of rippling muscles pushing out from beneath his immaculate formal clothing. In front of him—another screen and a console. He has sandy colored hair, perfectly shaped eyebrows, and a thick, well-manicured mustache. When he shook hands with me, I felt like a pygmy. He could have crushed my hand to pieces if he'd applied the pressure. I'm not sure, but I think I saw him unconsciously wiping his hand immediately after shaking mine, as though he didn't want any Primal germs to infect his skin.

His green, beady eyes look at me with a mixture of disdain and disgust, wrapped in an artificial politeness. It's very clear to me. Harry Shields is the enemy. I instinctively hate him and fear him.

I wish I was back in my familiar surroundings. Round about now, I should be giving a class to my tenth-graders on the American Indians. I miss my friends. I miss my cat, Jigger.

"Are you ready to begin, Mr. Franklin?" Harry Shield's cold, controlled voice brings me back to the harsh reality of the PEPS hearing conference.

"Yes, I am."

Harry Shields spoke up, looking at nobody in particular, as if talking to the air.

"We are on the record. This begins Session 7-224 of the PEPS hearing of the United Nations Authority on the Primal Species, known as UNAPS. I am Harry Shields, Special UNAPS counsel. Also present today is the Primal witness, named Eusebio Franklin, and his counsel, Naomi Aramovich."

He turned towards Naomi.

"Counsel Aramovich, can you attest to the fact that the Primal witness was brought here today strictly under the guidelines established in PEPS Session 4-136, incorporating the amendments per Session 5-89?"

"Yes, I can attest to that," responded Naomi.

The formality made me shiver. I hadn't expected this much formality. All my conversations with Naomi in the hotel room yesterday, even the late night visit from Yusef, none of that seemed as grave and heavy as what I was now experiencing. Yesterday, all my conversations, no matter how horrible the subject matter, seemed like nothing more than . . . conversations. Suddenly, today, in the formality of the conference room and Harry Shields talking "on the record," it began to sink in how serious and deadly was the situation in which I'd found myself. The words of Yusef last night echoed in the back of my mind: *"If you attend that PEPS hearing tomorrow, you will get yourself embroiled in something much greater and more disturbing than anything you can ever imagine."* I began to feel, for the first time, what he meant.

Harry Shields continued speaking. "Will the Primal witness now please raise his right arm and swear that he will tell the truth, the whole truth, and nothing but the truth, invoking GALT Section 1-11."

Confused, I turned to Naomi.

"Eusebio, GALT Section 1-11 is simply an invocation under international law. GALT stands for the Global Aggression Limitation Treaty, the foundation for modern international law. Section 1-11 states that each individual's belief in a higher power is legally subsumed to the ultimate values of peace and cooperation among individuals and nations."

Peace and cooperation sounded good enough to me. I raised my right hand and swore to tell the truth under GALT Section 1-11.

Harry Shields now turned to me.

"Eusebio Franklin—is this your correct name?"

"Yes, it is."

"And how would you prefer to be referred to—Mr. Franklin? Or just Eusebio?"

"'Eusebio' will do just fine."

"Then 'Eusebio' it will be," Harry Shields responded with an annoyingly patronizing tone.

I suddenly felt I'd just made my first mistake. Should I have maintained the formality of "Mr. Franklin"? But that seemed so absurd. Yet, now he could take an even more patronizing tone with me, using my first name. I vowed I would call him "Harry" right away.

"Eusebio, am I correct in understanding that you are a Primal living in the Humanist community of Tuckers Corner in the state of New York?"

"No, Harry."

"What do you mean, 'no'? What is not correct about my understanding?"

"Harry, I don't view myself as a Primal. To me, I'm a human being, and you are a d-human, someone different from me as a human being."

Harry's face, which was initially confused by my response, turned into a satisfied smile.

"Oh," he responded. "It's a question of definition. Well, Eusebio, under the PEPS Session 1-14, which dealt with the issue of definitions, someone like you, whose genes have never been optimized, is defined as a Primal."

I was beginning to feel the adrenaline of battle.

"I'm sorry," I responded, "but I wasn't part of that session, and I don't accept that definition."

"I have a suggestion," Naomi intervened. "For the purpose of this session, let's refrain from a definition of 'human being.' In the interest of clarity, can we agree that non-optimized humans will be referred to as 'Primals' and optimized humans will be referred to as 'd-humans'? That way, we can avoid getting hung-up on terminology."

For the first time, I saw Naomi in a new light. She was no longer the friendly d-human explaining to me how I'd been caught up in her fight to save my race. All of a sudden, she was an attorney, with a hard shell around her, in her legal element along with Harry Shields.

"That's satisfactory to me," responded Harry Shields. He turned to me. "And to you, Eusebio?"

"Yes, that's fine with me." I felt that I'd won a small battle. Would Yusef be proud of me at that moment? I wondered.

Harry shot me a satisfied smirk. "So, with our agreement on definitions, was my prior understanding correct regarding your identity?"

"Yes."

"Now, Eusebio, for the record: has anyone other than your counsel, Naomi Aramovich, spoken with you in any way about the session we're holding here today?"

I wasn't prepared for this question. I thought of Yusef. I didn't want to betray him to this d-human prosecutor.

"No," I replied.

Instantly, something changed in the room. Both Harry Shields and Naomi were suddenly intently watching the flat panel screens in front of them. Their expressions showed surprise and intense concentration.

Harry Shields looked piercingly at me.

"Let me repeat my question, Eusebio. Has anyone, other than your counsel, spoken with you in any way about the session we're holding here today? Anyone?"

"No," I replied, gritting my teeth.

Immediately, I heard a loud, alarming, repetitive beep coming from the two screens in front of both d-humans. Harry turned to Naomi.

"Counsel Aramovich, do you agree with me that we have a neurographic event?"

"I do, Counsel Shields," Naomi said with a resigned voice.

"For the record," Harry continued, "the neurographic analysis has just recorded an unequivocal neurographic event. The Primal witness is lying. I will now play back the neurographic recording of the witness' thoughts, monitored on neurographic level three, during the few seconds following my last question."

To my horror, Harry Shields pressed a button in front of him, and a computerized voice filled the room from unseen speakers. There was a crackling static noise in the background. After a moment of hesitation, I began to make out the words only too clearly:

"Yusef—last night—don't betray—human—called me 'brother'—bastard d-human Harry Shields—loyalty to Yusef—just don't tell him about it—just lie—say 'no.'"

The words were undeniable. I knew that they represented exactly what I'd been thinking when Harry Shields asked me that question. The neurographic machine had seen directly into my brain. I was caught out. I was naked, stripped and humiliated. I felt like one of the naked Jews shuffling into Auschwitz, their private parts open for inspection; like one of the African slaves coming off the slave ship to the auction block, stripped of every human dignity.

Naomi spoke up:

"Counsel Shields, I'm invoking the Primal witness' 5-89 rights for an immediate privileged consultation with me."

"That's fine, Counsel Aramovich," came the response from Shields.

Naomi turned to me. "Eusebio," she said gently, "you need to leave your seat right now and come with me."

I got up from my seat. I was stunned by what had happened, a rabbit caught in the headlights. Naomi took me by the arm and steered me through a door in the corner of the conference room, which she closed behind us. We were in another smaller room, with a table and some chairs.

Naomi spoke to me with barely concealed frustration.

"Eusebio, we're in a special room called the Privileged Room, with audio jamming on all frequencies. Our conversation here is absolutely private and you have no legal obligation to repeat it to anybody. Now, what the hell happened last night, and why didn't you tell me about it?"

At that moment, I realized that any damage had already been done. There was nothing left but to tell Naomi the truth, everything that had transpired the night before. I had tried not to betray Yusef, but the technologies of the d-human world had opened me up and gutted me. As I told Naomi what had happened, I watched her eyes roll upward as she shook her head and sighed audibly.

"I can't believe this happened to you," she said, after I'd finished my story. "These people are out of control. They're fanatics. They will stop at nothing to try to undermine progress and law. It's not your fault, Eusebio, I can see now what you were going through." She snorted derisively. "This Isotope 919 nonsense. It's a myth. It's the kind of thing these fanatics come up with to get more misguided humans to fight and die for their cause. I've heard the myth before, some years ago. We even researched it a few years back to see if there was anything to it, and we came up with nothing."

Naomi sat down at the table next to me and all of a sudden, grabbed hold of my hand. It was a warm, friendly grab. As if she wanted to infuse my being with all her knowledge about the world around me. She looked at me with her kind, brown eyes and continued talking.

"All that stuff, Eusebio, that he told you about the Great Global Wars and the Global Aggression Limitation Treaty—that's all true. GALT is the greatest step forward in human history. And the Rejectionists—well, they really are the biggest threat to world peace and prosperity. But that Isotope 919 myth . . . it's nonsense. You were being tricked, Eusebio. They were taking advantage of your openness and honesty to try to rope you into their cause. So he called you 'brother.' Eusebio, you know as well as I do, that doesn't make him your brother."

I wasn't completely convinced. After all, as Yusef himself had said last night, Naomi was a d-human who had abducted me from my life without asking my permission. But I had nothing to go on—and what choices did I have anyway?

Naomi continued. "I have to make a security report immediately about the unauthorized access to your hotel room 3-D imager. They'll have to sweep your room and review security clearances for the hotel technology staff."

My heart sank further. I thought of Eusebio saying to me last night: *"A number of people had to risk their lives for me to be able to speak with you tonight."* I dreaded the thought that my "neurographic event" would lead to dire consequences for someone I never knew.

Naomi walked to the opposite corner of the room and talked softly into her PDA for a couple of minutes. I couldn't hear what she was saying. Then, she came back to where I was standing.

"What's difficult right now is to get our session back on track," she told me. "Your integrity, Eusebio, was a major factor in you being chosen to represent your race. Now, we have a neurographic event before we've even begun." She mused for a moment. "Okay. I think I know what I need to say. I will have to tell the session what happened. You understand—there's no choice about that." She looked at me with one of her condescending smiles. "Don't take it personally, Eusebio, if you don't like some of the things I will have to say on the record. It's all just legalese to get things back on track."

She led me back from the private room into the main conference room. I resumed my position on the neurographic chair, which I had already begun to hate.

Naomi then proceeded to summarize, on the record, what I'd told her in the conference room. After describing Yusef's visit, she added:

"Now, Counsel Shields, I think you will agree that what we have here is an event that clearly falls under Section 7 of PEPS Session 5-89. As we agreed during that session, the Primal witness is naïve to the practices and protocols of our society, and can easily be manipulated. In this situation, the naïve Primal witness acted out of a misguided sense of loyalty to a concept of racial identity cynically placed on him by the Rejectionist intruder. As a Section 7 exclusion, we can agree that this neurographic event does not compromise the

Primal witness' integrity and therefore does not undermine the legal validity of the proceedings. Do you agree, Counsel Shields?"

"I do, Counsel Aramovich. I agree with your analysis."

Naomi looked extremely satisfied. "So, Counsel Shields, let's begin with the substance of the proceedings."

Harry Shields sat back in his chair, took a deep breath, and began speaking again.

"Now, Eusebio, do you have an idea of how many tigers were freely roaming the wilds of Asia during the late nineteenth century, just three hundred years ago?"

Which was how I found myself on the dock, defending our human race for the crimes of our ancestors, for the extinctions of the great mammals, for the genocides carried out against those unable to defend themselves against the onslaught of the European powers. For the devastation wrought on our planet by the overwhelming power of our technology.

Which was why I was yelling at Naomi Aramovich in the Privileged Room at the end of that first morning session. *"How could you have put me there?"* A lamb to the slaughter.

And all Naomi could give me back was a warm smile from her kind, brown eyes and a reassurance that everything would come together. All I needed to do was to be myself. To talk about our human soul. As if I knew what the hell that meant.

Naomi looked at her watch. "Now, I have to take care of some other things, Eusebio. There's a lunch that's been prepared for you." She pointed to a package on a table. "Try to relax for an hour. You might want to wander around the UN building for a little bit . . . see some of the different country exhibits. Don't worry about going anywhere unauthorized." She laughed. "No laser bars will come up. In the UN building, your authorization allows you to go into most places."

Her eyes lit up for a second as if she'd had a great idea.

"Do make sure to go up to the rooftop garden. It's one of the best places in New York. It's a botanical garden, where each region of the world is represented. The plants have been genetically engineered to thrive in the New York climate, regardless of their natural habitat. There are benches where you can sit and eat your lunch.

"Oh, and I almost forgot." She smiled as she handed me what appeared like a pair of old-fashioned spectacles. "These are special binoculars that will help you enjoy the view from the rooftop."

I couldn't help being struck by the contrast between her insouciant tone and the hours of mental agony I'd just suffered. Suddenly, I was being treated like a tourist having a lark in New York City. Before I could even say anything, Naomi was gone, and I was left alone in the Privileged Room with my lunch and my high-tech binoculars.

I walked out into the corridor and wandered around. Most of the rooms were utterly uninteresting—conference rooms similar to my own torture chamber.

I found the elevator to the Sky Garden, as it was called, and walked around. The fresh air was a delight. It was the first time I'd breathed air from the outside world since my abduction, who knows how many days ago. Naomi was right. The Sky Garden was beautiful. There was a cactus grove, a tropical area with a beautiful monkey pod tree and giant sago palms surrounded by exotic orchids, a grass section with spectacular tall flowering grasses, and a bamboo grove making beautiful rustling noises in the breeze.

I wandered to the railings at the edge of the roof and as I looked out on the massive spectacle below and around me, I drew my breath in awe, just as I had done when I first looked out of my hotel room window. Buildings and bridges were almost indistinguishable from each other as I gazed across the three-dimensional maze above the waters of Manhattan. I turned my head northward and saw a gap in the criss-cross of architecture. I realized that must be the famous Central Lake, with its amusement arcades, water sports and islands. Even from so far away, everything was a hive of activity. Everywhere was motion—countless air-borne vehicles buzzing in and out of the architecture. The high-tech binoculars took some getting used to, at first making me dizzy, but after a few minutes I found myself enjoying zooming in on a particular building or group, focusing on some d-human engaged in something, presumably very important to him or her but totally unknowable to me.

I looked farther north to the horizon. I began to realize that, over there, not so far beyond, lay my own community of Tuckers Corner, where the Barlows would be feeding Jigger, where Paul Huntley, my fellow history teacher, would be standing in for me teaching the tenth-graders about the American Indians. What would they all be thinking about my disappearance? They would know I'd never leave them like that. They must realize that something else was involved. But would they even guess, in their wildest imaginings, who had abducted me? No—no way. I missed them all so badly, it hurt me deep in my gut. I wanted so much to be back in my familiar surroundings, with my fellow human beings, trying so hard just to live our lives and keep the human spirit alive.

I thought about how our community had begun, over a hundred years ago. How our founder, Julius Schumacher, had seen what was coming and tried so hard to stop it. And I wondered, for the umpteenth time in my life, what had gone so terribly wrong with our world.

Julius Schumacher

[Excerpts from The Humanist Annals: The Book of Alison*]*

And I'll tell and think it and speak it and breathe it
And reflect it from the mountain so all souls can see it
Then I'll stand on the ocean until I start sinkin'
But I'll know my songs well before I start singin'

The Vultures of the Intellect

I first met Julius Schumacher in Sakété. A little town in the eastern part of Benin, close to the Nigerian border. The year must have been around 2030, when the Nigerian refugee crisis had gotten out of control.

He looked so out of place, stepping off the bus with the local villagers and chickens—I knew I had to find out who this person was. Night was falling. I was, as usual, trying to manage too many things at the same time. I was on my satellite phone, yelling at the supply center dispatcher that we needed yet more water purification kits. I was counting as a trucker unloaded U.S. army-supply MREs—meals ready to eat—to make sure we got the full amount. But Julius Schumacher caught my eye, and I walked over to the bus.

"Are you lost?" I asked him. "My name's Alison."

"Not exactly," he replied. "We've spent the last six hours getting nowhere—twenty-three miles to be exact. Landslides from all the rain."

This had been a dry part of West Africa, but climate change had been causing the clouds to drop their water too early in their voyage from the Atlantic, bringing mudslides to Sakété and drought to the forests.

He immediately attracted me. Was it the blond hair contrasting with his olive-toned skin and brown eyes? Was it the look in those eyes, which seemed to watch and absorb everything around him? Later that night, I discovered that he owed his looks to his German father and Brazilian mother. But at that first moment, I remember more than anything being amazed that he had no idea where he was. This was, after all, the site of one of the largest, most diseased and wretched refugee camps that Africa had ever experienced. Not the kind of place that tourists turn up to in a local bus.

We spent the night drinking beer together, finding out about each other. I discovered Julius had recently landed at the Ivory Coast after hitching a ride on a commercial boat from Brazil. He'd come here, not to check out the Yoruba and Igbo refugees from the Hausa onslaught in Nigeria, but to discover the source of the magical spirits that had imbued their life into him in Brazil. He was looking for the roots of *Candomblé* and *capoeira*.

Julius told me that night about the *Candomblé* dolls in Rio de Janeiro, the birthplace of his mother, Emilda. He'd stayed with a family in the *favelas* who managed a shop selling these dolls, and he'd come to treasure the different types: the Oshun of red, yellow, and amber, representing harmony and love; the black and red Elegba, bringing good luck; and his favorite, Obatala, pure white, standing for patience, knowledge, and wisdom. All these spirits, he whispered to me, had hitched a ride on the slave boats from West Africa along with the desperate, manacled slaves and had bloomed fresh meaning into the hardship of the New World. And he told me about the *capoeira* he'd learned in Rio, how it transformed the battles of life into a dance, a spiritual connection with his inner being.

We slept together that night. I thought I'd never see him again after that first, wonderful night—that he'd keep moving on, searching for his *Candomblé* shrines. And that would have been OK with me. Up to that point in my life, I'd never met a man who interested me for more than a day or so. My life was committed to helping the starving, desperate people in the world who hadn't had the benefit of an Ivy League education. I'd partnered up with the International Red Cross rather than a young, well-groomed investment banker wanting to start a family. And yet—Julius Schumacher did something to me in those first few days that would change my life forever. He touched a place in my soul that I never even knew existed. His spirit challenged everything I'd held sacred. He didn't challenge me directly. He didn't engage in arguments with me about social injustice, about helping the poor. His eyes just kept silently asking me "Why?" in response to everything I told him. Why did the Hausa rise up against the Yoruba and Igbo? Why were there not enough tents for the people? These were easy to answer. Why did the refugees keep arriving with tales of horror, murder, mutilation, rape, and desecration? Why was I here to help them? More difficult to deal with these questions. Why had I walked over to Julius as he got off the bus? Why was I falling in love with him? Why was he attracted to me? I've spent my life trying to answer these.

In those first few days, it slowly began to dawn on me that Julius was a genius. Not just some very intelligent guy. Nothing like that. A genius. Someone who lived in a world of perceptions and insights that barely touched our normal world. Ironically, the way he told the story, it sounded like the opposite—as though he'd grown up mentally disabled. He told me how his parents had both screwed up their careers to educate him at home because he couldn't handle regular high school. His father, Johann Schumacher, was a Lutheran minister who quit his charitable work to raise his son. His mother, a high-powered gynecologist, had cut her hours to part-time so she could do her part in child-rearing. He'd left Germany for Brazil, he told me, because he'd been kicked out of Humboldt University in Berlin after six months, flunking his first set of undergraduate exams.

Years later, when Johann and Emilda would visit us in the States, when everything in our lives seemed to be going relatively normally, I heard from them what it was really like raising Julius, how as he developed into his teens, he would pursue intellectual meanderings that defied normal reason. They told me how he would try to interpret Shakespeare's *King Lear* using evolution theory. How he'd take the human genetic code, apply different colors to each base letter, and create a computerized picture using each colorized base letter as a pixel. How he then created different pictures for different organisms and hung them on his walls. How he'd attempt to derive mathematical formulas describing the *Tao Te Ching* based on theoretical physics, utilizing theories of matter and anti-matter. How he once wrote a paper for his own amusement integrating the teachings of Confucius, St. Augustine and Aristotle into one code of social conduct and then related each chapter of the code to different Mozart piano concertos.

But there was no way to tell from Julius himself about any of that. He spent those first few days following me around the refugee camp, learning how to set up pipes and faucets for potable water, helping to distribute tents, blankets, and food to the never-ending flow of newly-arrived refugees, learning how to identify the weakest and diseased arrivals to send them to the make-shift clinics on the other side of Sakété. In the middle of the suffering, the mud and the putrid smell of human waste, Julius and I were passionately attracted to each other. At night, exhausted from a day of laborious work, from the agony of carrying a dead baby to the morgue out of the hands of a wailing mother, from the putrefaction of public toilets alive with flies, maggots, and flying cockroaches, we would hug each other so tightly that I almost couldn't breathe, and we would make love as if the thrusting and ecstasy could somehow flood away the misery we'd endured through the previous day.

One night, in our tent, after making love, lying together bathed in each other's sweat, Julius told me what I meant to him:

"It's your commitment, Allie, to compassion, to human kindness. Throwing yourself into a struggle for good against an infinitude of evil and suffering. There's a void deep within me, Allie, that my intellect is forever circling, like a flock of vultures hovering over an empty carcass. And your compassion has driven away those vultures. Here, here in the middle of despair and desolation, Allie, you've helped me find love and meaning."

It didn't last for long. One morning, Julius woke up violently shivering, trembling. He'd caught dengue fever and was suddenly transformed from one of the helpers to one of the diseased. I stopped everything I was doing, just to care for him. Every part of his body was in agony. In the middle of shaking and vomiting, he broke out in a burning rash. Then we received bad news from the medics. His strain was the increasingly frequent hemorrhagic dengue, known as DHF. This would be fatal, they told us, without receiving the most current anti-viral medicines, which were only available in the developed world. Julius' parents quickly arranged for emergency transport to bring their son back to the safety of Hamburg. If he'd been one of the Nigerian refugees, he would have died, but he'd been born into the developed world, so he could be saved. I watched him being carried by stretcher on to a helicopter and we both wondered if we'd ever see each other again.

Back in Hamburg, after weeks in hospital, Julius slowly recovered. He called me on the satellite phone, and I saw a person with a different affliction than the one he'd just been treated for. Depression. In the gray, rainy Hamburg winter, he told me, the routines of the world around him seemed fixed in place like rigor mortis. The doctors wouldn't let him come back to Sakété and his parents wouldn't fund any more world traveling. Here was Julius, they felt, almost 21 years old, without a college education, without any skills to propel him in the world—just another mixed-up adolescent with no sense of direction. Emilda found Julius a job in her hospital as a junior technician in the medical imaging department. None of us knew it at the time, but that was the step that would ultimately change, not only Julius' life, but the future direction of humankind.

The Soul Has Fled

The videophone calls gave it away. I should have known at the time. I think I did know, but didn't want to believe it. I've spent my whole life not wanting to believe it, because I've known the Julius Schumacher who got meaning from me and who loved me for that.

The first time I saw it was a few weeks after he'd begun working in the hospital's neurological imaging center.

"Allie, it's amazing," he told me on the phone. There was light back in his eyes, but a cold light that I'd never seen before. "They use this functional MRI—FMRI—to map the brain, but they don't know what they're doing. They get stuck in General Linear Modeling and their results are too vague and non-specific. I've already improved some of their software, but that's nothing. There's so much potential."

It all flew by me. I was more interested in the old woman I was trying to calm down because she'd just lost both her daughter and granddaughter to typhoid. But, as Julius later told me, the vultures of his intellect, endlessly hovering with gnawing hunger, had found a fresh carcass on which they could feed without end. Julius realized he could be a pioneer in an undiscovered land, the human brain, and that he could use his unique intelligence to map that land to a level of detail never before imagined.

He changed overnight. The phone calls became fewer. The seeker of spiritual fulfillment was transformed into a driven professional. It took him a year attending night school to get his undergraduate degree. After his MD with top honors from Oxford, he began a research fellowship at their FMRI center. Then Harvard, at their Center for Functional Neuro-Imaging Technologies, where he joined—and soon led—a team blazing a trail in developing a new science, known as neurography.

Harvard was good news for me. We'd be close to each other again. By that time, I was an officer at Wildlife Trust in New York. We were collecting the DNA belonging to those species doomed to extinction, creating a DNA bank with as much diversity as possible so that one day, perhaps, these species could be cloned and re-introduced to a better world.

I'd moved on from saving humans to saving animals. There had been a young Yoruba boy, perhaps thirteen, suffering from malnutrition and typhoid. I'd nursed him back to health. I loved the innocence in his eyes and agonized when they looked at me pleadingly. He regained his health, started running and playing again, and I felt a gush of fulfillment. Two years later, I returned to the same camp where an atrocity had just occurred—the Yoruba had turned on the

Igbo, massacring dozens of them. Some of the Yoruba youths doing the raping, killing, and mutilating had been captured by the UN troops. I walked past their make-shift jail and looked directly in the eyes of the little boy I'd saved two years earlier. Animals, at least, usually kill for good reasons rather than hate and malice.

So there we were, Julius discovering new ways to map the human mind and me trying to save the last DNA from doomed animals. Our common ground was our past, not our present or future. But we both refused to believe it. Our passion, kindled in Sakété, still glowed despite the lack of oxygen. We married, and I had our baby, Clarissa. A few years later, and we were divorced.

Julius had given himself completely to his research. There was not enough for me and Clarissa. He drove himself and his research team beyond their wildest imaginings. By taking millions of images a second of neuronal activity and applying his software, Julius became the first person to create a literal snapshot of a human thought. Then, shortly before our divorce, came his breakthrough of parallel imaging, allowing him to isolate the multiple thoughts that pass through a person's mind simultaneously and separate them out into different neurographic images. Now they could observe all the inner workings of the mind, both conscious and unconscious, at any given moment.

I remember one time, while we were still married, Julius taking me to his lab, showing me a computer screen of flashing thoughts along with what they called "thought vocalization," an eerie computerized voice speaking aloud the mind's unspoken thoughts with crackles in the background. I shuddered.

Clarissa meanwhile grew into a beautiful young woman but she missed her father's attention. I confess—and it pains me more than I can even bear—I spent too much time step-mothering my soon-to-be-extinct animals and not enough on my own daughter. Clarissa inherited my abhorrence of the suffering of others and her father's restlessness when he had been her age. But neither of us gave her the guidance she needed. Her name was meant to symbolize clarity. Clarissa's vision of the world was clear as mud.

I'd still see Julius from time to time. Our love for each other remained, like radio signals sent between two different planets. Neither of us re-married. I even accompanied him when he received his second Nobel Prize, for the discovery of the CONDUCTER as he called it—the "Cognitive Network Directing Ultimate Control through Electronic Relays." Julius hadn't been content with mapping out thoughts. No, he wanted to find where in the brain was the author of those thoughts. He finally realized that consciousness was, in fact, a continuous relay between different centers in the brain, centers in a never-ending discourse with each other, agreeing, battling, allying, debating with each other in an interminable neuronal relay race. The CONDUCTER. This was Julius' in-joke because, in fact, his CONDUCTER proved that human consciousness had no orchestral "conductor" waving a baton. It played its music more like a free-form jazz band.

It was after that Nobel Prize that something started going wrong with Julius. When I saw him, he seemed withdrawn and closed, even when talking about his work. In fact, *especially* when talking about his work. This was not Julius.

He didn't tell me what was wrong. Only years later, when we were close again, he explained to me about what became known as "Schumacher's smudge." Ever since Julius and his team had developed neurography, their pictures of human thoughts had contained wispy, shadowy smudges in the background. No one had given this much thought. This was the same as the crackling in the background of the thought vocalization that I'd heard in his lab, like the crackly noise of the ether in early radios. But Julius couldn't leave these crackles and smudges alone. What were they? What did they signify and why couldn't they be identified? He had seen the smudges on the neurographic images of other animals, too—with advanced primates, they were similar to human smudges, and with other animals like mice or rats, they were still there, only smaller and vaguer.

Things got disturbing for Julius when his team started doing research on the neurographic images of genetically optimized creatures. They were experimenting with the cognitive DNA of lab animals in the embryo stage, trying to create, for example, a genius rat, a super-aggressive rat or, a pacifist rat. When Julius saw the first images, he was shocked. No smudges. He checked his data; had his team re-do their experiments. Still no smudges.

Slowly, achingly, an awesome and awful hypothesis occurred to Julius. It was a hypothesis so terrible, so dreadful, he didn't breathe a word of it, not just to me, but to anyone in his team. He could barely even consider it himself. What if the smudges represented something innate in the creature, something primordial, something that had never yet been identified by science, something that was an integral part of the creature's consciousness? And what if the manipulation of the creature's DNA destroyed the delicate underpinning of the unknowable source of this primordial existence? In short, what if the smudges were images of the creature's soul? And Julius' lifetime work was succeeding in destroying the soul?

It was while Julius was beginning to conceive these awful thoughts, shuddering deep within himself, that the greatest disaster imaginable struck both of our lives. Our dear, darling Clarissa put an end to her own life with a drug overdose. She was a freshman undergraduate in Los Angeles at UCLA. They found her dead in a cheap hotel in the slums of East LA. Clarissa had inherited too much feeling and too much intellect from me and her father, and we had failed to give her the love and nurturing she needed to develop these gifts. They were too much for her to bear. She had felt only the pain of alienation and isolation. Her intellect had permitted her to see through the "bullshit" of everyone else's belief structures—but she hadn't been able to create her own. Rejecting our love, devoid of belief, feeling betrayed and ignored by us, and separated from the rest of the world, she couldn't stand the pain anymore and chose to free her soul from another day of aching.

It's taken me half a lifetime to be able to feel it from her point of view and to write that. All I felt at the time was hatred for myself and an equal hatred for Julius, for our betrayal of our daughter. At the funeral, we avoided each other's eyes until one moment when we could no longer harness our defenses and our eyes met. Our gaze burned a searing hole in both of our souls. And then Julius came closer to me and, with a haunted look, breathed a short sentence that I could barely hear.

"The soul has fled," he whispered to me.

And I thought he was talking about Clarissa. I didn't know he was referring to the human race.

On Being Human

I didn't see Julius for more than four years after the funeral. For a large part of that time, I really didn't care if I'd ever see him again. The thing is, nobody saw him. He'd gone AWOL. I didn't know it at the time, but as he later told me, he'd begun a search for the mystery of the human soul.

Julius had flown back to Boston from the funeral and spent three days and nights locked away in his lab. Then he left his lab and never returned. He left the United States with nothing other than his passport, his wallet, and an overnight bag with a change of clothes. And, as he described to me, with his mind seething in pain and a desire for a way out of his torment, searching for a greater understanding, an inner calm, to put an end once and for all to the circling vultures of his intellect.

His first stop was the village of Chajul in the highland of Guatemala, so remote that the inhabitants still spoke the ancient Mayan language of *Ixil* rather than Spanish. The men still grew onions and potatoes in small fields watered by an open irrigation system that still collected rainwater as it had done for thousands of years. The women still wove traditional clothing known as *huipils*. Julius watched the women weave and felt their gentle interactions with the children. He saw a ten-year-old girl looking after her six-year-old little brother, changing his clothes when he fell into a muddy puddle. He sat with the men in the evening as they got drunk on *couche*, the local alcoholic brew.

As the months went by and Julius became increasingly comfortable with the gentle, quiet people of Chajul, he knew it was time to leave. One day, with hugs, benedictions, and tears, Julius jumped in the truck of one of the merchants buying *huipils* from the village and returned to the hubbub of the city.

Julius felt compelled to travel to the furthest regions of the world, the places that modernity had ignored because of their desolation and their utter uselessness. Places where people still lived a life mostly untouched by the twenty-first century.

Next stop Challacota in Bolivia, surrounded on all sides by the desolate salt flats of the Altiplano. At thirteen thousand feet, the air was thin, the days were cold and nights were freezing. Julius went with the indigenous people on *Dia de los Muertos*, the Day of the Dead, to visit the ancient tombs of their ancestors, leaving food steaming on the ancestral stones, so the spirits of the dead could enjoy the nourishment of the living. After the spirits had taken their fill, the people would bring the food back to the village and feast on their ancestors' left-overs.

Julius continued his search. He found himself deep in the Amazon, in one of the last remaining patches of tropical rainforest, at a settlement of the Yanomami people. It took a long time for Julius to earn even a hint of trust from the Yanomami who had been fighting an eighty-year war of attrition with the modern world since gold had been discovered in their land in the 1980s. Many of their children were born with terrible defects from the mercury used by the miners and by this time there were just three thousand of them left. They knew their race was doomed, but they would fight to survive, to the last man, woman, and child.

Julius told me about the day he discovered from their *pajé*, or shaman, the Yanomami interpretation of the events that had destroyed their world. Their creator spirit, *Omamë*, had hidden a terrible secret called the *xawara* deep in the earth and had told his people never to go there, into the place they didn't belong. If they ever brought out the *xawara*, he warned them, all human beings would die. The white men had come and ignored this warning, taking the gold hidden deep in the ground. Now, the Yanomami knew, the sky would collapse in pieces over the earth; the sun, moon, and stars would fall, and the world would go dark.

Julius shuddered when he heard this story. He knew in himself that the *xawara* was none other than the misty smudges of his neurographic images, the hidden soul of humankind that had existed undisturbed through millions of years of evolution, and which he had managed to destroy with his manipulation of the cognitive DNA of the creatures he'd been experimenting on. The *xawara* belonged deep in the ground, undiscovered. But Julius had dug it out of its hiding place and he was afraid, just like the Yanomami, that the sky was about to fall.

Julius' search took him to Africa, to Asia, to Australia. To the Ogiek people of Kenya who had lost their forest to settlers, loggers, and tea plantations but who lived in the present and seemed calm about their fate. To the Konso people of Southwest Ethiopia, in constant battles with the neighboring Mursi and Bodi tribes over their dwindling resources. To the Bushmen of the Kalahari where the men were mostly drunk, the women mostly prostitutes for the truckers passing by, and the children mostly dying from disease.

He spent nearly a year in Western New Guinea where the loggers were still having trouble getting to those parts of the forest in the heart of malaria-ridden swamps. He came to know the Korowai in their tree houses and the Asmat, preoccupied with appeasing their ancestor spirits. In a bizarre trick of nature, they began to create ever more extreme and beautiful wooden carvings in the belief that, if they could only achieve a better design, their ancestors would use their spirit powers to keep the Indonesian military and foreign corporations at bay.

Finally, Julius began to understand some answers to the mystery he had set out to unravel. He had a message for the modern world. The time had come to return. He believed he needed to repay humanity for the sacrilege he had committed in unmasking the human soul. He needed to spend the rest of his life fighting to defend that soul.

He returned to his home in Boston. I was the first person he called to say that he was still alive.

"I'm writing a book," he told me. "It's going to change the world as drastically as my earlier work on neurography. It's called *On Being Human*."

The Coup of the Prefrontal Cortex

Julius sent me a draft copy of his book before he published it. I was awed and horrified. It encapsulated everything that was special in him. His neurographic research. His search for the mystery of the human soul. He had pulled it all together. He thought it would profoundly change society and my horror arose because I saw how wrong he was.

On Being Human attempted to explain what had happened to human consciousness since the early evolution of mankind. Julius saw a particular part of the human brain called the prefrontal cortex as the major protagonist in the story of human development. This was the area, Julius explained, that's used for abstract thinking, planning, suppression of primal drives, and what are known as the "executive functions" that separate mankind from other mammals.

Julius showed how in early societies, the CONDUCTER process of the human mind was in harmony, in balance. However, over generations, helped by the development of language and then writing, the prefrontal cortex began to gain strength over the other, more primitive parts of consciousness. This led to an imbalance that redefined the human race. It led to the great advances of mankind, from the invention of the wheel to the mapping of the human genome. But it also led to a contortion of the human spirit.

Julius described how, gradually, the human concept of what makes up the essence of life was transformed from the physical notion of "the spirit" to the abstract notion of "the soul." He talked about how, for indigenous people around the world, the spirits exist within all aspects of their consciousness. Their ancestors' spirits are all around them, in the forests, in the animals, and in the rocks; and during their ceremonies, their own spirits could commune with those of the world around them and of their ancestors.

But the prefrontal cortex carried out a coup in the human psyche and transformed the earth-oriented concept of a spirit to the universal abstraction of the soul. The abstract soul of monotheism, which then gave rise to science. Mankind's cognitive powers could have developed to enhance a person's relationship with his inner being. But since the coup of the prefrontal cortex, the spiritual healers and mystics of traditional cultures are instead viewed by our society as bizarre aberrations. The prefrontal cortex rules. Science rules. Abstraction rules.

Julius blamed the prefrontal cortex's domination for the breakdown of social cohesion, from the tribal group to the extended family, to the nuclear family and finally, in modern times, to the disintegration of even the nuclear family. I couldn't help but think of the agonies of my darling Clarissa when I read that part. But Julius went beyond our human breakdowns to global breakdowns—the catastrophes of climate change, our rape of the earth's natural resources, the ever-increasing extinctions of other species . . . all due to the domination of the prefrontal cortex over other parts of our consciousness.

Julius then described his discovery of the neurographic smudges and how they vanished when a creature's DNA was re-engineered, explaining his belief that the creature's soul was being destroyed by genetic manipulation of the embryo. Julius explained how only three per cent of human DNA was known to control the codes for creating the proteins that make up our bodies. This was the DNA defined in the human genome. The remaining three billion bases of DNA, the vast bulk of our human biological structure, he theorized, was a relic of earlier genes that had once controlled the codes for proteins but that evolution had made biologically irrelevant. But, he wrote, that didn't make them irrelevant to the structure of the human soul. When genetic engineers changed the genes within a human embryo, Julius hypothesized that they altered the sensitive dynamic between the bases of the other ninety-seven per cent of DNA and, when they did so, the human soul, the innate harmony of the relationship between all these ancient DNA structures, could evaporate.

Julius presented a bold manifesto for changing our behavior to balance the power of the prefrontal cortex. And he proposed an immediate ban on all manipulation of human DNA within the embryo because of the risk to that person's soul.

He thought he would change the world. That they'd listen to the great Dr. Schumacher, double Nobel Prize winner. He couldn't have been more wrong.

Christian groups around the world banned his book from their communities. The Chief Ayatollah issued a fatwa on Julius' life for his attack on the basic tenets of the teaching of Muhammad. The scientific community refused to have anything to do with him. Harvard University formally terminated their professional relationship with him. The members of Julius' co-op, where he'd been living for fifteen years, politely asked him to leave.

Julius had become a prophet with a growing number of followers and an outcast from the rest of society. His followers were called Humanists although they were unrelated to any previous humanist organizations. He and I became close again because I could once more see the Julius Schumacher I'd fallen in love with years earlier in Sakété. But I couldn't protect Julius against what was to come. His ideas were hijacked by a political force more massive than his own. He became a pawn in one of the great, inexorable conflicts of history.

I'll Stand on the Ocean Until I Start Sinking

It had all begun with the Elgin marbles. That is, when the International Court of Justice directed the United Kingdom to give back to Greece the sculptured walls of the Parthenon that had been stolen by Lord Elgin between 1801 and 1811.

They never thought that would lead to the greatest class action lawsuit in history, which became known as the Class Action to Rectify Global Injustice, or simply CARGI. A Tennessee law firm, Arbuckle, Stinson, and Hargreaves, realized that a precedent had been made. If the taking of the Elgin marbles was now considered theft, then how many other actions since the rise of European colonialism could now be viewed as theft? And how much money would be at stake? Untold billions. Arbuckle filed complaints against the nations of Western Europe on behalf of India, Pakistan, South Africa, Kenya, Brazil, and dozens of other countries. Within a few years, over a billion people in the developing world were represented.

The people of the Congo sought reparations from Belgium for the atrocities carried out a hundred and fifty years earlier, when Belgian soldiers would cut off the hands of Congolese natives who hadn't produced enough rubber. The Masai filed to get their land back which had been stolen from them by the British. The few remaining indigenous people of Nicaragua filed suit for the extermination of their ancestors, ninety-nine per cent of whom had died in the first seventy years after the Spanish conquest.

Things really got going with a new series of lawsuits against the United States and European nations for allowing their multinational corporations to commit crimes against the less developed people of the world. The oil industry was sued for leaving lakes of black oil where there had once been arable land. The bottled water industry was sued for buying up all the fresh water rights, drying up reservoirs, and leaving local people without water to drink.

My colleagues at the Wildlife Trust and I even tried jumping on the bandwagon. We tried to file suit on behalf of the great apes—the bonobos, chimpanzees, gorillas, and orangutans. For genocide and loss of habitat. Sadly for the apes, ours was one of the few suits ever thrown out of CARGI.

Meanwhile, the United States would have none of it. They threatened to pull out of the United Nations, the World Bank, and just about every other global institution unless all charges against their multinationals were dismissed. Americans could no longer travel to developing countries without armed guards. The Europeans tried to broker a middle ground but failed.

That was when disaster struck. In October 2063, as Columbus Day was being celebrated and the people of Columbus, Ohio enjoyed their long weekend, digging into their brunch or settling down to watch the sports on TV, a nuclear bomb exploded in their downtown. Over fifty thousand people were instantly killed. A hundred thousand others wounded and devastated by radiation sickness. The shining towers and proud skyscrapers of downtown Columbus were incinerated into a red-hot, radioactive crater containing two square miles of melted steel and pulverized concrete.

The Citizens Seeking Global Justice, a group nobody had heard of before or since, claimed responsibility along with an awful threat: if the United States didn't recognize and participate in the CARGI lawsuit, an even bigger nuclear explosion would take place in a major city exactly one year later. The Department of Homeland Security did everything imaginable to find the perpetrators. Everyone in the U.S. had to register with the Department and wear a tag so they could be monitored by satellite wherever they went. Every financial transaction, no matter how small, was registered and analyzed. But they were never found.

In solidarity with the United States, the International Court of Justice suspended all CARGI hearings for a year. Terror gripped the people of the United States as the anniversary of Columbus drew near. A week before the year was up, the United States announced they would no longer boycott the International Court of Justice. They had re-joined the global community. The United States had blinked. They never held the same power in the world from that day on.

The CARGI was the inexorable force that hijacked Julius. His book was published in the years following the Columbus explosion. In the view of the Department of Homeland Security, his book made him a potential enemy of the state and they never left him alone.

Two years after his book was published, the CARGI plaintiffs asked Julius to testify on behalf of the Yanomami tribe. Julius didn't want to—he was obsessed with spreading the ideas of his book and was worried that CARGI politics would pollute his message. But he received a subpoena and was forced to make arrangements to fly to The Hague to testify.

It was the second Sunday in November. The year was 2069. Julius spent the afternoon with me, brimming with enthusiasm about his new mission.

"I don't care if it takes the rest of my life, Allie, I'm going to get my message heard. There's too much at stake. The human soul. We mustn't lose that, Allie."

For the first time since Sakété, I found myself feeling a thrill of love for him. For his specialness, his laser-like energy now focused on something I thought was so right.

The following Tuesday, Julius stepped out of his New York hotel to take a cab to the airport to fly to The Hague. As he did so, someone in a motorcycle drove past him and shot him in the head with a high-powered pistol. Julius' brains, which had accomplished so much in six decades, were strewn over the sidewalk.

Clarissa gone. Julius gone. This story isn't about me so I won't go into the bleakness that will be with me to my dying day. None of us know who killed Julius. Maybe it was a fanatical Muslim carrying out the fatwa against him. It could equally have been a fanatical Jew or Christian. Sometimes I wonder if it wasn't the Department of Homeland Security wanting to silence a radical voice. May it was some nut trying to avenge the human soul for having been laid bare by Julius' technology. Only one thing is certain. Julius Schumacher is dead.

7 Reflecting Water

I saw a black branch with blood that kept drippin'

"**E**usebio, it's time to go back to the conference room and begin our afternoon session."

The gentle words of Naomi Aramovich come from behind me, shaking me out of my day dream. I'd been looking through the high-tech binoculars at a place at the horizon's edge, where I'd focused in on a grove of trees, hazy in the distance, thinking about my friends at Tuckers Corner, about Jigger . . . about Julius Schumacher and the last hundred years of a turbulent world he'd tried so desperately to change.

It takes me a few seconds to shake my mind from my reverie and remember where I am. As the awful present reality starts to fix itself into my consciousness, I shiver. Naomi continues with her encouraging tone.

"You did really well this morning, Eusebio. Now is your chance to talk about the things that matter to you the most. You're going to do great."

I neither understand nor care what exactly she means. I follow her through the roof garden and down the elevator into the PEPS conference room. Sit down once again in my own personal torture chamber, the neurographic chair. Why have I agreed to do this? Right now, I can't think of any good reason. I'm just here, and I don't have the strength or guts to stand up and walk away.

I try to pull myself together. Get my brain clicking into the here and now. I'm not going to help my fellow human beings by sitting here feeling sorry for myself.

Harry Shields passed his beady eyes over me and began to speak.

"Eusebio, at the end of our morning session, you stated that the PEPS proposal would be a crime greater than all the devastation caused by your fellow Primals because it would be destroying the human soul. Do you remember saying that?"

"Yes, I do."

"Would you care to elaborate?"

"Well, I don't know where to begin . . . " I wasn't prepared to take on such a vast topic.

Naomi intervened.

"Eusebio, let me ask you a couple of questions to help you get started. The founder of your Humanist community—Dr. Schumacher—what did he think genetic optimization might do to the soul?"

"It might destroy the soul."

"And is that the reason why the early Humanists avoided any genetic engineering?"

"Yes, exactly."

"And how, in Dr. Schumacher's view, is the soul most fulfilled?"

"When human consciousness is in harmony."

"And, looking back in history, where did Dr. Schumacher believe that this harmony occurred?"

"In the traditional tribes of the world, where the prefrontal cortex was still in balance with the rest of human consciousness; where it hadn't achieved its control over the CONDUCTER."

"Now, Eusebio, before you left Tuckers Corner to participate here in the PEPS hearing, weren't you preparing course work on the American Indians?"

"Yes, you know I was." I got unbelievably irritated that she referred to kidnapping me as "leaving Tuckers Corner." I tried to remind myself that she was meant to be on my side.

"Well, Eusebio, tell us about the American Indians. Who they were, what their lives were like. That would be a great way to answer the question from Counsel Shields."

Finally, it dawned on me what Naomi had repeatedly been trying to explain to me—that my whole life was a preparation for this hearing.

She wanted me to talk about what mattered to me more than anything in my life. To give utterance to what was special in our human existence. To be the mouthpiece for the millions of wondrous lives lived silently in centuries and millennia past. For the souls and spirits of our human ancestors who had lived in harmony with their world. I was going to record their existence here in the conference room of the PEPS hearing and by doing so, use the collective force of their spirits to make a stand for humanity.

For the first time since I was taken from Tuckers Corner, I became excited. I realized Naomi had chosen me for a purpose.

A swirl of energy took over me, and I began to talk about the American Indians. Falteringly at first, a little woodenly, and then more fluently, I talked about the lives of the great tribes. The Indians of the Great Plains, the Sioux, the Arapahoe. The Indians of the prairies, the Pawnee and the Osage. The Zuni and Navajo of the South West.

As I talked, I began to lose myself in my subject. The great seasonal buffalo hunts. The ceremonies and dances—the Sun Dance, the Snake Dance. *Wakan Tanka*, the Great Spirit. The *wakanpi*, the spirits that have power over everything we do. The great warrior way of life. I spoke the famous saying of the Lakota Sun Dance: *"That the people might live!"*

I was finishing describing the vision quest, how a lone warrior would spend days fasting up in the mountain, with the tribe below praying for him to make contact with *Wakan Tanka*, when it seemed that Harry Shields could stand no more. He stuck his head forward and interrupted my flow.

"Eusebio," he said, "thank you for your eloquent description of the native American Indians. That was both beautiful and informative."

I hated his phony compliments. But he kept going before I could interrupt.

"Now," he said, leaning back in his chair, putting his hands behind his head, so relaxed, "I think it's time to take a break from the cross-examination and admit into evidence an NVRX. It's called Reflecting Water."

Harry got up, walked over to a closet in the conference room, and brought out what looked like three motorbike helmets. As he presented one each to me and Naomi, I looked across with total bewilderment.

"NVRX? Reflecting Water?"

Naomi gave me one of her reassuring smiles.

"It's OK, Eusebio. Just put the helmet on, like this . . . It's a Neurographic Virtual Reality Experience. Sit back and let it take you. Don't try to fight it. Just go with the flow."

The helmet covered my face completely. Everything was black. But after a few moments, I began to see a complete scene in front of me. Like one of those ancient twenty-first century movies we watch back in Tuckers Corner. Only the scene was all around me and it wasn't just visual. I could see, hear, smell, feel everything as though it were real.

What I saw was a wide open plain with snow-covered mountains in the distance. The grass around me was blowing with a cool wind but the bright sun warmed my face, peeping above the horizon, rising into a deep blue sky. Over on the left and behind me were teepees and the buzz of people engaged in everyday activities. I could smell the delicious odor of buffalo meat smoking over a big fireplace.

Buffalo meat? How the hell did I know what it was? I'd never smelled buffalo meat in my life. Then, I began to realize the strangest thing. Thoughts were starting to enter my mind. But they weren't my own thoughts. They seemed to go with the scene. At first, I tried to reject them, and then I remembered Naomi telling me, "Go with the flow." So, I figured, I may as well.

It's an important day for my big brother, Waking Bear, the thoughts told me. *Today, he's going to ride on a full-grown horse for the first time. He's going to get thrown many times. I hope he doesn't break any bones. But he'll do well. I know it. The* wakanpi *are with him.*

By this time, I was beginning to let the scene, the feelings, the thoughts wash over me. It was easier that way. Just let myself *be* there.

I'm walking over to the corral with my big sister, Sun Behind Clouds. She's older than me and Waking Bear. She's almost a woman. I saw her kissing a boy the other day at the creek, but she wouldn't talk to me about it. She said I'm too young to understand. But I do understand. One day I'll be big, like Sun Behind Clouds, and I'll kiss a boy too.

Sun Behind Clouds is taking me to see Waking Bear become a horse-warrior today. We're going to give him our courage. My mama told me that once, a long time ago, there were no horses, just like there were no white men. But when *Wakan Tanka* wasn't looking, the white man came to our land. *Wakan Tanka* felt sorry he'd let that happen, so he gave us horses to make our lives better. Mama shook her head and told me "Better no white man and no horse." I couldn't imagine it.

I see a glinting stone on my right and bend down to pick it up. It's prettier than all the other stones around. I'll add it to my collection.

"Reflecting Water, come on!" Sun Behind Clouds tells me. "We've got to get to the corral before Waking Bear begins. We need to give him our courage. He'll need the courage of three to ride the full-grown horse today."

There will be hardly any warriors to watch Waking Bear this morning. They're out hunting along with our friends from the Arapahoe who are staying with us. It's OK to go out hunting today because our leader, Black Kettle, has made us safe. He's a great leader. He's been all the way to the other side of the world to see the Great White Father. He came back with so many special things: metal badges of honor with miniature eagles; important papers with all kinds of white man inscriptions on them; and most special of all, a flag from the White Father with red and white stripes and white stars in a blue sky. A flag with magic powers, Black Kettle told us. Powers from the Great White Father who would always protect us under the flag.

I hear shouting from the teepees. The men who are still in the settlement are mostly the older ones, but they seem very upset.

"Look," I point excitedly to my sister, "there's White Antelope. Look how fast he's riding!" No one in the Cheyenne is braver and wiser than White Antelope except, of course, Black Kettle.

Sun Behind Clouds isn't happy with what she sees.

"There are white men over there. White Antelope's riding towards them." Sun Behind Clouds gasped. "There are so many of them. They're the Bluecoats. They shouldn't be here. Oh no!"

"What, sister?"

"Can't you hear what White Antelope is singing?"

I can barely make out his voice wailing over the field.

"It's the Song of Death, Reflecting Water. White Antelope's riding to his death."

Almost as soon as I hear these words from my sister, I see puffs of smoke coming from the white men in the blue coats and White Antelope falls off his horse. A few seconds later, I hear the "putt, putt, putt" of the guns as the sounds finally reach us.

Now my sister is frantic. She grabs me.

"We must run back to the teepees. To Black Kettle's teepee. To the flag of the Great White Father. His magic will protect us."

"What about Waking Bear? He's going to be a horse-warrior today!"

"No time. We've got to get to Black Kettle's flag."

Now Sun Behind Clouds is dragging me as fast as she can. I'm half running, half flying in her grip. We're getting closer to Black Kettle's teepee. But the Bluecoat white men are riding all around us, shooting at people, setting fire to teepees. I see Yellow Flower, my cousin, running towards us and fall down, screaming in pain.

"Come, Reflecting Water, faster, faster!" my sister yells at me.

But, all of a sudden, she's no longer grabbing me. She grunts and falls on top of me. I think she's playing a game with me. But she doesn't say anything more, just makes strange gurgling noises. I feel her warmth all over me. Flowing over me. Her blood is flowing on me. Her body is still. Sun Behind Clouds is no longer breathing. My sister is no longer breathing.

I lie under my sister. Completely still. I hear terrible noises: screaming, tortured yells that I never thought could exist in our world. Everywhere around me is movement, running, horses neighing, white men yelling, my people screaming.

But I remain completely still. The spirit of the stone I picked up earlier has entered me. Still as a stone, I lie under sister's body, her blood no longer running, but congealing over me. My face is covered in her blood. I lick its salty taste in my mouth, sucking in the spirit of my beloved sister.

Hours pass. My eyes are closed. I hear shooting, wailing, screaming. I smell gunpowder, smoke of burning teepees, and then of burning flesh. I know it's human flesh I can smell. Slowly, silence returns. Eerie, dead silence.

Then, I hear white men around me, talking in their strange language. One of them comes closer to us. I hear him shouting to the other white men. I smell the sickening smell of alcohol from his breath. I try to stay still. I half open my eyes and I see the world through the red blood of sister. Everything red. The white man pulls my sister up. I remain still. I pretend to be dead. He cuts my sister's clothing open. He's not interested in me. He exposes the bare left breast of my sister. Her breasts that just grew two years ago, that I wished I were old enough to have. He puts his face to her breast and licks it. Then he takes a big knife and starts cutting her left breast. No blood. It stopped flowing hours ago. He cuts at it like a buffalo steak. I hear the tearing sound of my sister's dead flesh. Her breast is no longer soft. It's hard as leather in his hands. He cuts around her breast until, finally, it's separated from her chest. He holds it in his hand. One side still beautiful with my sister's nipple in the middle. The other side ugly and black with congealed blood. He lets out a snickering noise and smiles. He puts my sister's breast in his pocket.

I'm no longer scared. I want to join my sister on the other side. I hope he'll see I'm alive and put his knife through me. But one of his friends calls him and he turns away from us. From me and my sister, Sun Behind Clouds, whose chest is now open to the world with a big, black scar where once her soft left breast had been.

The world suddenly goes black. The thoughts of Reflecting Water vanish from my mind. I realize that I'm all me again. Eusebio. But the experiences of Reflecting Water are still in my brain. They've seared themselves into my memory. I know I'll never forget them as long as I'm alive.

"Eusebio, you can take off your helmet now." It's the soft voice of Naomi.

It takes me a few seconds to shake myself from the horror. To realize that I'm back in the UN building, with Harry Shields and Naomi Aramovich around a table in a conference room.

Naomi's looking still and somber. Harry's shaking his head with a plastic expression of sadness on his face.

"Terrible. Terrible," he mutters softly.

Then he shakes his head more vigorously, as if waking himself up. He turns to me, like I'm a fellow conspirator.

"Eusebio, you know what you were experiencing, don't you? Your specialty is, after all, the history of the American Indians."

I know only too well.

"Sand Creek, Colorado. November 1864. Colonel John Chivington. Led one of the worst massacres in American history."

Harry gave me a look of concern, as though he really cared.

"Now, I assume the American Government investigated this, right?"

"Yes."

"And of course Colonel Chivington was punished, put in jail?"

"No," I answered sullenly.

Harry raised his eyes to the ceiling, took a few breaths, and continued.

"Now, Eusebio, I'd like to ask you, roughly how many American Indians were there in North America in 1492, when the Europeans discovered the New World?"

I knew the answer to that. "As many as ten million," I told him.

"And four hundred years later, by 1900, how many American Indians were alive?"

"About four hundred thousand."

Harry paused, his forehead wrinkled, as though he were trying to calculate something in his head.

"So, in four hundred years, ninety-five per cent of the native population was wiped out?"

"Yes."

"Why was that, do you think?"

I began to get angry. "You know why it was. Because the Europeans that came to the New World annihilated the native Americans. Through disease, betrayals, massacres, stealing their land, and destroying the buffalo."

And that was how I found myself sitting in the neurographic chair, telling Harry Shields and his PEPS hearing how the Europeans had systematically devastated the native Americans, cheating and betraying them, manipulating their beliefs, killing them one by one, massacring them in their settlements, destroying their spirit and culture. And building cities and freeways over their sacred territory.

Finally, as the hours passed, Harry Shields sat back in his chair, obviously satisfied that he'd done enough to expose the cruelty and treachery that the American Indians had suffered. He took a deep breath and said:

"Now, I would like to refer back to our earlier discussion of the human soul. Which soul is it, exactly, that the PEPS proposal would be eliminating? The soul of those brave white men who destroyed the American Indians, mutilating their corpses? Or the soul of the indigenous people? Because, if it's the latter, it seems the Primals have already done a damn good job of eliminating it already. And if it's the former . . . well, please explain to me what's worth saving."

Naomi was ready for this. "On the contrary, Counsel Shields," she countered. "If PEPS is implemented, then one day hundreds of years from now, we may be viewed as perpetrators of a terrible crime, just like the Americans of the nineteenth century."

I felt like a hamster in a cage, listening to these two d-human lawyers wrangling about my fate and the fate of three billion of my fellow human beings. It seemed to me they were playing an intellectual game at my expense. At the expense of my race.

They kept debating while I felt an upsurge of anger rising in me. I was emotionally exhausted from the outpourings of the last few hours. I'd felt I was doing something meaningful to defend my race. Now, it was all transformed into a legalistic chess game, with these two d-humans, clearly enjoying themselves, sparring over who could make the best point for the record.

I got so angry that I was about to get up from my neurographic chair and walk out of the conference room in protest. The words of Yusef kept ringing through my mind: *"You will be their stooge."* And then, as soon I'd made the decision to end my part in this travesty, they called it a day. They'd beaten me to the finish line.

They'd both agreed that the crux of the issue was the true nature of the Primals currently alive. Harry Shields' position was that there's nothing left worth saving. Naomi argued that we still have a soul that shouldn't be destroyed.

Once they arrived at this point, Harry Shields said:

"Well, Counsel Aramovich, this appears like an appropriate time to adjourn for the day. Tomorrow, with our virtual field trip to the Primal settlement of Shaktigarh in India, we will hopefully gain more evidence to settle the issue."

Virtual field trip? What were they talking about? Where or what was Shaktigarh? I was, as usual, completely confused, once again realizing I was playing a game according to rules that nobody had bothered to explain to me. Only it wasn't a game. It was the future of my race.

Jessica Goodrich

8

[Excerpt from The Humanist Annals: The Book of Jessica*]*

Heard the song of a poet who died in the gutter

"Julius ... It's Julius ... He ... They shot him. He's ... he's dead. I just got off the phone with Alison."

That was how I first heard of it. From the hushed, broken tones of Brian Chang, Julius' most faithful research colleague. Along with the terrible dread, the feeling of my guts being sucked out of me, came another thought. That bitch, I thought to myself. She couldn't call me directly. Even in Julius' death, she had to tell Brian rather than me. I had to hear it secondhand.

Alison always hated me because there was a bond between me and Julius that she could never even come near. I saw the greatness in Julius that Alison could only resent. I could share his vision. We could blaze the trail together to save the human soul. And now, Julius was dead. He was gone. What was I to do?

It wasn't too long before a call came in from Jason Hilgard in Chicago. I was expecting it. I looked at his well-manicured features, that ever-so-appropriate look of bereavement on his face. Just a few minutes since disaster strikes, I thought, and he's already got the right look down.

"Jessica, you've heard the news?" he asked in his mellifluous voice. "We need to meet in person. The three of us. You, me, and Brian. That's what Julius would want. The Humanist movement is more important than any of us, even Julius. He'd want us to keep things going without him."

I finished talking with Jason, and then I was alone again. I'd never felt so alone. The emotion began to hit me. A wave that just kept coming and coming. I'd only known Julius for a few years, and yet he meant more to me than anyone in my life. I thought back to that time in Guatemala, in the little village of Chajul, where I first ran into him.

Chajul was the site of our water purification pilot project. If it worked there, we had plans for installing hundreds throughout indigenous parts of Latin America. Because it was so important, I wanted to see it for myself. Talk to the local villagers about how it was working. There's an American guy there, my staff told me, who speaks the local language and can act as an interpreter. He's a little strange but very helpful.

He was curious about me.

"So why, Ms. Goodrich, do you think these people from Chajul need your help to drink water, having made it through five hundred years since the Spanish conquest?"

His formality was playful; the look in his eyes was amused.

"Because the bottling companies are stealing fresh water sources from communities like this around the world. They'll be left with nothing unless they adopt new technologies for themselves." At that time, I was so filled with the energy to save the world.

"And why you, Ms. Goodrich?"

"Because I got lucky and can do something about it." I told him about my company, Applied Genomic Solutions. How I'd built it from scratch over fifteen years, developing nanochips that create new genes—genes that could strengthen tree trunks, make corn oil more combustible for fuel. Two thousand employees around the world. How I took the company public. How Nanogenic, the industry giant, bought us, promised me a position on their board. I told Julius how I felt like my own baby had been taken from me and murdered when they started dismantling everything I'd built to incorporate it into their plan for global industry domination. A year later and I was kicked off the board. Successful executive with two billion dollars to her name and an empty hole in her soul.

"So, Jessica, how do you fill a soul with two billion dollars?"

I was "Jessica" now, but the same amusement darted across his eyes.

"By using the money. To try to make the world a better place. For these people whose lives get ruined for the want of a few dollars."

I spent the following years pouring my money into water purification plants, internet access for remote villages, and trying to fill the hole in my soul. But I never forgot those few days with Julius in Chajul. That look in his eyes. As the years passed, I realized it was more than just amusement. He really wanted to know. He was searching for something. But I didn't know what. And all the time, his presence grew within me, almost into an obsession. But I had no idea where to find him.

Until I came across a new book, just published, called *On Being Human*. I read it, gasping for breath. This was the Julius Schumacher from Chajul. That one book nourished me more than those years spending my money trying to save the world. I finished the book and tracked him down in New York.

And now Julius was dead.

* * * *

"Julius would want us to keep building the Humanist movement. We're the ones who shared his vision. He always relied on the three of us, and now, in his death, he needs us even more. We've got to put aside our differences and work together to fulfill his vision."

Jason Hilgard seemed unable to speak without uttering noble statements. And here he was again. Just a few days after Julius' funeral. His ashes still warm.

"You're right about that," Brian Chang nodded sincerely. Always so literal. Never seeing the underlying motives of people like Jason. "I've received so many calls now from Humanists around the world. They're asking what happens next. They're distraught. Thousands of people a week are joining the movement but now nobody knows what they're joining. What are the Humanists without Julius Schumacher?"

Yes, I knew we needed to work together, but how could I

embrace a serpent like Jason? For the sake of Julius, I figured I'd try to do anything.

"Julius was going to give that major speech next month," Brian continued. "I was preparing the research for him."

"You mean the one on how genetic engineering affects the soul?" Jason asked. Brian nodded.

"Brian," he asked, ever so calmly, so self-assured. "Did Julius tell you what his position was going to be?"

"No."

My adrenaline started pulsing. I had known Jason had an ulterior motive. Now I saw what it was.

"How about the research he asked you for? Could you tell from that where he was going?"

"Not exactly."

I couldn't control myself any more.

"There's nothing to figure out, Jason. We all know Julius' position. It's clear in his book. It's clear in everything he said. It's what Humanism is all about. Genetic engineering can destroy the soul. Humanism is about nurturing the soul. You can't be a Humanist and alter the DNA of your offspring."

"Please, Jessica, don't get carried away now. We can't afford it."

Patronizing bastard.

"See, Jessica, I had a number of long conversations with Julius about the topic. You've met Rod and Charlotte, my two kids." A sweet little twinkle entered his eyes. "They're so precious . . . and they're both PNO babies—no risk of diabetes, cancer, heart disease when they grow old. What's wrong with that? So they have healthier genes. How can you hold that against them? Look them in the eyes, see them smile at you, and try telling me they have no soul." Jason chuckled ever so lightly. "The whole idea is ridiculous. And Julius as good as told me that he agreed."

I jumped at the chance.

"'As good as told you' means he didn't tell you he agreed, doesn't it?"

"Oh, Jessica, you're always spoiling for a fight. We've got to use some common sense here." Jason was a master at not answering the question. "The fact is, Jessica, at the current rate, we'll have a million people calling themselves Humanists by the end of the year. We'll be at five million three years from now. And I guarantee you, Jessica, ninety per cent of these people will have nothing whatsoever to do with Humanism if they're told they have to condemn their children to a lifetime of disease in order to protect their souls."

So now it was out in the open. Just a few days after Julius' death and the battle lines were drawn.

"Spoken like a true marketing consultant, Jason," I struck back. "You might do a great job with your firm back in Chicago, but this is not one of your plum marketing assignments. This is real life. It's got nothing to do with marketing. I don't care if ninety-nine per cent of Humanists leave the movement because they don't like hearing the truth. What I care about is telling the truth, just like Julius did, and dealing with the consequences. Not how many Humanists we have by the end of next year."

"Do you think, Jessica, perhaps because you don't have any kids of your own, that you can afford to be a little more cavalier with the health of the next generation?"

That cut me deep. There were no holds barred in this battle. He looked over to Brian.

"Brian, your lovely son, Thomas . . . he's a PNO child, isn't he?"
Brian nodded.
"Do you think he has a soul?"
Brian nodded back thoughtfully. "Yes, but . . . "
Jason wouldn't let him finish. He turned back to me triumphantly.
"Jessica, it's not about marketing. Julius didn't want me close to him because I'm a marketing consultant. It's because I understand people, Jessica, and the trade-offs involved in life. The simple matter is, Julius wanted to get the word out to all humanity, not just a few true believers. OK, so we all agree that at some point, genetic engineering can destroy a soul. And we don't know exactly where that point is. But we do know that we're nowhere near that point yet. So why destroy the growth of Humanism before it even begins, over a theoretical principle? If people can follow Humanism and still give

their children the chance of a healthier life, then in a few years our movement can begin to make a real impact on the world, we can affect the future course of humanity. That's what Julius wanted."

"Jason, why don't you change your name to Paul?" I asked him.

"What?"

"Well, aren't you trying to do what Paul did to Christianity two thousand years ago? Make it more convenient to the Gentiles, get rid of those pesky problems like circumcision, give them a better afterlife to look forward to, and before you know it, you've got a world religion. After all, wasn't Paul the greatest marketer our world's ever seen?"

I had meant to hurt Jason. No such luck. I think he got positively puffed up by the comparison.

"Well, Jessica, the truth is that without Paul, Christianity wouldn't have become a world religion. It's not enough to have an insight into the truth, Jessica . . . you have to be able to communicate it in a way that will inspire people, ordinary people, masses of people. Paul did that for Christianity. And I'm telling you, Julius would want us to do that for him. Let's not let his death be for nothing. Now, our Humanist movement has its own martyr, just like Jesus . . . "

We kept at it all day, exhausting each other with intellectual sophistries and emotional jabs. Brian, for the most part, just watched and listened to our duel. Finally, we turned to him. By the end of the day, Jason and I both agreed that Brian would be our tie-breaker. Whichever position he took would be in the majority and would become the official position of the Humanist movement. Could someone be a Humanist and permit any pre-natal genetic alteration of their offspring? Yes or no?

Brian, sincere and academic, rested on his integrity like a rock. His career was a testament to that. He'd been Julius' right-hand man in the research team at Harvard that developed neurographic imaging. In the four years Julius went AWOL with the indigenous tribes of the world, Brian had independently begun to worry about the same neurographic images without smudges that had sent Julius off on his voyage of discovery. Brian had stayed at Harvard and tried to pursue his own research on the smudges. He tried to find people whose genes had been pre-natally optimized and run neurographic scans of their thoughts to see if they had smudges or not. He never got a definitive answer. When he asked Harvard for funding to analyze the smudges more systematically, he was told by the head of the department that, if he valued his career, he should avoid any further discussion about "Schumacher's smudges." By then, Julius had been ridiculed in scientific circles and Brian was told he'd end up in the same place. Investigations into matters of the human soul, he was told, were better left to religious ministers than scientific researchers.

That was when Brian left Harvard, got in touch with Julius, and became one of the leaders of the movement.

And now, he was making the call for the future of Humanism. Jason felt confident he'd get the answer he wanted. After all, Brian had his own PNO baby. I was ready to walk out and leave the Humanists forever, rather than take part in undermining Julius' struggle to save the human soul.

"You know Julius' analogy about the soul, how it's like an orchestra?" Brian started speaking after lots of humming and herring and clearing his throat nervously. "You know, how over five hundred million years of evolution, as life on earth began branching off into plants, reptiles, mammals, a shared harmony existed between the DNA of every living object on earth?"

Jason and I both nodded silently, earnestly. You could hear a pin drop.

"And as creatures became more diverse, the harmony between their DNA and the DNA of other creatures became more complex, but it never disappeared." Brian's voice was taking on more authority with every sentence. "Julius theorized that the soul is not something that can ever be tangibly identified, but it exists as a series of relationships, patterns, vibrations, between different elements of a living creature's DNA and RNA."

We were both listening intently. Where was Brian going with this?

"So Julius saw the origins of the soul to be the Earth itself. The relationship between man and the Earth is integral to the existence of the soul. In fact, Julius believed this was the basis for the immortality of the soul." Brian was no longer talking to either of us. He was staring straight ahead, intently, into space. "If . . . if Julius is right, then . . . " Brian paused for a moment. His voice became more solemn. "If Julius is right, then right now his soul—that dynamic interaction of billions of strands of DNA within him—didn't die but has been transformed into billions of separate interactions now re-forming with other DNA belonging to other forms of life on Earth. So his undivided soul no longer exists as it did, but its component parts are helping create new souls in new creatures."

Brian turned to both of us with a strange smile on his face.

"That's what he meant with his orchestra analogy. Now that Julius is dead, his own symphony no longer exists. But each note of his symphony continues to exist and joins up with other notes on the Earth to become part of billions of other symphonies, for as long as life continues on this Earth."

I wanted so much to ask Brian where he was going with all this, but I held my tongue. I didn't want to break his spell.

But Brian broke his own spell. He shook his head and his voice returned to his normal academic sincerity.

"So," he continued, "I've thought a lot about that orchestra analogy. Julius used to talk with me about it. He used to say that pre-natal genetic engineering was like trying to create a square violin or a rectangular flute—you'd make the instruments fit better in a box but you'd kill the music. And he may be right. The thing is, think about an orchestra. If you eliminate one of the lesser violins, you'd hardly notice the difference in the symphony. But if it's a piano concerto and you destroy the piano, the music's over."

Now Brian looked intensely at both of us. The denouement was close.

"So the question is—is the PNO stuff that we do nowadays changing one of the lesser violins or is it changing the piano? Problem is, we just don't know. We haven't done enough research. I think it's just changing one of the violins. Or even less, perhaps it's just slightly affecting the acoustics of the music hall. But we don't know.

So, until we've done more research and come up with better answers, the only scientifically valid approach is Jessica's. We should avoid any genetic engineering on our children in case we end up inadvertently destroying their souls."

I'd won! Brian and I were on the same side. A flush of excitement pulsed through me. I had immediate visions of working with Brian—strange as he was—to build the Humanist movement in Julius' image. A real Humanist movement. One that didn't compromise.

*   *   *   *

The day was over. I was walking out of the building to catch a plane back to my home in Big Sur. Thoughts running through my head about what Brian and I were going to do next for the movement.

"Hi, Ms. Goodrich, would you mind spending a few moments with us? We have some questions for you about your meeting today."

Usually I was ready for them. But today, with the shock of Julius' death, the battle with Jason, I was totally unprepared. There were three guys, two of whom I knew from before. They had the dark suits and high-tech equipment of the Department of Homeland Security. Or, as we call them nowadays, simply the "Department." They hounded me incessantly. I knew it would backfire, but I couldn't stop myself.

"Will you guys just leave me alone? Julius Schumacher just died. I need to catch a plane back home. Don't you have any human sensitivity? Just leave me be."

"Ms. Goodrich, you know as well as I do that, as a USP, you have a legal obligation to answer our questions right now, without delay." The leader of the three was one I've dealt with before. A real prick. "You know that refusal to do so will land you in jail. Now do you want to cooperate or go to jail?"

So they led me into their van parked a block away, where they could wire me up with a lie detector kit before asking the questions. Yes, I was a USP, an Unaffiliated Suspicious Person. After Columbus, the Department had scored the whole American population with a gigantic computer algorithm, based on their activities and affiliations, as to their likelihood of being a member of the Citizens Seeking Global Justice. Since I'd left Nanogenic, I wasn't a member of a corporation, a church, a mosque, or a synagogue; I didn't belong to a union or a golf club; and to make matters worse, I continually went on trips to developing countries, spending my money trying to help the poorest people there . . . all those things put me through the roof on their USP list. I was under continual surveillance. They listened to every one of my phone calls, they analyzed every e-mail I sent. Someone in their Department was convinced I must have been involved with Columbus. And I was equally convinced they'd been involved in Julius' murder.

"Is it possible, Ms. Goodrich, that Dr. Schumacher's death has permitted you to try to take over the Humanist movement? And is it possible that you are now planning to direct the Humanists to subvert the U.S. Government? To plan another Columbus? Was it you, Ms. Goodrich, who killed Dr. Schumacher in an effort to take over his movement and use it to attack our homeland?"

They were nuts. Paranoid nutcases, every one of them. And they were the ones setting the agenda of our government. But I'd learned the hard way not to lose my temper with them. They had all the cards. I took some deep breaths and tried to answer them seriously.

Of course, I missed my flight back to Big Sur. But at least they didn't arrest me. Just wanted to know what we'd been talking about all day. They didn't believe for one instant that we could have spent the day arguing about the human soul. But I made it back to Big Sur the next afternoon.

* * * *

Now I'm sitting on my deck at home, watching the sun begin its descent behind the distant Pacific Ocean as fingers of fog roll their way between the green hills. A glass of chilled chardonnay in one hand, and a joint in the other. As I sit here, I feel myself hurtling down one of those unstoppable slides into depression. Maybe it's the wine and the weed together—sometimes it does that to me. I think it was

Jason's jab about me not having any children of my own. Patti and I could have had our own kids. We were partners for nearly twenty years and they have the genetic technology nowadays for us to have had our own child. But we never got around to it. Patti was too busy with her art and I was engrossed in building my company. Then as the demands of my company became too overwhelming, we split up.

So I find myself on the deck, alone with this scene of beauty. All alone. No Patti. No children. Even the company I spent half my life building has now disappeared. I think of Julius' remark that first time he met me: *"So, Jessica, how do you fill a soul with two billion dollars?"* Good question. I thought I'd had the answer but while it helped a lot of people around the world, I'm not sure it helped me. Then, Julius himself helped me fill that hole. Gave me something to live for. And now he's dead. And here am I, prime suspect of the Department, living my life like a well-endowed fugitive from justice.

That familiar feeling, when my heart sinks so low there's nowhere further down to go, which at least gives me a little comfort. A little security that I can't feel any worse than I do now. And I look out at the sun, now beginning to paint the horizon in an awe-inspiring red hue, at the fog busily pouring from the ocean across the valleys, at the graceful green oaks and cypress sitting still on the hillsides around me. Then—maybe it's the weed having an effect—I feel like the beauty of it has begun to swirl around into a life of its own and, along with the breeze across my cheek, has begun to paint itself over me. A fanciful thought enters my mind. It's Julius. It's his spirit. He's still here within me, to inspire me. Inspire me. Breathe into me. The wind is his breath. My lungs are breathing in some of those billions of notes of his soul swirling around the universe.

I think of Julius in one of his more lyrical moments. He used to compare the soul to an ecosystem. Every little part of the ecosystem, the vegetation and the rain, the mold and the bugs, the worms and the birds—they had all evolved together to maintain a harmonious whole. Then mankind came along with its prefrontal cortex and blew away those ecosystems, turning the rainforests into soy farms, the tundra into marshland. And now that prefrontal cortex is beginning to do the same thing with the ecosystem of the human soul. Chopping down the trees, one at a time.

Julius and me. We're going to save a little part of that ecosystem. Like one of those nature reserves that Alison has spent her life fighting for. Only this time, it will be a nature reserve for the human soul. Brian and me. We're going to build communities in different parts of the world for refugees from modern civilization to flee to. We'll fill our communities with the finest artifacts from the indigenous tribes whose flames have not yet been snuffed out. With Kalimantan masks from Borneo. With carved Torajan doors. With huipils from Guatemala. With Sepik River bark paintings. Future generations of our community will see and feel these things and know that they are not alone in trying to nurture their souls.

Brian and me. And Julius. Together, the three of us will create a Humanist community. And I won't be sitting on my deck alone.

9 The Department Agents

I saw a room full of men with their hammers a-bleedin'

B efore I could catch my breath, Naomi was steering me out of the conference room, down the elevator, out of the sanctity of the UN building and back into the cacophony of the New York skywalks. We stopped at Naomi's favorite Betelbar for a drink, where she gave me her usual encouraging feedback and told me about our "virtual field trip."

It was going to be a tour of a Primal community called Shaktigarh in West Bengal, in India. Only this tour was not going to be in person. We would be using virtual reality so we could visit Shaktigarh without ever leaving the UN building.

I felt a wave of childlike excitement at the prospect. The thought of traveling—even virtually—to another country, another continent . . . Up to that time, I'd spent my entire life in the sheltered community of Tuckers Corner. Now, I'd have the chance to see a completely different part of the world! For a brief moment, the gravity of the whole situation evaporated, and I felt a surge of anticipation.

"Now, the man who'll be our guide in Shaktigarh tomorrow," Naomi continued, "he's a d-human, but he's not exactly the same as me or Harry Shields. He's d2 rather than d3."

D2? D3? What the hell was d3?

As always, Naomi had the answer for me.

"A d2-human, Eusebio, is someone whose genes have been customized . . . their parents choose the features they want, their intelligence level, their main character traits. This is the technology developed last century."

Sure, I understood that much.

"Well, a d3-human goes beyond that. A d3-human is someone who's been neurographically optimized. Most Americans and Europeans are d3. I'm d3, and so is Harry Shields. In fact, so is almost everyone around us here in New York. But in places like China and India, most people are still d2."

What the hell's the difference? I thought to myself. A d-human's a d-human as far as I'm concerned.

We left the Betelbar and went back to my hotel room. Naomi had some leisure reading for me. She pointed to the coffee table, and there was a brand new copy of *Tuckers Weekly*. My disappearance had made the headline in typically straightforward terms. It read: "Eusebio Franklin Has Vanished." It pained me to think of my friends searching for clues in my house and in my office at school. I knew they wouldn't find anything. The d-humans were way too thorough for that.

Naomi left, telling me to make sure I got an early night. Shaktigarh was ten and a half hours later than New York, which meant we'd do our virtual reality tour very early in the morning to get the daylight hours in Shaktigarh.

I was alone again in my hotel room. And that was when the Department agents arrived.

It had only been about fifteen minutes since Naomi left. I was still browsing through the latest copy of *Tuckers Weekly* when I heard a knock on the door. I opened the door and two gigantic men, one white and one black, stepped into my room. They were dressed in dark suits, and they both wore versions of the high-tech glasses I had used when I was at the top of the UN building. One of them was carrying a briefcase. Because their glasses were reflective, I couldn't see their eyes. But I didn't need to see their eyes to get an instant sense of doom as they entered.

"Eusebio Franklin, we are agents from the Department of Homeland Security. We need your assistance for a few minutes. We appreciate your cooperation," the white man spoke.

"My assistance with what?" I was not feeling very cooperative.

"We understand that last night, you received a visit from someone who called himself Yusef. We need to know what this 'Yusef' looked like."

"Don't worry," added the black agent. "You don't need to do anything. We just gotta place our MNI around your head, and we'll do all the rest of the work."

"What's an MNI?" I asked, nonplussed.

The black agent smiled reassuringly. "Oh, it's a mobile neurographic imager, Eusebio. Once we've fitted it around your head, it will help you find the image of Yusef in your memory, and we'll be able to record it on to our 3DI screen."

I felt a surge of panic and anger as I remembered the humiliation of the "neurographic event" earlier in the day. I'd already betrayed Yusef this morning. I was damned if I was going to do it again. I would do everything in my power to stop them from invading my mind.

"Get out of here," I said to them both angrily. "I'm not going to help you and you've got no right to be in my room."

They both grinned back at me, like I was an ant they were about to step on.

"Eusebio," said the white man, "we have every right to be here in your room. In fact, you have no right not to cooperate with us. Based on what you just said to us, which is all being recorded, you could be facing five years in jail already. Non-cooperation with a Department agent is an automatic felony."

I didn't give a damn about five years in their jail. I wasn't going to betray Yusef, and I told them that.

"Get the hell out of my room. If you want to arrest me, go ahead. I don't give a damn. But you're not going to get an image of Yusef from me."

"Oh yes we are," said the black agent.

At that point, the white agent stepped towards me and picked me up, like I was a little girl. He was so much bigger and stronger than I was, that my attempts to fight him off were futile. I tried to hit him and kick him, but everything I did was useless. He held me in a grip so I couldn't free up an arm or a leg. He was obviously being gentle with me, because he could have broken my back in a second if he'd wanted.

He placed me down in a chair, and before I knew it, my hands were handcuffed behind the chair with a plastic cord, loose so they didn't hurt, but secure so I couldn't move them. I was still kicking and fighting to get out of the chair, like a fish flapping about vainly on the deck of a fishing boat. I started to scream at the top of my voice. The black agent put his hand over my mouth and gagged me with a cloth.

My adrenaline was pounding. I was being violated. I was going to fight to the death to stop them getting Yusef's image out of my mind.

The white man used more plastic cords to tie my ankles to the chair, stopping me from kicking. The black agent, meanwhile, opened his briefcase and took out a device. He unfolded something that looked like a set of headphones. Then he took out a soft metal strip—like a type of aerial—and clicked it together, so it formed a three-foot wide circle. Then he fixed the circular strip on a flat metal base, which he placed on the coffee table.

The black agent spoke to his partner, in a matter-of-fact tone.

"Jake, you ready to do the headset?"

"Sure, Mikey," Jake replied.

Jake then picked up the headset, and unfolded it further, so that now it seemed to have four different earpieces. He approached me, tied onto the chair, and placed the headset over my head, with each of the four ends pushing lightly against different parts of my skull—my forehead, my temples and the back of my head. I was helpless. I couldn't get the headset off, even though I kept struggling against my handcuffs, my leg binds and my gag. I was afraid they were going to torture me, but I was determined that, no matter what the pain, I wasn't going to give up Yusef's image to these bastards.

Jake and Mikey sat down on the sofa facing me, legs crossed, relaxed as though they were enjoying a cocktail with a friend. Mikey, the black agent, started talking to me in a menacingly soft voice.

"Now, Eusebio," he said, "we're not going to hurt you. You can relax. We just had to restrain you because you weren't being very cooperative. It's for your own good, because like Jake said, non-cooperation will land you in jail for at least five years. Think of what we've done to you as keeping you out of jail. You should thank us." With that, Mikey chuckled lightly. "We're just here, Eusebio, because someone came to visit you last night in the 3DI, and we need to know what he looked like. Because we need to find him and talk to him about why he came to visit you. That's all, Eusebio."

I was sitting there, gagged and tied up, my blood coursing through me in anger and fear. I couldn't have answered even if I'd wanted to.

"Now, all you've got to do, Eusebio, is remember for us what Yusef looked like." Mikey's voice became even softer, like a hypnotist trying to put a subject under his spell. "So, it was last night, and you were already in bed, right? And you suddenly saw Yusef over there, right?" He pointed to the 3DI receiver in the corner of the room.

I remembered Yusef's visit last night, and again I vowed not to give them any scrap of information, no matter what the consequences to me.

"So, you must have been surprised, seeing a stranger suddenly appearing in your hotel room?" Mikey continued. "What did he look like when you saw him? What was he wearing? You must have been angry at an intruder, like you were with us. Did you ask him who he was?"

Mikey continued talking in a trance-like voice for a few more moments. Suddenly, a flash of light appeared in the middle of the circular wire orb standing on the coffee table in front of us.

"Mikey, we got a register!" Jake exclaimed with restrained excitement.

"Very good, Eusebio, you're doing well," Mikey continued in his hypnotic voice.

I saw that suddenly, there were some specks of color appearing within the circular orb on the coffee table. At the same time, I started feeling a strange sensation, like flashes going off inside my brain.

Every few seconds, another flash sparked inside my head, and each time that happened, more specks of color appeared in the circular orb.

This kept happening for what seemed like several minutes, and to my utter horror, I began to realize that the specks of color were beginning to be identifiable as a human face. Flash by flash, more specks of color appeared and connected to each other, and I began to make out the beginnings of Yusef's face inside the orb. I felt a sinking sense of despair.

"You're doing really well, Eusebio," Mikey said again, with a sneer in his voice. "See, Eusebio, what happens is, our MNI finds the image your mind remembers of Yusef. As soon as it sees that image, it notes the neural coordinates of that thought. Then, it sends a message to your brain to keep replicating those neural coordinates. That's the flash you feel. Each time you do that, it picks up some of the image and translates it into pixels. All you need to do, Eusebio, is relax." Mikey chuckled again, menacingly. "Hey, that's the wonder of technology. If this were a few hundred years ago, we'd have to torture you to get the information . . . and you wouldn't like that, would you?"

I hated Mikey and Jake. I hated their d-human society. I hated the Department of Homeland Security. I hated Naomi Aramovich for taking me from my haven and putting me in this heartless, soulless hotel room under the power of these people.

I watched powerlessly as the image of Yusef began to form, ghost-like, in front of me.

Suddenly, as Yusef's face was about half-formed, the hotel door burst open. It was Naomi. She was furious. I'd never seen her like this. She thundered towards the two Department agents, shouting at the top of her voice.

"Get the hell out of here! Release the Primal right away! Get that MNI off the Primal's head. Get that 3DI dismantled! Immediately!"

Before either of the agents had even stood up from the couch, she was standing over me, pulling off the headset. The flashing in my brain stopped and the image in the circular orb froze, half-formed.

"I'm so sorry, Eusebio," she said to me softly.

Jake had stood up by this point.

"Hey lady," he said, "Do you know what you're doing? We're Department agents. What you've just done could cost you ten years in the slammer. You got some big problems coming your way."

"On the contrary," Naomi responded. Now, her voice was hard and cold as steel. "I have a Veto Authority Level 2A and if you don't release the Primal and get out of here immediately, you're the ones going to have big problems."

"You gotta be kidding," Jake retorted. "No one has a VA Level 2A."

"Well, what's this then?" With a flourish, like Merlin the magician, Naomi held out her PDA and hit a button. A virtual 3-D image of a certificate suddenly appeared in front of her, floating in mid-air. I could see it had some writing and some official looking stamps on it.

Jake turned to his partner.

"Hey, Mikey, authenticate that piece of shit."

Mikey walked over to the image and held up his own PDA to it. I heard some beeps, and Mikey sucked in his breath.

"Holy shit, it's for real," he said to nobody in particular. He looked over at Naomi. "Who are you, lady, that you can get a VA Level 2A?" Suddenly, his voice had more respect.

"That's none of your business," Naomi spat back. "Now this is your business—you get the Primal untied, pack up your toys, and get the hell out of this room in one minute, or I'm calling your boss, and you won't be Department agents for much longer."

The impact of this left me incredulous. Like meek puppy dogs, Jake and Mikey silently walked over to me, unlocked my ties, took my gag off, folded up their instruments, put them back in their briefcase, and walked out the door. They had literally left the room within Naomi's one minute.

"I'm so sorry for this, Eusebio," Naomi was now completely focused on me. "This should never have happened. It's an outrage. I can't believe what they did to you."

At this point, I was in shock. I could barely speak. I felt a surge of gratitude to Naomi for coming to rescue me.

"It's lucky I even heard about it. The hotel manager notified me when he saw the agents, and I came here as fast as I could," Naomi continued.

Absurd as it sounds, I felt guilty for my feelings of hatred for Naomi moments before she'd appeared at the door.

"Are you OK, Eusebio? Do you think you can still manage to get a good night's sleep and take part in the hearing tomorrow? If not, we can reschedule it for the next day."

I reassured her I'd be fine. She gave me a small device to clip onto my belt, and told me that if anything like this happened again, I should push the button, and she'd be right over. A few minutes more of apologizing and Naomi was gone.

* * * *

I was alone again in my hotel prison cell.

I sat on the chair where, moments before, the agents from hell had been piercing into my mind and forcing my neurons to betray Yusef once again. I tried to make sense of all that had happened to me. I kept coming back to the same question: Was I being set up as a stooge for the d-humans, or could I really do something to save my race? Although everything in me rebelled against the idea, deep in my heart I felt I was being set up, just as Yusef had warned me. What was Naomi's role in all this? Was Yusef right—that she was earnest but the system was taking advantage of her too, to add legitimacy to its genocide?

I thought of my gratitude in being rescued by Naomi. In the calm after the initial shock, I began to realize that she hadn't been rescuing *me*—she'd been rescuing her PEPS session. I realized she couldn't care less if Yusef's face had been finished and he'd been caught by the Department. In fact, she would probably have supported them. All she really cared about was the sanctity of her legal process. But then again—was that so bad? She was, after all, trying to defend my race. What was the importance of me—or Yusef for that matter—compared to three billion of my fellow humans?

I felt so powerless in every respect. Supposing I told Naomi I wanted to go back to Tuckers Corner? Would they even let me, with everything

I now knew? I had a strong feeling they would not. With another wave of despair, it began to dawn on me that my own life had changed forever. I would never see my friends again, never teach my class again, never stroke my cat again, never say "Good morning" again to the Barlows as I left my house to head off for school.

I felt so desperate and alone. I'd been violated, first by Harry Shields, then by the Department agents. I kept thinking about Yusef. What a fool I'd been to ignore his warnings last night. He had told me the truth. He was on my side—a fellow human being, rather than these d-humans in the process of eliminating our race. I hoped nobody had been caught for helping Yusef visit me. I wished, deep down, that I could talk with him again, apologize for my idiotic response last night. That I could ask him for advice.

I prepared to get my early night, feeling overcome by a growing sense of depression. I hated myself for allowing all this to be done to me and through me, to all humanity. I felt a heaviness in my heart, a dread for our future.

Suddenly, I heard a soft voice calling to me from the other side of the hotel room. To my amazement, I instantly recognized it. Yusef! He'd returned. I turned in the direction of the voice, and there he was. But his image wasn't as clear as the previous night. It was flickering a little. I was confused. He wasn't in the 3-D imager, but somewhere entirely different in the room. But more than anything, I was filled with a wave of relief and delight. I never expected I'd have the chance to see Yusef again.

"Yusef, I'm so glad to see you!" I blurted out.

He looked straight back at me. "How are you doing, Eusebio? How are you holding up?"

I knew I had to tell him the awful truth immediately. The neurographic chair. The Department agents.

After I'd finished, Yusef just smiled back at me, warmly. "Well, Eusebio, it seems you had a difficult day. But you survived it, with your heart and soul intact, thank God."

"Did anything happen to the people who helped you visit me last night?" I'd desperately wanted to know this all day.

"Yes, Eusebio," Yusef answered gravely. "Something did happen. One of our brothers, fighting for our race, was discovered. He lived in Bangalore, in India, and was part of the technology unit for your hotel. They came to pick him up for questioning in the middle of the night. But they never got him. We all have cyanide capsules inserted in our mouths when we join the freedom fighters, and we make an oath to God that the d-humans will never take us alive. So, our brother, Ashok Prakesh, took his own life in the battle for our race, and protected the rest of us from the d-humans. Praise be to God, may his soul have already arrived in heaven."

I felt like I'd been punched in the stomach. For the first time, I realized on a new level how gravely serious the role was that I'd been given—and had accepted—in this fateful process.

"What about now?" I said to Yusef. "Won't the same thing happen again? How did you even get your image here again?"

Yusef cracked a grim smile. "We have a lot of tricks up our sleeves, Eusebio. Right now, there are two helipods in the air above New York beaming their signals into your hotel room. They don't know who we are. They're just receiving our signals and transmitting them so they intersect in your hotel room. They've been told we're arranging a surprise visit from an old friend. That's why my image isn't anywhere near your 3-D imager. The Department has deactivated any signals that haven't been pre-authorized. But don't ask any more about that. That's all you need to know right now."

"Why are you going through all this—for me?" I asked him.

"Because I need to tell you more about who we are and the struggle we're engaging in. It's important you understand things a little better, my brother."

"But Yusef, won't they do the same thing to me tomorrow—invade my mind again, and know you came to see me again?"

"We'll deal with that a little later, Eusebio. There are some methods we use which I can teach you."

So Yusef started talking to me about the Rejectionists and his fellow human freedom fighters.

"Eusebio," he told me, "we are the last vestige of the greatest traditions of humanity. We blend our love of God with a love for the diversity of human ideas and beliefs. If you look across the human Muslim world, from Morocco in the west to Indonesia in the east, you'll see more variations of peoples, cultures and philosophies than you could imagine. And we don't just tolerate each others' beliefs—we value them. We respect them."

GALT, Yusef explained, had presented a zero-sum game to the world: on one hand, you could have continual war and human suffering; on the other hand, you could have global peace only by giving up the spiritual experience of life—the most important aspect of mankind's existence. But the Rejectionists believed genetic engineering could optimize the spiritual aspect of human beings, and in doing so, tolerance and love for others would naturally follow.

It seemed like we were talking for hours. Then, at some point, Yusef seemed to shake himself. "I'm afraid, Eusebio, I've been talking your ear off. But that's not the reason I'm here. I needed to give you a sense, Eusebio, of who we are and what we're fighting for. A future for humanity, a future that offers hope, where we can share the planet with d-humans, where we can stay in touch with God . . . where every person—human and d-human—can pursue their lives, their beliefs with respect and dignity, however they choose. And I've had to describe this all to you, Eusebio, because I need to ask you a question." He looked at me directly, straight into my eyes. "Are you willing to join our struggle, Eusebio? Are you willing to join our fight to save the human race, to give our race a future?"

I paused for a moment before answering. It may seem self-evident that of course I would join a struggle to save my own race from destruction at the hands of the d-humans. I'd spent the past two days learning of the greatest genocide in history being planned for us, and here was a fellow human being offering me a chance to take part in defending ourselves.

But I paused. I paused because some of the things I'd been hearing from Yusef were unsettling. Difficult to absorb. Here was a man who truly believed in one universal God, clearly willing to die for this belief. I found this strange enough in itself. But this man was now asking me to join him in his struggle. A struggle for what? For his religion? A struggle for humanity? Perhaps. But was this the only path that could lead to our survival?

I thought about the d-human society I'd been thrown into. It seemed to me so crazed and heartless. I thought of Tuckers Corner. I love my little community. I love my friends, my colleagues. I even love the people I don't like. We're like the mountain gorillas and bonobos of the twenty-first century, I thought, who lived out their beautiful, sacred lives while the crushing forces of human development eliminated their living space, acre by acre, tree by tree, life by life. We Humanists have no more chance against the d-humans than the mountain gorillas had of winning back their forest.

I thought of my last two days. Waking up in a luxury hotel prison. Taking part in the PEPS session. Harry Shields' smug, superior face. The way he used the things most sacred to me and subverted them to his own legalistic arguments, somehow making me feel responsible for the very destruction wrought by his own type on the most special things in the world. The humiliation of the "neurographic event," my own private and secret thoughts spoken out in public on the record. Then, I thought what had happened in this room, just a few short hours ago. The Department Agents. And an unknown technology worker, named Ashok Prakesh, far away in Bangalore, who had given his life in the struggle for humanity as a result of the neurographic invasion of my brain.

I knew I had to do everything possible to protect our race against these people. I wasn't a fighter. I was a history teacher. I'd never in my life taken part in any "struggle" against some other power. My struggle had been to live my life properly. Now, I had to take a stand.

"I think I'm ready to join the struggle, Yusef. What do I have to do?" I said to him.

"Right now, Eusebio, nothing that you're not already doing. Later . . . well, that will be up to you. For now, just go ahead with the PEPS session. Give it everything you've got.

"But there's one thing you need to do with me right now. You have to succeed in this, otherwise there's nothing more you can do to help us."

"What's that?"

"When you go into the PEPS session tomorrow morning and Harry Shields asks you the same question as yesterday, you've got to respond without triggering one of their 'neurographic events.'"

"How am I supposed to do that?" I knew I couldn't protect my thoughts against the neurographic chair.

"I'm going to teach you right now."

And that's how I spent the next couple of hours.

Yusef taught me the way to protect my thoughts against neurographic invasion was to control consciously two levels of thought simultaneously and try to think on these two levels with the highest amount of "volume," in order to drown out any other thoughts.

The most successful approach, Yusef explained, was to fill one level of thought by silently singing to yourself a favorite song, preferably one with a catchy tune and lyrics you know well. At the same time, you need to fill the next level of consciousness with a very strong feeling, preferably directed to someone or something in your immediate environment.

Yusef told me to choose my favorite song and sing it to myself out loud. So there I was, in the middle of the night, in a hotel room in New York City, looking at the image of Yusef in front of me, singing a song to myself written two hundred years earlier. The era we call the Age of Denial. A song called "Mind Games." I began to understand what Yusef meant. As I sang, it brought out feelings and emotions in me, and for a few moments I forgot the realities around me.

Then, we moved to the second level of consciousness. That was an easy one. My hatred of Harry Shields. I could look at him and put all the anger, the rage, the disgust I felt for what I saw in his face, into the dead center of my mind.

Yusef had me practice and practice. We did some role playing. He pretended to be Harry Shields, asking me if anyone had talked to me about the PEPS session since yesterday. I kept saying "No," directing all my energy into the song and my hatred for Harry Shields.

Finally, Yusef was satisfied. He explained to me there was no guarantee this approach would work, but I should be OK.

If it didn't work, Yusef told me, he'd know about it, because the Department would immediately track down the helipods beaming Yusef's signal into my hotel room. But their trail would go cold from there, and Yusef would survive intact. Naomi would protect me from any further invasions by the Department into my psyche. The PEPS session would go on, because none of the d-humans wanted it to end prematurely. And I would never see Yusef again. They would carry on their struggle without me.

I desperately wanted to succeed in defending against a "neurographic event." Now that I'd told Yusef I would join the struggle, I didn't want to fail before I even began.

Yusef finally bade me farewell. "Good luck, my brother. May God give you the strength to defend yourself against the d-humans. I pray you will succeed, and if you do, I'll be talking to you again tomorrow night."

It was past one o'clock in the morning. I knew Naomi was going to come and pick me up at five. That gave me not much more than three hours' sleep. This time, I didn't need the Monazepam. I fell asleep the moment my head hit the pillow.

WEALTH MONTHLY

June 11, 2069

The New Offshore Baby Boom

The rush for designer babies brings a new line of business to the offshore banking centers

Aretha and William Johnson are on their way home from the Cayman Islands. But this wasn't a vacation, and Aretha and William weren't interested in the sun, sea, and sand. Instead, they spent the past few days on their second visit to the largest, most state-of-the-art in vitro fertilization (IVF) clinic in the world, run by the industry heavyweight, Advanced Germline Engineering (AGE) Inc.

The Johnsons are a typical young, middle-class couple living in Atlanta. They are well-educated; both have good jobs and are part of the country's largest urban African-American middle-class community. They want to make sure that their children have every advantage they can give them, and they are coming back from a trip that is rapidly becoming a normal part of the American way of life.

This IVF clinic isn't focused on helping infertile couples. Instead, it's one of the leading centers in the world for enabling couples to create their own "designer babies," or "d-babies" as they're affectionately referred to by clinic employees.

The Johnsons are not alone in thinking that taking two trips to an off-shore paradise is worthwhile for their future offspring. Recent estimates suggest as many as ten per cent of Americans born this year will be the result of this offshore baby boom. America is on its way to becoming a country of "designer babies."

This is a development that means big business for the leading companies in the industry, who claim they're helping create a healthier and happier nation.

How designer babies went offshore

But why do the Johnsons have to fly to the Cayman Islands to do their part to create a healthier and happier America? Back in the 2050s, the so-called "designer baby" industry was burgeoning in the United States. But then it got hit by a double whammy of setbacks. First, a militant evangelical Christian group, the "Jesus Germline," believing that any changes to the human germline would be a sacrilege since man was created in God's image, began a militant campaign against domestic "designer clinics," blowing up three of them and killing two embryologists. But, painful as this was, it wasn't enough to stop the industry in its tracks. The knockout blow came when a disgruntled couple sued their IVF clinic, claiming their child was not growing up to resemble the child they had been led to expect. The judge, himself a fundamentalist Christian, imposed massive punitive damages on the clinic, which bankrupted it. From that point on, all liability insurance companies withdrew from the market, and it became impossible for a doctor to perform human germline engineering in the United States without taking on unacceptable financial risk.

That was when the offshore industry took notice. For nearly a century, the offshore banking centers of the world– the Cayman Islands, Bermuda, the British Virgin Islands, and about fifteen others– had built their economies on legally friendly domiciles for financial services. For several decades, however, the attractiveness of these offshore banking centers had begun to decline, as global anti-terrorist politics put pressure on these small countries to open up to international law enforcement.

All of a sudden, the offshore industry saw a new opportunity and began to pass laws that made it impossible for a client to sue practitioners of "designer IVF" for anything other than gross negligence. Before too long, AGE Inc. and its competitors were setting up shop in these offshore islands, building the most advanced clinics in the world, and providing housing, education and other services for the coterie of professionals they needed to relocate there. New airports were built, permitting the airlines to schedule non-stop flights from California, Texas, Chicago and the east coast to the offshore centers.

All this investment in the late 2050s has paid off in the 2060s. A basic designer baby can cost a couple as little as $100,000, no more than two months' salary of an average American dual-income family. But with the add-ons that are offered, a top-of-the-line designer baby can come in at over $1 million, still very affordable for an upper-income middle-class family but highly lucrative to the industry. AGE's Cayman Island clinic– the biggest of the breed– can process as many as thirty couples a day with average fees of $300,000, leading to $3 billion in annual revenues from this clinic alone.

So how does it all work? The process has become remarkably straight-forward and user-friendly. There are two steps: Step 1 is called "Genetic Screening" and Step 2 is called "Genetic Donor Enhancement" or GDE.

Designing the Johnson's baby:
Step 1– Finding the best little Baby Johnson

When Aretha and William Johnson arrived at the AGE clinic, the first thing they had to do was contribute some sperm and eggs. William had the easier job, but retrieving the eggs from Aretha was no more than a 30-minute painless procedure. The clinic then fertilized the eggs with William's sperm to create what are called "zygotes," simply fertilized eggs. Each zygote starts dividing, forming a cluster of embryonic stem cells called "blastocysts." This is where the technology magic kicks in. The embryonic stem cells are harvested and cultured, creating thousands of colonies of new blastocysts.

Meanwhile, Aretha and William have some work to do while their zygotes are busily dividing. On day two of their visit, a consultant meets with them to discuss their hopes and desires for their baby. The discussion is divided into four distinct categories: Health, Physical Features, Intelligence and Personality. Each category contains dozens of characteristics. For example, under Physical Features, there are questions about height, skin color, eye color, shape of nose, hair color, weight, etc.

Once this consultation is completed, the data is entered into the clinic's proprietary software, and the consultant gives the couple their first Off-spring Characteristic Probability Report, known in the trade as the OCPR. This is a description, in everyday language, of the child most likely to emerge from the criteria the couple chose. Frequently, it's an interactive process. The consultant gets feedback from the couple and a revised OCPR is created.

That's when the fun begins for Aretha and William. The revised OCPR is now re-entered in the computer and a virtual representation of their child-to-be is created. At this point, Aretha and William take part in a Virtual Offspring Interactivity experience. This is like a virtual reality computer software game, with an avatar. But the avatar is the theoretical child created by the Johnsons' criteria. The Johnsons can now see their desired child at different ages, from infancy to adolescence, all the way to adulthood. They can even talk to their "avatar child" and see how he or she would respond.

Once Aretha and William are fully satisfied, they sign a contract, requesting the clinic to design their child as closely as possible to their desired characteristics.

And that's when the waiting begins. The Johnsons' first trip to the AGE clinic happened nearly three months ago. Since then, the blastocysts have been busily dividing, creating many thousands of potential "baby Johnsons." The blastocysts are automatically screened and compared to the Johnson's OCPR until one blastocyst emerges that sufficiently meets the criteria. This can take as little as a few days, or as much as a few months, depending on the couple's preferences.

In the Johnsons' case, it took about two months. When they were notified that their Base Blastocyst had emerged, they were very excited. They both scheduled time off from work, and within a couple of weeks they were back at the Cayman clinic for the second step of their designer baby process.

Designing the Johnsons' baby:
Step 2– Adding those little extras

So last week, the Johnsons were at the clinic for the second visit. The consultant met them and presented them with a new computer simulation of their baby. This part of the process was somewhat disappointing to the Johnsons. The avatar in the new computer simulation didn't appear exactly as they had expected.

This is the moment where the consultant begins to morph from psychologist to salesperson. Now, the consultant showed the Johnsons on the computer what their child *could* become, depending on what packages of GDE they elected to buy.

It's the GDE process that creates a touch of magic into the process of designer babies. GDE is a step where patented "genetic panels" are inserted into the blastocyst that will become Baby Johnson and will have a dominant effect on chosen features of the Johnsons' child.

The technology for doing this was first developed over fifty years ago, and has since been perfected through practice on animals. At this point, in fact, the global agri-business is wholly dependent on GDE for enhanced productivity of farm animals: cows are given "genetic patterns" for enhanced milk productivity; sheep are optimized for wool productivity; chickens for egg productivity, etc.

The first human GDE was made public over twenty years ago, and stirred a ton of controversy and an even greater amount of revenues for the companies that pioneered it.

The consultant guided the Johnsons carefully through this momentous decision process. He started by showing them the effect that certain basic, inexpensive GDEs would have on their future child, whom they had already decided would be a son called Gary. If they left Gary's Base Blastocyst without any further enhancement, the whole process would have ended up costing them $100,000. But Gary would only be about five feet and seven inches tall. William is six feet tall and wanted his son to be about an inch taller than him. An extra six inches of height would cost the Johnsons a mere $18,000.

These were the one-off items that the consultant initially took the Johnsons over. Then he moved on to the more expensive, branded packages. For $40,000, the Johnsons could get the "Steve Harbright" genetic panel. For those of you who are not football fans, Steve is one of the Top Ten stars of the National League this season. This branded panel would insert certain of Steve's physical features— his height, bulk, strength, and endurance— into the Base Blastocyst, so that Gary Johnson would grow up with features combining the Johnsons' own genes with these particular genetic patterns of Steve Harbright.

Gradually, the consultant moved up the pricing ladder, to the more expensive panels, ending with the "Hal Burton" panel. Hal, as everyone knows, is the world's Number One football player and owns the second most popular patented genetic panel to date. This panel alone would cost the Johnsons $300,000, which would have blown the Johnsons' budget, leaving very little to spend on Gary's other features, including his health, his intelligence, and his personality.

These were the kind of trade-offs that the Johnsons spent days agonizing over. Eventually, they chose the Steve Harbright panel, along with five other panels, at a total additional cost of $250,000 over the initial $100,000 for the Base Blastocyst.

Finally, one last step. Before they left, Aretha underwent another procedure. Once again, she had an egg retrieved from her ovaries. The clinic then removed the nucleus of this egg containing its original DNA, and inserted the new GDE-enhanced Base Blastocyst for which the Johnsons had paid their $350,000. They then re-inserted the newly enhanced egg into Aretha's uterus. With all this completed, Aretha and William Johnson flew back to Atlanta as excited, expectant parents.

Two more satisfied customers

"I couldn't be more pleased with how everything went," Aretha told us with a sparkle in her eyes.

William nodded emphatically. "This is the best investment we're ever going to make," he added.

In fact, William's not the only one looking at his designer baby as an investment. Several mortgage companies are now actively marketing "d-baby loans"– home equity loans to finance the cost of the designer baby, payable back over twenty-one years.

These loans are just one part of a widespread, aggressive marketing strategy that has succeeded in helping AGE Inc. corner forty per cent of the offshore designer baby market. Wedding-related web sites are filled with AGE's marketing. Not sure what wedding present to get for your friend? That's easy, buy them a GDE certificate that can be redeemed at any of AGE's offshore clinics.

But this aspect of AGE's marketing pales in comparison to their bombardment of the obstetrician/gynecologist community. Throughout the U.S., gynecologists are engulfed with offerings of free gifts, interactive computer marketing videos to be given to young women thinking of having a child, seminars and conferences in (of course) AGE's delightfully sub-tropical offshore domiciles. All this generosity has one aim: to persuade a woman's gynecologist to give his or her seal of approval on the designer-baby process. This approval has been identified by the AGE marketers as the single most important endorsement necessary to win new customers.

It's an approach that seems to be working. AGE's business has been growing at forty-five per cent a year for the past four years, and the growth only seems to be increasing. The biggest constraint on growth right now, in fact, is the limited number of qualified embryologists, lab technicians, and client consultants that are all necessary to produce more designer babies.

The real winners: celebrity superstars

Lucrative as this business is to AGE and its competitors, it pales in comparison to the big bucks made by the celebrity superstars with patented "panels" of their DNA. Since the landmark Supreme Court case of 2041, it has been illegal for anyone to patent any single gene. However, in most cases, it is a unique pattern of related genes and associated proteins, rather than one single gene, which leads to a person's major attributes, and these unique patterns, whether developed artificially or retrieved from someone's DNA, are completely patentable.

Wealth Monthly has done some research into this aspect of the business and has compiled the first Top Ten list of celebrity DNA panels, along with estimated revenues received. It's a telling list of America's preferences for the next generation *(see next page)*.

Mark Harvey, spokesperson for AGE, explained to *Wealth Monthly* some of the demographic trends the company has seen.

"Most people are conservative about how they want their children to turn out," he told us. "They don't want their children very different from them, especially in intelligence or personality. They tend to go for slightly

Top Ten celebrity DNA panels

OWNER	BACKGROUND	KEY FEATURE	EST. REVENUES
Kelly Hendrick	Film star	Female beauty (blonde)	$2 billion
Hal Burton	Football star	Physical prowess	$1.5 billion
Carmen Gonzalez	Film star	Female beauty (Hispanic)	$1.2 billion
Chris Templeton	Film star	Male features & physique	$900 million
Marcus Forbes	Real estate developer	Personality and intelligence	$700 million
Steve Hurliss	Baseball star	Physical prowess	$500 million
James Powell	Evangelical preacher	Personality, religious ethics	$400 million
Bonnie Prescott	Supermodel	Female beauty and physique	$250 million
Peter Meeks	Multi-billionaire entrepreneur	Personality and intelligence	$150 million
Isaac Sorensen	Self-promoter – genius level IQ	Intelligence	$100 million

higher IQ levels and slight changes in personality. But when it comes to physical features, it's completely different. They all want their daughters to look like beautiful film stars and their sons to have physiques like their favorite sports personality."

Some watchdog groups have spoken out against this "celebritization" of America. Indeed, there are some who even claim that the whole process of designer babies is a social evil. The oldest of these organizations, Genetically Optimized America, argues that the current approach to designer babies will only increase the gulf in our country between the "haves" and the "have-nots."

"This is a forty-year trend we've been fighting, and it's only getting worse," said Martina Bergman, spokesperson for Genetically Optimized America. "In the past generation, the widespread use of d-panels has already led to an uninsurable underclass in our society, who have not been prenatally optimized for health. The health profile of this group is actually getting worse, even while the overall health of the country has made incredible gains. Now, with the growth of designer babies, there will be an even greater chasm between those who can afford to give their children genetic enhancements and those who can't. Our society is beginning to split into two: the genetically enhanced and those still in a natural state."

Genetically Optimized America argues that the state should mandate basic health d-panels for all children, regardless of their financial status. They believe that the long-term benefits for the country would easily repay the initial investment, pointing to the European experience.

AGE Inc. sees things differently. "America has always been a country of contrasts and diversity," says Mark Harvey. "We're simply continuing a tradition that has been the bedrock of our society from the outset. Wealthy parents have always had the freedom to give their children a good education, feed them nutritious food, send them to an Ivy League school, and give them any other advantage in life. That's a fundamental principal of a free society. Why should this be any different?"

What the future holds

The offshore jurisdictions that enabled this incredible growth in designer babies may well turn out to be victims of their own success. So many Americans are signing up for an enhanced next generation that there is an increasing groundswell for building clinics on America's own shores.

In the past year, three leading insurance companies have begun offering liability insurance again for U.S. practitioners, given the remarkably safe track record established by AGE Inc. and its competitors offshore. At the same time, there's been a dramatic turnaround in fundamentalist religious thinking about designer babies. To quote James Powell, the evangelical preacher, one of the loudest voices for designer babies (and who has made some decent money himself from the process as our table above shows):

"The act of genetic optimization is doing God's work. God created Man in his own image, and gave us the intelligence to understand our own DNA. If God wanted Man to remain imperfect, he would never have given us this ability. Each step we take to improve our genetic make-up will only get us closer to the true image of God. We're not fulfilling our destiny on this earth if we fail to take advantage of the powers God has given to us."

It seems that lots of Americans believe him. There is little doubt that every one of the $400 million that Mr. Powell has made from selling his own patented genetic panels has come from the majority of Americans who believe in God and faithfully live their lives according to His will.

Indeed, AGE Inc. has plans to establish seven new state-of-the-art clinics in Los Angeles, New York, Chicago, Atlanta, San Francisco, Miami and Houston, over the next five years. It's estimated that within ten years, fifty per cent of American babies will be d-babies, most of them conceived within the boundaries of the U.S.A. It's not surprising that AGE Inc.'s stock price has quadrupled in the past two years.

— Wealth Monthly *Reporters:*
Henry Stoddard; Julie Goodsill; Mike Moran

10 Shaktigarh

Where the people are many and their hands are all empty
Where the pellets of poison are flooding their waters
Where hunger is ugly, where souls are forgotten

It's 4:15 in the morning and the alarm wakes me up. Three hours' sleep. Too little sleep even to feel tired. Three cups of coffee. A shower, with the super-soft genetically optimized cotton towels. Eggs and bacon with the super-tasting genetically optimized flavors. Another cup of coffee. Adrenaline racing. I'm going to beat Harry Shields and the neurographic chair.

Naomi comes to pick me up. Her usual cheery self. Did I have a good night's sleep? Yes, I lie to her. We make it through Skywalk 4 to Skywalk G, just like yesterday. I'm even beginning to get used to the hubbub of noise, pictures, activity, and M3DIs racing through the air. Amazing how adaptable we humans are.

We stop at the Betelbar. This time, I'm the one pushing the button that gets rid of the 3-D image trying to sell me a Nanolite. No more embarrassing episodes. Whatever the hell is a Nanolite, anyway?

Into the UN building. Roboguard scans Naomi's and my irises. Just like yesterday. Through the metal detector. Back up to the 146th floor. I'm going to beat the damn neurographic chair.

Here I am again. In the neurographic chair. Harry Shields opposite me. Naomi to my right. Harry begins the session with his usual sneer.

"We are on the record. This begins Session 7-225 of the PEPS hearing of the United Nations Authority on the Primal Species, known as UNAPS. I am Harry Shields, Special UNAPS counsel. Also present

127

today is the Primal witness, named Eusebio Franklin, and his counsel, Naomi Aramovich."

Harry turns to me with a bored expression.

"Now, Eusebio, for the record: since yesterday's session, has anyone other than your counsel, Naomi Aramovich, spoken with you in any way about the PEPS session?"

OK. This is my moment of truth. I look at Harry Shields and bring all my loathing of him to the surface. I hate his smug expression, his feeling of superiority. I hate the way he twists the facts and tries to make me feel responsible for crimes against the world that his own ancestors committed. I hate his legal sophistry. I hate that his race of d-humans have stolen our world from us and don't even admit it. I hate his soullessness, his complete lack of caring for anything of sensitivity, for anything that couldn't be measured and scientifically optimized. I hate his physical perfection, his height and his strength. I hate his invulnerability to my hatred.

At the same time, just as I had practiced last night, I start singing to myself John Lennon's "Mind Games." I fill my mind with the words and the music.

So keep on playing those mind games together
Faith in the future out of the now . . .
Love is the answer and you know that for sure
Love is a flower—you gotta let it, you gotta let it grow . . .

I feel the words and music infuse me, so incongruously, fusing into the conscious and intense hatred I was feeling for Harry Shields.

In the middle of my overflowing thoughts of hatred and music of love, I answered very matter-of-factly to Harry Shields' question: "No."

I saw, through the noise of my own mind, a look of quizzical surprise in Harry Shields' face. Obviously, he was reading the neurographic output on the screen in front of him, and he didn't understand what he was seeing. He looked over with a questioning expression to Naomi.

I turned my attention for a moment to Naomi, keeping up the barrage of feeling and music in my own mind. She, too, was surprised. She looked at me with a question mark. But I was too busy singing "Mind Games" to myself and feeling hatred for Harry Shields to respond to her gaze. I looked away.

Harry Shields took a deep breath, puffed himself up and said:

"Let me just ask you again, Eusebio. Since the end of our session yesterday, did you or did you not speak with anyone other than your counsel, Naomi Aramovich, about the PEPS hearing? Please think carefully before answering."

I could feel my adrenaline pumping. I knew that I couldn't keep this up indefinitely. Already, thoughts were beginning to creep into the back of my consciousness that would betray me. I increased the volume of my hatred for Harry Shields. I started to think awful, terrible thoughts completely out of character for me. I started to imagine I was a foot taller and twice my weight, and I was swinging my right fist into his cold, emotionless face. I imagined the blood coming out of his nose. I even started to imagine that my right swing broke his neck, and his head was hanging loosely, half off his shoulders.

At the same time, I upped the volume of my song. I started blaring it into my brain:

Yeah, we're playing those mind games together,
Projecting our images in space and in time . . .
Yes is the answer and you know that for sure.
Yes is surrender, you gotta let it, you gotta let it go . . .

It occurred to me for a brief moment how inappropriate the words of the song were, given the situation, but I immediately banished the thought from my mind and kept up the singing to myself:

Keep on playing those mind games together
Raising the spirit of peace and love . . .

As I was going through this, in a small voice, I once again answered Harry Shields:

"No."

I didn't want to put together a more complex sentence, since I was sure that as soon as my brain started forming a grammatically correct answer, it would give the game away.

Harry Shields' eyes widened in shock, presumably seeing my violent thoughts about him. In another situation, the sight of his face would have seemed funny. But not now. There was too much at stake.

Harry began to bristle. He didn't want to leave the subject. He began, again, to formulate another question.

"Now, Eusebio, I must ask you again . . . "

I knew I couldn't keep this up for more than a few more seconds. Then, suddenly, my rescue came from an unexpected source.

"Counsel Shields," Naomi intervened. "I have to ask you to stop badgering the Primal witness. It's clear from the neurographic record that he is stressed from your line of questioning. It's understandable, given the neurographic event that occurred yesterday, that the repetitive nature of your questioning on this subject is stirring up memories of yesterday, which are being transformed into anger against you. The Primal witness is obviously trying to soothe his own eruption of anger with music. You have no reason and no right to increase his anguish at this point."

Harry Shields paused for a moment. He sat there, thinking. I kept up my own internal barrage of hatred and music. Finally, he nodded and answered Naomi.

"Yes, Counsel Aramovich, I believe you are right. We have an answer from the Primal witness on the topic, so let's move on."

I couldn't believe it. I'd beaten the neurographic chair! But Yusef had warned me not to relax too quickly. They were still watching my thoughts, and any stray thought could still give Yusef away. I kept up my music and my hatred for Harry Shields until the session moved on.

Finally, after what seemed like an eternity, Harry spoke again. The pomposity was back in his voice.

"Our plan for today's session is as follows. We have convened early in the morning because we will soon be commencing a virtual field trip to Shaktigarh, a Primal community in the district of Bardhaman in the state of West Bengal in northeastern India. The purpose of this field trip is to experience the living situation of a typical Primal community. Through this shared experience, we can dispel certain factual disagreements and thereby focus our attention on the ethical issues.

"Once the field trip is completed, we will reconvene here in the conference room and continue our session.

"Any questions? No? In that case, let us commence our preparations."

I was just thrilled to be out of my neurographic hot seat. Naomi led me to a room down the corridor. It looked like a waiting room, leading to several private cubicles. These, Naomi explained to me, were the virtual reality cubicles.

The three of us, Naomi explained, were going to meet Subrata Bammarjee, the UNAPS field supervisor for the Bardhaman district. He would meet us in the town of Bardhaman, a "civilized" d-human town, and then drive us to Shaktigarh.

Subrata, Naomi explained, had not been told the reason for our visit and wasn't aware that one of his visitors was in fact a "Primal." He'd been told just that three senior UNAPS officials from New York were on a fact-finding mission, and he was to be their guide. So I was expected to act out the role of a d-human. Strange! I realized that, once in a VRU—a virtual remote unit—there would be no way to distinguish me from a d-human. But how was I to act? Should I leave my soul at the door? No, I would just be myself. If Subrata saw through the act, the hell with it.

The cubicle seemed like an empty box, with a little closet for my clothes. In the middle of the room was something that resembled a black, rubber diving suit, with a "tail" coming out of the lower back region, a long, thick electrical cord connected to the wall. This, Naomi had explained to me, was called my "skin." I saw that it only went up to the neckline. Where was the attachment for my face? I looked around and there was a hood, made of the same material, suspended from the ceiling by another electrical cord; only this cord had been curled for flexibility.

I put on the skin-tight suit. I could see why they called it a "skin." With some trepidation, I pulled the hood down over my face, and attached it with four snaps to the "skin."

As soon as I attached the last of the snaps, I saw a kaleidoscope of lights and heard an announcer-type voice saying to me:

"Welcome, Eusebio Franklin, to the exciting world of virtual reality, brought to you by Vireon Incorporated through a licensing arrangement with UNAPS. Vireon—enablers of global virtual reality."

A moment passed. I began to feel a tingling, like millions of tiny little pin-pricks, starting from my toes and gradually extending up my body all the way to my scalp. The tingling stopped, and was followed by a heat sensation. Naomi had warned me about this part of the initialization. The "skin" was establishing contact with each of the millions of nerve endings on my own skin. The heat sensation was followed by a feeling of pressure. I felt that someone was giving me a massage, again starting with my toes and creeping up through my legs, through my torso, and up to my neck and head. It felt quite pleasant. Next, I began to hear different sounds, ranging from a very high-pitched whistle, down to a low rumble. Then, I smelled a range of different scents, from a beautiful perfume bouquet to a disgusting smell like excrement. Finally, I began to see a kaleidoscope of colors. It felt like a drug-induced hallucination.

After a few seconds, the kaleidoscope began to stabilize. It was like millions of pixels were joining together to form a complete picture. Finally, the picture was fully formed, and I realized I was in what seemed like a conference room with soothing lights. Opposite me was a glamorous-looking woman with tight-fitting modern clothing and long black hair. She smiled at me and stretched out her hand to shake mine. Without thinking, I held out my hand and shook hers. It felt completely real. She spoke to me.

"Welcome, Eusebio, to the world of virtual reality. My name is Virea, and I'm here to help you initialize your virtual reality experience. It will only take a few moments, and then you'll be on your way. Please sit down."

There seemed to be a soft, leather padded chair behind me. I sat down on it. I couldn't believe this experience. The chair felt as real as the one I'd been sitting on a few moments ago in the PEPS conference room.

"Now, I'm going to ask you some questions, Eusebio, about how you'd like to experience your virtual reality."

Virea began to ask me bizarre questions I had no idea how to answer. On a scale of one to five, with five the highest, how much odor sensation do I want to experience? I told her "five." How much strength did I want? I thought of my fantasy of punching Harry Shields in the face, and I answered "five" again. How much pain experience did I want, on a scale of one to five? Again, I answered "five." Why not? I wasn't planning on getting any dental work done in Shaktigarh.

The questions went on like that for a while, until Virea gave me a smile and told me we were done. I was now ready to begin my virtual reality experience. This whole time, I kept wondering if Virea was real, or was she an avatar? She seemed too perfect to be real, but too real to be an avatar. I couldn't stop myself.

"Virea, are you real?" I asked her.

She gave me a big smile. "Eusebio," she replied, "I'm as real as you want me to be. I'm an avatar, but this is a world of virtual reality. Everything here is real . . . as real as you want." She shot me a look with her eyes, and suddenly there was an air of sexual tension in the air. My heart started pulsing. I couldn't believe what I was feeling—turned on by a virtual reality avatar! I pulled my eyes away from hers and politely said:

"Thank you. I guess I'm ready now to meet the others in Shaktigarh."

Virea held out her hand again to shake mine.

"Have a great time, Eusebio," she said with a smile. "With the compliments of Vireon, enablers of global virtual reality."

At that, the image of Virea disappeared. I was back into initialization. I felt a more rapid repeat of the tingling, heat, and pressure sensations. Only this time, the heat remained high. I could feel a hot breeze blowing around me. The sound initialization began again. It ended, not with silence, but with a cacophony of foreign-sounding noises—vehicles honking their horns, people talking in a foreign language, even the sound of a cow mooing. Then the smell initialization, ending with a strange smell, combining a faint whiff of industrial exhaust with an exotic presence of unrecognizable food odors. Finally, the kaleidoscope of colors returned as the pixels gradually formed a complete picture.

I looked around me and saw I was standing on a street in front of a foreign-looking but modern office block. There was a hubbub of noise and activity around me. The heat was still intense. I now realized I was feeling West Bengal in May. Only a couple of times in my life, on the hottest days of the hottest summers in Tuckers Corner, had I felt such an intense heat. The wind itself was hot, like a hair drier. The sun burned down on my face. It must have been well over a hundered degrees Fahrenheit. The sounds and smells were, in fact, coming from the street. I saw the vehicles in a traffic jam in front of me honking their horns. Incredibly, I saw a cow walking, unattended, right in front of me, alongside the road. Everywhere around me were people. But these people were completely different from the cacophony of people on the New York skywalks. There was a certain crazy aliveness that they had, which seemed so different from New York. It reminded me of looking at an ant's nest. So much activity, with such obvious organization, but such a complete mystery to me.

Then, I realized there were three figures standing next to me. Two of them—a man and a woman—seemed like lifeless, moving waxworks. Of course—these were Naomi and Harry in their VRUs. The VRUs were close enough to their real likenesses to be easily recognizable, but there was no attempt to make them appear like real people. There was no question that these were merely the vehicles for a person, rather than the real person. I realized I must look equally wax-like, in my own VRU. It would certainly be easy enough for me to pass as a d-human, looking like this.

The third figure, talking excitedly, gesticulating with his head twisting in a curious way with each expression, was obviously Subrata Bammarjee. I got two immediate impressions of Subrata. First, I saw how he was d2-human. He didn't have the robotically, digitally-perfected motions of Naomi or Harry. But equally clearly, his physical characteristics were optimized. He had none of the quirky, idiosyncratic features that make us humans so clearly human. His features were obviously Indian and attractively articulated, like the features of a Bollywood film star. Not surprising—they were probably modeled after a Bollywood film star, I thought to myself. At the same time, I got another strong impression of Subrata. I liked him. Perhaps because he wasn't d3-human. He seemed more alive. His eyes seemed to have something within them. His expressions seemed infused with his feelings. He was so earnest—but in a very different way from Naomi's earnestness. It seemed more real, like it hadn't been digitally created.

They all noticed that my VRU had come alive—that I was now with them. I guess my initialization had taken longer than theirs, because this was my first ever virtual reality experience.

"Hey, Eusebio, welcome to Bardhaman! What took you so long, buddy?"

I couldn't believe it. This was Harry Shields talking to me. His sudden friendliness was more surprising to me than any of my new surroundings. What was up? Could it be that really he wasn't so bad, that he was just playing a role at the PEPS session? Then, it dawned on me. He wanted Subrata to think I wasn't a Primal, so he was pretending to treat me like one of his own. He sickened me.

Naomi immediately intervened.

"Eusebio, I'd like to introduce you to our guide, Subrata Bammarjee."

Subrata came towards me with an eagerly outstretched hand. I shook it.

"I'm so very pleased to make your acquaintance, Mr. Franklin." Subrata spoke with a strong Indian accent. "As I was just saying to Ms. Aramovich and Mr. Shields, it is a very special occasion for our remote region to be visited by officials from New York. We are indeed most blessed by your presence today. I am absolutely honored to be your guide."

I politely responded to Subrata that I was pleased to make his acquaintance.

"I must apologize for the absolute awfulness of the noise and congestion here in Bardhaman. This is a very booming business center nowadays, and unfortunately we experience the effects of this all the time. This is a common problem here in India nowadays. That's one of the costs of being the world's largest economy. But of course there are also many benefits." Subrata smiled to me and moved his head in a strange way, something between a nod and a shake.

We all climbed into the hoverpod parked on the road in front of us. The hoverpod, Subrata explained proudly to anyone interested, was the perfect vehicle for our trip. It was called an MPV or a "multi-purpose vehicle." On the paved road, it drove like an automobile. However, if you needed to go off-road, it used air-compression to hover slightly above the ground, enabling you to drive smoothly wherever you wanted without regard to the underlying terrain.

We began our drive on the main road out of town, with Subrata acting as both our driver and guide. He spent more time pointing out the sights than he did focusing on the road, which made me a little nervous at times.

"You are lucky that you met me here and not in Asansol, further west. That is where the heavy industry is situated. Especially Durgarpur. That has now become one of the major steel manufacturing centers in Asia," Subrata continued talking without regard to anyone's expressed level of interest. "Here, it is more agriculture—we call it the granary of West Bengal." He laughed. "Although you wouldn't know it from the amount of traffic on the road nowadays. I am responsible for all the Primals in the district of Bardhaman, from the Ajay River in the north to the Bhagirathi River in the east . . . which is also known as the Hooghly River when it goes further south. But we are going no more than fifteen kilometers east to Shaktigarh."

I took advantage of a momentary pause in Subrata's monologue to ask him more about his comment that India had the world's largest economy.

"Oh, it has been over fifteen years now that we have surpassed China," he answered and then he chuckled. "I think my esteemed visitor must spend so much time worrying about the Primal question that he fails to keep up on world events as much as perhaps he should!" There was no malice in his voice, only a sense of humor.

"Our Indian renaissance began in earnest after the horrors of the Great Global Wars," he continued. "India's infrastructure was hurt more by the Wars than any other major country. We had tens of millions of Bangladeshis invading our borders in the northeast because there was no more Bangladesh. We had the nuclear attacks from Pakistan. Oh, so awful! But after the wars ended, we had the biggest investment in our new infrastructure than any other country. So our technology and infrastructure now is the most modern in the world. China's whole infrastructure is completely twenty-first century and so decrepit. They haven't modernized fast enough. Our growth rate has been faster than theirs for over thirty years now."

"But, there are downsides to our progress," Subrata continued. "This traffic is certainly one of them." We were, indeed, completely stopped in a gridlock of traffic. Cars were honking their horns, but no one was moving. "I'm afraid you arrived during the afternoon rush hour, when the traffic gets absolutely out of control. There is an increase of forty thousand people in Bardhaman in the last ten years, but they haven't built any new roads. It's most ridiculous. I'm getting worried I won't be able to get you to Shaktigarh by 17:30, which is the time of the Afternoon Gathering."

What was the Afternoon Gathering?

Before I had the chance to ask, Subrata had started talking again. He looked across at each of us in the vehicle.

"I am hoping that you will all have time after the visit to Shaktigarh to come back to my humble house for a taste of Bengali hospitality. I would be deeply honored if you would find the time to enjoy my invitation. My beautiful wife, Mumtaz, has been preparing some delicacies for our distinguished guests." He chuckled. "I understand that you will only be able to enjoy the tastes of her cooking *virtually*, but that should not stop you from the enjoyment. Mumtaz is known far and wide for her homemade *rasmalai*. Oh, if you don't know about *rasmalai*, you are in for a treat. They are delicious cottage cheese cakes. You will love them."

Naomi made some kindly sounds to Subrata in response to his gracious invitation, ending in "Let's see how the time goes." We were still stuck in the traffic, going nowhere.

Subrata kept talking, as though trying to melt the frustration of the stopped traffic with his warmth.

"That would be so wonderful if you could grace us with your presence, even if it's only for a few minutes. You can meet my two most precious little ones—Anil, my son who is four, and Anita, our baby girl who will be two next month. They are both d2. We are very proud of our genetic choices for them.

"We still plan to have another one. Only for our next son, we want him to be d3, just like all of you. We are so looking forward to having a neurographically optimized member of the Bammarjee family. Of course, d3 is still very expensive for us here in West Bengal. It's not the usual thing, as it is in the United States. But I think I have a good chance of a promotion, and then we will be able to afford it. That's what we're waiting for."

He looked across once again at each of us, focusing on Harry Shields. He seemed to have gotten the signal that Harry had more authority within UNAPS than either Naomi or me.

"You see," Subrata went on, "the position for regional field supervisor has opened up." Subrata's voice suddenly took on a more serious tone. "There are seven other district field supervisors in the region, but I think I have the best chance of the promotion." Then Subrata's brow furrowed for a moment. "With the possible exception of the supervisor from Bankura. He has a little more experience than me, but I think I am viewed as having more initiative."

Then Subrata's eyes lit up, as if had just had a flash of inspiration. "Oh, perhaps you are in a position to put in a good word for me back in New York. I'm sure a simple word from any one of you would make a very big difference. It would be so appreciated. It's initiative that they are looking for. Initiative."

Naomi made a few more kindly sounds. Harry Shields remained silent. Everybody was getting increasingly frustrated by the stopped traffic.

"I know," Subrata suddenly exclaimed with glee. "We'll go off-road. Technically, you're not supposed to do this, but we're a UNAPS vehicle so the traffic police won't stop us. It's a more roundabout route, but it will get us there quicker than staying in this ridiculous traffic."

With that, there was a whooshing sound, and I felt the vehicle raise itself from the ground. Subrata steered us out of the traffic, between two modern high-rise apartment blocks, squeezed us through an alleyway, and then we were gliding above a watery field towards some forested hills.

"These are the rice fields that make this part of Bardhaman famous as the granary of West Bengal," Subrata told us, above the whooshing sound of the compressed air. "I know these back ways very well, because I've been the field supervisor of this district for six years now."

Subrata smiled at everyone. "Now, this way you will get the scenic tour, and we can expect to be at Shaktigarh in no more than fifteen minutes."

We reached the end of the rice field and entered the forested hillside. Subrata had to slow the hoverpod down to a crawl to steer carefully around the trees. As we made our way across the hill, Naomi suddenly startled everybody by saying to Subrata:

"Subrata, stop for a moment, please. What's that? It looks like a group of giant monkeys." Naomi was pointing out the window, a few hundred yards ahead of us.

I looked in the direction she was pointing. It was, indeed, a bizarre sight. There seemed to be seven or eight creatures, but I couldn't make out what they were. Some were on all fours; some were standing, stooping slightly. If they were monkeys, they seemed very large and human-like. But they certainly weren't humans.

Subrata brought the hoverpod closer to the group of creatures and then stopped the engine. He started to explain what we were looking at, but as we got closer to them, the explanation was superseded by the horror of what we saw. These creatures were, indeed, some form of human. They were naked, except for a couple who wore loin cloths. But every one of them had bizarre contortions of the human form that were unimaginably horrific. I felt like I had entered into a waking nightmare of the wildest kind. One creature had no neck—his head was placed squarely between his shoulders where the collar bone usually exists. Another creature had a perfectly normal body, but with two completely separate heads growing from the torso. A couple of the creatures had arms almost twice as long as normal and were squatting on all fours on the ground. One creature had no arms at all, but instead you could see a huge tail rising behind her from her coccyx. This was the ultimate freak show. The shock of it was quickly overwhelmed by nausea and fear. What was this?

Meanwhile, Subrata cheerfully continued his explanation as he brought our hoverpod to a halt by the creatures.

"These people are called the New Harijan by some—the New Untouchables. They are also known as the Tribe of Hanuman. Hanuman is our monkey god, who sometimes appears with four faces and six arms. They were originally the result of pirated d-panels purchased by very poor people. All that happened about a hundred years ago. Of course, nowadays, there are no more of these d-panels around. Tragically, many of these faulty d-panels had inheritable germlines, so when these unfortunate people mated with each other, their offspring tended to have a combination of their physical misfortunes."

We all continued to stare in disbelief at the horrific sight of these deformed creatures.

"How many of these people are there?" I asked Subrata in a whisper.

"Oh, nobody knows for absolutely sure. They are definitely numbered in the millions, but perhaps no more than five million.

You must realize that this is a tiny percentage of our population in India—less than one half of a per cent."

"Why hasn't the government done something about them?" I asked. I was still in a state of shock.

"Oh, but the government most definitely did try to do something about them. The problem began during the Great Global Wars, when there was a temporary disruption in central authority. Terrible, terrible times. After the Wars, when things returned to normal, the government started to round up the unfortunate New Harijan, and keep them in institutions. But this didn't last for long. A lawyer took the case to the International Court of Human Rights in The Hague and won. He was too clever by half, if you ask me. The Indian government had to release all the New Harijan, and now they wander the countryside."

The New Harijan appeared to be communicating with each other about the presence of our hoverpod, and a couple of them started to shuffle over towards us.

"Thank goodness for the piety of the Indian people," Subrata was continuing his monologue, even as we were all watching the New Harijan through the windows of the hoverpod. "We Hindus believe that this is all the result of a little mischief played on us by Hanuman, the monkey god, who became angry when we started to improve our genetic make-up. So, Hanuman punished us by permitting the faulty d-panels to spread. When the New Harijan started to wander the countryside, they found refuge in all the temples devoted to Hanuman. There are thousands of these temples spread around India. People in the local communities donate food and money to them through the temples and keep them alive. That is why they are called the Tribe of Hanuman."

By now, the two representatives of the Tribe of Hanuman, one of the males with long, loping forearms, along with the female with the long tail and no arms, both completely naked, had arrived at our hoverpod. They appeared expectant and had no sign of aggression. I didn't know what was going to happen. Then, abruptly, Subrata got out of the hoverpod, walked towards them, reached into his pocket, and brought out what appeared to be some paper money. He held it out to them. As though we were watching a circus trick, the female brought her tail up and used the end of it to take the money from Subrata's hand. It was probably the strangest thing I have ever seen in my life, and yet to Subrata and the female with the tail, it seemed like a normal, daily transaction. The two members of the Tribe of Hanuman started shuffling back to their group, and Subrata got back in the hoverpod.

"I can't believe my luck today," Subrata exclaimed with a big smile. "First, I have the opportunity to be a guide to three distinguished guests from UNAPS in New York. Now, I've had the chance to make a donation to the Tribe of Hanuman. You see, we believe that if you give money to them, Hanuman looks kindly on you, and permits you the genetic optimization you want for your children. Now I'm sure we will succeed in having a son who is d3."

At this point, Harry Shields pointed out that we were getting late for the Afternoon Gathering, and Subrata started driving the hoverpod through the trees with renewed vigor.

There was silence for the rest of the journey to Shaktigarh. I think all three of us "distinguished guests" were suffering from shock at the sight of the Tribe of Hanuman, and Subrata now seemed so satisfied with life that there was nothing left to talk about, at least for now.

We finally cleared the forested hills and found ourselves on top of a ridge. Subrata brought the hoverpod to a halt and we all got out. There was somebody waiting there for us. He looked small and wizened, his face was pockmarked and scarred, and his clothes were barely more than dirty rags. At the same time, it was almost a relief to see someone with two arms, two legs, and one head, after our previous encounter. Scruffy and dirty, perhaps, but one look at his eyes told me something unmistakable—this was a human being.

It was a strange moment for me. This was the first human being I had actually seen "in the flesh" since being abducted from Tuckers Corner. Yet, to him, I was anything but human. What he saw in me was simply a VRU inhabited by another d3-human from New York.

As we got closer to him, I realized he had a strong body odor—a smell of dried sweat that seemed to waft around him like a swarm of buzzing flies. He was barefoot. The whites of his eyes were more red than white. His skin was dark and I couldn't tell where his natural skin color ended and where the dirt began. And yet his red eyes were bright with life, and his broad smile, which revealed an incomplete set of yellow, half-broken teeth, was earnest and warm.

"Let me introduce to you Mr. Peshawarti Sabrakhatan, the leader of the Poonoo gang which currently holds the power in Shaktigarh," Subrata announced with such formality that he may as well have been introducing a prince of the Raj. "Mr. Sabrakhatan only speaks Bengali," Subrata continued, "but your virtual reality software will automatically translate into English, so please feel free to talk with him directly."

Peshawarti Sabrakhatan started to speak to us in Bengali, but as Subrata had said, I could hear a simultaneous computerized voice giving me the English translation. It was a strange combination: the voluble outpouring of incomprehensible words spoken with passion and feeling, accompanied by a smooth, computerized, emotionless translation in a perfect American accent.

"I am very pleased to make your acquaintance," the computerized voice spoke in my ear. "Please, do not try to pronounce my full name. Everybody just calls me Pesh." With that, Pesh vigorously offered his right hand to shake. Each of us shook hands. I couldn't help thinking of Harry Shields' obvious distaste when he was forced to shake my hand, the hand of a Primal. He's lucky he's in a VRU, I thought to myself. I couldn't imagine him even coming near a person like Pesh in real life.

Subrata intervened. "Everybody," he spoke to us urgently, "the time for the Afternoon Gathering has come. I had hoped that Pesh could explain this procedure to you beforehand, but now there is no time. Quick, let us go to the edge of the ridge, so we can see what happens. Then, we can talk about it later to our hearts' content."

We followed Subrata and Pesh along a trail which took us to the edge of an escarpment. As we got to the edge, we could see that a valley lay below us. A foul smell wafted up from below, a smell of old sewage mixed with other unfathomable odors. The valley seemed to be strewn with debris of some kind, but I couldn't make out exactly what it was.

Naomi whispered to me. "Eusebio, your virtual eyes are just like the spectacles I gave you for the rooftop of the UN building. If you focus on one area for a few seconds, it will automatically start magnifying for you."

I did what Naomi suggested, and I began to realize that the debris was garbage. Tons and tons of garbage. Garbage as far as the eye could see. All kind of garbage. Over here a pile of rotten vegetables. Over there, broken pieces of construction materials. Somewhere else, a jumble of fragments from various high-tech pieces of machinery. Mostly, unrecognizable, random pieces of garbage.

I pulled my eyes away from the close-up view and looked around the edges of the valley. On the other side of the garbage, I saw some movement. Once again, I focused in on the movement, and as the area became magnified, I could see that the movement was, in fact, a large group of people. There seemed to be hundreds of people. They looked like other versions of Pesh. They were obviously human, and equally obviously, they were small, dirty, and dressed in rags.

What was going on? Why had we been brought to a garbage dump? What in hell was the Afternoon Gathering?

"They're coming, now. They're coming," Subrata told us in hushed tones. The rubbish lorries are coming." He chuckled. "But, for my distinguished guests from New York I should call them garbage trucks."

There they were—a convoy of large trucks, multi-purpose vehicles like our hoverpod, making their way into the garbage valley, towards an area close to the crowd of people. The convoy—it looked like about seven trucks, each filled with heaping piles of garbage—came to a stop and hovered a few feet above the garbage-strewn ground. Then, as if by command, they all simultaneously began to roll over in mid-air. Second by second, each truck turned until they were hovering almost sideways. As they turned, the garbage in each truck began falling into the dump. By the time they were sideways, it was falling in a massive crescendo, like seven gigantic waterfalls of trash. After a couple more seconds, the crashing sound of the garbage hitting pay dirt wafted up from the valley to our virtual ears.

The hoverpods kept rolling until they were upside down and all the garbage had fallen out. Then they continued their roll until they had fully rotated back to their normal position. At that point, the convoy started moving again, turned around and left the garbage valley.

I was still wondering what the big fuss was all about. Watching garbage trucks dump garbage didn't seem especially significant. Then, as I watched, I began to see why we had been brought here, and my heart sank even further within me.

As soon as the hoverpods left the valley, the hundreds of people waiting at the edges started clambering through the garbage-filled valley to the freshly dropped trash. They made their way in haste, half-running, half-climbing over the randomly strewn unrecognizable objects that formed the ground of the valley. As they reached the fresh trash, they started jostling each other to get at various pieces important to them. It was a frantic scene, like a flock of vultures flapping at each other to get a bite of a fresh carcass. I used my magnification vision to close in.

I could see one woman, who had found some packaged food, tearing at the package to open it. As soon as she did so, she wolfed it down in a second. I saw a man holding a big canvas bag over his shoulder, diligently searching through the trash for pieces of plastic, stepping on them to make them more compact and putting them into his bag. I saw a young man pick up something that looked high-tech, with a monitor and various dials. As soon as he did so, two other men rushed at him, knocked him over, picked up the high-tech object, and ran off with it. I saw several other young people holding big plastic bottles, searching through the garbage, and then, every now and then, pouring some liquid they had discovered into the bottles. There was another man who appeared to be collecting small pieces of metal. He had a pair of shears with him and was hard at work cutting pieces of metal from various objects in the trash.

The scene was both fascinating and awful. As time went on, the order seemed to degenerate. An increasing number of fights broke out, with small groups struggling with each other to get hold of a particular piece of garbage. In one area, a particularly vicious group was running at people with metal rods, swinging the rods into them, and knocking them down. One of their victims was hit so badly that he didn't get up. He just lay there, spread out over the garbage where he had fallen.

So this was the Afternoon Gathering. The most valuable resource to the human community of Shaktigarh was the garbage of the d-humans. As I looked, with my magnification vision, at the dreadful desperation of the people, frantically searching through the garbage, fighting each other for a piece of rotten food or a broken piece of machinery, I felt a surge of anger for what this world had done. How had they let my fellow human beings degenerate to this level?

And yet I felt so distant as I surveyed the scene. Here was I, in a VRU, looking at these people fighting each other in the stench of d-human waste for the rejected trash of d-human society. I kept remembering, in spite of myself, how, in reality, I was standing in a cubicle in the UN building in New York, watching this scene playing out halfway around the world. My anger was diluted by my distance. Part of me could see how the d-humans had distanced themselves so much from this world that it was no more than a theoretical annoyance, a statistical disturbance, a virtual reality sideshow.

My reverie was broken by Subrata's voice.

"If you would all be kind enough to gather around now, Pesh will explain to you what you have just seen and answer any questions for you."

I turned towards the others, and as I did so, I caught Naomi's eye. She was looking straight at me, and even through the distance of virtual reality, as the digital vision sped through the satellites from New York to Shaktigarh and back to New York, I saw the look of sympathy in her face for the people in the valley below, as she slowly shook her head, gazing directly at me. "You are a human like them," she seemed to be saying to me, "and your fate is inextricably linked. I'm so sorry." That's what I thought I saw in the movements of her virtual reality face.

Pesh spoke. Once again, there was a bizarre combination of his sharp voice, filled with passion, spitting out incomprehensible phrases, followed by the cool, dispassionate American accent in my ears, translating the words into a hygienic, grammatically correct sentence.

"This moment is the glory of the day," the automatic translator spoke to me. "It used to belong to the Khopali gang, but we fought them hard, we sacrificed many of our young men, and now thanks to the great Lord Shiva, we alone have the right to the Afternoon Gathering. The Khopali gang is now reduced to harvesting whatever food they can from the fields. They are left impoverished." With that, Pesh spat on the ground, and looked sad at the fate of his erstwhile rivals.

"Why is the Khopali gang impoverished with food from the fields?" asked Naomi. "Are there not enough fields to grow food?"

Pesh looked fiercely back at Naomi. "Of course there are enough fields," he answered back. "But for generations now, the fields don't yield their crops. They are overwhelmed by the GM weeds from the d-humans. The d-humans have made our fields worthless."

Naomi looked across at Subrata. "What does he mean?" she asked.

Subrata put on a professorial tone as he addressed all three of us.

"Pesh is correct in what he says," Subrata explained. "As we developed ever stronger strains of wheat, soy, and other crops last century, some of these strains mutated into equally strong strains of useless weeds. During the Great Global Wars, many of these genetically modified weeds took hold in the fields of the poorest communities and strangled the crops. Of course, our d-agriculture technology developed new strains of crops that outgrow the GM weeds. But these were very expensive and the Primals couldn't afford them."

"Why hasn't the government subsidized this—or just given the new strains to the Primals?" Naomi persisted.

"Things have gone much too far for that," Subrata responded. "The Primals won't accept anything any more from the d-humans. Only our rubbish." Subrata almost laughed with a bitter irony. "They look at the fate of the New Harijan, they look at their fields overgrown with GM weeds, and they think that the d-humans only want to destroy them. So, whenever we try to give them anything, they reject it, thinking it must be poison to them."

Subrata shook and nodded his head at the same time. "In fact, things have become so bad that there is now a rumor among the Primals that we wish to put an end to them entirely. They have a ridiculous idea that we are going to make their women sterile and slowly there will be none of them left. Absolutely ridiculous. But there's nothing we can do to put an end to their silly ideas."

Naomi looked across at me. For a moment, I almost told Subrata and Pesh that this rumor was true. But I stopped myself. I thought of their desperation and their struggles with each other for the right to scavenge the d-humans' garbage. What purpose would it serve to put more terror in their lives? If I was going to fight for my race outside the rules of UNAPS, let me do it with Yusef. I was sure he had far more important plans for me than to blurt out the truth to a helpless, desperate human village chief. I shut up.

Suddenly, Harry Shields spoke up. "Pesh, we would like to pay a visit to your home, so we can gain a better understanding of how you and your community are living."

Pesh immediately responded with an intensely emotional jumble of Bengali.

"I would be honored to receive my guests in my house," the dispassionate translator spoke in my ears. "One of the greatest acts in our lives is the act of hospitality. Everything that is mine will be yours. However, I must give you a terrible warning. There are many in our community who believe that you d-humans are our enemies and wish to destroy us. I have control over my Poonoo gang, but right now they are busy distributing the rewards of the Afternoon Gathering, and the warriors available to defend my home will be very few. If anyone from the Khopali gang sees that you are visiting my home, they will rise up in a mob and attack us. They will think I am conspiring with you, and it will lead to terrible things. Therefore, before I can welcome you into my home, I must give you this warning."

Subrata became extremely agitated. "Mr. Shields, it would be most terribly against UNAPS protocol to enter their community and visit Pesh's home. It would be very dangerous, as Pesh has said, and it would also break the rules of UNAPS. Please understand, Mr. Shields, I could lose my job if it were ever known I led you into the Primal community."

Harry looked back at Subrata. "I wouldn't worry about losing your job, Subrata. As you know, we're from central UNAPS, so we would take the responsibility. It seems to me that it's more a question of where your job is going in the future. It's very important that we get the fullest experience of Primal conditions. You told us you have more initiative than the other district field supervisors. Now is your chance to show this to us. Use your initiative to work out with Pesh how to get us safely into his home."

Subrata's face contorted with a mixture of fear and calculation. His face was so transparent that his thoughts seemed to be given voice as though he were himself in a neurographic chair. As I looked at him, I saw his mental calculations: he needed his promotion so he and his wife could have a d3 member of the Bammarjee family; this was his golden opportunity for a "good word" from central UNAPS; if he didn't take the UNAPS officials to Pesh's home, he would blow this one chance, maybe even get a "bad word" from central UNAPS—no promotion, no d3 Bammarjee baby. What was the danger of the visit to Pesh's home versus the loss of his chance of promotion?

Subrata finally spoke. "Let me discuss with Pesh if there is a safe way in which we can visit his home. Please give me a moment, my distinguished guests."

With that, Subrata walked over to Pesh and they talked quietly together. After some intense discussion, and many nods and shakes of their heads, along with violent gesticulations of the arms, Subrata came back to us with a triumphant look on his face, attempting to hide the obvious fear underneath.

"I think we have found a plan to visit Pesh's home safely, without taking too much risk of something going badly," he announced. "I think my honored guests will be very pleased. You must understand this is very difficult, and not a little dangerous. I hope you will remember what Subrata Bammarjee has done for you when you return to your 'real' existence back in New York.

"Here is our plan. We cannot go on the direct route to Pesh's house, because the lookouts from the Khopali gang will see us, and they may attack the house by the time we get there. We will go the back route. You should understand that it is not a very pleasant way to go. We will pass through where the outcasts live, and it is not pleasant." He held his hand up to his nose and smiled grimly. "It certainly does not smell pleasant," he added with irony in his voice.

"Who," Naomi asked, "are the outcasts?"

"Oh, they are the people who are not members of the Poonoo gang, nor are they members of the Khopali gang. Either they did something wrong and got thrown out of one of the gangs, or in many cases they are orphans with nobody to look after them. Very sad."

I could hardly imagine how things could be even worse for a group of people, after witnessing the desperate battle for garbage that had just taken place in the Afternoon Gathering.

With that, we all got in to the hoverpod, and made our way along the ridge and down to a clearing. Pesh's presence filled the hoverpod with a heavy odor, as though we were in a stable.

Subrata stopped the hoverpod in the clearing. He turned to us and explained the next step.

"Here we must disembark from the hoverpod and walk to Pesh's house. The hoverpod will be very obvious anywhere past here and will advertise our presence. Now, please make sure to stay together. It's easy to get lost."

Pesh led the way, followed by Subrata. The three of us followed their lead, in single file. There was a small stream in front of us, which we crossed by jumping from one boulder to another. The water appeared green and soapy. I hoped this wasn't their drinking water.

On the other side of the stream, we could see signs of a settlement ahead. It quickly became clear there were no real houses. Each shelter was made of a combination of randomly shaped pieces of different metals, plastics, and other flat building materials. Instead of walking directly to the settlement, Pesh led us sideways, down a narrow path. We came to a big, dark concrete tunnel. Pesh continued unhesitatingly into the entrance.

Subrata looked back at us. "This is the unpleasant part," he whispered.

We entered the dark concrete tunnel. There was an instant, unbearable stench of sewage and decay. My virtual eyes immediately adapted to the darkness, and in a moment I could see almost as clearly as if it were daylight. I wished I couldn't see so clearly. Here were the outcasts, who had made their homes in the sewers. The center of the tunnel was filled with dank, filthy water. The sides of the tunnel were damp. It was clear that, at other times, the water rose much higher, because I could see a high water line on each side. Above the high water line, there were holes in the concrete, each one just big enough to fit a human. And there were humans in most of these miniature caves. They were lying there like bats in a cave, squeezed between the concrete, listless, looking at us as we walked by. Additionally, there were some hammocks, made from random strips of rope and nylon, hanging from metal hooks in the concrete ceiling. Some of these hammocks held more of the outcasts, lying from the ceiling above us, staring down at us. The outcasts seemed to be mostly young children. They were small and skinny, with big heads and eyes, dressed skimpily in rags, filthy, their bodies all covered in what seemed like boils, open sores, and scars.

The stench was terrible. The sight of these outcasts was even worse. But worst of all was the look in all of their eyes. It was a haunted, empty look. A look of utter hopelessness. There was no life in their eyes. Only emptiness, gigantic black holes of emptiness. I had never in my life experienced such an awful, gaping blackness as that which I saw in the eyes of these outcasts.

After a few moments, I couldn't stand it any more. My own stomach, sequestered away in a cubicle in the UNAPS offices in New York, felt a sickening wrenching from the hopelessness of these children's faces. I looked away from them and focused on my trail through their sewer.

We walked for several minutes. It felt like an interminable torment. Finally, Pesh turned into an opening in the tunnel, and we climbed up a crumbling concrete staircase back out into the daylight. The sun was getting low, and dusk was imminent, but it still seemed bright compared to the blackness of the sewer.

We had emerged in the middle of "tin pan alley"—makeshift houses were all around us, a medley of different colors and materials all patched together like a quilt. It was hard to imagine these constructions holding people, never mind keeping out the rain. Pesh led us down a side street and through a door. There was a man who appeared to be a guard standing outside the door. He acknowledged Pesh with a sign of respect as we walked inside the home. Pesh lit a kerosene lamp. I couldn't believe it, but it seemed these people didn't even have access to electricity.

We were in a small room, but it had the warmth of human habitation. There were wooden chairs to sit on, a table, and pieces of material strewn around. There seemed to be a shrine of some kind in the corner of the room, with candles and incense.

"I must apologize," Pesh said to us as we sat down. "My wife would normally be here to offer you some food and drink, but she is with the others, dividing the spoils of the Afternoon Gathering. She should be back shortly.

"It is a difficult life, but we make do, thanks to Lord Shiva," Pesh told us. "Last month, I celebrated my fortieth birthday. That makes me the most senior warrior in our gang. I have now been their leader for over four years. It was under my leadership that we beat the Poonoo gang four years ago." His face lit up with pride.

I was astonished that Pesh was forty years old. His face was so wizened, I had assumed that he was at least in his sixties. I thought of my surprise just a couple of days earlier—it seemed like half a lifetime ago—when I realized Naomi Aramovich was in her seventies, although she looked only half the age of Pesh. This world made no sense to me.

Naomi and Harry Shields began asking Pesh questions about how his people lived. I wasn't really concentrating. I was looking around at his hovel, trying to reconcile all this with the busy street in Bardhaman where we had met Subrata, with the sights of the New Harijan, and the outcasts in the sewer, all the time trying to remember that my real body was sitting in a "skin" in a cubicle on the 146th floor of the UN building in New York.

The conversation was interrupted by an anxious call from the guard. Pesh jumped up, talked with him briefly, and came back to our group. There was fear in his face.

"They saw us," he said with alarm. "The Khopali gang spotted us. One of our spies just came and warned my guard outside. They're on their way right now."

Subrata's eyes were wide with fear. "What shall we do?" he asked Pesh breathlessly.

"Let me check the back way, see if that's safe. I'll be right back. You all stay here until I get back," Pesh responded.

Pesh disappeared into the back. We were all silent. Subrata was looking at each of us with a mixture of terror and anger. This lasted only for a moment, as the silence was broken from noise outside. First, we could hear a couple of people yelling, then it became clear that there was a mob forming out there. There was a beating of sticks, chanting, stamping of feet. Every now and then, a particularly loud shout was picked up by my auto-translator, and bizarrely translated into an emotionless English sentence.

"Kill the d-human enemies," my auto-translator said.

"Kill the Poonoo traitors who plot with the d-humans to poison our fields."

Subrata kept looking back to where Pesh had disappeared. I

could see the question in his eyes: should he try to make his escape that way? Why hadn't Pesh returned? Had he run away or had something happened to him?

The noise from outside turned into an uproar. There was a sound of fighting, and an ear-piercing shriek filled the air. Subrata's eyes became even wider. It was the sound of death. We all knew what it must mean—Pesh's guard had been killed. A moment later, there was a crashing sound. I turned around to see that a Molotov cocktail had been thrown through the small window into our room. The flaming kerosene spilled onto the floor. The back of the room, where Pesh had disappeared, started burning in a wall of flame. No escape in that direction.

Subrata was panicking. He was panting, gasping from fear. I looked over at Naomi and Harry. Strangely, they were absolutely motionless, as though there was no one home. I didn't know what to do. Without thinking, I put my arms around Subrata and hugged him.

Subrata whispered to me. "What shall I do? What about Mumtaz? Anil? Anita? Help me!" I could feel his heart beating so fast and hard, it seemed like it would jump from his chest.

Another Molotov cocktail crashed in. The room was burning up. Flames were everywhere.

"We've got to go outside or we'll burn up!" I said to Subrata. "Come on!"

We pushed open the front door and staggered outside together, through the smoke. There was a wild roar, stamping, beating. I looked at the faces of the people. They were frenzied, eyes staring with hate, faces contorted with violence. We took no more than two steps, and someone swung a heavy pole directly at Subrata's head. It seemed to break his neck instantly. Subrata fell into my arms. His head rested on his shoulders at an impossible angle. His eyes were rolling up into his head. Blood was pouring from his scalp over his body and onto my arms. The mob's roar got louder. Another swinging stick hit Subrata in the chest. I heard his ribs crushing with a sickening sound.

A second later, I felt an excruciating pain in my own ribs. I'd been hit. I fell onto the ground next to Subrata. The mob roared on.

Somebody's heel came down onto my face. The intensity of the pain was an unspeakable agony.

And then, blackness.

* * * *

And then, silence.

And more silence.

After a few more moments, I began to realize that my virtual reality experience had ended. I felt no pain, even though I had a terrible memory of the agony a few moments ago. I realized I was lying in my "skin" in the cubicle in the UN building. I kept lying there for a minute, as though I were waking from an awful nightmare. I sat up. Then I stood up. I took off my "hood" and looked around at the high-tech cubicle. I began to peel off my "skin." I walked over to where my clothes were hanging and put them back on.

As I was doing all this, it slowly dawned on me that, although my virtual terror had ended, this wouldn't have been true for Subrata. For Subrata, it was his life that had ended. I had held him as his neck broke and his ribs crushed. There was no doubting it. Subrata had died a terrible death.

I was in shock. I was shaking with grief for Subrata's end. It was so far away from the quiet cubicle in the UN building, and yet it was so immediate.

I walked out of the cubicle. There was Naomi, looking a little disturbed, but otherwise the same as usual.

"Eusebio, I'm so sorry . . . " she began.

I was exploding with anger.

"Where did you go?" I interrupted her violently. "How could you leave Subrata? He's dead. They beat him to death. I was holding him. They broke his neck. How could you leave him to die?"

I let out a cry of anguish.

Naomi responded with a staccato voice.

"We didn't leave him. We did an ETP so we could file a PDR ASAP and send for an ERT."

I looked at her with puzzlement as the acronyms flew right past me.

Naomi calmed herself down and rephrased her speech for me.

"I'm sorry, Eusebio," she said. "It's been highly disturbing for all of us. What I'm saying is that, as soon as it became clear that the situation was getting out of control, both Harry and I activated what's called an Emergency Termination Procedure, which de-activates the virtual reality. We then instantly filed a Primal Disturbance Report. That's a special procedure that goes to the closest UNAPS enforcement division in the region. Each UNAPS region has an Emergency Response Team, called an ERT, which can get to a place in minutes. By now, they're probably already there on the scene, breaking up the mob."

"Too late for Subrata," I said bitterly. "They can't bring his life back now."

"Eusebio, what happened was tragic. It's very disturbing. But both Harry and I did everything we could to try to save Subrata.

"As soon as we filed the PDR, I deactivated your VRU," Naomi continued. "I'm so sorry, Eusebio. I should have explained the Emergency Termination Procedure to you in advance, but I never dreamed it would be necessary. I looked at your settings, and I saw your "pain experience" was five. I should have told you never to set it at five. You must have been suffering terribly."

She was right. I had suffered moments of unimaginable pain. But a few moments later it had all become just a memory. For Subrata, his unimaginable pain had ended in his death.

Naomi led me back into the PEPS conference room. She explained to me that the legal protocol called for the three of us to re-start the session on the record and discuss what we'd seen. This was all part of a process called RTVD, which stood for Real Time Virtual Discovery.

I was still in shock as I was led back to my neurographic chair. All I could think of was Subrata's neck breaking in my arms, and the sound of his ribs crushing.

Harry Shields began with his usual formality.

"We are going back on the record. This is a continuation of Session 7-225 of the PEPS hearing of the United Nations Authority on the Primal Species, known as UNAPS.

"The three participants of this session have just completed a virtual visit to Shaktigarh as part of our Real Time Virtual Discovery process, known henceforth as RTVD. A tragic incident occurred during our RTVD. A UNAPS colleague, the district field supervisor of Shaktigarh, named Subrata Bammarjee, was caught up in a Primal disturbance. I have just received confirmation from the Emergency Response Team who arrived at the site that, in fact, Mr. Bammarjee was killed by a Primal mob. Let me take this moment to express on the record the deepest regret that we all feel for this tragic loss of life. Mr. Bammarjee died while performing his UNAPS obligations, and he will be appropriately honored. At this moment, I understand that Mr. Bammarjee's body has been recovered and is being transported back to his family. Our deepest sympathies go out to Mr. Bammarjee's wife, Mumtaz, and his two children."

As Harry spoke, the anger in me began to foam and build up like a volcano. So this was how they clean up their screw-ups, I thought. A couple of "deepest sympathies" expressed on the record, some "appropriate honors," and everything's back in order. Then we can go on with the hearing.

I thought back to that moment of truth, when Subrata had told us it was too dangerous to go into Shaktigarh. It had been Harry who had goaded Subrata into taking us there. *"A question of where your job is going in the future,"* he'd told him. I began to realize how cynically Harry had manipulated Subrata into risking his life. For what? For a little extra evidence of the miserable existence of Primals? *"It is very important that we get the fullest experience of Primal conditions,"* Harry had told Subrata. *"You told us you have more initiative than the other district field supervisors. Now is your chance to show this to us."* Harry Shields had used Subrata's desire for his promotion, his dreams of a "d3 Bammarjee" son, to get his way without regard for Subrata's own safety. Yes, it was the mob that ultimately killed Subrata, but it was Harry Shields who murdered him.

As these thoughts filled my being, I couldn't stand watching Harry get away with his empty expressions of sincerest regret. He was getting away with murder. I felt I had to stop him. This had gone too far. Now was my only chance. Here we were in the PEPS session, on the record. It was my one and only moment to get the truth out.

"How dare you sit there and ignore what really happened!" I yelled at Harry across the table. "It was you, you, who caused his death! Subrata didn't want to take us into Shaktigarh. It was too dangerous. Pesh clearly warned us all what could happen. You manipulated him. You made him believe you'd get him promoted if he took a risk with his life. You're the one responsible for this! You're a murderer! Now his wife is a widow, and his two little children are orphans because of you!" By this time I was almost screaming at the top of my voice.

Harry barely missed a beat. He sat back in his chair, turned his face slowly towards Naomi and said, in a cold, neutral voice:

"Counsel Aramovich, would you like to take a little time with your client before we proceed?"

"Yes, I would, Counsel Shields," Naomi responded.

"And Counsel Aramovich, with your agreement, I would suggest that we delete the Primal's outburst from the record."

"You have my full agreement, Counsel Shields."

I was in a state of apoplexy. How could the two of them just switch off the truth with a flick of the wrist? At least, I'd thought Naomi had some conscience. How could they do this?

Naomi led me to the Privileged Room where I exploded in anger. After letting me vent, she took hold of my arm and gently started speaking.

"Eusebio," she said, "there are so many things you don't understand. That's not your fault. How could you understand? Let me try to explain to you. You're right to feel anger at what happened. I'm angry at what happened. In my view, Harry Shields is morally responsible for Subrata's death. I agree with you completely. But accusing him of Subrata's murder here doesn't help anything. If we left that on the record, the only person you'd be hurting would be Subrata's family."

I was incredulous. How could the truth hurt Subrata's family?

Naomi explained to me. The current view of what had happened within the UNAPS administration was that it had been a tragic accident. Subrata would be seen as having died in the line of duty, and as such, his wife would receive a large one-time payment along with double the usual pension for the rest of her life. However, if it were established that Subrata had led us in to Shaktigarh against the advice of Pesh, then he would viewed by the UNAPS administration as having been negligent. His wife would have to forfeit the one-time payment, and her pension would be the minimum. If I raised the idea, on the record, that Subrata had been manipulated by Harry into taking us into Shaktigarh against his will, the official responsibility for that decision would rest with Subrata, not with Harry.

"I can't stand Harry Shields any more than you," Naomi added. "But Eusebio, this is not the time to try to win an empty victory against him. We're fighting a much bigger battle here, Eusebio. We're trying to save your race. Let it go. The only person you'll be hurting will be Subrata."

"He'll never get to have his d3 Bammarjee son that was so important to him," I said dejectedly.

"On the contrary, Eusebio. If his wife gets her one-time payment and the double pension, she'll be able to have his d3 son, and she probably will."

"But he's dead," I cried out with frustration.

"Yes, he's dead. But their embryology clinic will have his sperm frozen from his past two conceptions. They'll have enough sperm to create thousands of Bammarjee sons. His wife can donate an egg whenever she's ready, and now she'll be able to afford the extra cost of a d3 neurographic optimization. The only person who can stop this now would be you, by trying to accuse Harry Shields like you just did."

Checkmate. Of course, there was nothing more I could do. The last thing I wanted was to hurt Mumtaz Bammarjee after holding her husband in my arms as he died. How could I do anything to stop Subrata's greatest wish of a d3 son coming true? Harry Shields was going to get away with murder. The system had me beat.

* * * *

I was back in my hotel room. Harry and Naomi had spent hours sparring over the visit to Shaktigarh. Harry arguing that the lives of the Primals were so dismal that the PEPS proposal was a kind solution. Naomi arguing it was a genocide disguised as a solution to avoid paying the cost of improving their lives. I was so tired I could barely follow the debate.

Naomi left me, with more reassuring and encouraging noises, and told me to get some rest. I was happy to oblige. I fell onto my bed, fully clothed, and went straight to sleep.

I slept through the afternoon. I woke up hungry, and ate my room service dinner greedily. Right on cue, a few minutes after I'd finished my dinner, I heard the now familiar voice of Yusef calling me from the other side of the room. I turned to him with relief. I'd been hoping he'd return, but there was no way I could know for sure. I realized momentarily he must have some contact in the hotel, to know so accurately the right time to visit me.

His face was warm. I felt he was my only friend in this insane life into which I'd been thrown.

"Hi, my brother, how have you made it through today?" he asked, with a twinkle in his eye.

I told him about the events of the day. Yusef shook his head slowly as he heard the story.

"I'm not surprised by any of it," he told me, "and I'm sorry you had to undergo such traumatic experiences. But, you've now been able to see first-hand the cold-blooded hypocrisy of the d-humans. They wrap everything up in their high-minded values and legal procedures, and then they can do whatever they like as long as it doesn't breach their protocol. You no longer have to take my word for it.

"That," he continued, "is the PEPS proposal in a nutshell. They create a UN hearing, complete with the token Primal, and they know they can get away with the biggest genocide in history just because their proceedings were completed."

Yusef began to tell me about his own family. They lived in Peshawar, in northwestern Pakistan, an area that was still mostly human. Yusef taught comparative linguistics at the University of Peshawar. He'd joined the fight for a human future, he told me, when he saw so many of his students, initially filled with hopes and ambitions, lose their way in despair because they could make no progress in a society dominated by d-humans.

He told me his wife, Yasmina, had given him three children that he loved dearly. His oldest, Abdul, was in his late teens and was beginning undergraduate studies in nano-genetics at the same University of Peshawar where Yusef taught. His second, a daughter called Ishmalia, also a teenager, wanted to be a doctor. Finally, his second son, Ibrahim, was only twelve, but Yusef had great hopes for him. Ibrahim showed a deep spiritual side, and already read the Koran with passion. Yusef hoped that Ibrahim might one day grow up to become an imam, a spiritual teacher of Islam.

Yusef told me how, over the years, he'd become a type of "human ambassador" for the Rejectionists. Because of his language skills, he'd been asked to reach out to humans in different parts of the world. He'd made contact with humans all the way from South America to Europe and Australia. However, in all these years, he told me, there had never been a contact as important as me.

I felt a cold finger of dread make its way up my spine. I didn't want to be so important. It scared the hell out of me. I asked him why.

"Eusebio," Yusef answered, "you remember only two nights ago, I pleaded with you not to take part in this PEPS session. I tried to explain to you there were huge forces at work that you couldn't comprehend, that might overwhelm you. Do you remember?"

I acknowledged that, yes, he'd tried to stop me and I'd decided to participate anyway.

"At this point, Eusebio, there's a role for you to play that may, without exaggeration, alter the course of history. There are decisions you will need to make and things you can do, which could literally save the human race from extinction. At this point, there is no way you can ignore the train that you stepped on. You can stay on the train or you can jump off it, but whichever it is, the train is moving and you have to make a decision one way or the other."

I didn't understand what he meant. After all, he had been telling me two days ago that I was a mere stooge for the PEPS session, that my role was meaningless. I asked him to explain.

"There will be time enough for that, Eusebio," Yusef responded. "Right now, it's getting late and you need to prepare for your neurographic challenge tomorrow morning. You've got to come up with a different song to hide your thoughts from the neurographic chair, and we should practice again against Harry Shields' questions."

I thought of my close call this morning. I'd made it through without my mind betraying Yusef, but it hadn't been easy. I tried to think of a song that would fit with my hatred for Harry Shields when he was interrogating me. Then it came to me. I sang aloud the lyrics from a song I'd loved as a youth, another one from the counter-culture movement of the mid-twentieth century:

They paved paradise and put up a parking lot
With a pink hotel, a boutique, and a swinging hot spot
Don't it always seem to go
That you don't know what you've got till it's gone
They paved paradise and put up a parking lot

I would enjoy singing this to myself tomorrow morning so the lyrics would show up on Harry Shields' screen as he was interrogating me.

They took all the trees and put 'em in a tree museum
And then they charged all the people twenty-five bucks just to see 'em
Don't it always seem to go
That you don't know what you've got till it's gone
They paved paradise and put up a parking lot

I knew all the words by heart. I used to listen to this song with my friends when I was younger. I was already looking forward to watching Harry's eyes when I directed my anger to him at what he and his fellow d-humans had done to us all.

Finally, Yusef was almost ready to go. He paused and spoke with a very different tone in his voice. His voice was grave and steady.

"Eusebio," he said, "before I go tonight, I need to leave you with a question. Don't answer it now. Answer it when I see you again, God willing, tomorrow evening. But you need to think hard and think deep about the answer."

"What's the question, Yusef?"

"Are you willing to give your life, if need be, to do what must be done to save our human race?"

I already knew the answer. But I did what Yusef had asked and remained silent. We said farewell to each other, and Yusef's image disappeared.

I prepared for bed. Naomi would be picking me up early again tomorrow morning. I thought about Yusef's question and was a little surprised by the clarity of my inner response. There was no doubt about it. I have lived through great and wonderful things in my life. I have loved, and I have lost. I have experienced the greatest wonders and deepest despair that life can offer a human being. I've done my time on this earth. I'm ready to get off if the time is right and join my love, join Sarah, on the other side, in the spirit world.

I went to sleep, thinking of the love of my life, dreaming of Sarah.

11 Sarah

I met a young girl, she gave me a rainbow
I met a young woman whose body was burning

I was making my way to Jerry McHadden's house filled with excitement and anticipation, all tinged with fear. I'd just turned eighteen and it was my Vision Day. Jerry was my Spirit Guide who was going to lead me through my journey on Perception. This was supposed to be the most important day of my life. What would happen? What would it be like? Most of all, I just hoped it would be something meaningful. My biggest fear was that it would be a flop, that I'd finish the day disappointed, saying to myself "What was that all about?"

I thought back to that other milestone of life in our community—Initiation Day. At thirteen years old, everything had seemed so special. That day, in front of all the people of Tuckers Corner, I'd prayed to *Wakan Tanka* in my ancestor language, the ancient language of the Nez Perce Indians, known as *Nimipuutimpt*. In my own little voice, first in the original language and then translated in English, I'd uttered the words of Chief Joseph as he surrendered to the U.S. army after months of leading hundreds of Nez Perce on a haunted march for freedom ahead of thousands of American soldiers hunting them down.

"I am tired of fighting," Chief Joseph had said. *"Our chiefs are killed. Looking Glass is dead. Toohoolhoolzote is dead. It is cold and we have no blankets. The little children are freezing to death. Hear me, my chiefs! I am tired. My heart is sick and sad. From where the sun now stands I will fight no more forever."*

That day, I'd become part of my Humanist community. I'd felt so special, in touch with Chief Joseph from hundreds of years ago; in touch with everyone around me. Even at that age, Sarah had been special to me, and I'd looked around at the audience until I'd seen her eyes filling me with encouragement, with pride.

Now, Sarah was thousands of miles away. It was her Year Away, and she was staying with our sister Humanist community in Wales. I had to go through my Vision Day without the person most important to me. How would I do it? What would it mean to me without Sarah?

Jerry's wife was at work; his children were at school. There was no one in his house but him and me. He gave me one tiny pill of Perception. Within fifteen minutes of nervously swallowing it, things started changing. I'd been told about this, the period of transformation while neural pathways that were usually blocked were gradually opening up. I started seeing strange patterns in the walls along with other continually changing visual hallucinations. Jerry was sitting there with me in his living room, but his face started changing shape and looking weird. Still, I was already glad he was there.

Before too long, the transformation was over, the neural pathways were open, and the hallucinations went away. I was seeing in a way I had never seen before. I looked at Jerry, a face I'd seen literally thousands of times. But I had never *really* seen his face before. It was as though I was looking at an X-ray of his soul. As he looked back at me with a steady gaze, I saw the face of Encouragement. Then, moments later, it morphed. I saw the pain of his life. I saw a hardness in the lines around his face, in the way the edge of his lips curved. I knew in a flash he was having difficulties with his wife. I'd seen those signs for years but never realized what they meant. Then, without any warning, his face morphed again. I saw in his eyes his struggle to reach Serenity, how he used his craftsmanship with wood to achieve an inner peace. I saw his warmth and how he tried so hard to live a decent life. Then, everything went even deeper. As he watched me watch him, with his steady gaze, I saw my Spirit Guide, I understood that he was ahead of me exploring an unmapped wilderness, looking back at me, waving me on to catch up with him. All this happened without a word passing between us.

Now I was in Jerry's backyard. I'd been there hundreds of times, but this was the first time I'd ever experienced it. It was a warm day in early summer. I found myself getting to know a friendly oak tree in the yard. I hugged it and felt its strength and inner calm. I felt its roots locking it in place and pulling up nutrients from the soil. I sat on the lawn and watched the grass grow. Literally. I saw each blade quivering with life, basking in the rays of the sun, sucking up the moisture in the earth. I watched the afternoon storm clouds begin to gather and move in towards us. I felt the grandeur of the weather. As I did so, some thunder roared out its warning. As I experienced its greatness, something came into my mind. It was the name of Chief Joseph, whose words I had spoken years ago on my Initiation Day. In Nez Perce his name was *Hin-mah-too-yah-lat-kekt*, or Thunder Rolling in the Mountains. I thought of him dying of a broken heart after sixty years of resisting the white man, exiled forever from the land of his ancestors. I'd read and thought about him so many times before, but for the first time in my life, my heart broke with his.

Sitting there, in Jerry's little backyard, I felt the generations of lives that had lived in the cycles of nature; I felt the heartbreak of their loss at the hands of the white man. I thought of the reality out there, beyond our little enclave of Tuckers Corner, the freeways criss-crossing the land in every direction, the planes overhead, the satellites monitoring every movement of everybody, the once wild lands that had become genetically engineered farmlands, the digital signals that controlled the whole world. I felt the loss of so much, I couldn't bear it. I started sobbing uncontrollably. With each heave of my chest, it seemed like the earth was sobbing with me. In the middle of my sobs, I noticed my Spirit Guide, Jerry, sitting in front of me, watching me. I cried out to him, "Where has it all gone?" He slowly nodded his head in response, silently telling me that he himself had gone through this terrible path of despair and come out the other side.

Tears came dripping out of my eyes. The thunder clouds were now above us and started shedding their warm raindrops on both of us. I kept sobbing there in the rain, as my clothes absorbed the water and clung against my skin. I knew that the earth was weeping with me. It was sharing its grief with mine. Then, gradually, the raindrops slowed and turned into a gentle drizzle. Something began to change in me. I realized, in a moment of awareness, that the ancient spirits of the land were telling me something as the soft drizzle enveloped me. They were saying that *"Life goes on!"* They were all around me. They *were* the gentle rain drizzling on me.

I found myself back in Jerry's living room, warming up from the rain. Gradually, the state of Perception was beginning to fade. I could feel the building blocks of my consciousness getting ready to re-assemble themselves. Only this time, I could shape how they would reconfigure. I could seal them together with my own meaning. I began talking, slowly, to Jerry, with words that seemed to fill the whole room with resonance. As I did so, a famous saying of Chief Joseph filled my mind: *"It does not require many words to speak the Truth."* My words were few. I spoke to Jerry of the beauty of the world, the wonder of life, the despair of what has been taken from our world. As I did so, I realized that the ancient spirits had given me a role to play. I could do something to keep their memories alive. I could teach others of their lives and their sacred activities. It was at that moment, talking to Jerry of what I had experienced, that I realized I would spend my life as a teacher of history, making sure the great wonders of the past would not be forgotten.

As Jerry saw my mind was beginning to re-assemble itself, he told me it was time to choose my totem. Your totem can be anything that exists in the natural world that is non-human: an animal, a tree, a mountain, a rock. It's something that has a spirit akin to your own. You choose your totem at the end of your Vision Day, as a reminder of the experiences you've had. In future years, when you're uncertain of what to do, of who you are, it's our tradition to remember your totem, to use that memory as a lifeline to your inner consciousness, connecting your own spirit with the strength of the external spirit world.

At that moment, it was easy. I didn't need to think about it. I had known it all along, but it needed Jerry's question for it to hit my consciousness. The friendly oak tree was my totem. Its roots took life from the earth; its leaves took energy from the sun; its branches bent with the wind; its trunk remained solid. It gave me the strength to make it through my life.

I returned to a normal state, with my new consciousness sealed in place. In my heart, I found myself thanking Dr. Julius Schumacher for creating Perception, for allowing me to partake of this experience, and Jessica Goodrich for making Vision Day part of our community's life. I felt there was a meaning to my life that I'd never dreamed about before that day.

I longed to tell Sarah about my Vision Day, about the thunder, the rain, the oak tree. But she was thousands of miles away. By the time she came back, many months later, my oak tree totem had taken root deep within. But my thoughts had moved on. All I cared about was Sarah.

* * * *

Sarah. Sarah, I miss you so much. It hurts almost too much to think about you, but I must. You are so much a part of who I am. Where are you, Sarah? Are you here, around me now? I know you are. As you said to me, years ago, you are always here, deep inside me. Our spirits joined, and nothing can separate them. Not even death.

Sarah. When I first met her, I was just a little boy. Probably no more than ten years old. Sarah was in the class above me. Unreachable for a ten year old. Why she even talked to me, I'll never know. We found ourselves walking home from school together. Our homes were in the same direction, and before too long, this became a habit. Just a boy and a girl, walking home, pointing out things to each other as we went.

One day, after several months, as we were walking home from school, I realized I'd left my pens back in the classroom. I asked Sarah if she could loan me a pencil. We sat on a wooden bench next to the corn field, as she looked through her bag. She pulled out a brand new pencil.

"This is my only one," she said. "So, we're both going to get half."

Before I could say anything, she broke the pencil in two. She took out her pencil sharpener and sharpened the broken end. Now, there were two smaller pencils. Then she said something to me that stayed with me forever.

"Eusebio, the spirit of this pencil has now been split in two. We'll both have part of the spirit. Now, we've always got to be close to each other, or the spirit will get mad at both of us, and who knows what he'll do."

I couldn't tell if she was joking or serious. We'd all been taught that everything around us contains spirits. But a pencil? I looked at her. Sarah Connor. She still had her Irish bloodline intact. With her reddish, wavy long hair, her fair skin, her little nose, her freckles, and her green eyes. I looked at those eyes, and they seemed to be dead serious. Looking back at me, waiting for an answer.

"So, are you going to take your half of the spirit, Eusebio Franklin? If you take it, you'd better remember what I said about it."

I decided to take what she said seriously. After all, who knows? And, already, by then, I was happier being with Sarah than anyone else.

"I'll take it, Sarah. I'll remember about the pencil spirit."

And remember I did. To this day. As I look back through the years, I know that was the moment I began to fall in love with Sarah. I didn't know it at the time. I had no clue what love even meant. But from that moment, there was something special I saw in her, that balance on a razor's edge between a sublime, unique understanding of the world of the spirits on the one hand, and that touch of Irish humor, that playfulness about the most important things in the world on the other hand. It was a tightrope that Sarah walked between these two spaces, and sometimes I felt I was her balancing pole, that the things she said to me helped her to keep upright on that tightrope.

But none of those thoughts passed through my mind at that time. I was just struck by the possible importance of the pencil spirit, and I knew I'd made a promise I had to keep.

We kept walking home together after school. During weekends

and Ancestor Days, when our whole community would get together to commemorate the Incas, the Mayans, or the Aboriginals, I found myself always seeking out Sarah, because whatever I did, it always seemed to have an extra meaning, it seemed to quiver with a special life, when Sarah was around.

Sarah and I were best friends for many years before we became lovers. As I grew into my later teens, I would fantasize about Sarah at night, in the privacy of my bed, hormones raging. But during the day, when I was with her, our friendship seemed to have created a barrier that not even the force of teenage male hormones could shatter. I was afraid that one move as a male would do something to our friendship that couldn't be undone. And our friendship had become more important to me than anything.

Then, Sarah went through her Vision Day. I had just turned seventeen at the time. For a few weeks after her Vision Day, Sarah seemed strangely distant. I didn't know what had happened. Something had changed in her, and she wasn't telling me about it. I felt hurt, almost betrayed. I'd already come to rely on Sarah to share the world around me and give it meaning. When anything happened during the day, it didn't really have meaning until I'd told it to Sarah and heard her laugh about it or tell me something about it that would never have entered my own mind.

More than a month passed after Sarah's Vision Day. I'd already made up my mind to confront her with my feeling of hurt, to ask her what had happened. But I hadn't yet plucked up enough courage. We were walking one Sunday afternoon in the cornfield, where years earlier Sarah had given me half of the pencil spirit. Suddenly, she seemed gay and light. It was early summer, and the world was alive around us. We started laughing and playing around. Before I knew it, we were tumbling together on the ground, holding each other. In a moment, everything changed. I realized that Sarah was holding me, not as a friend, but as a woman. My face was right next to hers. Our breath stroked each other's faces. Sarah's eyes looked into mine, and I saw something I'd never seen before. I saw Sarah's womanhood. Her eyes beseeched mine. The moments passed. It was as though she were calling my maleness out from my loins. I felt a stirring within me as I looked right back at Sarah's beautiful, female green eyes. She didn't need to say it, but she did. Her lips moved, and a whisper, barely audible, came from her.

"Take me," she whispered.

And I took her. I took her like an erupting volcano. I couldn't restrain my actions. I ripped her clothes off her, not caring as buttons were torn off. I felt her soft breasts for the first time in my life. I kissed her and felt her tongue greet mine. I smelled her beautiful scent, I licked her lovely breasts, I kissed her between her legs and was overcome by her femaleness, her softness, her scent of sex. Then, she yielded to me. For the first time in my life, my maleness took over everything else in the universe. I was a wild animal taking my mate. I thrust and thrust, and Sarah gasped and yielded further. We exploded together in a moment of ecstasy that I had never dreamed possible.

We lay there in the cornfield, in the warm sunshine. Nothing would ever be the same again. We touched and stroked each other. There were no words. Only our feelings caressing each other's being. Our eyes met and our gaze locked. Then, something very strange happened.

As I was holding Sarah, looking into her eyes, her face seemed to start changing shape. I was transfixed. I felt like I was in a trance. Sarah's face seemed to encompass all womanhood. She looked like Cleopatra, like the Queen of Sheba. She looked like the essence of love, of sex, of female beauty. She looked as though every woman from thousands of years of human existence was touching her spirit and putting their essence into her. I gazed and wondered momentarily what Sarah was seeing in my face. I got lost in the profusion of female essence that looked back at me. And then, there was a flash. It was as though two electrical wires had short-circuited. I threw back my head, as did Sarah. Deep in the back of my brain, it felt like some circuits had flashed that had never before come to life. I had no idea what had happened. I looked back at Sarah, and she was no longer every-woman, she was back to being Sarah, my love Sarah.

I broke the silence.

"What just happened?" I whispered to my love.

"Our souls just touched," she whispered back, matter-of-factly, as though something like that happened every day.

"That was for real, wasn't it? We didn't just imagine it?"

She nodded ever so gently. "That was for real, Eusebio. Yes, it really happened."

As we lay there, in the cornfield, as I felt Sarah's soft flesh around me, as our breathing enveloped each other's breasts, I realized that something very special had taken place. There was a bond that had formed between Sarah and me that was beyond any ordinary meaning. Our souls had touched. Part of me was now in Sarah, and part of Sarah was now in me. Nothing could ever undo that.

For the next few months, I felt I was sailing on air. The world had become a place of extraordinary sensation. The sky was bluer and the earth seemed to give me a spring in every step. I lived for my time with Sarah. I was engulfed by my love. Nothing else mattered to me. My family, my friends, all wondered what had become of me, because nothing had any meaning anymore unless it was with Sarah.

Then, the summer months began to fall, and it was time for Sarah to go and spend her Year Away. The day of Sarah's departure approached for me with the impending doom of a funeral. Sarah was going to spend her year with the Humanist community in Wales. Her ancient language was Irish Gaelic, and she was excited at the prospect of spending time closer to her Celtic roots. I dreaded it.

The day arrived and Sarah left, with hugs, kisses, and tears. Sarah would write to me, frequently at first and then more rarely. Our method of communicating with each other was cumbersome. Sarah had to send an e-mail to a community neighboring Tuckers Corner, which had access to InfoCore, the system that all digital communication had to go through in the United States.

Our Humanist community never signed up to InfoCore, so about once a week, one of our Outside Guides would pick up print-outs of any e-mail messages received for us, and I would get my treasured letters from Sarah. Every time she would mention another man in her letters, I would squirm with jealousy. I dreaded the notion that she would meet somebody there, and that I might never see her again. I was hopelessly in love with her.

The only respite to this year of deprivation was my own Vision Day, which gave me a renewed strength and sense of my inner self. I began to harden myself to the notion that, just possibly, Sarah's life and mine might not remain intertwined forever.

Then, finally, Sarah returned from her Year Away. She was back. At first, we were a little distant from each other, but as the weeks passed, I could see that our separation had not touched our love. We grew together again. After some time, when we felt as close to each other as before, Sarah confessed to me that she'd had a relationship with another guy in Wales. They had spent about three months together, and she had broken it off, she told me, because I was the person she loved. I went through all the anger, the hurt, the confusion, and finally the reconciliation that could be expected of an eighteen-year-old who hears such a thing from the girl he loves. Ultimately, she had broken off the relationship, and most importantly, she was telling me about it.

That was when I asked her for the first time to marry me. We were sitting on the edge of the same cornfield where we had first made love. I wanted, more than anything to know we would be together forever.

"Eusebio, I love you," she responded, warmly. I had the feeling I wasn't going to hear what I had hoped for.

"I love you," she continued, "not because you're the smartest person around, because you're not. Not because you're the best looking, or have the best body, because you don't. Not because you have the best personality, because that's not necessarily true."

We were sitting on the grass together. I wasn't enjoying what I was hearing. She turned and pointed to a mound of earth not far from us. It was a little hillock, covered with grass, completely unnoticeable.

"I love you, Eusebio, because you're like that mound of earth right there."

A mound of earth! This was not my idea of a romantic response to a marriage proposal.

"I love you because you're always there, Eusebio, like that mound of earth. I know what you are, and I can trust that you'll always be that. You're reliable. You don't bullshit around. You don't try to be what you're not. You're part of things, and that gives me more comfort than anything. When I left for my Year Away, that mound of earth was just sitting there, and now I'm back, and it's still there. In the rain, it gets muddy, and in the spring it gets a new layer of grass. It does what it should do, and I trust it. That's what I love about you, Eusebio Franklin."

I wasn't sure how I felt about what I heard. But that was part of my love for Sarah; she was always taking me to some new place in my mind and soul that I hadn't even dreamed was there. At least she was telling me that she loved me.

"So will you marry me?" I asked again.

"No, Eusebio. Not right now."

"Why not?" I felt a terrible surge of disappointment. I wanted Sarah so badly to be part of my life.

"Because you're not ready yet. I need to know that I'm right about you, that you really are as reliable as that mound of earth. Next year, it's your Year Away. Go away, spend that year. When you come back, if you still want to marry me, then I'll know I was right. Then we'll see. Right now, let's just love each other and enjoy being with each other."

She put her arms around me and started kissing me.

And so it came to pass, as Sarah had predicted. I went to Argentina for my Year Away and came back wanting more than anything to marry her. I had my own infidelities in Argentina, which I admitted to her. They taught me the difference between having sex and making love. I could have sex with any woman who would have me; I could only make love with Sarah. And that was all I wanted.

Sarah was good to her word. She accepted my proposal the second time. We got married in a joyful ceremony in Tuckers Corner. We struggled like all young couples everywhere to make ends meet.

174

I began my career as a junior history teacher at our school. Sarah, like so many others in Tuckers Corner, began her own crafts business. She had a fascination for ancient Viking art, and we put together a little metal workshop for her in the back of our small, two-bedroom house.

I felt that the spirits had smiled on us. I couldn't quite believe that life could be so good, so right. Sarah became pregnant, and we had a beautiful baby girl, Sally. The years passed. Life wasn't easy, we had to watch every dime of our money, but we had each other and we had Sally, who grew into a spirited and beautiful little girl. It seemed like nothing could spoil our daily routines. We tried to have another baby, but we kept waiting without results. That was OK. Sally was our delight.

And then, Sarah began to notice that her abdomen was swelling a little, but it wasn't because she was pregnant. She tried doing more exercise but started to find that she would quickly get tired. This went on for months and just didn't seem to go away. One day, when we were making love, she shuddered and let out a gasp of pain. We both felt there was something wrong. But we didn't want anything to disturb the peace and happiness of our lives. We just waited for Sarah to feel better again.

She began to get terrible indigestion and found herself going to the bathroom more frequently. Then, one day, she found that she had some vaginal bleeding in the middle of her menstrual cycle. We knew we couldn't ignore her symptoms anymore. We went to the Tuckers Corner Medical Center together. Sally was nine years old at the time.

I wish I could forget the look on the doctor's face after he had performed some tests on Sarah. He walked into the waiting room where we were both sitting nervously. He brought us into his consultation room. He looked seriously at both of us and then turned his attention to Sarah.

"Sarah," he began gravely, "you have ovarian cancer. It's beyond the early stage, and we can't yet tell if it's in stages two, three, or four, without doing surgery. If it's stage two, we can treat it here at Tuckers

Corner. If it's a later stage, we're going to have to arrange for you to visit the Albany Medical Center. We would need an Outside Guide to help arrange the visit."

A terrible sinking feeling pulled me in my gut. I looked across at Sarah and held her hand. I could only imagine what she was feeling.

She went directly into surgery. They came out and told me the bad news. It was at least stage three. They couldn't treat it here in Tuckers Corner. We needed to plan for a trip outside, to Albany.

While Sarah was recuperating from her surgery, I talked with the Tuckers Corner Financial Administration. I had never in my life spent a moment thinking about these things. The Financial Administrator explained to me that the Tuckers Corner Emergency Fund was available to pay for us to go with the help of an Outside Guide to the d-human Medical Center in Albany.

I can barely remember the details. All of a sudden, life was a daze. I just remember us being driven in one of our rickety fifty-year-old automobiles by an Outside Guide, Stacey, to our neighboring d-human community. There we got in an automated, high-tech taxi which took us to the Albany Medical Center. I barely looked out the window at the world around me. I could only think of Sarah's pain and fear, and hold her hand.

Stacey had arranged everything for us. She led us through the maze of strange, high-tech passageways, to an automated check-in area. I went with Sarah into the examination room, where they put humming machines around her and watched computer screens. It barely took half an hour, and then we were in another doctor's consultation room. Only this time the doctor was a d-human.

He looked at us with something like benign pity. He spoke to us slowly and simply, as though we were both ten years old. Obviously, he'd had experience dealing with Primals before, and this was the style he'd developed.

"Sarah, the type of cancer you have is not likely to be responsive to the old-fashioned approaches available in your community. It's an advanced cancer, known as 'late stage three.' I'm sorry they put you through a surgery at Tuckers Corner. We could have used nano-surgical techniques here to eliminate the tumor without having to cut you open. But even here, we can't easily stop the cancer from growing back.

"You see, Sarah," he continued, "this type of cancer is unheard-of nowadays. The genetic patterns that permit this have been screened out of everyone for generations. Everyone except Primals. I've never seen a cancer like this before. We had to go into the archives to identify its genetic fingerprint. The problem, Sarah, is that our whole medical infrastructure is set up to manage d-human health problems. We couldn't even begin to treat this here in Albany."

It wasn't sinking in. It didn't make any sense. This was the d-human world. They had all the scientific answers.

"What are we supposed to do?" I blurted out.

"Well, if Sarah had this cancer a hundred years ago, it would have been easy. Any medical center like ours would have identified the genetic fingerprint in a moment and created a designer protein to attack that particular cancer. The treatment would have been easy and non-invasive. It would have led to a complete cure in a matter of weeks.

"Of course, the technology still exists to do all this," he continued. "It's just not normally used. We'd have to get in touch with the CHD in Atlanta."

"The CHD?" I asked, puzzled.

"Sorry—the Center for Historical Diseases. They're the national center for the archives of diseases that used to affect Primals. They're mainly a historical research unit. But they might still have some of the equipment needed to create the right protein to kill the cancer. You see, each cancer like this has a unique genetic structure, and a protein has to be individually created to eliminate the cancer."

"So they can cure Sarah?" I was jumping to the conclusion I wanted to hear.

"Well, they should be able to. I'll have to speak with them and see what they can do. And how much it will cost. I have to warn you, this approach may be very expensive. It's not just a matter of applying a standard treatment. They may have to retrofit certain machines and possibly even construct a machine from scratch to create the proteins that are needed. The machines used a hundred years ago for this are just historical curiosities nowadays." He stopped and thought for a minute. "Alternatively," he continued, "they may be able to import a machine from somewhere in the developing world. If they can find one."

Sarah and I left the Albany hospital with Stacey. We were bewildered. We didn't know what to think. Sarah's life, it seemed, was in the hands of a d-human doctor and the archives of the Center for Historical Diseases. We jumped between hope and fear. But we seemed to spend most of our time with the fear. It crept into our beings and hung there, spreading its black tentacles into all our thoughts and feelings.

A couple of weeks later, Stacey led us on another visit to Albany. The doctor had the answer from the CHD. We were back in his consultation room.

"I spoke with a doctor in Atlanta whose historical specialty is twenty-first century oncology—that means the treatment of cancers. He told me he can construct the machinery to identify and create the protein that would eliminate your cancer entirely, Sarah."

The relief swept over us. That was until his next sentence.

"The only problem is, it's not inexpensive. He estimated the total cost for the treatment, including the specialized equipment, would be in the region of fifty million dollars."

I felt that I'd been hit in the stomach. I didn't know what to do. It would take Sarah and me a lifetime to earn fifty million dollars. We had no savings. The whole Emergency Fund of Tuckers Corner, which had paid for us to come here to Albany to visit the doctor, only had about thirty million dollars in it. Where would we get the money?

"There's one other possible alternative, if you can't find that kind of money," the doctor continued. "In Europe, they have more Primals, and they still have some of this historical equipment in use in some of their medical centers. I've got a friend in London. I'll give him a call and see if there's anything they can do for you there. I expect it would be a fraction of the price."

We returned to Tuckers Corner in a daze. How had it come to this? How could Sarah's life be at stake over money? We're not going to let this happen, we're going to do something about it, I kept saying to Sarah. But I had no clue what we were going to do.

The days passed. We seemed to be in suspended animation. Word spread around Tuckers Corner. Everybody was especially friendly to Sarah and me. But no amount of warmth and friendship could metamorphose into fifty million dollars. We kept waiting for a message from the doctor in Albany. Perhaps Sarah's salvation lay in Europe.

The message came from the doctor. Stacey brought it to us. Europe wouldn't work. It seemed they had all the equipment, but the bureaucracy wouldn't permit it. There was a lot of political pressure in Europe to reduce the expenditures on Primal health care. It would be impossible for Sarah, as a Primal, to enter Europe for the purpose of medical treatment. If she went to Europe as a tourist, they wouldn't treat the cancer; they would just send her back to the United States. We were checkmated by politics and bureaucracy. The doctor said he'd check into the cost of importing the machinery from a developing country, but we got the sense he was getting bored with this project, and we weren't going to hear from him again. Not unless we found the fifty million dollars.

Things were becoming critical. Sarah was getting increasingly tired. We feared the cancer was growing back. One day, we were visited by one of the Tuckers Corner councilors, Vanessa Pilger. Vanessa was a matriarch of our community, well respected and liked. When she spoke, you knew she spoke for Tuckers Corner. She sat down with us in our living room.

She told us that the Tuckers Corner council had met to discuss Sarah's predicament. Everybody in the community was desperate to find a solution for Sarah. A few months earlier, a tourist from Boston had visited Tuckers Corner and had fallen in love with our collection of ancient Peruvian and Bolivian weavings on show in our ethnic museum. He had offered Tuckers Corner seventy million dollars to buy the whole collection. The council had, of course, instantly refused. It has been a basic tenet of our community since inception never to lose the original collections of ancient ethnic crafts that Jessica Goodrich had spent so many years building in the early days.

However, the council had now voted to override this basic principle and had agreed to sell the entire collection to raise the money to pay for Sarah's treatment. For a moment, I was excited. I felt the stirring of hope inside me. It would work. We would get our lives back. I would have my wife. Sally would have her mother.

Then, I looked at Sarah, and I saw her shake her head. She kept shaking her head. Softly, she spoke.

"No," she said, "I'm not going to accept that. Thank you. I mean, thank you from the bottom of my heart. I can't believe what everyone would do for me. To save my life. But I can't accept it."

"Why not? What's the matter with you?" I almost yelled out at Sarah in frustration.

"I can't accept it, Eusebio, because to do so would be to begin unraveling everything Tuckers Corner is about. I want my life. Trust me, I don't want to die. But I'm not going to stay alive at the expense of Tuckers Corner."

This was a Sarah that I had never known. I didn't even understand what she was saying.

"Sarah, how can you say this?" My voice was still raised. "Your life is worth more than weavings. That's what they're saying. What's the problem with that?"

"Because it's the first step to unraveling everything our community is based on. I've thought about this for a while. And I've already made up my mind."

All these years, I'd never known Sarah to keep something important from me. We'd always shared our thoughts about anything. I was shocked. Sarah continued talking.

"Don't you see, Eusebio? If I accept this from the Council, then we'll get to pay for the treatment. And I'll live, and we won't have the Bolivian and Peruvian collection any more. That's great. Then, what happens a year from now, or ten years from now, when someone else gets sick from a disease that costs tens of millions of dollars to cure? They will say, 'If you could pay for Sarah Franklin, why can't you pay for me?' And the next thing you know, we'll sell the Sepik River bark paintings, and the Dogon masks, and the Torajan doors. And soon there won't be anything left that Jessica Goodrich spent all those years collecting, that we've all used for our inspiration for generations. And so we'll start selling bits of land that we don't really need. And before you know it, there will be nothing left of Tuckers Corner. Just a bunch of useless, sick Primals who mean nothing to anybody, not even to themselves. I'm not going to be part of that unraveling. My life means almost everything to me. But our community means more."

Sarah sat back, and a grim smile passed over her face.

"Look, it won't be the first time a Celtic girl sacrificed herself for her community," she said with sadness and irony in her voice.

Vanessa, who'd been observing this dialogue between Sarah and me, spoke in a soft voice.

"Sarah, the Council is aware of everything you're saying. You're right that we've never sold anything in our collection before, because we haven't wanted to set a precedent, just like you said. But this is a unique situation. We've never seen something like this before, where someone so young, so full of life, is now sentenced to death, and we know there can be a complete cure if we can only pay for it. This is a one-off situation, and the Council is willing to do it, so don't refuse it."

"Thank you, Vanessa, but I've already made up my mind," Sarah responded with a strong voice. "I couldn't live with this burden on me, knowing I've started the process of destroying Tuckers Corner. How am I meant to feel, years from now, when someone is dying from breast cancer, and they're in their fifties, and they say, 'Why should Sarah Franklin get her life and not me?' How am I meant to watch that person die, knowing the community paid for my life and not for hers? We can't get into this path. And the only way to stop it is never to start it."

So Sarah rejected the offer from the Tuckers Corner Council to pay for her treatment by selling the weaving collection. For weeks, I tried everything in my power to get her to change her mind. All of our friends would visit and add their voices to the arguments. I tried logical reasoning. I tried to appeal to our love. I even tried guilt. How could she leave her little daughter Sally, to grow up without a mother? Never in my life had I been so angry with Sarah. How could she give up her life for a theoretical principle? How could she do this to me? To herself?

The weeks turned into months. Sarah became weaker. The good days became fewer, and the bad days were more severe. Finally, one day, Sarah begged me to stop haranguing her to do the treatment.

"I need you, Eusebio, to help me through my last few months," she whispered to me, lying in bed. "I need you as my husband, my love. I can't stand your anger anymore. Let it go. Please. Be there for me. Hold my hand and be with me until I get to the place where only I can go."

From that day on, I never tried again to get Sarah to change her mind. I just gave everything I had to help her through those final months. My anger didn't go away. But it metamorphosed and became anger at Julius Schumacher and Jessica Goodrich for creating the situation that we found ourselves in. Why did they reject something as basic as the d-panel for genetic screening? Something as simple as that would have prevented Sarah from getting this cancer. I hated Jessica Goodrich for never compromising on this. I blamed her in particular for what Sarah was suffering.

"Don't do this, Eusebio," Sarah said one day as I vented my anger at Jessica Goodrich. "Suppose she was right? Eusebio, that day, years ago . . . That day, when our souls touched . . . " She looked at me, and I nodded back. "That has meant more to me than anything. All these years, we've shared our lives together in a way I never dreamed was possible. There have been so many times when I've said to myself, if I should die today, that's OK, because I've felt such happiness on this earth. If Jessica was right, and their genetic engineering does something to the soul, then we might never have known life the way we've known it, never have known love the way we've known it if they'd optimized our DNA before we were born.

Would you have been willing to take that risk? I don't think I would. I'd rather have it the way it's happened, cancer and all. I wouldn't lose what we've had together, not for anything."

I looked straight at her and tried to pierce the veil of her sickness to see if she really meant what she had just said. I just couldn't tell. Was she trying to believe it to make herself feel better as she lay there in her living hell? Was she just saying it for my sake? I couldn't know.

The months continued their relentless ride. Sickness was all about in the house, in the smells of the carpet, the mess of soiled clothes, the pervading gloom. And hiding in the corners, behind closed doors, in the shadows, Death was lurking. Sarah was losing her battle to stay alive. The worst days were the days when she felt better. Occasionally, she seemed to get her energy back, and we'd go for a walk or eat a real meal. She'd help Sally with her homework. For a few hours, we'd have a glimpse of life as it once had been, as it was meant to have been for us for so many more years. For a moment, we'd forget the fate that had been seared on our family's life. We'd get a momentary lightness of heart, even a smile or a laugh. And then, without warning, Sarah's body would start shuddering, she'd try to make it to the bathroom, but before she could get there, her stomach would convulse and the vomit would swarm over the carpet and the walls, as if Death had jabbed Sarah from its dark corner, to make a mockery of our moment of good cheer.

Month after month. The only consistency was Sarah's continuing spiral of weakness, weight loss, and pain. Every day was a physical agony for her and an emotional torment for Sally and me. One afternoon, I was watching Sarah as she slept. Her eyes opened weakly, and she gave me a thin smile.

"Eusebio," she whispered. I got closer to her to hear what she was saying. "When I die . . . Take my ashes . . . Wait until the first rainy day . . . I mean, real rain . . . Take my ashes to your friendly oak tree . . . Your totem . . . In Jerry's backyard . . . Pour my ashes into the roots, mix them with the rain. That's where I want to be." She was gaining her strength back as she spoke. "I'll always be there, with you, with your totem, Eusebio. I'll become part of your oak tree, and I'll never be alone. Our souls will stay connected, even after I die. Part of my soul is already in you. And another part will be one with your totem. Then I'll never be alone." She looked intensely at me. "Promise me, promise me, Eusebio."

I promised her, as the tears flowed out of control, down my cheeks and splashed onto Sarah's soft, hollow face.

And then, one day, I woke up and walked over to Sarah. I was now sleeping on a make-shift bed next to Sarah, because she was beginning to convulse in her sleep and needed the space of the whole bed to herself. I knelt down to check on how she was doing, and I saw that she no longer had any breath. Sarah was dead. She had been freed from her torment. My insides let out a silent scream that echoed through the universe. For the first time ever, I got a glimpse of that dark, cold, infinite vastness of eternity, that awful void that had sucked Sarah's life from her body and from me. Where had my Sarah gone?

The next days of my life, a different form of life without my love, without my ever present Sarah, were all just a daze of frozen emotion. Family and friends, long faces, ceremonies. Sarah's ashes in an urn. If I hadn't had the responsibility of helping Sally make it through this time, I don't know what I would have done. I was numb. How would I deal with the world without my love? How could I be both a mother and a father to Sally?

One Saturday, I was cleaning out our bedroom. Sorting through Sarah's underwear drawer, there, in the back of the drawer, behind the bras and panties and socks, was half a pencil. It was the pencil that Sarah had broken, years ago, when we were children. She had kept her half all through the years. That afternoon flooded back into my mind, so long ago, sitting on the bench, wondering if this girl really meant that we had to be together or we would make the pencil spirit angry. That moment, I realized, that was the moment when I had fallen in love with Sarah. I sat on the floor and started sobbing. My body convulsed in big, heavy sobs as the tears started flooding my face. All the memories, all the moments of love, all the special things, they all kept tumbling into my mind, and there was no Sarah there to be with me anymore, to make more memories together. I wept for my love, I wept for myself. Then, softly, I felt an arm around me. It was Sally.

"It will be all right, Daddy. We'll be all right. Mommy wants us to be strong and to be happy. I know it."

How did she know what Mommy wants? It was right then, with Sally hugging me and trying to comfort me, on the bedroom floor, I realized to what extent Sally was her mother's daughter. That same quality, that ability to seem to know things that I could never understand, that quality that had made me fall in love with Sarah so many years ago, was now expressing itself in Sally. I felt the same quizzical surprise I had felt countless times in Sarah's presence. Did Sally know what she was saying? Was she just saying it to make me feel better? Was there another source giving her this clarity that I could so rarely find?

From that day on, Sally's presence began to fill the void in my heart. As she grew into a young woman, she began to resemble Sarah so closely in her physical appearance, in her movements, and the way she spoke, that occasionally I would find myself momentarily confusing whether it was Sally or Sarah talking to me. A father's pride began to mend the gaping hole that had once been a husband's love. Sally was full of boundless energy. Yes, we had our share of fights as I tried to set down the parameters for a teenage girl, and she would get angry. What would hurt me the most was when she was really mad at me, she would spit out the words to me that she knew would pierce through all my defenses: "Mommy would have understood what I meant . . . " But those battles of adolescence were just punctuations in our lives, and for the most part, as Sally's days and months filled up with academic challenges, sports, social crises, boyfriends, all the normal milestones of a healthy growing girl, her energy swept me up in its flow and kept my heart from breaking.

That was until Gareth Lewis appeared on the scene. Not that I hold anything against Gareth. In fact, I like him a lot. He's a good man with a good soul. But he took my Sally away from me.

Gareth was staying at Tuckers Corner on his Year Away. He came from the Humanist community in Wales, the same community that Sarah had stayed in during her Year Away, a long, long time ago. It hadn't taken long for him to become a regular fixture at our dining room table. At first, I was happy for the company. I could see Sally's eyes light up in his presence. I should probably have figured it out sooner. If Sarah had been around, she would have told me what was going on months before it ever occurred to me. Sally and Gareth were falling in love.

Gareth was twenty-three years old. He'd waited on his Year Away for as long as possible, a full five years from his eighteenth birthday. That was because he was so involved in his art. Gareth is a kinetic sculptor, a throwback to the twenty-first century style of art, which uses "smart ceramics," a material that transforms its shape, color, and texture within a three-dimensional space. Gareth's art always centered around a particular theme—the assimilation of indigenous cultures into the modern world. One sculpture he gave me, still there in my living room, shows a fierce tribesman from Borneo throwing a spear. The spear then transforms into a cloud which rains onto the tribesman. As the rain falls on the tribesman, it gradually melts his features and turns him into a modern looking man, sitting down at a desk. By the end of the transformation, the tribesman's face has lost all character and just smiles passively into space.

That's where Gareth is at. He's moody and passionate. His art had already created quite a following in Wales among d-human society. They would sometimes come to the Humanist community of Llandovery in southwest Wales with the sole intent of buying a work by Gareth Lewis. Apparently, in Europe there's a sizeable group of d-humans who romanticize Primals and believe they're worth preserving. These people, mostly young and liberal-minded, found that Gareth's work spoke to their political and cultural ideals.

During the year Gareth was visiting Tuckers Corner, we came to know each other well. We would sit around, after dinner, drinking too much whiskey. I would reminisce about times with Sarah;

Gareth would talk about the new project he was working on; and Sally . . . Sally would watch me watching Gareth talking, sizing up my feelings, wondering how I would react to the coming turn of events. By that time, Sally was twenty years old. She'd gone through her Vision Day and came out the other side a strong, caring woman, but at the same time, a loyal daughter who loved her father and knew she was everything to me.

One night, about three months before the end of Gareth's Year Away, it was clear something was up. Gareth was already on his fourth glass of whiskey, but was still nervous. His voice, usually filled with feeling, was taut. He followed me into the kitchen as I was making some coffee for the three of us.

"Mr. Franklin, there's something I want to discuss with you," he said.

That's right—Mr. Franklin. In our Humanist communities, there still exists an atavistic tradition of respecting our elders, and although Gareth would call me Eusebio when we were both relaxed, it was quite normal for him to address me as Mr. Franklin if there was something important to talk about.

"Look," he continued, "I don't know how to say it, so I'll just say it. I love Sally, and she loves me. We want to marry each other. I know that she means the world to you. I want to ask you, Mr. Franklin, for your permission to marry Sally."

By this time, even I had figured out this was going to happen at some time. And I had thought through the consequences. So I wasn't surprised at Gareth's answers to my questions. Not surprised, but devastated nonetheless at the knowledge that I was going to lose my Sally, and there was nothing I could do about that. Nothing that wouldn't cause untold misery to the very object of my love.

"Where would you plan to live, Gareth?"

"It would have to be in Llandovery, Mr. Franklin. I've got to go back there to carry on my art. I've got a following there. People are waiting for me to get back. Here, nobody knows about my art, and nobody cares."

I knew that was true. There was no arguing about it.

"So you'd propose marrying Sally and both of you going to Llandovery?"

"Yes, Mr. Franklin. But only if you give us your permission. And your blessing."

"What's more important to you, Gareth?" I asked him, looking into his eyes. "Your art or Sally?"

"It's a fair question, Mr. Franklin," he replied, "but I can't answer it. At least, I can't answer it honestly. I don't know. I love Sally. I love my art. It's everything I am. I don't know how I'm meant to compare the two."

He had answered honestly. I told him I needed to speak alone with Sally. She told me she'd been fearing this day for many months. She hadn't known what to do. She knew she shouldn't leave me alone, but she loved Gareth so much. She wanted to spend her life with him.

What was I meant to do? There was only one way to go. I made a toast to their love, and we all finished the bottle of whiskey. As time went on, I noticed that my drinks were getting bigger than Gareth's. There were tears aplenty, and hugs. Then, in the early hours, they disappeared into Sally's bedroom. And I disappeared into mine. Mine and Sarah's, only there was no Sarah. But there were more tears. Only these were different tears than before. Tears of loneliness. Tears accompanied by an aching, gnawing knowledge that I would soon be losing the living memory of Sarah, the young, happy face that had shooed my loneliness away.

So we had a great wedding celebration. And the weeks passed too quickly until it was time for them to go. And I hugged Sally and made Gareth promise to look after her, or her mother would haunt him forever. And I believed that Gareth would do as he promised.

And I went back to my quiet, lonely house. Where there were only memories. Of Sarah. And now, of Sally. And I went back to my teaching, telling my young pupils about the lost souls of the great warriors of the American plains, about the lost souls of the great wanderers of the Australian outback, about the vast mysteries of human existence that have now been all but forgotten. And each day, I would go back to my quiet, lonely house of memories. And I would miss Sarah. And I would miss Sally.

So it was an easy question for me to answer, when Yusef asked me if I would be willing to give my life to save the human race. The answer was right there on the tip of my tongue. I have had my days of sunshine, my moments of unbelievable joy, of wonder, of excitement, of satisfaction. I've loved, I've felt, I've created another special human life with the woman I loved. Would I be willing to speed up my return to the infinite, to join the other side where Sarah's waiting for me, in order to save what's left of our human race? That was one of the easiest questions of my life.

The Kelly Hendrick Game Reserve

I've stepped in the middle of seven sad forests
I've been out in front of a dozen dead oceans

D id Sarah visit me last night, in my dreams? Or was it just that I'd fallen asleep thinking of her? Did she know I am close to joining her on the other side? Did she come to welcome me?

A chime swept these thoughts out of my mind and a recorded 3D image of Naomi Aramovich appeared in the corner of the room.

"Good morning, Eusebio," her image said. "I hope you slept well. I'm leaving you this message so you'll get it first thing in the morning. I want you to listen to something while you're having breakfast. The guide who'll be showing us around the game reserve today—he's half Tobo. I wanted you to know what that means before you meet him. Hit the play button over there when you're ready."

Naomi's image gave a grimace.

"I'm sorry for what you've got to hear. Prepare yourself—it's not easy listening. You'll see why I didn't give it to you last night—I wanted you to sleep well."

With that cheery introduction, Naomi's image disappeared. I ordered my breakfast and started listening. Naomi was right—it wasn't easy.

It started with a few clicks and then a woman's voice. A strained, tormented voice. She seemed to be whispering nervously.

"My name's Mutamba Kabende. I hope someone can hear this. Sure hope I'm not risking my life for nothing. Date's 2097. September, I think. Not sure any more."

There was another click. Silence. Then she started whispering again.

"Raped eight times today. All Tobo troopers. Can't move around. I'm always tied up. But it's better than the TBK."

Another click and silence.

"Can only talk when guards aren't around. If they catch me, torture me to death. Seen them do it to Telesa. Still hear her screams."

Click.

"Telling this in hope someone will pick up signal. Tell the world what's happening here. What Tobo is all about."

Click.

"My husband's Nkulu Kabende. Was. Dead now. Heard him die. Dentist. That's how he got transmitter in my mouth. Disguised as a tooth. He had one too. So we could communicate with each other on the run. Heard him die. Every scream. Every groan. And the silence after."

Click.

My breakfast arrived. I was already having trouble eating it and listening at the same time.

"Tobo's propaganda playing all the time around us. Zulu master race gonna take over Africa. Our races all gonna disappear. Nkulu and me—we're Bemba. Lived in Zambia. All gonna die."

Click.

"Third day of transmitting. Hope someone's hearing me out there."

Click.

"Tobo invaded Zambia last year. Same as with Zimbabwe, Mozambique. Threatened to nuke Lusaka, like he did Harare. Our government . . . just let Tobo troopers in. Without a fight."

Click.

"Nkulu wouldn't submit like the others. Genetic cleansing, Tobo calls it. Put an end to all African genes except Zulu master race. Nkulu wouldn't line up at Tobo-clinic to let them surgically castrate him. We ran from our home. Hid out in the bush. Thousands more like us."

Click. Her voice was sounding weaker. Anguished.

"He was bringing water back to our camp when they found him. I heard it from his transmitter. They made him strip naked. Saw he still had his testicles. Hands tied behind his back. Ankles tied together. Took their laser scythe and cut him in one swipe. Everything. Testicles and penis in one swipe."

Click.

"They collect them. Like scalps. Ten sets—they get promotion. Fifty—they get best reward—they get their own clone. Every Tobo trooper wants his own clone."

Click.

"When you don't submit—like Nkulu—they use you as example when they catch you. Leave you to die in your blood. Tied up, naked, bleeding your guts out. Anyone tries to help—they kill them too. If you're lucky, you die quick. If not, it can take days. The rats come and eat your guts at night. Nkulu took two days to die. I heard every minute."

Click.

"Six hours of Tobo propaganda today. How he's saving Africa. Africa needs warrior mentality. If only all Africans had nobility, power, and ferocity of great, historic Zulu warrior, then Africa united in greatness. Africa pay rest of world back for centuries of devastation at their hands. So clone master race of Zulu warriors on clone farms. Millions of Tobo clones, but his generals—they get lots of clones too."

Click.

"I made it four more months after Nkulu died. They found me one day looking for food in garbage dump. Thought they'd kill me like Nkulu. No—TBK for me."

Click.

"If you're good conquered woman, you check-in to Tobo clone farm. Ovaries and tubes removed surgically. Then, your womb implanted with fertilized egg containing Tobo clone. Imprisoned in clone farm nine months until give birth to Tobo baby. After birth, hysterectomy—make sure you can't have no more other children of rival tribe. Then, free to return to castrated husband and family."

Click.

"Morning spent being raped. Six Tobo troopers. Afternoon of

propaganda. Tobo's cleared the rainforests. Drained the marshes of the Congo. Now Africa's breadbasket of world. Second only to Brazil."

Click.

"Me—I wasn't good conquered woman. So for me, it's TBK. Tobo Baby Keeper. They don't trust me not to put an end to myself, so they put Tobo clone egg in me and control every movement for nine months. Every movement."

Click.

"TBK. Movable bench with tubes, manacles, treadmill. Oh, and a drain. I'm completely naked. Wrists and ankles permanently manacled to TBK for nine months. At night, bench pivots horizontal so I sleep lying down. During day, bench pivots vertical so I have to stand. Treadmill starts up for hours so I have to exercise—make sure body stays healthy to feed Tobo fetus."

There was silence for a moment. Then her voice started up again, whispering.

"When I have to pee or shit—no choice but just let it go and it drops down the drain. Like an animal. Twice a day, overhead shower rinses me clean. Food three times a day through tube forced down nose."

Click.

"After giving them Tobo baby, get complete hysterectomy. Then, my reward. Spend my days in R&R center. I get to give Tobo troopers pleasure."

Click.

"Hope someone out there hearing this. Recording it for future. Hope someday there'll be an Africa—not just Tobo clones."

The recording went dead. I was gasping with shock. I couldn't believe what I'd just heard. How could anything in the world have ever been so depraved? So evil?

Naomi came to pick me up. I didn't get a chance to ask her anything until we stopped at the Betelbar.

"How could the world have let this happen?" I was almost yelling at Naomi.

"This was the time of the Great Global Wars," Naomi sighed. "Probably the darkest period in the history of the human race. Tobo used the strategic balance of power. He played China and India off against the West. As his empire grew, he used his mineral deposits, oil and gas, diamonds . . . he funneled his raw materials to China and India, and every time the West tried to stop him, he turned it into a form of global brinksmanship—stalemate. "

Naomi looked straight at me. "Eusebio, you have to realize, Tobo was a Primal, just like Hitler, Stalin, Genghis Khan." She paused for a moment and leaned closer to me. "Why do you think people like Harry Shields want to put an end to the Primals?" she asked me. "After the Great Global Wars were over, the whole world wanted to make sure that the words 'Never Again' would finally mean something. This is what GALT was all about. Now, people like Harry Shields say, as long as there are billions of Primals walking on this planet, there's always a risk something like this could happen again."

Maybe they have a point, I thought to myself. My insides were erupting with disgust at what I'd heard this morning.

"So what happened to Tobo and his clones?" I asked Naomi.

"After more than twenty-five years of Tobo's rule," Naomi told me, "The Americans, the Chinese and the Europeans finally achieved a global alliance. They sent an international force into Africa. There were a few fierce battles, but it didn't take long."

"And Tobo himself?"

"Strung up from a lamp-post in his capital city of Johannesburg and had his own genitalia cut from his body by the Zulus."

"The Zulus? I thought this whole horror was done in their name?"

"No, Eusebio, it was done in the name of primal evil, in the name of the human desire for power," Naomi explained. "There were countless Zulus who died fighting to preserve the true spirit of their culture, trying to depose Tobo. Tobo's evil was technically done in their name, but it was never what the majority of them wanted."

"But the legacy of Tobo's horror still exists in Africa today," Naomi continued. "In the aftermath, there were tens of millions of young Tobo clones populating Sub-Saharan Africa. Vast areas effectively depopulated except for the aging, castrated locals and the young generations of Tobo clones.

"For decades after the Great Global Wars," Naomi continued, "the biggest project of UNAPS was to cross-fertilize Africa again with a newly diversified gene pool. It's been partially successful, but there are still millions of third- and fourth-generation Tobo clones all around Africa."

Naomi shook her head. "The awful irony is that, now, the Tobo clones suffer the worst discrimination of any part of African society. They're hated by virtually everyone. They find it impossible to get jobs. Is it their fault that their genes are the same as the greatest perpetrator of evil in history?

"That's why our guide today is half-Tobo. He's one of the millions who can't get a job, except in government organizations. So if you get a strange feeling from him, you'll know why. But don't worry. He's d2-human and the original Tobo aggressive gene set has gone. He'll be harmless.

"Now, we're getting late for the session." And with that, the subject was wrapped up, and we were on our way to the UN building.

* * * *

We're back in session. Harry Shields is performing his usual oration for the record.

"Today," he announces, immensely pleased with himself, "we will be conducting a virtual field trip to the Kelly Hendrick Game Reserve in Masailand. The objective of this field trip is to establish for the record the quality of life attainable in a well-run, modern reservation. The Primal reservations after the implementation of PEPS will be based on this model. Our society can be proud of what we've achieved in reservations such as the Kelly Hendrick Game Reserve. And we will be equally proud of our humane and respectful treatment of the Primals after the conclusion of PEPS."

And then I'm back in the virtual reality cubicle. In my *Resistex* "skin." Going through the weird initialization process. Only, this time,

I know what to expect and it all seems so much less bizarre. And a few moments later, I'm standing on marble steps in front of a modern-looking, sleek building. I look around and see savannah stretching out in front of me. I turn to my side and I expect to see Naomi and Harry in their VRUs. Instead I see three small, machine-like objects with metallic arms and legs, each with a face that looks like an ancient twentieth-century image of a robot. Not even close to human-looking. I look down at myself, and I realize I'm one of these robot-like creatures myself.

"Hi, Eusebio, this is me, Naomi." One of the robot-like creatures raised its arm. It pointed to the right. "This is Harry." Then, to the left. "And this is Ojimo Nkruma, who will be our guide today. Ojimo, can you explain to Eusebio the reason for these specialty VRUs?"

"I'll be happy to, Naomi." His voice was slick. I could hear the African accent, but most of all, I could hear smoothness emanating from the voice. It sounded like he'd been through this rap too many times before.

"These VRUs, Eusebio, are specially designed for safari. They're made to look as different from human beings as possible, and they're small enough that they aren't particularly noticeable to the game. Our wild animals in the Kelly Hendrick Game Reserve hardly ever get to see human beings in the flesh, and we want to keep it that way. But they're used to seeing these specialty VRUs. The VRUs are infused with a scent that's attractive to most game. For this reason, don't be surprised if one of the wild animals comes right up to you and licks you." There was a chuckle. "Up close and personal. This enhances the safari experience for our visitors. Any questions before I continue?"

I had too many to list. Apparently, neither Naomi nor Harry had any at all. Ojimo Nkruma, the half-Tobo safari guide, whom I still hadn't actually met, except in the form of robotic VRU and a slick voice, continued.

His voice took on the timbre of a well-rehearsed speech.

"Before we begin our safari, I always like to pause here for a few moments, on the steps of what we call Reserve Central. Let's look around and take in the beautiful scene."

I obediently followed Ojimo's direction. It was, indeed, a beautiful scene. So beautiful, in fact, that I realized I'd never seen something as spectacular in my whole life. We were on the edge of a plateau, and could look down at a huge valley below and around us. Miles upon miles of grassland. Broken up here and there by clusterings of trees and bushes. The trees themselves were beautiful. Flat-topped for the most part, they gathered together to form vast, wide swathes of greenery. It seemed to be mid-afternoon, with the sun baking the grasslands, causing a hazy shimmering in the distance.

In the wavy haze, I saw patches of what seemed to be thousands and thousands of black dots. I double-blinked to focus in on the dots. I was getting used to this virtual reality magnification trick from the day before. As my vision closed in on the dots, I sucked the air in awe. Each dot was an animal. Gigantic-looking animals, grazing calmly. Looking up every now and then. Flicking their tails. Mothers nuzzling their calves.

Ojimo caught my gaze.

"Wildebeest," he told me. "It's the time of the annual wildebeest migration. One of the greatest sights of the African savannah."

I had no disagreement with him on that. I pulled back my focus to take in the whole scene again. It was glorious. It was magnificent. I felt a surge of wonder at the vast and beautiful existence laid out in front of me. A wave of gratitude to whatever twist of fate had allowed me to experience this moment.

Ojimo's voice shook me out of my reverie.

"Believe it or not, seventy-five years ago, this whole area was nothing but dried-up desert," said Ojimo. "A century of global warming, combined with the loss of the tropical rainforest, desiccated this region. The grasslands vanished, replaced by baked fields of dry, cracked mud. The wildebeest herds, the water buffalo, the Thompson gazelles—all the animals began to disappear. Their predators died out because there were simply not enough animals to keep them alive. The savannah had become a desert. A wasteland."

"I don't understand," I responded. "How did it get like this?"

"UNPRES," came back the response.

"UNPRES?"

"The United Nations Project for the Re-establishment of Extinct Species," Ojimo explained further. "After the Great Global Wars came to an end, UNPRES was formed to perform the greatest act of geo-transformation ever seen. The first job was to get the rains back again. Global warming had changed the wind patterns so the rain clouds never made it over land. So UNPRES used a creation of nanotechnology, called *Nanonets*. These nets are hundreds of kilometers wide and a few kilometers high, attached to thousands of motorized weather balloons. Their texture is so fine they're invisible to the naked eye. A bird can fly right through the net and not even notice, and the fabric just closes back. But the fabric of the net is electrically charged to attract the droplets of moisture in clouds. When the weather balloons slowly start driving the net towards land, the rain clouds follow. As they get over the Masai Reserve, the balloons rise to a higher altitude until the rain clouds drop their precious cargo. And, hey presto, the Masai is green again."

Ojimo's slick style grated on me. But I was fascinated by what he was saying, and I was listening intently.

"But that was just the first part of the project," Ojimo continued. "What about the animals? Most of them were completely extinct. Luckily, a few organizations had collected the stem cells of virtually all the major species before they disappeared, and these had been frozen and stored, in some cases for nearly a hundred years. This was the source of Project Regenesis, one of the greatest achievements of this century."

I thought of Julius Schumacher's wife, Alison. But it was a different woman's name that came out of Ojimo's mouth.

"Thanks to Kelly Hendrick, it all came together," Ojimo was clearly enjoying his soliloquy. He had spoken it so many times that every phrase, every intonation glided out like melting butter. "Kelly Hendrick was, as every schoolchild knows, the wealthiest woman of the twenty-first century. A billionaire by the time she was thirty, because every parent in the Western world wanted their daughter to look like her. By the time she was in her sixties, her beauty had become the most valuable female asset since Cleopatra."

I could tell from the little snicker in Ojimo's voice that he loved that line.

"Kelly Hendrick was the first woman to become a trillionaire late in her life. But she didn't waste her money. For years, Kelly had been accused of being an empty-headed beauty, a symbol of the frivolity of the Western world. Then, she spent the final decades of her life proving everybody wrong. She cared passionately about the loss of the natural world around her, and she used her billions to recreate a game reserve in Africa, filled with the creatures that had once lived there.

"Yes, it was one of the greatest projects in human history, and the result is the Kelly Hendrick Game Reserve today, filled with the healthiest, most diverse set of wild creatures ever seen in this part of Africa.

"Look down over there at the wildebeest. Over three million of them in Masailand at this very moment. Fifty years ago, you could count them with the fingers of two hands."

I had to confess, much as I hated Ojimo's voice, I was impressed by what he was saying. Quite honestly, I couldn't wait to get on with the safari.

Which was the next thing we did. We marched our little, robotic stick figures into an MPV, similar to the one that Subrata had driven for us the day before, when he took us on his expedition to death. I wondered for a brief moment if something equally disastrous would occur again. I knew I wouldn't shed as many tears, though, for Ojimo as I had for Subrata.

After a short ride into the bush, we stopped and got out of the MPV. It seemed like a grassy knoll, like any of the others we'd passed. After a few moments, though, I noticed something weird. It was quiet, standing there, and yet I was hearing more than I'd ever heard in my life. I began to make out the sounds of different bird calls, the chirp-chirp of cicadas and who-knows-what other insects in the grass. I could hear the sounds of branches creaking in the gentle breeze. A call that sounded like a monkey from somewhere far away, and then another call in response. The world was silent, and yet it was abuzz with more sonic activity than I'd ever dreamed possible.

And then I noticed something even weirder. I started smelling different odors. Not just a general smell, but a whole array of different scents. I could distinguish the smell of the grass around me; a musty smell of mold coming from a shady area on my right; a smell of fresh dung from my left. But the dung smell didn't disgust me—instead it smelled interesting, as if it had a story to tell.

The only time I'd ever had a similar experience was when I had taken Spirit Broth at Tuckers Corner, during an Ancestor Day. But this was different. Spirit Broth makes you feel more primal, it makes your feelings temporarily dominate your consciousness. Right now, my consciousness was still fully functioning, but it was receiving a whole new range of meaning from what I could hear and what I could smell.

Ojimo's voice, as usual, interrupted my reverie. "By now," he intoned, "you will be enjoying the experience of what we call the "Safari setting" of your aural and olfactory perceptions. These are automatically set to maximum in your VRU system controls, and give you a perception of the world more closely matching that of the animals here in the reserve. Some people find these settings a little uncomfortable, but most enjoy it. If you have any discomfort, don't hesitate to tell me, and I'll have your perception controls turned down a little."

I felt a momentary pang of disappointment. I'd thought I was experiencing something special. Now, I realized it was just another high-tech manipulation.

We followed Ojimo's stick figure down towards some bushes. Before I could see anything there, I started to hear the sound of some creatures, something between mewling and barking. Then, I saw movement behind the undergrowth. We followed Ojimo right into the middle of the bushes and there, to my amazement, was what looked like a leopard, along with two half-grown cubs. I thought it must be a leopard, because the first thing I saw was its spots. Ojimo put me right.

"We're fortunate to have come across a cheetah family, a female cheetah and her two cubs. The cubs are half weaned, which means they still nurse from their mother, but they also eat any fresh meat mother can catch for them."

I was fascinated. The only animals I'd ever seen "in the flesh," apart from my cat, Jigger, were the other dogs and cats of Tuckers Corner, along with the usual farmyard animals. That was it. I was so absorbed that for a while I forgot everything other than this moment. I forgot why we were there. I forgot about Harry Shields and Naomi Aramovich. I forgot about Yusef. I forgot about UNAPS and PEPS. All I could think of was the magnificence, the beauty, the splendor of the cheetah mother; the innocence, the cuteness of the cubs playing on the ground together.

One of the cubs noticed our stick figures. Its curiosity got the better of it and it ambled towards us. I remembered what Ojimo had told us about the attractive scent of our VRUs. In spite of this, I confess I was a little scared. The cub came right up to me and—yes—it licked the robotic leg of my VRU! I could feel the sensation so strongly, I almost shivered. It was a big, raspy, friendly lick. Like a sandpaper kiss. I never would have believed that, in my life, I would be licked by a wild cheetah cub. Even if it happened virtually.

For a while, we watched the cubs playing and frolicking. Ojimo kept intoning his lecture about the lifestyle of the cheetah.

I began to lose interest in his lecture and started to watch the magnificent cheetah mother. While the cubs were playing, she was constantly on alert. She wouldn't rest for a moment. Every now and then, she'd spring up and climb to the top of the slope above the bushes. Look around intently. Sniff the air. Then, nervously, come back down to be with her cubs.

I was transfixed by the cheetah mother. How could a hunter, a savage killer, seem so beautiful, so nervous, so vulnerable? Suddenly, after yet another sniff of the air, she started prowling off, away from us and the cubs.

"It's possible," Ojimo told us, "that the cheetah mother may be after some prey. Let's climb to the top of the hill to see what happens."

He was right. From our new vantage point, we saw some animals grazing, not far from us. They had beautiful, sharp, curved horns.

Just like the cheetah mother, they seemed incredibly nervous. On a knife-edge. Every couple of seconds, they'd pull their heads up from the grass and look around, sniff, and continue grazing again.

"These animals," Ojimo said, "are Thomson gazelles, known as 'Tommies'—the cheetah's favorite food."

For a few moments, everything seemed calm, as though the world had just paused in time. Then, suddenly, everything was moving. All the gazelles threw up their hindquarters at the same moment and began darting around, first in one direction, then another. I caught sight of the cheetah mother streaking across the grass. My adrenaline was pounding. I watched them zig, then zag, then zig, then zag. There was a flurry of kicking. They had run behind some trees, so I couldn't see exactly what was happening.

A moment later and there they were on the other side of the trees. The cheetah mother closing in on her chosen gazelle. You could see she was making it. Closer and closer. Finally, with a leap, she clamped her mouth around the gazelle's throat. Both down on the ground. A few moments of flopping, and then the gazelle was still. They were lying there on the ground together, engaged in a deadly hug.

We walked our stick figures over to the kill. The cubs seemed to think this was a great idea, too, and were jumping and bounding around, following us.

With my "Safari setting," I could smell the fresh kill before we even came close to it. Fresh blood, raw, intoxicating. The cubs seemed to think so, too. They sprinted ahead of us and started tearing at the carcass. The cheetah mother had already torn open the hindquarters, so the cubs could dig into the soft, bloody tissue. Their faces turned red with blood. They started hissing and growling at each other. They were transformed from sweet, little cubs; now blood-hungry, savage, obsessed by one thing alone—fresh meat. The same was true for the mother, her face also painted red with blood. Except that, in her case, she would periodically pause from gorging and look around, sniffing the air. I thought of the gazelles doing the same thing, only moments before. One of them was now lying here, dead. Fresh meat.

We were now standing so close, we were almost part of the orgy. I could hear, smell, see every bite, every tear, every swallow of the warm flesh. It was so awful and so real at the same time. Terrifying and grand. It was life and death. The world at its most raw, bereft of all trappings. Just one life that became death. One heart that was beating one moment, giving life to its owner, and dead the next moment, giving life to its killer.

Suddenly, the cheetah mother sprang away from the kill and started pacing nervously. There, no more than a few hundred feet from us, was the ugliest-looking creature I'd ever seen. Like a huge dog, but with a fearsomely ugly face and mongrel-like markings. It let out a blood-curdling, other-worldly howl and kept moving closer to the cheetah family where the cubs were still gorging on the kill.

"Here comes a hyena," Ojimo told us. "Now let's see what happens. The cheetah has more to lose than a hyena if they actually fight. Just one injury to the cheetah will mean certain death for her and her two cubs. And the hyena has the strongest jaws in the animal kingdom."

What happened was a stand-off. The hyena kept closing in. The cheetah mother kept swerving towards it, but never getting too close. Finally, the hyena turned and ran.

"The cheetah has bought herself some time," we heard from Ojimo. "But soon, the hyena will come back with other members of its pack and then there will be no contest. From that point on, the kill will belong to the hyenas. Unless a lion pride discovers it first."

And this was the end of our safari adventure. Harry Shields pointed out the time to Ojimo, who herded us back to the MPV, and towards Reserve Central.

* * * *

It's no more than a half hour after the wild, smelly, bloody orgy of the kill, and here I am, standing in a civilized, humanoid VRU, along with Naomi and Harry, gathering round the real Ojimo Nkruma. We're standing in a vast marble, steel and glass atrium, filled with virtual reality images celebrating the re-born animals of the safari.

Ojimo in the flesh gives me the creeps even more than his voice. A slick smile, eyes that keep moving, never resting in one place for more than a second. So this, I think to myself, is the face of the greatest tyrant in history after appropriate genetic treatment from modern science. The killer genes turned into genes of institutional slime. No more overt violence in those genes. Just covert hatred of everybody's soul. Including his own. If, indeed, he has one. But that's not for me to say.

Ojimo took us down a corridor and opened a door to another great room. Only this room was filled with banks of computers, and dozens of earnest, youthful-looking men and women, mostly Africans, intently looking at computer screens or talking to their virtual reality assistants. The place was humming with work and technology. The young technicians closer to us looked up at us briefly with polite smiles and then all went back to their work.

"This," pronounced Ojimo, "is the hub of our Safari park. Here we can monitor, analyze, and control what goes on in the wild; make sure the creatures are healthy and the environment remains in balance."

I was intrigued. How did they analyze what goes on out there? How can they control anything? It seemed pretty wild and uncontrolled to me.

Ojimo gave a big grin. "What seems to you like primal Nature in the reserve is in fact one of the greatest technological achievements in history," he explained. "You don't think, after the hundreds of billions of dollars and decades spent re-creating the wilderness, that we'd just let it go on its own and hope things turn out right? Of course not."

Ojimo was really getting excited. He seemed different from the composed, documentary-like narrator out on safari. Obviously, this stuff turned him on.

"You see," he went on, "there's a constant interaction of information—trillions of bits of information—between us and every living organism out there. How do we get this information? Every organism in the park has genes implanted in their DNA that create "monitor" and "receptor" enzymes. And there are signal transmitters planted every ten meters from each other in the park. Sometimes, they look like a pebble, sometimes they'll be part of a tree trunk. You don't see them, but they're everywhere, creating a grid of information, with millions of grid-units.

"Each second, we get signals that tell us everything we need to know to keep the reserve running smoothly."

"So you mean you know which animal is where in the park at all times?" I asked naïvely.

Ojimo gave me a patronizing snicker. "That—and about a million times more. We know each animal's metabolism, hormone levels, the state of their liver, their kidneys, their adrenaline. You name it—if it affects them in any way, we're picking up that information."

"But I don't get it . . . What do you do with all this information?" I continued my naïve set of questions.

"That's where the 'receptor' enzymes come into play. Let's take the case of elephants. When male elephants enter a state of enhanced sexuality, it's called 'must.' It makes them very aggressive. Now, if we have too many male elephants entering 'must' at the same time, they can cause damage. So we send a message to the receptor enzyme to reduce production of the elephant's testosterone. Within a day, the elephant is no longer in 'must.' Things are back under control."

Ojimo was loving this. For the first time, I saw passion in his face. "Think about the lovely cheetah family we just saw. Now, suppose the cheetahs weren't catching enough 'Tommies' and their population started dwindling. All we need to do is transmit a signal to the receptor enzyme of one of the 'Tommies' to reduce its adrenaline response. Lo and behold, the next time the cheetah mother's trying to catch dinner, she succeeds. And before too long, the cheetah population comes back into normal range."

There was no stopping Ojimo at this point. He was breathless. "You see, Nature is an infinitely complex, infinitely delicate balance between multiple dimensions. It's a miraculous ecology, interfacing the climate, the carnivores, the herbivores, the vegetation, the insects . . . even the mold. This is what we've had to re-create here. This is the great achievement of the Kelly Hendrick Game Reserve."

I was about to throw up. Literally. In my virtual reality cubicle in the UN Headquarters in New York, I felt my stomach churning. This jerk thought he and his crew were playing God. What he was telling me was that what I'd thought was real was in fact an artifice. That the whole Safari park was just another version of virtual reality.

I couldn't control myself. Any politeness vanished. "So you guys think you can sit here in your control center and play God with those animals out there? What do you think gives you the right?" I shot out at him.

Ojimo looked at me with a patronizing smile. "Are you aware, my friend, of the concept of 'culling'?" he asked me.

Culling? I was vaguely aware that it was some primitive form of livestock management, but not much more than that. I admitted this to Ojimo.

"Culling was how they used to manage the number of animals in a nature reserve. It might be hard for you to imagine, but culling was nothing other than the savage cold-blooded slaughter of animals when there were too many of them. If there were too many elephants, you know what they used to do? Simply kill the innocent creatures, until the number of elephants came back into range. Now I don't know what you call playing God, but I know I call that barbarism. What we do nowadays isn't playing God, my friend, it's managing one of the greatest assets God gave to this world, keeping it healthy and in balance. Mankind almost wiped out this precious resource. With the miracles of technology, we've been able to bring it back to life. We're not going to make the mistakes our Primal ancestors made, and lose this treasure again."

I felt like I had felt so many times in my debates with Harry Shields. Checkmated. What he said sounded so reasonable. But I couldn't stand it. I thought about the awesome sights, sounds, and smells I'd experienced minutes earlier. The cheetah mother, the Thomson gazelles, the kill. It began to dawn on me that things had worked a little too much like clockwork. How had we been lucky enough to find the cheetah family? How had it happened that, within moments of us turning up, the cheetah mother had gone for a hunt? Was it a coincidence, that she'd caught a gazelle right then? Or was it just for our entertainment?

I thought of a phenomenon that occurred during the Age of Denial. It was called Disneyland. Fantasy parks that millions of people would visit, where they would pretend they were part of life in other worlds or earlier historical periods. I was beginning to realize I'd just been participating in the d-human equivalent of a Disneyland. Only in this case, they had done such a good job that they'd completely tricked me. I'd thought it was for real. But it was a creation of computer algorithms. Just like my enhanced smell and hearing. It sickened me. I had to find out if this was true.

"Tell me," I asked Ojimo, "about the gazelle that just got eaten. Did one of your technicians transmit a signal to decrease its adrenaline levels so the cheetah mother would catch it? Was that arranged for our entertainment?"

"These computer algorithms are way too complex for me to answer a question like that," was Ojimo's response. I could tell he was just avoiding answering. His eyes were darting everywhere. "How would I know that?"

I was so angry. Angry at being manipulated. Angry at the way they could plan for the death of a creature without a moment's care. For the entertainment of their safari tourists.

Ojimo was getting rattled, beginning to lose some of his slimy calm. "I don't understand what you're so upset about, my friend. Our visitors to the Safari park love to see the wildlife and take part in Nature. If they're lucky enough to witness such dramatic events, they appreciate it. They don't accuse me of arranging things for their entertainment. In all the years I've been a safari guide, I've never heard anything like this."

In all those years, I thought to myself, you've never had a real human being as one of your "visitors." Hell, I thought, all your visitors have been genetically manipulated as much your wildlife animals. Of course they wouldn't see anything wrong.

I'd had it with Ojimo and his Safari park. I just shut up after that. I'd seen enough. This was what Harry Shields wanted for my human race. Another managed reserve, maintained in good health and balance by yet another computer algorithm. My hatred for Harry Shields and the society that produced him found a new depth. I hadn't known myself capable of such hatred. An emptiness, a coldness, and—I had to face it—a fear. Yes, a fear of the power that these d-humans had to turn our human race into another managed computer algorithm.

13 Warrigal Killara

Heard the sound of a clown who cried in the alley

We're back in the UN conference room on the 146th floor, having lunch before re-starting the PEPS session. Naomi and Harry enjoying small talk about political and sports events that mean absolutely nothing to me. I'm still seething with anger about the manipulation of the Safari park.

And I was given a chance to speak my mind. I can't deny it. When Harry began the formal afternoon PEPS session, his first question was to ask me what I thought of his wonderful wildlife reserve. I told him straight. I told him how disgusted I was. That, in my mind, there was nothing "wildlife" about it. It was a Disneyland, an artifice, a paean to the spectacular power of technology, but it had nothing to do with the real world of Nature that had spent millions of years evolving. It was Man's creation, not Nature's. The cheetahs, the gazelles, even the flies buzzing around the fresh kill—none of them had any free will, none of them truly existed other than as puppets of the technology hub of Reserve Central. It nauseated me.

For the first time since the PEPS session began, I think Harry was truly disappointed. The expression on his face was like an uncle giving a birthday present to his favorite niece and getting it rejected. When I finished my tirade, he turned to Naomi and said:

"Counsel Aramovich, I am very surprised at the negative response of the Primal witness to the wildlife reserve. Are you sure there has been no prior attorney/client interaction on this issue, per our agreement in PEPS Session 4-136?"

"I can assure you of that, Counsel Shields," came the response. "Other than a brief discussion about the history of Toboism, as agreed upon in Session 5-89, there has been no attorney/client interaction regarding this morning's virtual field trip."

"It's certainly an intriguing response," Harry continued, wanting to take the session back under control, "but from a rational perspective, it seems completely unfounded. If the Primal witness were telling us he's nauseated by the destruction wrought by his own species . . . that I could understand. Instead, he's nauseated by our attempts to manage what we've recreated, to make sure that the delicate balance created by Nature over millions of years is maintained. That—I don't understand."

"I think," Naomi offered tentatively, "perhaps Eusebio is objecting to the level of control that we have over the lives of the animals. You remember the emphasis on "free will" and "individuality" in late Primal culture? There seems to be some point where the degree of control asserted by society over the individual becomes unacceptable to Primals."

"Thank you, Counsel Aramovich," came the response. "That's a helpful elucidation. If this is what the Primal witness is concerned about, that shouldn't present a problem. We've already established in the series of PEPS Sessions 3-2 to 3-7, that the residual Primals would be free to accept however much assistance from us they might choose. They will be free to police themselves, even to fight among themselves to a limited degree. But we need to establish parameters to avoid their self-annihilation if things get out of control, as we've seen happen too often in Primal history."

Harry Shields stirred, seeming a little irritated.

"But as you know, Counsel Aramovich," he continued, "these are mere details and procedurally outside our current scope. They're scheduled for discussion and resolution in PEPS Session series 8 and 9, so I think we can put this matter to rest for now."

With that, my objections to the Kelly Hendrick Game Reserve were whisked away into nothingness. A mere detail. To be resolved in a later PEPS session. Yusef's words came back into my mind: *"You would be legitimizing their process. You will be their stooge,"* he had said to me. And so far, everything had proved him right.

After a short break, Harry put us back "on the record," saying he would now continue where we had adjourned yesterday. As always, I thought I was ready for anything, and he took me completely by surprise.

"Eusebio, I'd like you to tell me if you recognize this," he said and switched on the 3D-imager. There, in the conference room was an image of one of the most special and sacred places in this world.

"Of course I recognize it. It's Uluru." I replied.

"Uluru?" Harry Shields looked puzzled. "What did you call it?"

"Oh, you would know it as Ayers Rock. We refer to it by its real name, in the local aboriginal language of Arrente."

Now, I don't speak any aboriginal languages myself. But every year, I've participated in the Ancestor Day commemorating the aboriginals of Australia. On this day, those people in Tuckers Corner who speak some of the five hundred or so aboriginal languages that once existed, all get together and take the rest of us on a journey into the Dreamtime of the aboriginal people. I've drunk the Spirit Broth and I've come to grasp just a little bit of the meaning of the *"Tjukurpa"*—an aboriginal word for what's commonly called "the Dreaming."

So, when Harry Shields asked me why Ayers Rock is special, I didn't tell him it's because it's the second largest monolith in the world, a gigantic piece of rock five miles in circumference, almost a thousand feet high, extending one and a half miles into the ground. I didn't tell him how beautiful it is, turning red and violet depending on the weather. No. I told him it was one of the most sacred sites to the aboriginals of Australia. That for over a thousand generations, aboriginal people told stories of the sanctity of the site, the meanings that it holds. That important songlines traverse the site and that several of the ancient Creative Ancestors took their final resting places as part of Uluru, and their spirits remain there.

"Tell me about the songlines. What are they? Who were the Creative Ancestors?"

For once, Harry Shields seemed genuinely interested in something important to me. So I explained to him what I've picked up in Tuckers Corner from those who have spent their lifetime as part of the Dreaming. Knowledge is a very different thing in aboriginal culture. It's viewed as something special and sacred, only to be passed on to those who have proven themselves worthwhile. Something that takes a lifetime to learn. There are sacred meanings to things, some of which I've been told in confidence that I would never pass on. But there are other public elements shared by all the different aboriginal groups and those were what I spoke about to Harry.

In the beginning of time, I told him, the world was a formless place inhabited by Spirit Beings called the Creative Ancestors. These beings were part human, part animal, and all spirit. They wandered aimlessly across the unformed terrain, and as they did so they sang the world into existence. As they uttered words for animals, plants, mountains, water, each of these came into existence. Their actions formed the timeless landscape of what we now know as Australia. As they wandered across the terrain they were creating, singing the world into existence, they left trails behind them, known as songlines. The paths taken by the Creative Ancestors as they sang formed the world of the "here and now." But the Creative Ancestors never went away. They grew tired of their work, and they merged their spirits into the land they had created. Some became part of the rocks and the hills; some transformed into the animals; some merged with the wind and the rain; others imbued themselves within the humans who were conceived in a particular Creative Ancestor's resting place. So it was that the aboriginals were part of the land they were conceived in and shared it with their Creative Ancestors.

Harry seemed fascinated. Naomi seemed entranced. She had that beatific look on her face that she only seemed to get when I was talking about something near and dear to my heart.

Finally, Harry took advantage of a pause in my explanation and looked at me with a sincere expression in his eyes. As though we were members of the same team.

"Eusebio," he said, "that was a fascinating description of something

I've known almost nothing about. But tell me, you don't actually believe this nonsense, of course, do you? I mean, all this talk about spirits, Creative Ancestors, and singing the world into existence. It's a great metaphor, I'm sure, a wonderful mythology, but of course you agree that's all it is? Right?"

Now, when Harry Shields said this to me, he was attacking the very essence of my existence. He was undermining the reality that keeps me alive from one day to the next. Something Dr. Schumacher explained in his book, *On Being Human*, is the very special nature of aboriginal beliefs. Their understanding of the world arose in an era when human beings were part of the earth from which we've evolved. An era before agriculture, when the human species had not yet begun to separate itself from its world. Their knowledge, passed down from one generation to the next, is the closest thing we have to an original human consciousness. It represents an understanding of our place in the universe from a time many thousands of years before any of the world's major religions were conceived. Because of Australia's isolation, this understanding could thrive and remain completely untouched by the coup of the prefrontal cortex that eventually took place in what is now known as the "cradle of civilization."

The prefrontal cortex couldn't allow stories of spirits to co-exist with it. That would subvert its drive to dominance. The spirits had to be banished and replaced by abstractions that originated only in the higher level of consciousness—the concept of monotheism, later supplanted by the concept of the scientific method.

This coup never took place in the consciousness of Australia's aboriginal population. The prefrontal cortex remained in balance. And the knowledge of the Dreamtime remained unbroken.

As Humanists, we're taught to reach out and touch this glimmer of ancient understanding with awe and wonder. It infuses our lives with meaning. On my Initiation Day, when the ancient spirits of the land came to me in the form of gentle raindrops, telling me *"Life Goes On"* at the moment of my deepest despair, nothing could be more important to me. When I looked into Sarah's eyes, the first time we made love, and our two souls touched each other in a flash, this formed the foundation of meaning in my life. When I gently poured Sarah's ashes onto the roots of my oak tree totem, in the rain, and saw her spirit give nourishment to the earth and the tree, this was a comfort that has warmed my soul ever since. And now this d-human piece of shit was reaching into the very essence of my life and trying to take it away from me.

But I wasn't going to let him see me sweat. I was in his PEPS conference room, with a neurographic scanner around my head analyzing every thought. I kept my cool. I just responded:

"Actually, Harry, it's more than a metaphor or a myth. And I do believe it."

Harry seemed a little perturbed. Or perhaps it was just a performance he was putting on for the record.

"Oh come on, Eusebio. You can't mean that. You're an intelligent, educated Primal. You're a history teacher. You're well read. You're not an aborigine, even if you'd like to have been one. You know as well as I do that Ayers Rock is just an unusual and beautiful piece of rock. You know it wasn't put there by 'Creative Ancestors.' Get real."

"I don't believe that one version of reality invalidates the other version," I answered.

"Look, Eusebio, we've got to try to reach some sense here," Harry continued. "Now, you've told me the world was formed by 'Creative Ancestors' who sung it into existence. On the other hand, there's a pretty solid body of evidence that the universe was created billions of years ago, and our earth is part of a solar system in the galaxy called the Milky Way." There was a barely concealed sneer now on Harry's face. "Geological science has explained in detail how our landscape was formed. Evolutionary science has shown how other species and the human genus evolved. You're not seriously questioning this reality, are you?"

"So how was the universe actually formed?" I shot back at him.

Harry was startled for a second and forced to think.

"Well, I'm not an astrophysicist, so I can't tell you much about that." He looked across at Naomi, part quizzically, part humorously. "But isn't the theory called Dimensional Slippage? I'm not sure I understand it too well, although I've seen enough VR shows about it."

Now I was on to something. I was remembering a lesson from my classes on Julius Schumacher when I was a kid.

"And in the twenty-first century, wasn't there a completely different theory called the Big Bang?"

"Yes," Harry responded, "I think I remember something about that."

"So, back then, everybody thought the Big Bang was the true way the universe began, and they also thought the 'Creative Ancestors' was a cute myth . . . right?"

"Yes," came Harry's response. I could see he didn't like it when I asked the questions.

"But now, everybody thinks the Big Bang theory is ridiculous, I guess?"

"Yes, they do," came the response.

"So, if you're asking me to choose between a theory that's held constant and made sense for tens of thousands of years, and another that may well look ridiculous within a hundred years, I think I'd put my money on the first one."

I was on a roll now, and I wanted to keep going.

"But I'll tell you what I do believe, now we're on the subject. When it comes to the concept of infinity, the human mind is simply unable to grasp it. The best we can do is create metaphors our minds can deal with. So any version of creation mankind comes up with is never more than a metaphor. It tells us more about the dominant cultural forces in that society than it tells us about the creation of the universe. The story of the 'Creative Ancestors' gives us an opening into the aboriginal mind. The story of God creating the universe from the Old Testament tells us a lot about the monotheistic religions of the last two thousand years. And the story about the 'Big Bang' or 'Dimensional Slippage' tells us about the dominance of the scientific method in today's world. That's all."

Score one for me and for Julius Schumacher. I could see I had trumped Harry Shields on this one.

"I think we've gone off subject a little," was his response. "Let's get away from the creation of the universe, to something more tangible. Back to Ayers Rock. Now, you were telling me before that, back in the Dreamtime, there were two blue-tongued lizard men, called Mita and Lungkata, who killed an emu, and because they didn't share enough of it with the 'Bell-Bird brothers,' they were killed by them, and their bodies now exist in the form of two half-buried boulders around Ayers Rock. Did I get your story right?"

Yes, Harry Shields had been listening carefully, I could see.

"So, there are these rocks in the earth. Now, you can't be seriously trying to tell me that the geologists are wrong, and the rocks are anything other than remnants of geological transformations. Please, Eusebio, you're under oath, and I'm asking you to give me your serious answer."

He just wouldn't leave this subject alone. I guess he figured, if he could humiliate me for showing respect to the Dreamtime, he could ridicule the very notion of the human soul. I wasn't going to let him get away with it.

I reached back in my memory to the aboriginal Ancestor Days in Tuckers Corner. I remembered something that had been said to me while I was intoxicated by the Spirit Broth.

"Nothing is nothing," I spoke solemnly.

Both Harry and Naomi looked up, surprised.

"There are no things in this world that have no meaning," I continued. "There is no one animal, human, bird, mountain, or river that knows everything. The purpose of much that exists will be known to some but will remain obscure to others."

I was quoting what I'd heard from my friends who had steeped themselves in the Dreamtime. But I was also remembering another lesson from my classes on Dr. Schumacher.

"You see, Harry, your very question betrays an underlying belief about knowledge. There is not necessarily such a thing as a universal truth. Something can have multiple meanings and multiple forms of existence all at the same time. That's something the aboriginal people understood, but you completely fail to. But it's not your fault, Harry. You're just a product of your culture."

I was enjoying myself now. I thanked Julius Schumacher for his smarts—there was no way I could handle this attack from Harry Shields without him.

"You see, Harry," I continued, "when the prefrontal cortex pulled off its coup and took control of the human consciousness, it wanted absolute control. It couldn't stand the idea of multiple aspects of consciousness, each with its own validity. Then, it wouldn't have control. Then consciousness would be more like a democracy. No, it needed totalitarian control. It had to ridicule and marginalize all other forms of knowledge. At first, it used mono-theism for that. *'There is no other God than the Lord'* and all that stuff from the Old Testament. Destroy the idols. With Christianity, the prefrontal cortex had a field day. Burn the heretics at the stake for thinking other thoughts about reality. Destroy Galileo if he dared to tell the Inquisition that the earth revolved around the sun. But, science proved too powerful, so the prefrontal cortex changed its allegiance to the scientific method. Ridicule all other approaches to reality. Make them irrelevant and foolish. Above all, don't ever allow the mind to touch the idea that there might be multiple ver-sions of reality, and that for each of us, in the words of the aborigi-nal wise men, *'The purpose of much that exists will be known to some but will remain obscure to others. There are no things in this world that have no meaning.'"*

"Wow, that was quite a speech. I'm impressed, Eusebio."

Harry's response was made with his usual sneer. But I knew I'd won this particular battle. Thanks to Julius Schumacher and the Ancestor Days at Tuckers Corner.

"So, these holy places like Ayers Rock . . . I guess the aborigines liked them a lot, spent a lot of time hanging out there, worshipping their ancestor spirits?"

I hated his snide, superior tone, but I wasn't going to let him get to me. I knew that was his goal.

"No, Harry. In fact, these places were so holy that, in some cases, only certain people were allowed to visit at certain times, and in other cases, no one could enter an area that was especially sacred."

"So, explain something to me," Harry continued. He pointed to the 3-D imager. It was closing in on Ayers Rock. "You see all those little black dots on the rock face? What do you think they are?"

For a moment I was reminded of the black dots I had seen only a few hours earlier, as I had looked out at the annual wildebeest migration on the plains of the Masai Mara. Artificially recreated wildebeest on an artificially recreated game reserve. Now, as the 3-D imager got closer to the real Ayers Rock, I saw that the black dots were people—dozens and dozens of people, possibly even hundreds. Some walking up the path, some propelling themselves up the vertical part of the cliff face. I was aghast at the sight. They had turned Ayers Rock into an adventure park.

"People . . . " I began to say.

"In fact, Eusebio, some people, but for the most part, VRUs," Harry corrected me. "Ayers Rock is a favorite place to experience the virtual reality of rock climbing and the beauty of the Australian wilderness, without having to leave your own home. But I wanted to ask you, Eusebio . . . if Ayers Rock is so sacred, and no one's permitted there, why is it filled with people and VRUs?"

A phrase came back into my mind from the various Ancestor Days of the past, when I would be under the influence of Spirit Broth and felt with my soul what I was hearing. It was something once said by an aboriginal wise man, describing the white man's rape of his country.

"White men just came up blind, bumping into everything, putting up a flag." I uttered the words before I'd even realized I was speaking.

"So what are you telling me, Eusebio? The white man came and destroyed the aborigines' culture and their spirits? When did this happen? Who were these white men? Were they Primals or were they d-humans?"

I'd fallen right into his trap. Now, he was going to use the abomination performed by my race centuries ago as a justification for his PEPS proposal. Just like the American Indians the other day. How could I get out of this one? Once more, I felt like standing up and walking out of the conference room. Why should I endure this? But who was I helping by doing that, other than myself? I looked at Naomi, who gazed back at me with sympathetic eyes. I briefly thought of Yusef, telling me to play their game for the time being, if I wanted to help him. Then I got that thought out of my mind as soon as I could. I didn't want another "neurographic event." I said, plaintively, to Naomi:

"Do I really have to answer that question?"

"Yes, Eusebio," Naomi responded softly. "Remember, you're under oath."

I sighed and quietly said, "Yes, they were Primals."

"I'd now like to admit into the record the NVRX known as *Warrigal Killara*." Harry spoke calmly and powerfully, the way someone says "checkmate" as they move their rook decisively down the chess board in a final flourish.

And just like the previous day, we're putting on our NVRX helmets. What horrendous massacre will I see this time? But as I open my eyes inside the helmet, I realize I'm not looking around at some battlefield. Instead, it's a bar. It's got that smell of old booze and dirt. Of tables wiped down too many times. There are a few old geezers scattered around in small groups, chattering away. Over in the corner, some noise coming from a small black and white TV. Mid twentieth-century, I tell myself.

I realize that "I" am leaning on the bar itself. Just like yesterday, I let the NVRX thoughts wash over me. But they're not clear and crisp like the thoughts of Reflecting Water. No. They're vague, fuzzy, blurred. In a moment, I realize why. I'm drunk as a skunk.

"Drink to forget," I tell myself, in the form of an all-pervading thought that remains over everything, like a cloud settled as fog over the landscape.

I'm cradling a beer in my hand. "Drink and bloody forget. Forget all. Forget what them did. Them took me. Them gutted me like fish."

In spite of the "drink and forget," I realize I'm remembering something. From long ago.

Take my life and let it be
Consecrated, Lord, to Thee

I'm hearing the powerful sound of young voices singing in unison. A hymn. In a chapel. I'm one of them. But others are singing and I'm not. The sweet power of glorious music.

Take my voice, and let me sing,
Always, only, for my King.

The voices keep flowing. I'm silent. I'm thinking of a little dirt yard where I used to run after the chickens before my mother would catch me and take me in.

Take my will, and make it Thine.
It shall be no longer mine.

Ow! My thigh jolts with pain. I've been hit with the bat. From the Super. Him balding and crusty. He got that mean expression that most wonks have. Hard, cold mask of a face.

"Sing along, Luke! Sing along!"

That's what they call me here. Luke. But Luke's not real name. Real name is Warrigal Killara. Means something. Not like Luke.

The memory blurs and re-forms. Now, I'm walking behind the schoolyard, talking to my friends in Warlpiri. Having fun.

"Luke, come here!" It's the Super again.

"Wassup, Mr. Worthington?"

"How many times have I told you—don't speak in your native language! It's obscene. Disgraceful. Why have we spent all this time teaching you a civilized language, for you to waste our good charity with this filth!"

I'm getting my mouth washed out with soap. It tastes so awful . . . I'm gagging. Almost throwing up. The taste stays with me for days. It tastes like English. Like the Captain Cooks.

And I'm back in the bar. Holding a new can of grog. Gulp down in one go. Head fuzzier still.

Remembering again. Remembering. Night time. Cicadas chirping. Called to Mr. Worthington's room. No one around. Punishment. Hit on the bum. Stinging. Stinging. Mr. Worthington's trousers down.

His cock big and hard. He pulls my face to his hard cock. Smell of old sweat on his balls.

"Now you do a good job or I'll never leave you alone, you worthless half-breed."

I do good job. His spunk fills my mouth.

"Now you swallow it. Do you hear? Every last drop."

And again. And again.

I'm holding another bottle. Drink to forget. Nearly there. Nearly falling down. But the remembering starts again.

I'm eight years old. It's my birthday today. I'm playing with my little brother and two little sisters in the yard. Momma looking over us. Trying to catch the chickens. I got my present today. A cricket bat. I'm going to be a great cricket player one day. I'm holding cricket bat with one hand and catching chickens with other.

Two Captain Cooks turn up in motor car. One of them's Mr. Worthington, but I don't know it then.

"There he is!" cries Mr. Worthington.

I'm grabbed by them.

"He's the half-caste! He's the one we can civilize!"

My momma screaming. Fighting the Captain Cooks. Little brother and sisters hitting them. Them carry me, kicking and punching, to the motor car. Smells of leather and cigar smoke. Never smelled that before.

Momma hitting the car window.

"They're always like that," Mr. Worthington says to the other wonk. "But they soon forget their offspring and turn their attention to their other abo pups."

All I can think about is my cricket bat. It fell on the ground. I want my cricket bat.

Momma yells through the window:

"Never forget your name, Warrigal Killara. Never forget who you are."

Another grog. I feel myself slipping from the stool. Warrigal Killara. *Wild One Forever*. Pissed forever.

I take off my helmet. I feel sick. Sick to my stomach. Sick in my soul. Silence fills the room. Broken by the calm, victorious voice of Harry Shields.

"Once again, Counsel Aramovich, I fail to understand how you can use any argument in defense of the Primals that relates to the specialness of their soul. I think we've established beyond a reasonable doubt that the Primals themselves had already done a magnificent job of eliminating anything special and sacred from those ethnic groups around the world that had maintained a link to the early forms of human consciousness."

Naomi made her usual arguments. But I was too wasted and demoralized to listen. I was disgusted. I couldn't stand this much longer—watching Harry Shields take everything sacred to me, eviscerate it, and then use it to his ends; take everything horrific about our history and then manipulate it to argue his case. I wanted out. The only thing I was looking forward to was my evening meeting with Yusef. He, at least, was another human. I felt I could confide in him. I felt I could glean a little comfort from him.

I couldn't have been more wrong.

14 The Choice

I've stumbled on the side of twelve misty mountains

Sure, I got my evening meeting with Yusef. The PEPS session ended; I found myself back in my hotel room prison cell, eating another taste-enhanced room-service dinner. All I could think of was giving Yusef the answer to his question. Yes—I was ready to give my life to save what was left of our human race. What did I need to do?

And right on cue, when dinner was over, only a few minutes passed before I heard the warm, friendly voice of Yusef calling softly to me:

"Hey, Eusebio, my brother. How did it go? How did you make it through another day?"

I turned and saw his virtual figure sitting in a different corner of the room from last time. His engineers must have been working hard—his image was clearer this time, no flickering. I felt I could walk up to him and hug him.

A surge of warmth and relief infused me. I was so glad to have my confidant back. I told him about the day, starting with Naomi's revelations about the grotesque evils of Toboism. Was this really true? All day, I'd wanted to get a reality check from Yusef.

He gravely nodded his head.

"Yes, Eusebio," he said, "I'm afraid what you heard from Naomi about Toboism is completely true."

"Then how can people like Harry Shields be so wrong? Why should we fight so hard for our existence if our species is capable of doing such evil?"

Yusef paused and thought a while.

"You know, Eusebio," he said to me softly, "a genocide can occur on different planes than the gross, physical plane of Toboism or Nazism. During the Age of Denial, the Western societies began their own genocide, which PEPS is completing now. The genocide of the soul. Their entire society was a concentration camp where the soul was kept in chains. You couldn't hear it. You couldn't see it. There were no pictures of starving, skeleton-like figures staring out at you from behind barbed wire. But that's exactly what was happening to each person's soul—strangled, starved, left to wither away. Eventually, as the children turned into adults, the soul became too weak even to be heard. It might call out, from its corner, in a tiny voice, *"Help me! I'm hurting, I'm starving, please help me!"* but the voice was drowned out by the daily combination of video games, business meetings, schedules, rules, and regulations. There was no place left to hear the muffled shrieks of the soul as it lay, dying of starvation, in the corner. It was, Eusebio, genocide on a grand scale. And it was one that never made it to the history books. Everyone just kept going on with their lives, fixed smiles on their faces and emptiness deep inside as their souls finally gave up the struggle for survival and withered away into nothingness."

Yusef looked piercingly at me. "And that's what led, Eusebio, to the d-humans."

I was shocked by what Yusef had said. By the intensity of it. I thought of the Kelly Hendrick Game Reserve that afternoon—no soul there, that was for sure.

We kept talking for a while longer, but at some point, as I'd expected, Yusef changed the subject.

"Eusebio," he said somberly, "last night I asked you a question that, in a better world, one would never have to ask. You've had a day to think about it. Do you have an answer for me?"

I was ready for this. I had never wavered from my initial feeling.

"Yusef, I'm ready to die, if necessary, for the cause of saving the human race. I'm certain of it."

Yusef's face remained calm.

"I expected to hear you say that, Eusebio."

Then something changed. I could feel it from Yusef's expression, even though he was just a virtual image. There was a stiffening, a grimness that came through.

"Eusebio," he said, "I now have to ask you another question. This one, I fear, will be much more difficult."

There was a pause. A shiver went through me. What would he ask?

"Would you be willing, Eusebio, to kill d-humans, if necessary, to save our human race?"

No. I was just as sure of the answer this time as I was yesterday. I'm not a killer. It's not who I am. I would give up my own life if I needed to, but certainly not take the life of someone else. I don't care whether they're humans or d-humans.

I'm the kind of guy who finds a spider in the bath tub, and takes five minutes trying to catch it with my hands and throw it out the window to avoid having to drown it with the water. I don't like to kill anything. When I go to the market in Tuckers Corner, and the butcher asks me which chicken I want for dinner, I look at the live chickens, clucking and squawking in their cages, and I feel the dread of an executioner as I point out which chicken he should kill for me. Sure, I'm a hypocrite like the rest of us, and I enjoy eating my chicken. But I hate the thought of being responsible for its death. And that's just a chicken. A human being? A d-human? No way!

Before I had the chance to answer, Yusef spoke some more.

"Eusebio," he said, "I don't want to hear a final answer from you until I see you tomorrow evening, God willing. But I need to hear what you're thinking."

"Well, that's easy, Yusef," I spat out at him. "You've got the wrong guy. The answer is no. There's nothing to discuss. I'm not a killer, and I never will be. You'd better find someone else to do your dirty work for you."

Yusef seemed unperturbed.

"Eusebio, I expected you to react like this, and quite honestly, if you hadn't, I would have been disturbed. Killing another human being is not something to be taken lightly. Anybody who would readily do that is someone who should never be given such a heavy responsibility.

"But, Eusebio, supposing you'd found yourself in a room with General Tobo before he began his massacre of a continent. Suppose you knew what Tobo was going to do, and you had a gun in your hand and the opportunity to kill him, to prevent the grotesque devastation he brought to the people of Africa. Would you use the gun and kill Tobo?"

"Of course I would. But that's different."

"Then you're not against killing another human being as a universal principle. It depends on the situation."

"Well, I guess so, but it would have to be a very extreme situation."

"Why would you have killed Tobo?"

"Well, obviously, if I knew he was going to murder millions of people, then of course the trade-off between killing one evil man versus saving the lives of millions of innocent people—it's obvious," I replied.

"And how about if Tobo was there with his top five cronies, and they were all plotting together to devastate their continent, and you had to kill all five of them?"

"Well, if I knew that was true, it would be the same thing. What's the value of five evil lives compared with millions of innocent ones?"

"So now, Eusebio, you already have a set of ethical rules where killing might be justified. The ratio of killing versus the lives you'd save; the guilt of the people you'd kill against innocent lives; and how certain you are that killing would save their lives. Right?"

Now, I'd never thought about these things in my life. It's not the kind of thing that comes into your mind as you're walking down the street. At least, not in my case. But everything Yusef said so far did make sense to me. At least in theory. So I told him that.

"So, Eusebio, it's not enough just to tell me that 'you've got the wrong guy.'"

I was getting angry again. I felt I was being manipulated.

"Well, it's enough for me. I don't have to answer your damn question if I don't want to."

"No, you don't have to, Eusebio," came the answer. Yusef looked dead serious. "At least, not to me. I can be out of your life in a moment, if that's what you want. But you will have to answer that question to yourself. For the rest of your life."

There was silence. I was shocked by the heaviness of Yusef's words, and his expression. Yusef broke the silence.

"It's your choice to make, Eusebio, right now. If you want me out of your life, just tell me, and I'll be gone. I will literally just vanish, and you'll never hear from me again. You can go ahead with your PEPS sessions, your Naomi Aramovich and Harry Shields, go on your virtual discovery tours, and not have to think about what it all means. Just give me the word, Eusebio, right now. I'm waiting."

He sat there, looking at me, dead serious. I looked for the cheery, warm, brotherly smile. It was gone. Even though it was just an image, I felt I saw in his eyes the struggles of humanity, the lives lost over the centuries fighting injustice. He kept looking right back at me, waiting.

Yes, I realized, it really was my choice. I knew if I told Yusef to go, he'd be gone in a moment, and I'd never see him again. How would I feel? I thought about the first day of the PEPS session, when I didn't think I'd ever see Yusef again, how vulnerable and alone I'd felt in the world of the d-humans; how relieved I was when his image appeared the next night, as though I'd rediscovered a long-lost friend. How much more vulnerable would I feel if I told Yusef to get lost now?

But I couldn't stand what Yusef was doing to me. He was pulling me, bit by bit, into a world I'd never known and wanted nothing to do with. A world that recognized the devastation carried out in the name of progress and fought against it with everything. A world where moral clarity dissolved into a fog of trade-offs. When I had sat in Jerry's backyard, feeling the despair of all that had been lost, when I cried to Jerry, my Spirit Guide, through the emptiness, *"Where has it all gone?"*, and the ancient spirits of the land enveloped me in their soft raindrops to tell me gently that *"Life goes on,"* at that moment I'd made my peace with the relentless devastation brought on our humanity by our own progress.

And now Yusef was trying to get me to undo that peace. He was forcing me to throw myself headlong into the front ranks of the struggle against that relentless force.

I just wanted my old life back. My simple, solitary life. Teaching a new generation of Tuckers Corner children about the great tribes of the American plains. I wasn't cut out to be a warrior. I was no hero. On an impulse, I began to tell Yusef I wanted him gone, that his moral dilemmas and heroic struggles were not for me.

Then, I stopped myself in mid-breath. I thought of Harry Shields in the conference room, with his intellectual sophistries. How he'd manipulated Subrata into his death. I thought of the Kelly Hendricks Game Reserve, a world where the only human beings left were controlled by a gigantic computer program. I thought how, that afternoon, Harry Shields had tried to mock forty thousand years of aboriginal spirituality and undermine everything sacred to my own life.

I couldn't kick Yusef out right now. I couldn't leave myself open to the manipulations of Naomi Aramovich and the attacks of Harry Shields, when the future of my own race was at stake. I hated Yusef for doing this to me, but I knew I needed him right now. I made my choice.

"Yusef," I said, "I want you to stay. I don't want you to go."

And he stayed. And we kept talking about subjects I never wanted to grapple with in my life. The struggles of millions of humans to help the Rejectionists and create a future for their children. The daily battles in areas of the world I'd never heard of, where d-human troops swept into human Muslim towns on search-and-destroy missions against the Rejectionists.

But I was still holding out. I couldn't get past the notion that it was wrong to kill the other side if they weren't actually killing us. Yusef was getting exasperated.

"Eusebio, you don't understand, they are killing us every day. You just don't see it, and nobody talks about it. They're called GALT

Enforcement, or GE. The most powerful army in the world. They use VRUs—just like the ones you use for your virtual field trips, only these ones carry deadly weapons and kill real people. Every day, in dozens of human towns, their virtual soldiers swoop in, force our men, women, and children outside our houses. They search everywhere, looking for underground bunkers. Because that's where they know they'll find the Rejectionists. And if anyone resists, they shoot them down mercilessly.

"If only you understood," Yusef continued, "what was really going on. Then, Eusebio, I know you'd be there. You'd know who you're really fighting against; you'd know your enemy."

Suddenly, his eyes lit up.

"I know what to do, Eusebio!" he exclaimed. "I have an idea. Suppose I can get you to see it with your very own eyes, to see what they do to us every day. Then, would you be prepared to fight back and do what you need to do?"

"How could you do that?" I asked him.

"With your PEPS session 'virtual field trips.' We'll get UNAPS with their own game."

I didn't understand what he was talking about. But when he explained further, it made sense. It was a great plan. I had to be bolder than I'd been. But as Yusef went over the details of his plan with me, I liked it. I felt I could carry it off.

I was ready for the next PEPS session. Things were going to turn. I would see for myself what Yusef was talking about. Then, maybe, I'd have a clue. About what to do.

FOREIGN AFFAIRS

September 2093

Defending America's Homeland: The Genetic Solution

Dr. Henry Wallright

The author, who has served in two Homeland Party administrations as National Security Advisor, presents his case for incorporating required genetic modification (RGM) as part of the set of proposed constitutional changes in the upcoming Homeland Security Bill of Rights.

It was nearly one hundred years ago, this month, that the first warning shot came across the bows of the American ship of state, telling the people of our great country they were not invulnerable to the currents of global history. On September 11, 2001, a Muslim fundamentalist group, known as Al-Qaeda, perpetrated what, at that time, was the greatest act of terrorism against the American people. Two thousand innocent American civilians were killed as two hijacked planes were flown into the World Trade Center, in those days a symbol of America's global power.

This event occurred in the mid-point of what is now nostalgically referred to as America's Century—that began with the end of the Second World War and ended with the nuclear devastation of Columbus. At the time, legislators and media in our country believed their response to "September 11", as it became known, was adequate. A series of Patriot Acts were passed. The Department of Homeland Defense was created. However, as the decades passed, the pendulum swung back towards the reassuring truisms of earlier times.

The mistake made by the administrations of the early twenty-first century was to view American's vulnerability to a nuclear terrorist attack through the lens of Islamic extremism. This was understandable, given that "September 11" was perpetrated by Islamic fundamentalists, but it was a tragic error. By the mid-twenty-first century, the threat of Islamic fundamentalism was fading. However, America's vulnerability to nuclear terrorism remained high, while a new generation of Americans forgot the terrible lessons that September 11 had taught them.

By the middle of the twenty-first century, a new threat had arisen, which our leaders ignored until the nuclear catastrophe of Columbus forced them—too late—to acknowledge it. This threat, as we now know, was the rising expectations of the developing countries as they began to compete with the developed world for an ever-shrinking pool of global resources. When the Class Action to Rectify Global Injustice ("CARGI") began to develop global momentum, the United States was too comfortable in its hegemony to realize the impact this movement could have on its security. Our leaders looked at the growing middle classes of the developing world, and saw only rising prosperity and greater global integration. They failed to see that the poorer underclasses of the developing countries were being left further behind and that these groups, instead of blaming their own local governments, were blaming the world order that had left them out, and ultimately, the driving force behind that world order—the United States.

The nuclear bomb that devastated Columbus, Ohio in 2063 finally taught a lesson to the American people they should have learned two generations earlier. This was the defining moment of our century. It pointed out the true vulnerability of a society that based its constitutional foundations on the concept of liberty rather than security. From this moment on, America's global hegemony was over. The United States had experienced the first military defeat in its history. Our leaders had no choice but to back down and succumb to the threat of more nuclear terror.

What was the lesson, then, that our country had tragically failed to learn? Quite simply, that in a world of nuclear proliferation, security and individual liberty are irreconcilable concepts. A country can have one or the other, but not both. Until Columbus, the United States chose liberty over security, and we paid the price dearly. Since Columbus, we have come to terms with the modern age, and have succeeded in securing our homeland from further terrorist outrages.

The people of the United States have grown up. We have had to learn that sacrifices of individual liberty are necessary, that the Founding Fathers lived in a different world where ideals of liberty were consistent with—not antagonist to—the security of the people. We are finally at a stage where the individual's right to security will soon be enshrined in the U.S. Constitution above all other rights. With these changes, our country will be ready to face the future with confidence.

Or will it? Are we in danger of making that classic military mistake of "fighting the last war"? We are inexorably slipping into a new form of world war that is engulfing the globe, a war being fought in new arenas, and once again we need to make the difficult decisions now. If we wait two generations, like our predecessors did after September 11, we are in danger of suffering a global defeat even beyond the proportions of Columbus.

In this new global war, it is axiomatic that our enemy is China. More controversial, however, is identifying the new arenas where the war is being fought. A generation ago, China's leaders realized that genetic modification was the most powerful military weapon that has ever become available to a nation—even more powerful than nuclear technology. Nuclear weapons have their structural limitations—the threat of retaliation; the development of satellite-based missile shields. Genetic modification, on the other hand, has the ability to create a nation that is militarily superior to other nations in the most important sphere of all—the human sphere.

Twenty-five years ago, China enacted legislation requiring that any genetic enhancements must incorporate a set of four genetic modifications. These had been identified by China's leadership as fundamental to creating a generation of super-warriors, capable of dominating the globe militarily and economically. The four enhancements were: prioritizing both the *core aggression* gene set and the *doctrinal belief* gene set in the genetic hierarchy; increasing *average IQ*; and speeding up *instinctual reaction time*. In the minds of China's leaders, this would lead to a generation of designer babies, now known as d2-babies, who would grow up to be unyielding Chinese patriots, aggressively pursuing the country's goals, leading the world technologically and beating its enemies in the heat of battle.

While China was planning for a new generation capable of global dominance, here in the United States we were busy with legislation to permit Americans to choose the nature of their offspring according to our cherished values of the free market and individual liberty. While a generation of d2-warriors were being born to Chinese parents, American parents were spending their money making Kelly Hendrick and Hal Burton the wealthiest two individuals in history, creating a generation of beautiful women and strong, good-looking men, incapable of competing with their Chinese counterparts.

In the simplest terms, while we in the United States looked at the new powers of genetic optimization in terms of freedom and choice, the Chinese leadership saw these powers in terms of military and economic global domination.

Now, the first of the d2-generation are becoming adults and the choices made by our respective nations are only too apparent. It is not an exaggeration to say that global leadership is now, literally, in the Chinese DNA.

The leadership of all of our nations will, in the future, rest in the hands of these d2-optimized humans. In recognition of this, Pew Global Research recently compared the characteristics of d2s, aged between 18 and 21, in the major nations of the world. Their results are predictable—and disturbing. The average IQ of China's d2 population is 14% higher than their counterparts in the U.S. Their instinctual response time is 18% faster. In anonymous answers to its questionnaire, 96% of Chinese d2s said that they would "be prepared to die for their country" versus only 36% of American d2s.

These are not mere statistics. They are already flowing into the realities of our lives. China's top universities no longer accept candidates unless their DNA has undergone RGM. Furthermore, while it is difficult to conceive in a country as militaristic as China, two years ago the Chinese administration abolished the draft. Their military is so overwhelmed by top d2 applicants that they are able to select only the most highly qualified. Our own experience in the United States, by contrast, is only too well-known. Twenty years ago, the first Homeland Administration was forced to re-introduce the draft because of the inability of the military to attract and retain enough troops to meet our global military commitments.

China's ever-increasing lead is far more than an issue of national pride—it is ultimately a struggle for global dominance in the next century, a struggle that the U.S. is steadily losing to its faster, stronger rival.

As a nation, we need to understand the new realities of the current world order: economic power, military power and the genetic make-up of our citizens are all integrated into one vast battle for global supremacy. This is a battle that the United States is in serious danger of losing to China unless we take immediate and bold steps. In Southern Africa, General Tobo's troops are committing outrage upon outrage, and the civilized world is unable to prevent further atrocities because of Tobo's links with China. Europe is in paralysis, terrified of the economic risks of taking sides against the Chinese powerhouse: they can no longer be viewed as our committed allies in this global struggle. Japan, our strongest and closest ally, is increasingly threatened by the possibility of another Chinese stranglehold, repeating the experience of China's economic conquest of Taiwan.

Looking back at our period, historians will identify this decade as the beginning of the greatest ever struggle for global dominance.

Year by year, we are slipping from economic and cultural hostility with China into military conflict. The use of tactical nuclear weapons in more than one of the current regional conflicts is imminent. The United States must be on a total war footing if we are to avoid the twenty-second century becoming the "Century of the Dragon."

As a result of the efforts of successive Homeland Party administrations, we are now investing appropriate amounts in our military to maintain leadership in this arena. The missing factor, however, is the genetic make-up of the American people. We must ensure that the next generation of Americans is capable of defending our nation's interests against the Chinese bid for global supremacy. The only way of achieving this is to implement immediately the policy of *required genetic modification* that the Chinese introduced a generation ago.

Our RGM program would parallel that already introduced successfully by the Chinese government. It would compel American parents who choose d2 enhancement for their offspring to incorporate the "American Homeland" panel into their other genetic choices. The panel would, like the Chinese RGM, include a dominant role for the *core aggression* and the *doctrinal belief* gene sets, along with an increase in IQ and a faster instinctual reaction time. Many parents already find these genetic enhancements attractive for their children.

Atavistic liberal critics have fought against the introduction of RGM in the United States for two decades, arguing that it is a violation of the right to privacy enshrined in the U.S. Constitution. These arguments echo the liberal denunciations of increased Homeland security earlier this century, prior to Columbus. In those heady days, mainstream Americans still believed our nation's security could be maintained without disturbing the civil liberties that had been our national tradition since the birth of our country. The complaints of the liberal critics compromised the efforts to improve Homeland security for decades, leading to the disaster of Columbus. We cannot afford another compromise in the struggle to maintain our nation's leadership in an increasingly hostile world.

Within the next year, we can expect passage of the Homeland Security Bill of Rights, at which point the Supreme Court will be empowered to give priority to the security of our citizens above all other rights enshrined in the original constitution. We can then begin implementation of RGM and prepare a new generation of Americans to defend against the Chinese threat.

After Columbus, Americans finally acknowledged that their inalienable right to security was incompatible with the individual liberties they had enjoyed in the past. At this point in our nation's history, we need to accept a new version of this lesson before it is too late. We cannot fail our children and permit them to grow up in a world dominated by Chinese power. With the implementation of RGM, we can look forward to a future for the United States where we maintain our nation's global leadership and continue to fight for the values of democracy and freedom over the tyranny that would be imposed by a Chinese global hegemony.

15 Pannakot

I saw guns and sharp swords in the hands of young children

Things were going to change in this PEPS session. I was taking control. I'd had enough of Harry Shields' legalistic aggression and Naomi's patronizing benevolence.

I was going to use the rules of their PEPS session against them. Find out for myself what was really going on in this world of ours. Find out if Yusef was telling me the truth about GALT enforcement troops. Find out if Harry Shields' cool, legitimized process was as bloodless and civilized as he claimed.

I knew I had a hard road ahead. But, that morning, I felt bouncy. I would finally be taking charge of my own destiny.

I could see Naomi was a little surprised at my breeziness when she picked me up for the day's session. At the Betelbar, I felt she wanted to ask me if something had happened, but she stopped herself.

It wasn't too long before my moment arrived. We're sitting in the UNAPS conference room on the 146th floor of the UN building. Just like always. Me in my neurographic chair, with scanners all around my head. Harry Shields, beginning in his pompous drawl, to take me through another day of existential agony. I waited until he went on the record, and started his usual formalities. Then I interrupted.

"Excuse me, Harry, I have a question for you about these virtual field trips we're doing."

Harry looked back at me, slightly amused. Like his pet cat was playing with the catnip.

"What's that Eusebio? How can I help you?"

"Well, what's the purpose exactly of these virtual field trips?"

"To demonstrate the relevant context for the discussions we are having here in this conference room," Harry replied in his bored drawl.

"So how do you choose where we go on the field trips?"

"We've studied the issues at stake in these sessions and identified the environments that best represent the external realities being discussed."

So far so good. I was concentrating intensely. Now the important turning point.

"So do you make the choice of where we go based on supporting your own point of view, or are they meant to be neutral observations permitting a fair and balanced dialogue on the issues?"

I'd spent a while last night memorizing these lines. It's not how I usually speak, but it was important to get the legalistic point across. I watched Naomi raising her eyebrows as I was talking.

Harry still appeared not to notice anything unusual.

"It's the latter, Eusebio," he drawled back. "Neutral observations fairly reflecting the issues under discussion."

"Well, in that case, wouldn't it be procedurally fair for other participants, such as Naomi or me, to choose what we see on the virtual field trips?"

I was beginning to close in on the kill. But Harry Shields still hadn't clicked. I guess he thought there just wasn't any threat from a Primal, so he didn't need to be alert.

"Certainly, Eusebio. Counsel Aramovich had full input into the choice of virtual field trips. These were all covered in earlier PEPS Sessions 6-53 to 6-61."

"But I didn't get any input," I responded.

"Of course, Eusebio, as a Primal living in isolation from modern society, you didn't have sufficient knowledge of current events to play a meaningful role in the selection."

"But if there was a place I wanted to visit, as part of this session, then that would be a legitimate procedural step?"

At this point, Harry Shields actually smiled.

"Well, sure, Eusebio. If there's some place you'd like to see in a virtual field trip, we would do everything possible to make that happen."

It sounded like he thought I wanted to have some fun. Maybe get a day in the Caribbean, going scuba diving or something. It amazed me how it seemed impossible for him to take me seriously.

"In that case, could I please take a look at a map of the world?"

The plan was working better than I'd dared expect. Naomi was looking at me quizzically, her eyes narrowed and focused. But she still wasn't saying anything.

Harry spoke to the 3-D imager on the conference room table, and a three-dimensional image of a globe appeared in front of us.

Yusef had prepared me in detail for this moment. I pointed to the country of Pakistan.

"Could we close in on that area there?" I asked.

Harry began to get a little uncomfortable. Suddenly, too late, he was becoming aware that something was going on.

Now, I was looking at a close-up map of Pakistan. I pointed to an area at the top of the map named—as Yusef had told me—the North West Frontier.

"Can I see that area in more detail?"

Harry's eyes began to widen. His smile was wiped off his face. But he went ahead and told the 3DI to close in on that area.

I saw what I was looking for.

"Could we close in on that area called the Chitral Valley?"

By now, both Harry and Naomi were wide-eyed with surprise. The cat was out of the bag. Something was up. But they both seemed paralyzed in their surprise. Harry wasn't putting up any resistance yet.

The map closed in on the Chitral Valley. There it was. Just as Yusef had said. A tiny little dot on the map, with the name of Pannakot.

"See that place called Pannakot," I said. I could barely hide my excitement. "I want us to visit there. Now."

Finally, Harry was starting to compose himself again. He put his patronizing smile back on his face. Only this time, it was clearly forced.

"Well, now, Eusebio, it's not as easy as that. These virtual field trips are planned months ahead. We can't just decide on a place in the middle of nowhere and expect there will be three VRUs waiting there for us, now, can we?"

"Are you telling me there are no VRUs whatsoever in that area?" I was ready for Harry's delaying tactics.

"Well, now, how would I even know that? It's not like I'm an expert on the technological capabilities in the Chitral Valley." Harry gave a nervous snicker, trying to hide his anxiety. "And even if there were any VRUs, who's to say whether they'd be available to UN staff?"

This was the moment where I turn to Naomi. So far, everything going to plan.

"Naomi, you're my legal representative, right?"

"Of course, Eusebio," she answered, her voice tight and unusually hard.

"Well, in that case, I'm asking you, as my representative, to check right now whether there are any VRUs in the Pannakot area which are, in any way, related to the UN."

"Well, I can certainly do that, Eusebio, and I will. But you know, it's really a long shot."

"That's OK. Let's just see what you find out," I answered.

The session went off the record. Naomi pulled out her PDA and started talking into it. As she got some answers, her eyes widened even further. I thought I even saw her trembling slightly. She kept looking at me, part quizzically and increasingly with anger in her eyes.

Finally, she closed her PDA. She looked over at Harry Shields, who had been sitting there, nervously humming.

"Counsel Shields," she said quickly, "I need to talk with you privately, off the record."

I could barely conceal my glee. So far, Yusef's plan was working to perfection.

They left the room. I got out of my neurographic chair. I didn't want the neurographic scanner to find Yusef in my brain and give the game away.

They came back in, like conspirators. Naomi walked straight over to me.

"Eusebio," she said, coldly and formally, "I need to talk with you in the Privileged Room."

I followed her into the room where, just a couple of days earlier—it seemed like eons ago—I'd been forced to tell Naomi about Yusef's original visit after the neurographic scanner had caught me naked. How things have changed since then, I thought.

"Eusebio, what the hell's going on? How did you come up with Pannakot?" she said to me sternly.

"Why?" I pretended innocence. "What's so special about Pannakot?"

"I'm sure you must know. Don't even try to tell me it's a coincidence. At this moment, there's a significant GE SCUOP going on there."

"Naomi, what's GE and what's a SCUOP?" I was really enjoying myself.

"GE stands for GALT Enforcement. They're the UN troops who enforce GALT and protect the world against the Rejectionist extremists. SCUOP stands for "surveillance and clean-up operation." But I have a feeling you know all about that. Now tell me, how did you come up with Pannakot?"

I was ready with my story.

"Well, what happened, Naomi, was . . . you remember when we were on the skywalk going back to the hotel yesterday?"

Naomi nodded.

"Do you remember, at one point, somebody bumped into me?"

"No," Naomi said, "but it was so crowded, I don't think I would have noticed."

"Well, when I got back to the hotel room, I discovered he'd slipped a piece of paper into my pocket. It just said the words 'Go to Pannakot—in Chitral, in the North West Frontier of Pakistan.' That's all it said. And then, the strangest thing happened. Within five minutes of reading it, the paper just disintegrated and turned into dust."

"Yeah, that's smart paper. They use that a lot. It's a low tech way of getting messages to each other. The paper disintegrates and there's no way to trace where it came from or what was on it."

It worked. I was lying through my teeth, and she was believing it. After all, how else could I have known about "smart paper"?

Now Naomi took a different tack.

"Eusebio, they're trying to use your openness to undermine our PEPS session. You can't let them do it. We've come so far. We're making such good progress. Don't let them do this. They're going to undermine all the work, all the effort you've put in to these sessions."

"But why would this undermine anything?" I responded. "What's wrong with doing a virtual field trip there? If these GALT enforcement troops are there, then maybe they have some VRUs available."

"Eusebio," Naomi answered grimly. "They are all VRUs. That's how the GALT enforcement troops work. They never go to those places in person. It would be too dangerous. There are literally thousands of GE VRUs around Pannakot in the Chitral Valley right now."

"Well, that's great, then. It shouldn't be difficult to get access to three of them."

"That's not the point, Eusebio. They're trying to deflect our attention from the real subject of the PEPS session. Whatever the GE troops are doing around Pannakot has nothing whatsoever to do with PEPS or UNAPS. It has nothing to do with our session. They're trying to link their Rejectionist movement with PEPS in the hope of politicizing it."

Politicizing it? I thought to myself, a session on the subject of exterminating the Primals from the face of the earth could hardly be more political. But I didn't say anything. I had a role to play, and so far it was working well.

"Eusebio, you've got to understand. When we go back in session, Harry Shields is going to argue it's a misallocation of our time to go to Pannakot because it's not relevant to the subject at hand. And I can't argue against that because he's right. We're just going to have to move on from here."

"OK, Naomi, let's go back to the session, in that case." The plan was still right on track.

We went back into the conference room, back on the record, me in my neurographic chair. As Naomi had predicted, Harry launched a legalistic argument about how it was out of the question to go to Pannakot. I let him finish. And then I stood up from my chair and started to make my way to the door.

"Where are you going, Eusebio?" Naomi asked, panicky.

"I'm leaving," I responded. "You both told me this PEPS session was meant to be unbiased and open, and I was here to take part in a meaningful way. Now I can see that's not true. I'm not going to take part in your PEPS hearing any more. It's a travesty of justice. You're going to exterminate my people, real humans, from this earth, and you're going to make sure you get your way whether it's legitimate or not. I'm having nothing more to do with it."

"Eusebio, what are you talking about? That's not true."

"Eusebio, please reconsider. This makes no sense."

Both Naomi and Harry blurted out their responses together. They were equally distraught.

"There's nothing to reconsider," I said. "If we don't go to Pannakot now, I'm not continuing with the PEPS hearing. That's it."

Harry took the session off the record. But it was too late. I'd made my point on the record. They couldn't erase it. They both went into the Privileged Room and came out a few moments later.

Harry took the lead.

"Eusebio," he said, "Counsel Aramovich and I have conferred, and we've agreed that, given your strong desire to visit Pannakot, we will make immediate arrangements for that to happen. We will both, however, note that neither of us believes a visit to Pannakot is relevant to the subject of these hearings, and this virtual field trip will be undertaken solely to demonstrate to you as the Primal witness that this hearing is conducted on a fair and open basis, and that your remarks a few moments ago are completely baseless." He turned to Naomi. "Are you in agreement with my comments, Counsel Aramovich?"

"Fully in agreement," Naomi said, with a trace of anger in her voice.

It had worked. Yusef had explained to me that, since the veneer of legitimacy was the primary goal of these PEPS hearings, my ultimate weapon against the d-humans was accusing them of acting illegitimately. If the hearings broke down in the middle and I walked out calling the whole process a travesty, they would have wasted years of preparation. They simply couldn't allow that to happen.

So I got my trip to Pannakot. I hoped it would be worthwhile.

* * * *

It didn't take too long to arrange. Naomi told me there was a platoon of GE troopers who were going to be leaving the VRU station in Chitral in half an hour on their way to Pannakot. The platoon had been told that three members of UNAPS wanted to join them to get a better understanding of how the GE was doing its enforcement work in the area. They were happy to oblige and were preparing three suitable VRUs for us right now.

What was I going to find in Pannakot? I had no idea, but I had a strong feeling it would be something important. How would it affect my feelings about Yusef? Would it help me answer the terrible question he had posed to me last night? One way or another, I felt that it would.

We put our "skins" on and went through the regular initialization phase of the virtual reality. I was getting to be an old hand at this now.

My first sensation coming through on the other side was a brisk, cool breeze against my skin. I looked around. I was on some kind of military base. That was obvious. I was standing on tarmac. There were nondescript buildings all around . . . noise of machinery and people yelling orders at each other . . . dozens of VRUs around me instantly recognizable as soldiers, all decked out with uniforms, helmets, high-tech glasses, guns.

I raised my head and looked beyond the troopers—and caught my breath in awe. Beyond the base were some forested slopes.

Beyond those slopes were some barren, brown steep hills. And beyond those hills were mountain peaks that looked like something out of a fairy tale. Spectacular. Sharp, jagged peaks, towering over us even though they were miles away, covered in snow, creating a crisp, clear outline in the horizon against a deep blue sky. They seemed so vast, so serene. Like they would have nothing to do with the bullshit we were all engaging in. From the same earth, but from a different reality. I hated to take my gaze away from those peaks, but I reminded myself, I wasn't here for the scenery.

I turned around and saw Naomi and Harry in their VRUs. There was another VRU standing with them—it looked like a young man.

"Hi, pleased to make your acquaintance. My name's Russell Dean. I'm Second Lieutenant, GE Regiment 4-21, Central Division. I'm going to be your escort for the trip to Pannakot." The VRU called Russell Dean had a relaxed, southern American accent. He walked snappily and cheerily over to me and put out his right hand. His left hand was holding some kind of laser gun. I reciprocated and we shook hands. His grip was firm and precise. Real military.

"We're going to give you guys full coverage, we got Code Green clearance for y'all. That means you'll get full audio on all team communication. If we want to talk together, turn down the dial on your left forefinger, and then we'll hear each other more easily."

I looked down at my hands. I had gloves on, and they were certainly high-tech—filled with buttons, dials and gauges. I briefly wondered what they were all for.

"Let's get going. We're due to take off for Pannakot in four minutes and counting. There's our transport. It's a LAM."

He pointed to our left, and I saw a plane of some kind. It had long wings and various helicopter-looking blades.

"By the way, LAM stands for Low Altitude Mobility. It can get us anywhere over difficult terrain; it can fly as low as you like or as high as you like; it's speedy and it's quiet. We use a lot of them around here."

We clambered into the LAM. There were eleven other soldiers—or more precisely—military VRUs already inside. It was surprisingly comfortable for a military aircraft. Everything seemed clean and well organized. The other soldiers gave us all a cheery nod. They were relaxed, joking with each other. It seemed like they were going on a sightseeing tour.

"Why is everyone going to Pannakot today?" I asked Russell. I was determined to find out as much as I could. Given that Naomi and Harry were hardly enthusiastic about coming on this trip, I wasn't expecting them to pipe up with any questions. If I was going to find anything out, I needed to do it myself.

"Yeah, it's an exciting time here in the Chitral Valley right now. Last week, we managed to snag a Rejo alive—that's a rare event."

He saw the look of confusion on my face.

"Oh, Rejo is the name we use round here for the Rejectionists. Usually, they suck themselves down the drain before we can get our hands on 'em alive. But last week, we found one sleeping and managed to capture him."

I assumed that "sucking themselves down the drain" was a euphemism for suicide, based on what Yusef had told me the other day about Ashok Prakesh, whom I had sent to his death through the neurographic scanner's invasion of my brain.

"So we got this Rejo under twenty-four-hour neuroscan. He's fighting hard against it, but there's not a lot he can do when the neural coordinates lock in."

I thought of the visit I'd received from the Department Agents who had tried to get the picture of Yusef from my brain with their MNI.

"So we already got three hot spots identified in the last forty-eight hours. One of them's in this little village called Pannakot. I didn't even know the damn place existed until yesterday."

"What's a hot spot?" I asked Russell, the Second Lieutenant.

"It's an area the computer identifies as a high probability site for a tunnel entrance. Where the Rejos are hangin' out. The imager scans the Rejo's brain for visual images and then tries to match them against a database of the area. When it comes up with a possible match, we send GE troopers in to scan the chimps and see if any of them squeal."

246

Russell saw that I was completely puzzled by his last description. On my right, I saw Naomi roll her eyes and look up at the ceiling in disgust.

"Oh, sorry for using GE slang. I know you guys from 'political central' have your way of talking. The 'chimps' are the Primals. You know, they're called chimps because their DNA is closer to chimpanzees than to us. Hard to believe, huh?"

Now I understood why Naomi was so disgusted. I was barely able to control myself. This bastard opposite me . . . calling me a chimp. If he'd been there in the flesh, I might have punched him directly in the face. But what was the point of hitting a VRU made of high-tech plastic and electronic circuits? That was hardly going to accomplish what I needed. I steeled myself and kept going, as though I were another d-human prick checking out how well the GE troopers were doing their job.

"So how do you get the chimps to squeal?" I asked, trying to hide my nausea.

"Well, when we get to a hot spot, we herd up the chimps and put them through an MNI one-by-one. That way, we try to close in on where a tunnel entrance might be situated. By the way, an MNI's a mobile neurographic imager, in case you didn't know, pal."

Yes, I thought to myself, I knew only too well what an MNI was, pal.

"So, is it dangerous, herding up the chimps?"

Russell chuckled. "Well, it sure would be if we were here in the flesh. These chimps have some pretty high-tech weaponry. They get them from the Rejos they protect. Y'know, the Rejos have some pretty good funding. You'd be surprised what they can get their hands on."

"But we gotta be careful even with our VRUs," Russell continued. "These are sophisticated bits of machinery. If a VRU takes a hit, that can be fifty million bucks down the drain. That ain't chump change, even in Nashville, Tennessee. We have a saying in the GE: 'If you're VRU gets hit, you get hit.' What that means is, you're liable to miss your chance for promotion. A couple of badly damaged VRUs can ruin a GE trooper's career. So, you try to protect your VRU as if you're here in the flesh. And you need to be careful with these chimps. They can be dangerous. Even the women and children. You never know what they're up to."

"So is that where you are—Nashville, I mean?" I asked.

"Sure, pal, that's where the whole 4-21 Regiment is located. We have a giant virtual reality center outside Nashville. We're all there right now, in our skins, hunting down Rejos in the Chitral Valley. It sure beats doing it in person. At the end of the day, we go have a drink with the guys, enjoy our kids at home. I've got a six-year-old. I wouldn't miss him growing up for anything."

All this time, while we were talking, Naomi and Harry seemed paralyzed in a fixed grimace. Every now and then, I would sneak a view past them, at the countryside outside our LAM. It was awe-inspiring. One moment, we'd be flying through a deep valley with sheer rock walls on both sides of us. The next moment, we'd pass over a cliff face and see waterfalls crashing down next to us. How could we live our lives in such a mean, nasty world, I thought to myself, while such natural magnificence exists all around us?

All of a sudden, the chatter in the background between the other GE troopers changed character. They were getting excited. Something was going on.

"We got a squeal in Pannakot," I heard the breathless words coming through on the audio channel.

"Oh boy—did y'all come at a good time!" Second Lieutenant Russell Dean was sharing his good cheer with all. "We're going to be heading straight for a fresh squeal. Maybe we'll find a tunnel entrance while you're on SCUOP with us. That'll be something to tell the folks back home about!"

I started to hear directions coming in on the audio, presumably meant for the LAM pilot.

"Come in above the main drag, then take 278 degrees, target GPS six fifty-four slash seven nineteen," I was hearing on the audio. "Get a visual on a chimp settlement complex, six mud huts. Link up in hut number four."

The rest of the GE troopers were getting positively excited, grinning at each other. I guess they all wanted to be the one to find the tunnel entrance and catch another Rejo before he could suck himself down the drain.

Moments later and the LAM found itself outside the "chimp" settlement complex. We clambered out and entered mud hut number four. What a different world we had just walked into.

Mud hut number four was surprisingly big inside. It was dark, but it didn't take more than a second for my military VRU to adjust itself to the darkness. Everything was different. I felt I'd just gone back in time a thousand years. I could smell the smoke of a fire and saw food cooking in a big clay pot over a fireplace in the corner. On the other side of the hut, there were nine or ten local people. It looked like an extended family. They were wearing traditional clothing, some with beautiful old weavings. The women had brocaded shawls around them, with faded reds and yellows. The men wore baggy white pants and decorated waist-jackets. There were a couple of old men, an old woman, a few younger men and women, and some children. One woman was holding a baby who was crying.

Next to this group was another grouping, comprising two GE troopers, who looked Chinese judging by their VRUs, and one of the local men. The local man had around his head the tentacles of a MNI—something I recognized only too easily. He was wailing, as though some terrible event had occurred. He kept swaying his body forwards and backwards. I noticed his hands were tied behind his back, so it seemed to be the only movement he could make. I thought of my ordeal the other day at the hands of the Department Agents, and I instantly knew the meaning of his wailing. The MNI had forced him to give up the location of the tunnel entrance, and he was suffering the same sense of betrayal that I had felt giving up Yusef. He knew it wasn't his fault, but meanwhile the information had come out of his own brain.

One of the Chinese MNI operators started barking out directions to our platoon of new arrivals.

"Tunnel entrance somewhere behind that wall," he was yelling, pointing to the wall behind the group of local people. "Get them outta here. Get them neutralized. Move it. Before they can signal the Rejos. The entrance will self-destruct if we don't move quick."

The leader of our platoon started shouting at the group of locals. "Get to the side." He was screaming at the top of his voice. "Move it. Move away from that wall. I'm counting to five. Anyone still at that wall at the count of five is history."

For a second, I wondered how these people would understand him, and then I realized that, of course, the words were being automatically translated into the local dialect as soon as they were uttered by the VRU. So the locals knew exactly what he was saying.

The adrenaline everywhere was palpable. The GE troopers were all aiming their lasers at the group of locals.

"One. Two." The platoon leader was counting at the top of his voice.

One of the younger men, too brave for his own good, started to yell back at them.

"You bastards. Get out of our home. May God spit on you and your children!"

"Three."

A GE trooper took aim at him with his laser gun. "One more word and you're vaporized!" he screamed.

"Four." The platoon leader was shouting each number louder than the last.

The group was already moving away from the wall and the young man backed down, spat on the ground, and started to join them.

Suddenly, a little girl caught my attention. She must have been about ten. She reminded me of Sally at the age when her mother died. The age when she'd put her arms around me to try to comfort me in my loss. She had a face of innocent beauty. I had the feeling she was the daughter of the young man who had just cursed the GE troopers.

The little girl started running towards the troopers. I saw she had something in her hand. I couldn't tell what. It seemed like some sort of stick.

"Sayyida!" I saw her mother cry out to her.

"Five." The platoon leader yelled out.

The little girl raised her hand towards the platoon leader. Everything happened in the same second. There was a flash. The little girl collapsed on the floor.

Sayyida's mother let out a terrible shriek of pain and rushed to the little girl's lifeless body. The sound of her cry cut through me like a blade of ice. It was only too clear. One of the troopers had shot Sayyida with a laser gun.

There was pandemonium. The whole group was now huddled over Sayyida's dead body. The women were wailing. It was the worst sound I'd ever heard in my life. The men were howling. Cursing. Calling to Allah.

"May God strike you all down until you are dirt in the ground!"

"May the Heavens rain down pestilence on your family!"

"You followers of Satan! Go back to Hell where you belong!"

All these screams were being translated into my audio in perfect English. But the sounds and the feelings needed no translation. This was a terrible, terrible moment. A beautiful little girl was dead. Killed for what?

One of the men suddenly held up a piece of firewood. He had forgotten all fear in his overwhelming anger. He walked towards the GE troopers, brandishing the piece of firewood.

"This is what she was holding, you evil bastards! She was trying to give it as a gift to you, you followers of Satan! Hospitality—that is what we teach our children from birth. She saw how you were acting to her father and she thought, if she could give you a gift, you'd treat him more kindly. This was her gift. A piece of firewood. It's all she had. You evil murderers of innocence!" He screamed all this at the top of his voice, while the sanitized automated translator gave it all to me and everyone else in calm, grammatical English.

"It looked like a gun, Chief," the guilty trooper who had shot the laser said in a plaintive voice to the platoon leader. "The Pre-HAP showed up as a gun, like she was going to shoot at us."

The Pre-HAP? What the hell was that? But I had no time to ask. Events were moving too fast.

"What's the big fuss about one dead chimp?" one of the Chinese MNI operators yelled from the other side. "We're losing precious seconds before the Rejos self-destruct the tunnel entrance. Get them the hell outta here now."

As if on cue, a loud but muffled bang suddenly shook the hut. The ground vibrated and shook, as though an earthquake had just occurred. This was followed by another muffled bang, only a little softer. Then another vibration of the ground.

"Shit! They got the tunnel entrance. We've lost the squeal. Operation aborted!" the Chinese MNI operator yelled out in disgust.

"You assholes let the chimps screw us all again!" the other Chinese MNI operator shouted at our platoon.

The first MNI operator continued. He sounded like he was superior in position to the others. "SCUOP 17-352 Central Region aborted. Proceed with settlement obliteration."

Our platoon herded up the local tribespeople, who by now had retreated into muttering curses among themselves. Resignation had trumped anger. We all filed out of hut number four. One of the tribesmen was carrying the little, dead body of Sayyida. The platoon, the tribespeople, the MNI operators, all of us walked up a path, on a slight incline until we were a hundred yards or so from the grouping of huts. Then, moments passed while we all stood there, looking at the huts.

"Proceed with obliteration!" This time it was our platoon leader who called out the order.

Two of the GE troopers aimed some kind of grenade launchers at the huts and shot. A moment later, there was a loud explosion, and all six of the mud huts exploded in a ball of flame and fire. The fire immediately engulfed the whole complex. Moments later and we could feel the heat of the fire, bright and furious, in our faces.

The group of tribespeople started wailing again. Only this time, they were no longer cursing the troopers. They were praying to their God.

"God is great."

"God has created Heaven and Earth."

"God is with us in our suffering."

"God Almighty! Be with us in our loss!"

Again, their wailings were translated into calm, American sentences that seemed so out of place in this scene of horror.

What the hell was going on? What the hell was happening? Why? My mind seethed with anger, with horror, with a terrible sense of the loss of Sayyida. Where were these tribespeople going to live? Why did the troopers obliterate their huts? I could barely keep myself under control. But I had a job to do. I had come here to understand better what Yusef had been talking about. Well, I sure hadn't expected a lesson as brutal as this one.

As I was looking at the burning huts, one of the tribesmen must have seen that I was acting differently from the rest of the troopers. He was standing, just a few feet away from me, and out of the blue, he caught my eye.

He looked at me, not with anger, but with terrible sorrow. He seemed to understand that I was not like the rest. He was old, his face was lined. I could see the years, the decades of suffering that life had carved into his skin. He held out a scrawny arm to me and waved it over to the burning hut, and then to the man holding little Sayyida.

"See!" he said to me. "See what has been wrought on us! How do we endure? How do we endure?"

He shook his head, in disgust. Or in wonderment? I don't know. And then he turned away from me and walked back to his group. Was he sent by Yusef? I asked myself. Or was it just a chance encounter? To this day, I don't know the answer. But his words struck deep in my soul.

We made our way back to the LAM. In silence. Each in our own thoughts. The troopers disappointed that their "squeal" had failed to result in finding a tunnel entrance. Naomi and Harry, presumably, worried about the effect this experience would have on their "Primal witness." And me, I felt a hard anger, steel in my heart. I thought of what Yusef had been trying to explain to me. The suffering of his people, fighting for humanity. The hypocrisy and cruelty of the d-humans. Now, I'd seen it for myself. But I wasn't going to remain silent. I was going to glean every bit of information I could from our cheery Second Lieutenant, Russell Dean.

On our way back, through the awe-inspiring scenery, the disappointment of the troopers, the grim silence of Naomi and Harry, I kept quizzing Russell Dean about what had happened. To him, I was a UNAPS observer, and he'd better answer my questions honestly.

What was a "Pre-HAP"? I asked. Pre-Hostility Anticipation Protocol was the answer. Pre-HAP, my second lieutenant explained to me, was the way modern military technology got an edge over the enemy in real time. When a trooper experiences his virtual reality, he's not actually seeing reality as it is, but rather as his supercomputer is predicting it *will be* a second from then. Ninety-nine per cent of the time, Russell told me, this works great. Sometimes, though, the computer gets it wrong. In this case, the trooper who shot little Sayyida was actually seeing her holding a gun and aiming to fire at them, because that was what his Pre-HAP had anticipated. So, Russell explained with his cheery ethical ease, the trooper really had no choice—he was just responding to what he'd seen.

I kept my cool, as Russell casually told me about the unfortunate occasional side-effects of Pre-HAP but explained that this was far, far, better than permitting their precious VRUs to be shot at and damaged by real guns. So, what's the life of a "chimp," I thought to myself bitterly, against the risk of a damaged VRU? Obviously, that's an issue the programmers of the Pre-HAP computers had long ago answered very clearly.

And finally, I discovered why the GE troopers obliterated the houses of the local tribespeople.

"You gotta do something to get these chimps to understand they can't just protect the Rejos with impunity. What the hell do they think they get from the Rejos? Nothing. If they only helped us track down and clean out the Rejos, they could get back to their chimp lives, doing their cooking, drinking their goats' milk, and whatever the hell else chimps do to make it through the day. We gotta punish those pesky critters for protecting the Rejos. Well, we're not gonna kill them in cold blood. But at least if we blow away the huts they use to hide their Rejos, then maybe they'll think twice the next time a Rejo comes along and asks them for help."

"Do you think maybe you just alienate them more, and make them feel more support for the Rejos when you do that?" I asked the second lieutenant, Russell Dean.

He just shook his head, as though I were asking him about the mystery of creation.

"Hell, there's no telling how these chimps think. Don't ask me. All they ever do is curse us and pray to their goddam Allah. All I know is, it's official policy. When a SCUOP is aborted, the next thing you do is always 'settlement obliteration.' That's just how it gets done 'round here. Don't ask me. Ask one of your friends in New York at the UN. They're the ones who set the policies. We just do what we're told."

He sickened me. They all sickened me. I was seething with rage inside. But I was cold on the outside. Steel. Yusef was right. If I could make a difference in this battle, I had an obligation to my race, an obligation to Sayyida, and countless more like her and her family, an obligation to fight for us all.

16

The Accusation

I saw a newborn baby with wild wolves all around it

Naomi was waiting for me as I walked out of the virtual reality cubicle. Her face was hard and tight, but contorted with kindness. She was putting on the psychologist routine, trying to head me off at the pass.

"Eusebio, how do you feel about what we just experienced at Pannakot?"

Yes, she was playing the shrink game well. Always begin with an open-ended question.

"How do I feel? Well, how the hell do you expect me to feel when I see your people murder an innocent little girl in cold blood, because she's one of us, a human being? Because she's a 'chimp.'"

I spat out the last words with venom.

"How do I feel about seeing your UN troops burning up their settlements, leaving them homeless, because they didn't get a successful SCUOP? What kind of dumb question is that?"

I was sick and tired of being their dupe. I just had to be careful. Yusef had plans for me, and I didn't want to blow them at this point.

Naomi didn't rise to the bait. "Yes, you're right, Eusebio. I'm sorry, that was a dumb question," was her response.

"But," she carried on, "something you have to understand, Eusebio. I'm just as horrified as you are. I'm going to make a report to UNAPS as soon as we're finished today. They're not my UN troops. Remember, Eusebio, I may not be a Primal, but I've spent my life fighting for Primal rights. Give me some credit."

I just shook my head in disgust.

"Eusebio," she continued. Her voice was back to normal now. That earnest, confidence-winning tone. "Eusebio, you've got to listen to me. You're being manipulated by the Rejectionists. I don't know how they've been able to do it, but they've managed to mix up in your mind their cause with our cause. They're two completely different things. We're fighting to protect your race, the Primals, from the PEPS proposal. We're trying to keep your race alive and free. The Rejectionists are not Primals; they're d-humans. And what they're trying to do ultimately has nothing to do with Primals. They're trying to undo the last seventy years of peace and progress. They're trying to take us back to the conflict and hate that consumed our world until this century. Our society needs to do everything it can to stop them. They're dangerous. They'll stop at nothing—nothing—in trying to destroy our society, to undermine seventy years of global peace."

So now I was getting the world from Naomi's point of view. It all sounded so reasonable. But there was something I wanted to hear from Naomi. Something that would affect my own inner turmoil.

"So, Naomi, you support the GE troops trying to root out the Rejectionists?"

"Of course I do," she responded. "They're defending our society against people who want to bring back intolerance, wars, hatred. I don't support killing innocent little girls. And I can't stand people like Second Lieutenant Russell Dean. But what they're doing out there is necessary."

"And Naomi, if it were necessary for innocent people to die in order to get rid of the Rejectionists for ever, to completely eliminate them—I mean really necessary, not like little Sayyida—would you support that?"

Naomi's brows furrowed. She gazed at me with a piercing look.

"I don't know exactly what it is you're getting at, Eusebio," she replied quizzically. "But in principle, you know as well as I do that sometimes battles have to be fought for a society's values; and in those battles, sometimes innocent people have to die."

Naomi shook her head as if rejecting her own words.

"I would sure hate to be the person who had to make that decision," she continued. "And in truth, Eusebio, I'd do everything I could to avoid it."

Thanks a lot, I thought to myself sardonically. You've managed to put me in just that position that you'd do everything you could to avoid. And I don't see any way out of it. But at a deeper level, I knew Naomi had just answered for me the question roaring through my mind since Yusef had posed it to me the night before.

And then I find myself back in the hot seat. The neurographic chair. Session whatever of the PEPS hearing. Only it's a different Eusebio Franklin sitting there now. No longer the naked native coming off the slave boat. It's a Eusebio with a mission. I don't know what it is, but I know Yusef's got something planned for me. Something that will make a difference. And I'm sure as hell not going to make a difference acting as Harry Shields' patsy, no matter how well-meaning Naomi might be in her intentions.

Harry Shields has his usual patronizing smirk on his face. Only, this time, I think it's a little forced. Maybe he got rattled by the trip to Pannakot. By my nearly walking out on his PEPS session. Or maybe it's just my imagination. Wishful thinking.

"Let the record state," Harry's formal drawl rolls on, "that the Primal witness demanded a visit to Pannakot in the North West Frontier of Pakistan; and that in order to validate the principals of these hearings, he was granted his demand. In this virtual field trip, we were witness to a failed surveillance and clean-up operation, during which a young Primal girl was accidentally shot and died immediately.

"I wish to state for the record that this virtual field trip was outside the normal range of the procedural agenda for this PEPS hearing, and was undertaken solely to fulfill the desire of the Primal witness. Since there are no issues arising from the Pannakot field trip that have any bearing on the subject at hand, I move that we waive discussion of this field trip and return to the agenda for today's PEPS hearing. Counsel Aramovich, do you have anything to add or do you agree with this motion?"

Stony as before, Naomi responded.

"I do agree with this motion, Counsel Shields. I have nothing further to add, other than to state for the record that I will be filing a report to UNAPS on the killing of the young Primal girl after this session has ended today. Please proceed, Counsel Shields."

And that was that. Just like the death of Subrata Bammarjee two days ago. You've got to hand it to these d-humans. They have a great protocol for acknowledging murder, calling it a tragic mistake, putting it on the record, and then getting on with the real agenda. The stuff that really matters. Like formalizing the extinction of my human race.

And this time, when Harry Shields pushed a button like Merlin the magician, and up came a spectacular three-dimensional image of the mysterious peaks of Machu Picchu in Peru, I was ready for it. This time, it didn't take me by surprise. I might be suckered once. I might be suckered twice. But by the third time, Eusebio Franklin has gotten wise to what's going on.

Machu Picchu. Beautiful, mysterious, steeped in the clouds, hidden away nine thousand feet up in the Andes. It means "Old Peak" in the Quechua language and it was a religious center for the Inca people before the Spanish arrived to destroy their civilization. By that time, the Incan people had turned the place into a small, secret, self-contained spiritual community. Two thousand feet above the roaring Urubamba River, Machu Picchu was so well concealed and so remote that the Spanish never found it.

And their failure to find Machu Picchu had great spiritual significance for the Quechua people who survived the Spanish holocaust. Because Machu Picchu's *Intihuatana* stone remained intact.

The *Intihuatana* stone was the most sacred object in the Inca religion. The Incas believed that if it were destroyed, the gods that belonged to that particular area would depart forever. Once the Spanish discovered this, they knew what to do to break the spirits of the people forever. They began a "search and destroy" mission to find the *Intihuatana* stone in every Inca shrine and smash it to pieces. They were only too successful. Within a generation, there were no *Intihuatana* stones left intact anywhere in the Andes.

Except for Machu Picchu. Because, try as they might, they never discovered the site of Machu Picchu. And for that reason, the *Intihuatana* stone remains there. Intact. And the Quechua believe that when a person rests his head against the *Intihuatana* stone, for that moment he is in contact with the eternal spirit world.

And it's not just the Quechua who believe it. During my Year Away in Argentina, one of my closest friends there, Ignacio Herrera, spent hours with me through the night, telling me about the moment he had touched the stone. It reminded me my own Vision Day when I felt the ancient spirits fall around me in the gentle rain, telling me that *"life goes on"* in the middle of the devastation that we call our modern world.

So, when Harry Shields brought up the 3-D image of Machu Picchu, this all went through me in a flash. I thought how, the day before, he had tried to ridicule the aboriginal songlines. And then, when I came to their defense, how he turned the tables on me and accused my race of the genocide that took place against the very people who are so special to me. I sure as hell wasn't going to let him do this to me again. I wasn't going to be accused of murdering the millions of indigenous peoples whose lives and spirits were disemboweled at the hands of the Spanish conquest. I thought of my friend, Ignacio, telling me of his moment at Machu Picchu. I saw, in my memory, the fire in his eyes. I wasn't going to let Harry Shields anywhere near those eyes.

"Do you recognize this image, Eusebio?" Harry Shields began in his usual slick tone.

I didn't have a plan. I barely gave it a thought. I just started saying whatever came into my mind.

"I sure as well do, Harry. Yeah, I recognize it. And I know what you're going to try to do, and I'm not playing your game anymore."

Harry's eyebrows raised in an amused gesture of mild surprise.

"Yeah, that's right. I know the way it works. First, you'll ask me to tell you about the mysteries of Machu Picchu. Then, you'll try to ridicule the beliefs of the Incas. Then, when I try to defend them, you'll start accusing my race of destroying them. We've been there before, Harry, and I'm not going there again."

Naomi's frozen silence seemed to be melting. I was surprised. I thought that, just like before, she'd react like Harry, because I wasn't playing their game. Instead, she seemed delighted. Her eyes were beginning to show that warm gleam. I kept going. It didn't really matter to me what either of them thought.

I felt the anger rising in me. My voice was getting more and more agitated.

"You know why I'm not going there again, Harry? Do you know why? I'll tell you why. Because it's not me and my race who did all those monstrous things. It's you, yes, it's people like you who did it all. People like you who were responsible for massacring millions upon millions of indigenous people in the Americas."

I didn't really know what I was saying but it sounded good, so I was just letting go.

Harry remained unperturbed.

"Responsible for doing what, exactly, Eusebio?"

I knew I was losing it, but I kept going. Anything was better than getting caught in Harry Shields' web of fallacious logic.

"For doing what? I'll tell you what. For arriving in 1492 on the island of Hispaniola where millions of Arawak people were living happily in peace, and destroying them within a generation so that forty years later there were six hundred—yes, just six hundred—of those Arawak still alive on the island. You know what Columbus said about these people when he landed? Do you know what he said?"

I was literally yelling by this point.

"No, Eusebio, what did he say?" came back Harry's calmly dispassionate answer.

"He said, in his diary, 'They are so artless and free with all they possess, that no one would believe it without having seen it. Of anything they have, if you ask them for it, they never say no; rather they invite the person to share it, and show as much love as if they were giving their hearts.'"

I knew these lines by heart because they had been the subject of many a history lesson I'd given to my tenth-graders over the years.

"And you know how Columbus ended that sweet little journal entry about the innocent Arawak people?"

Harry Shields just shook his head silently.

"'They have no iron,'" I quoted. *"'Their spears are made of sugar cane. They would make fine servants. With fifty men we could subjugate them all and make them do whatever we want.'"*

"But Eusebio, wasn't it really just disease that wiped out most of the indigenous people in the New World?" Harry Shields asked.

Was he baiting me? Trying to get me to lose my temper further? If so, he did a damn good job. A lifetime of history lessons on the subject took over any other part of my reason. I'd completely lost control.

"Are you out of your mind?" I yelled back. "Do you know the atrocities they did? Do you want to know about the time in Cuba, when a hundred Spanish soldiers had a competition to see who had the sharpest sword. You know what they did? They went to the little village nearby and ripped the bellies open of every man, woman, and child, to see who could do it with just one swipe."

Years of anger were welling up in me. Anger at what Harry Shields' world had done to all the good people. Anger at Sarah's death because her life simply wasn't worth the cost of retrofitting a hundred-year-old machine. Anger at being kidnapped from my home. Anger at these grinding days of bullshit and torment. At Subrata's death resulting from Harry's callousness. At the murder of Sayyida that I'd just seen with my own eyes less than an hour earlier.

I blamed it all on Harry Shields, and I let him have it. My only weapon against him were the facts. Facts that I happened to know very well. The facts of what happened to fifty million indigenous people suddenly bombarded by the viciousness, guns, and diseases of the Europeans.

The minutes rolled into hours, and still I continued. I had a lifetime of teaching to fit into this session. My voice stopped yelling, but my anger at Harry Shields and all the various Harry Shieldses throughout history, who had planned, legitimized, and bankrolled the greatest outrage the world had ever witnessed—that anger remained on full throttle.

I went region by region, massacre by massacre. Finally, saving the best for last, I got to Potosi. Potosi, the mountain of silver. Potosi, the city that briefly became one of the grandest cities in the world, built on the blood and suffering of millions of indigenous slaves. The mines that caused the deaths of eight million tortured human beings over three centuries, far and away the greatest single site of human suffering the world has ever seen.

Finally, when even I could stand it no longer, I paused for a moment. I looked at both Harry and Naomi, and I spoke to them the earliest known poem written in the language of Nahuatl by a native of central Mexico, from the early decades of the sixteenth century.

Worms are swarming in the streets and plazas,
and the walls are splattered with gore.
The water has turned red, as if it were dyed,
and when we drink it,
it has the taste of brine.

My voice deepened and slowed. I looked across at both Harry and Naomi, as I spoke the words. They both looked back at me with solemn expressions.

We have pounded our hands in despair
against the adobe walls,
for our inheritance, our city, is lost and dead.

By this point, the room was silent. It remained silent. Moments passed. No one knew what to say. Both Harry and Naomi looked appropriately somber.

In a different voice, grave and deadly quiet, I spoke up again.

"I accuse you, Harry Shields, and the countless, faceless, calm, civilized, Western-educated sophists just like you, of causing this crime against humanity, the greatest crime that the world has ever witnessed."

For a moment, Harry seemed taken aback, as if he didn't know what to say, what to do. Just for a moment. Then, predictably, he settled back into his cynical, amused sneer, and as if I wasn't even worth the effort of responding to, he turned his attention to Naomi.

"Counsel Aramovich, perhaps you can help me reconcile a logical inconsistency that seems to have arisen. For some strange reason, the Primal witness appears to have confused the vicious, primitive urges of the Primal conquistadors with our current d-human society. I've been trying to understand the connection, but I confess I've come up short. Perhaps you can enlighten me."

What a bastard. Harry Shields' pomposity knew no bounds. He was doing everything in his power to make me look utterly ridiculous on the record.

"I think, Counsel Shields," came Naomi's response, "that the Primal witness has shown himself perfectly capable of putting his arguments together without any assistance from me. I suggest we ask him."

What was Naomi doing? Was she giving me respect and trying to undo Harry's attempts to humiliate me? Or was she simply clueless how to answer Harry's question and passing the hot potato back to me? I'll never know which it was.

All I knew at the time was that the ball was back in my court, and I had no idea what to do with it. I'd burned myself out on the description of the conquest and the genocide of the Indians. I was tired as hell. The image of little Sayyida, gunned down in innocence a few hours earlier, came back into my mind. I didn't want to let her down. But here was Harry Shields, scoring another victory, making me, the representative of the Primal race, look as stupid and irrational as he could ever hope to portray me.

I paused. I hummed and herred. The silence became embarrassing as it grew longer. And then it happened. I swear, the spirit of Dr. Julius Schumacher must have entered the room and touched my consciousness. There's no other way I could have thought of it. Not in a million years. But it arrived in my mind, and I had the answer.

"The Valladolid Controversy." The words came out of my mouth as if I were in a trance.

"The what?" replied a confused Harry Shields.

"The Valladolid Controversy. In 1550." I was coming back alive again. The ideas were beginning to form in my mind, and I was back in control. "King Charles I of Spain—King Charles held his Renaissance version of this PEPS session.

"You see, his counselors were telling him he was permitting so much horror and devastation in the New World that there was just a chance his immortal soul might be at stake, that maybe he might just burn in Hell for eternity for letting it continue. Well, King Charles took this threat seriously, so in April 1550 he suspended all new conquests in the New World until he held a conference of his top theologians and lawyers to come up with an answer to the question at hand. And you know what that question was? It might sound familiar to you, Harry Shields."

Harry just shook his head passively.

"The question was, are the New World Indians really humans? Do they have souls that are worth saving? Or are they sub-humans, not even worth treating as anything other than slaves and beasts of burden?

"Yes, it's hard to believe, but these civilized Christians really took this question seriously. And they had their sixteenth-century versions of Harry Shields and Naomi Aramovich."

I looked across at both of them with a vicious grimace.

"Yeah, Harry, you'd really like this guy called Juan Gines de Sepulveda. He was a man right after your heart. He was the chief prosecutor. According to Sepulveda, it was very simple. The natives shouldn't be treated as humans but as natural slaves. In fact, he wrote a book called 'The Just Causes for War Among the Indians.' His ideas were very legitimate. In fact, they came all the way from Aristotle. Oh, and the Bible too. He found a line in Proverbs which says 'He who is stupid will serve the wise man.'

"So Sepulveda stood there in front of the Council of Fourteen in Valladolid in Spain, and made his argument, that because of their *natural rudeness and inferiority*, the Indians *require, by their own nature and in their own interests, to be placed under the authority of civilized and virtuous princes or nations, so that they may learn, from the might, wisdom, and law of their conquerors, to practice better morals, worthier customs and a more civilized way of life.* You see, Harry, just like you, he was really thinking of their interests, and trying to do what was best for this inferior sub-species."

My sarcasm may have been over the top. But it was worth it. For once, I was enjoying myself.

"And there was no doubt in Sepulveda's mind that they were inferior. In fact, in his words, the Indians were as inferior *'as children are to adults, as women are to men, as different from Spaniards as cruel people are from mild people.'* Yeah, Sepulveda had a really clear sense of right and wrong."

I'd truly hit pay dirt. Thanks to the spirit of Dr. Schumacher, I'd come across an argument that trumped anything Harry Shields could think of. I could see it in both of their faces. And it was all on their goddam record. So I kept going.

"But Sepulveda didn't have it so easy. See, there was a self-appointed attorney for the Indians, making the case for them, even though none of them had the slightest idea that, thousands of miles from their land, these learned gentlemen were debating whether they had souls worth saving from eternal damnation. But there was a guy, a Dominican priest, who had once been a colonialist with his own slaves, who realized what an abomination he was living and spent the rest of his life fighting for the rights of the indigenous people of the New World. He was one of the greatest people in the sordid history of our world. His name was Bartolomé de las Casas. And he was a little bit like the sixteenth-century version of Naomi . . . "

I looked over at Naomi. I thought I saw her blush as she returned my gaze. Yes, there was some humanity there, I thought to myself.

"Las Casas," I continued, "spent decades fighting against the depraved actions of his countrymen. He told them they would go to Hell for treating the Indians with such cruelty. In fact, two years after the Valladolid Controversy, he wrote a book called *"A Very Brief Account of the Destruction of the Indies,"* which was the first time somebody had the temerity to tell it like it actually was. It was translated into all the major European languages, and it told chapter and verse, with details and statistics on the number of Indians killed, complete with graphic drawings showing the butchery of the Spanish.

"So Las Casas was ready to make his arguments in Valladolid, in front of those fourteen wise judges. He spent days taking them through a five hundred and fifty page Latin manuscript, with sixty-three chapters and no end of citations from the Bible. He made his point, sure enough. That the Indians were human beings with souls, and they needed to be treated as such. He even went so far as to compare the Aztec civilization favorably to ancient Greece and Rome."

"What happened, Eusebio? Who won?"

The question came from Naomi. I saw that she was truly interested. This was no game for her.

"It was a stalemate. The judges didn't know what to do. So they did nothing. Later on, both sides claimed to have won. Sepulveda continued a successful career as an apologist for the murderous colonialists. Las Casas kept writing his denunciations until he retired to a monastery and died in his nineties. The Spanish kept destroying what was left of the native peoples. Basically, nothing changed. The only winner, I guess, was King Charles of Spain, who could now sleep soundly at night, knowing he still had a good chance of making it to heaven when he died."

Things were getting a little too quiet and relaxed. Harry Shields took advantage of the moment and tried to pierce his dagger of sophistry into my diatribe.

"Well, thank you, Eusebio, for enlightening us on this interesting historical vignette. I will ignore your attempts to compare me with this character, Sepulveda. It is of course ridiculous to try to compare a senior UNAPS counsel with a Primal from the sixteenth century who obviously suffered from many of the superstitious delusions of the time. But I understand, Eusebio, you're angry and emotional, so I take no offence."

One thing you can really count on from Harry Shields—he'll always find a way to one-up you, no matter what. He kept going, now he'd found his footing again.

"However, Eusebio, I'm afraid I still fail to understand the relevance of your fascinating story."

I could feel myself slipping. Just like I said on that first day to Naomi, *"I'm not cut out for this."*

"The simple fact remains that the Primal witness has accused me and others like me of being responsible for the worst genocide ever conducted by the Primal race. This accusation is not only without merit. It is prima facie ridiculous. The terrible events he has described occurred hundreds of years before the first d-human was ever conceived. Far from accusing me for these atrocities, the Primal witness should be appreciating the progress made in our human genetic structure and feel secure in the knowledge that, under GALT, such evils can never happen again."

Game, set and match to Harry Shields. Again. He turned to Naomi.

"Counsel Aramovich, unless there is anything to add, I suggest we adjourn our session for the day."

Naomi looked across at me. I could see the turmoil in her eyes. The kindness, the caring. But I could see that she felt powerless, that she couldn't do anything to stop my humiliation, once again, at the hands of Harry Shields.

"Is there anything, Eusebio, that you'd like to add to the record before we adjourn?" she asked me.

And at that moment of defeat, something happened. Some synapses went off in my brain that had never fired before. You can call it what you want. An epiphany. A stroke of brilliance. But the truth is, I really don't get strokes of brilliance. I will believe, to my dying day, that Dr. Schumacher's spirit was with us in that room, and there is no one in history better qualified than Julius Schumacher to know which synapses to turn on when they're needed. And that's what I think he was doing to me. Not just for me. But for the human race that he'd given his life trying to save.

It was clear to me, and my voice was now calm. No hint of anger.

"Yes, Naomi, there is something I would like to add."

The room was silent.

"You see," I continued, calm and strong, "every accusation that Harry Shields has made since this PEPS session began, every argument he's made against the continued existence of my race, has been based on the idea that, because d-humans have an altered genetic structure, they're innocent of the crimes of their ancestors, but because we 'Primals' have the same genetic structure, the guilt of our shared ancestors remains with us."

I was talking like someone possessed. I'd never been clearer, more logical, in my life. Harry and Naomi could see that. They were silent and, for once, Harry was listening intently, concentrating hard.

"On that basis," I continued, "we should hold Ojimo Nkruma, our safari guide yesterday, guilty for the atrocities committed by General Tobo, because of their shared genetic make-up. I suppose the children of the Nazi concentration camp commanders should have been strung up and hanged along with their fathers at the Nuremberg trials in the twentieth century. It's an absurd argument that just doesn't stand up to reason."

"No, you've got it all wrong, Eusebio." Harry Shields' voice sounded anxious. Suddenly, he was speaking more quickly. His pomposity had evaporated. "You're focusing on guilt, which has nothing to do with what we've been discussing in these hearings. You are no guiltier than I am of the terrible things the Primal race has done in the past. The point is, your genetic make-up, and that of all other Primals, permits these horrors to happen."

I was unfazed. I knew where I was going.

"Harry," I said, "you and your society are obsessed with genetics. That obsession has caused you to miss the real cause of evil in our world. It's not our genetic make-up. Sure, that can lead to a predisposition towards certain behavior. But we still have free will. We can choose what we do with our lives, with our minds, with our bodies. You know that. No, the real cause of both good and evil in our world is what Dr. Julius Schumacher discovered over a hundred years ago—the CONDUCTER—the control we all exercise over our own consciousness."

Harry kept trying to parry every move I made.

"Look, I think this session is going nowhere. We don't need any academic discussions on the nature of free will to move forward on this hearing." Harry turned to Naomi in his usual tactic to avoid dealing with me directly. "Counsel Aramovich, I reiterate the Primal witness is unable to back up his absurd proposition accusing me of somehow being responsible for the atrocities of the Spanish conquest. I therefore move that we bring this session to an end."

"Counsel Shields, I don't think the Primal witness has had a chance to finish his line of reasoning yet."

Thanks, Naomi, I thought to myself. But quite honestly, at this point I don't even need your help. I know she can read my thoughts through the neurographic scanner, so I don't bother to speak them.

"Harry, have you read the book written by Dr. Julius Schumacher called *On Being Human*?" I was on track, and I wasn't going to let Harry trip me up.

"Yes, of course I have," came the response. "It was part of the background research on your Humanist society, Eusebio."

"Then maybe you remember the section where Dr. Schumacher describes the dominance achieved by the prefrontal cortex over the other areas of human consciousness?"

"I remember that part in general, but not necessarily every detail," Harry answered. "But I really fail to understand what this has to do with today's session."

"Please, Counsel Shields," Naomi intervened, "Let the Primal witness follow through on his discussion."

So I continued. "Well, Dr. Schumacher identified ancient Egypt and Mesopotamia as the time when the prefrontal cortex began to dominate, but then an event occurred in the collective consciousness of Eurasian society which solidified its control forever. Do you remember what that was?"

"No, actually, I don't recall."

"It was the alliance between the prefrontal cortex with the basest elements of the animate part of our consciousness: the primal desire for power."

"From the beginning of time, humans have always killed other humans, just like they've killed other animals. For food, for power, for sex, for any of the basic animate motives that exist. Just like cheetahs have always killed Thomson gazelles for food. But, a thousand years before Christ, and maybe even earlier—nobody knows for sure—a new idea emerged in Persia, in our so-called 'cradle of civilization.'"

"What was that idea, Eusebio?" Naomi asked in an encouraging voice. She clearly wanted me to keep going down my path.

"It began with the great prophet, Zarathustra, and led to the religion known as Zoroastrianism. But more importantly, it also led to the monotheism of Judaism, Christianity, and Islam. It was the idea, expressed for the first time in history, that there was a single God, and this God was involved in a struggle for good against evil.

"For the first time in history," I continued, talking calmly, almost in a trance, "a duality had entered human consciousness. The struggle for good against evil. And this was the historic opportunity for the prefrontal cortex. Now, it could latch on to monotheism. And even better, whenever a tribe or a kingdom wanted to go looting, kill their neighbors and steal their possessions, they could do it for a higher purpose. They could do it in the battle for good against evil."

"Of course, it took a while, but once Christianity took over the ancient power of Rome, this idea really got going. And it changed history forever. Now, when humans killed other humans, they believed they were doing it for a greater purpose. Not just for power, not just for vengeance. No, they started to believe they were killing other humans for God. That they were actually doing something great and purposeful while they killed other soldiers, raped their women, and massacred the innocent overrun by the tides of brutality. This was how the Muslims found themselves creating the greatest empire in history. Then came the Christian reaction, called the Crusades. So, for the first time, on a large scale, the prefrontal cortex, which had conceptualized this notion of an abstract all-powerful God, began to link this abstraction to the primal urges of human beings to fight for power and status. This is the alliance I'm talking about."

Harry Shields was getting increasingly irritated.

"Look, Eusebio, fascinating as this is, you seem nowhere nearer answering the basic question. What relevance does this have to your earlier accusation of me?"

271

"Well," I continued unfazed, "as we entered the Age of Reason, and the scientific method began to gain power, it was time for the prefrontal cortex to switch allegiance from one set of abstractions to another. This was easy enough, since the scientific method was itself a creation of the prefrontal cortex, just like monotheism.

"Now there was even less room in human consciousness for dissent. Those few people whose errant minds permitted a more balanced perception of the world were now marginalized, dismissed as freaks: yogis, witch doctors, tree huggers—none of them taken seriously by the world at large.

"So now, Europeans could kill both in the name of God and Enlightenment. The 'white man's burden' of the British colonialists. The 'manifest destiny' of the Americans as they laid their railroads and murdered the American Indians. The light to be brought into Africa's 'heart of darkness.'"

I looked across at Harry.

"I bet you're beginning to see now, Harry, where this is going. With your superior intelligence, I'm sure you've already got it."

I couldn't resist the dig. Harry just looked back at me with a stony silence.

"Do you want to finish the story for me, Harry? No? Okay, I'll do it then. We can fast forward into the twenty-first century. Colonialism is over, because now every country in the world has bought into the 'scientific method' in one form or other. Now, the alliance between the prefrontal cortex and the forces of greed takes the form of globalization—spreading the values of freedom, democracy, and free trade. Once again, the bottom line is the same: get rich, get powerful, and do it believing that it's all part of the greater good. Your greed is morally unassailable.

"Well, Dr. Schumacher never made it beyond that period. He was shot in the head on the streets of New York. So, I guess I've got to fill in the gaps now, based on what you and Naomi have told me in the past few days. It's pretty easy. I don't have to be a genius to do it."

At this point, both Naomi and Harry were watching me intently. I continued calmly. I didn't want to blow it right at the end.

"I guess your Global Aggression Limitation Treaty was the next step in the domination of the prefrontal cortex. Now, it's using its new weapon, genetic optimization, to literally make sure that each new d-human mind that comes into existence is structured with the prefrontal cortex fully in control.

"But that left a few messy loose ends. The Rejectionists. And those pesky Primals, those 'chimps,' still kept reproducing. So here we are now, at the end game. The Proposal for the Extinction of the Primal Species. The PEPS proposal. This hearing."

I raised my hand and pointed my finger accusingly at Harry.

"Yes, that's why, Harry Shields, I'm accusing you directly, you and everyone who's working behind the scenes to put you here, I'm accusing you and all the neatly trimmed, business-suited, clean, elegant, legalistic rationalizers and legitimizers of conquest, colonialism, capitalism and killing—I'm accusing you all of being party to the greatest conspiracy of genocide, destruction, and devastation of the human spirit that the world has ever seen. There's no difference between you and Christopher Columbus, writing in his diary, *'With 50 men we could subjugate them all and make them do whatever we want'*—other than he was braver than you: he risked his life and was ready to watch the agony his victims felt when he cut them to pieces."

I was done. The room was silent. Game, set, and match to the Primal race. At least as far this session went. I thanked the spirit of Dr. Schumacher for visiting me. I began to feel his presence depart, and once again, I was just Eusebio Franklin, history teacher. I knew there was no way I could have said that all over again.

17

The Jihad

I'll walk to the depths of the deepest black forest

W e're on our way back to the hotel through the hustle and bustle of the New York skyways. Naomi is chattering excitedly. I've never noticed before how beautiful she can look, her brown eyes filled with passion. I have to pinch myself to remember she's in her seventies.

I can hardly hear her through the noise of the videos, announcements, and conversations all around me. But I can make out enough sound bites to know what she's talking about.

"I knew you could do it, Eusebio!"

"I told you at the beginning—your whole life was a preparation for this hearing!"

"I knew we were right to choose somebody from the Humanists!"

No doubt about it. Naomi was happy about how that afternoon session went.

Her enthusiasm was infectious. By the time Naomi left me in my luxury hotel prison cell, I was feeling pretty pleased with myself. Yes, I'd really scored against that sonofabitch Harry Shields. Score one for the Primals.

But as time went on, and I sat there drinking a whiskey, reflecting on the day, as I ordered my automated room service dinner and savored the genetically optimized tastes, the sense of satisfaction faded away, leaving a deep, empty dread within me. The image of Sayyida kept coming into my mind, running to the soldiers to offer them the only gift she had, a piece of firewood. And moments later, she was a little dead body in the arms of her raging father.

But it was worse than that. The excitement of the day—the horrors of Pannakot, the verbal battles with Harry Shields—had at least had the effect of keeping to the periphery of my mind the heavy decision placed on me last night by Yusef. Now, as the day faded into the past, the weight of it came right back into the center of my consciousness. And even worse was the realization of what I'd said, so eloquently, to Harry Shields.

I couldn't escape the bottom line. If there were any truth in what I had just said in the PEPS session, in all those arguments that had made Naomi so happy, it came with an inescapable conclusion. I was, in every sense of the word, caught up in the great historic battle between those conquistadors, colonialists, d-human conquerors, and the human victims who have been suffering at their hands for centuries. If this were, in fact, part of the same battle, then I couldn't escape my role in it. My final words to Harry Shields rang in my ears. *"There's no difference between you and Christopher Columbus, other than he was braver than you."* By the same token, there's no difference between me and the millions upon millions of victims of those savage conquests—other than Yusef is giving me a chance to fight back. And I'm not ready to handle the implications.

It was a sickening and sinking feeling in my heart. I knew the answer I had to give to Yusef when he appeared. I knew I had to tell him I would be ready to do my part in the struggle. And, if necessary, to kill.

The very thought of it made me sick to my stomach. I stopped eating my dinner after a few bites and returned to my whiskey. Waiting for Yusef. My fellow human, my brother. My harbinger of doom.

And he came on schedule. We went through what was now becoming our standard routine. I began by telling him about the day.

I expected him to congratulate me for my victory over Harry Shields in the afternoon PEPS session. I couldn't have been more wrong. The more he heard, the more agitated he got. By the end, he could barely control himself. I had never seen Yusef so angry.

"Eusebio, how could you have done this? What do you think you're doing? Playing some debating game? What's the matter with you? Have you ignored everything I've told you these past few days?"

Yusef wasn't waiting for me to give him any answers. He was almost shaking in intensity.

"Eusebio, you were meant to just go along with their sessions and play their game. Don't you understand what this means? Now, I have no idea how much longer they'll keep the session going. Tomorrow may be the last day, for all I know. God forbid. After all we've been through. You may have blown it before we even have a chance!"

Blown what? A chance of what?

"Eusebio, I thought more highly of you than this. You let your ego get the better of you. Do you really, truly, think it matters if you score a point against Harry Shields? Do you really think it makes a difference to UNAPS global policy if one little Primal from a quaint community that nobody's heard of makes some argument based on a version of history that's barely understood by anyone? Do you really think anyone cares? What have you been thinking these past few days?"

There was a pause.

"How could you have let yourself be manipulated so easily, Eusebio?" Yusef continued. "And you even went so far as talk to them about Bartolomé de las Casas. He spent half his life fighting for Indian rights. He was a respected monk. He worked within the system. He wrote books that were read throughout Europe. He had the ear of the King of Spain. And how many Indians do you think he saved, with all his good work? Dozens? Maybe, at a stretch, hundreds? Out of the twenty five million killed. The difference he made was a speck of sand in the Sahara. And you had the temerity, the arrogance, to think that by winning an argument you could make the slightest difference in the implementation of the PEPS proposal? What's going on, Eusebio? Please, tell me."

By this time, Yusef's voice had calmed down. He just seemed sad. I felt like a piece of shit. What he said made so much sense. I couldn't believe it myself, how stupid I'd been to think I'd actually accomplished anything.

Then, his tone changed. His voice had warmth and encouragement back in it.

"Eusebio," he said, "do you understand why I became so angry about what you did? Harry Shields won't like being humiliated. You're becoming too dangerous for him. So, he's going to want to put an end to things before they get out of hand. I'm terribly afraid that tomorrow they'll be summing everything up and concluding the session.

"And if they do . . . " Yusef paused, thinking and looking at me, "if they end tomorrow, there won't be time for us to carry out our plan. The thing is, Eusebio, we need twenty-four hours before we can get you what you need."

Yusef sat there, silent, for what seemed like an eternity. I wished the floor would eat me up. But I just kept sipping my whiskey. I poured myself another one.

Finally, Yusef spoke. Now his voice was stronger, more decisive.

"There's only one way to go. I need to tell you everything about our plan. Right now. Listen carefully. The survival of the human race may depend on this. That is . . . if you're prepared to do what has to be done."

And so Yusef began to tell me, earnestly, forcefully, about the grim plight of the Rejectionists and the humans helping them. I hadn't realized, until then, that the situation was so desperate.

"Imagine," Yusef said to me, "you're Crazy Horse or Sitting Bull, one of the great Indian chiefs in the 1880s, watching your resistance drift into hopelessness. But now we're talking about the loss of something even greater than the entire American Indian culture. We're talking about the loss of the human race."

I'd spent a lifetime imagining the feelings of these great Indian warriors as they saw the end of existence as they and their ancestors had always known it.

"Now," Yusef continued, "imagine that *Wakan Tanka* offered magical powers to these Indian chiefs, powers both great and terrible. Powers that would lead to the death of untold numbers of white settlers in their cities in the East, but allow the American Indians to maintain their lives as they had been for hundreds of generations, to keep their freedom, permit the buffalo to roam as they always had. Imagine that, even now, three hundred years later, the Dakotas, Montana, and Wyoming were all separate Indian country, with no freeways, no cities to intrude on the native Indian tribes. Hard to imagine, isn't it?"

Yes, it was almost impossible to imagine.

"Now, would Crazy Horse or Sitting Bull have used those magical powers to save their race, their culture, their way of life, from extinction?"

"Of course they would," I answered. It seemed so obvious.

"Well, God has offered us this power, Eusebio. Nuclear power. The power of a nuclear bomb."

I was listening intently. The whole situation seemed to have nothing to do with me. Maybe it was a defense mechanism. It just seemed like an abstraction Yusef was describing.

"We've had the technical capability for decades. A very sophisticated nuclear bomb—small and virtually undetectable. The only thing that's stopped us so far has been the ethical consideration."

Yusef paused and watched me. He seemed to want to make sure I was following him closely. I said nothing. Just nodded. Yes, I was following.

"About thirty years ago," Yusef continued, "two Rejectionist scholars, Dr. Ahmed Baharraff and Professor Rangar Singh, circulated a rigorous study on the use of the nuclear option in war. This has been the core of our thinking ever since then."

Yusef's tone took on a new gravity.

"Their work ended with the conclusion that there was only one situation where the nuclear option could be justified. Where it became clear that the very survival of the human race was at stake.

"And now, it has become terribly clear to us that this time has come."

"The nuclear option." The words jolted me.

"A couple of years back," Yusef continued, "one of our undercover agents, Budhiman Raharjo, was given the post of Indonesian ambassador to the UN in New York. A Rejectionist with diplomatic immunity and access to the heart of the second biggest city in the United States. God had smiled on us."

I was in free fall. I had a terrible feeling of what might be coming next. I was trying hard to control a sensation of nausea sweeping up from the pit of my stomach.

"It took a while, but Budhiman finally succeeded in smuggling into the UN building a nuclear device. A hundred kilotons. Seven times more powerful than Columbus. And it's no more than two centimeters in diameter. Concealed carefully in a piece of furniture in the UN building. Ready for the trigger to be inserted whenever the need might arise."

Yusef's calm, inexorable voice kept going.

"And then disaster struck. Budhiman's cover was blown. He managed to end his life before the Department Agents could get to him. May God rest his soul in heaven. So our secret remained. But we had no method whatsoever of inserting the trigger into the bomb."

Yusef stopped, as if to calm himself down. He took a deep breath, like he was thinking back to those days.

"After Budhiman's death, God rest his soul, we began to gain intelligence on the PEPS proposal. We were desperate. We saw the end in sight, the end of everything we'd fought for, the end of the human race. And we had no way to fight back. No way to get that trigger into the UN building.

"And then God responded to our prayers with a miracle. In the form of Naomi Aramovich's PEPS session. In the form of you, Eusebio. The Primal witness, who has the highest level security clearance to enter the UN building. This could not have happened, Eusebio, except that it was God's will."

I knew what he was going to say, but I had to ask it anyway.

"So what is it, exactly, that you want me to do, Yusef?" I said it as calmly as I could manage, trying to keep the quiver out of my voice.

"What you need to do, Eusebio, is insert the trigger into the cartridge, until you hear a click. Within moments, there will be a hundred kiloton nuclear explosion in the center of Manhattan."

"So let me get this straight." There was horror in my voice. "You're asking me to set off a nuclear bomb in the middle of New York. To kill millions of innocent people; torture millions more with radiation sickness; obliterate entire families, whole communities. You're asking me to turn people into dust; leave millions dying and vomiting blood with their insides rotting within them? This is what you want me to do?" The more I talked, the angrier I was getting.

"There's no need for the rhetoric, Eusebio," Yusef answered back softly. "There's no one you need to impress here. No Harry Shields. Nothing on the record. Just you and me talking about saving the human race. And, Eusebio, you don't need to tell me about the effect of a hundred kiloton nuclear bomb in New York. I know only too well. Much more, in far more detail, than you would ever guess. You didn't mention the massive tidal wave engulfing the coastal cities. Along with everyone else in my group, I've studied Baharraff and Singh's work in detail. And let me tell you, they didn't leave anything to the imagination."

"But why?" I cried back to Yusef. "What good will it do? How will all this devastation save our race?"

"Remember Columbus?" Yusef answered gravely. "Remember how the U.S. backed down because of the threat of an even worse nuclear explosion exactly one year later? That's what we'll be telling them after you detonate the bomb. They must agree to our demands or another nuclear bomb will explode. They won't know if we're bluffing or not, but they can't afford to take the risk. And our demands are very reasonable: publicly destroying all stocks of Isotope 909 and 919; allowing genetic enhancement without destroying the ability to know God; giving humans and Rejectionists democratic rights to autonomy in what they call the Believers' Belt. Allowing us all to live together in peace—d-humans, Primals, Rejectionists . . . "

Another pause. I was trying to process what Yusef was telling. To make sense of it. Yusef began again.

"If you don't do it, Eusebio, then all the struggles of hundreds of thousands of years, all the journeys we've taken as human beings to understand our place in the universe and to know God; all the human children still to be born, to be raised, and find their place in the cosmos; all the moments of love between a man and a woman, wonder at the color of a flower, awe at the creations of God, all the feelings of fear, love, happiness, the infinite complexities that our Lord created us to feel . . . all the past and all the future that has ever had meaning to you, Eusebio, and to me, and to every other human being . . . all that will become as nothing, Eusebio, if you reject what you have to do, if you allow the d-humans to put an end to the human race."

"I just don't know, Yusef. I really don't think I can do it. I hear what you're saying. But this . . . no, I really don't think I can do it. Not for anything."

Yusef didn't seem surprised in the slightest.

"Eusebio, have you heard of the word 'jihad'?"

"Yes, sure I have," I answered impatiently. "It's a Muslim holy war, warriors fighting in the name of Allah against the infidels and all that stuff."

Yusef shook his head slowly and smiled.

"Just as I thought. You have no idea of what jihad really means. It's the most important battle you'll ever have to fight; the most difficult struggle you'll ever face. And it's beginning right now. And the future of our human race will depend on you winning this struggle."

I thought he was talking about the struggle of the Rejectionists against the d-humans. I soon found out that I was totally wrong.

"The 'lesser' jihad is the one that you and all Westerners think of: the battle against the enemies of Islam. The 'greater' jihad is the one I'm talking about. It's the battle within yourself. Within each human being.

"You, Eusebio, have become a *'mujahid'*—a 'struggler.' It's a role placed on you by forces beyond our comprehension, ultimately by God. Remember that first day I met you, Eusebio, when I begged you not to take part in this PEPS session?"

As I nodded, I remembered it only too well.

"I wanted to give you every chance not to take part in this struggle. It has to be something you enter of your own free will. And that's what you chose, Eusebio. Now you have to choose whether to save humanity. I know that you will."

"I don't know that, Yusef, I really don't." I was terrified. About any scenario that I could imagine.

"Eusebio, if an evil man, like a General Tobo, was asked to detonate a nuclear bomb, he wouldn't have a moment's hesitation, would he? Or any other fanatic. But in your case, Eusebio, your very nature, which is good and humane, makes this struggle so much more difficult. What this means for you, Eusebio, is that once you've chosen to go ahead, it will be all the greater an act, because of the terrible struggle to get there. That's why the internal jihad is known as the 'greater' jihad. Once you've made the decision, the actual detonation is smaller on the cosmic scale than the act of deciding to do it."

I think I got the general gist. Basically, the more terribly I suffered, the better it was, as long as I ended up deciding to go ahead and blow the whole of Manhattan to smithereens.

By now, Yusef was done. He told me how he felt profound sorrow for me for the struggle I had to endure; but after this, I would find my soul in the upper reaches of Heaven for eternity.

And then, calling me "brother," he left me in what was already a living hell.

I didn't sleep a moment that night. I couldn't stay still. I couldn't sit. I couldn't stand. I kept pacing, pacing, pacing. I walked to the window. I'll tell you the truth. If you could open the damn windows in that hotel room, I would have taken the easy way out and jumped to my death. I already couldn't stand the hell Yusef had placed on me.

How could I be responsible for the death and suffering of millions? But how could I be responsible for the end of the human race? How could I make the right decision? How could I stand dealing with this for even one more moment?

I ordered another bottle of whiskey from the automated room service. But no matter how much I drank, it didn't seem to help. Nothing could touch the torment in my soul.

18 Llandovery

I saw a highway of diamonds with nobody on it

Naomi saw the next morning that I'd been suffering. She just had no clue what I'd been suffering about. And no idea how intensely.

But she was doing everything in her power to make me feel better. Perhaps she just thought the sensitive Primal was suffering from culture shock in the big bad world of the d-humans. She was putting on her warmest, irritatingly condescending voice.

She waited until we were in the Betelbar before she told me.

"Today's our last day of the session, Eusebio. You've done a great job. You did everything that we all hoped. You should feel so proud of yourself."

She could have no idea of the feelings shooting around my body. I was off the hook! It was over. It was out of my control. It didn't matter what happened. I didn't have to make my fateful decision. Yusef would have to try some other way to carry out his plan, but it wasn't going to be with me. I tried, with everything I could, to keep my face passive, not to show what was going on inside me.

"You must feel relieved, Eusebio, that we're finally coming to an end. We have one more virtual reality trip planned for this morning, and then a concluding session this afternoon. Then, tomorrow, when you're rested, I'll come round to your hotel room and we'll talk about what happens next for you."

At this point, I didn't give a damn what would happen next for me. My life was over, as far as I was concerned. The relief that I was off the hook for the fate of humanity mattered more to me than anything Naomi could tell me.

At least, I thought so. Until I heard what she told me next.

"The virtual reality trip we have planned for today, Eusebio . . . this will be a very special one for you. We're going to visit your daughter, Sally, and Gareth in their home in Llandovery. And your little granddaughter, Sara."

I thought I'd been through so much by now that nothing could touch my emotions any more. How wrong I was. I almost fainted at the notion of seeing my darling daughter, Sally, again. The tears welled up in my eyes. Before I knew it, before I could control it, I started sobbing, my body shaking, right there in the Betelbar. The other commuters, drinking their Betel juice, watched with curiosity at the bizarre image of a Primal sobbing in his chair. Not that I noticed them. All the terrible, pent up feelings of the past days, the mental agony of the previous night, the relief that I was suddenly off the hook for the fate of my race, all those feelings were suddenly siphoned into an overwhelming gushing of my love for that one person left in this world who meant everything to me. For my daughter, Sally. And for her two-year-old baby daughter, Sara. My granddaughter. I'd never seen little Sara with my own eyes. Just in a blurry picture delivered to me one day last year by one of our Outside Guides. I'd grown accustomed to the realization that I would pass from this world without seeing Sally again, without seeing my granddaughter, Sara.

And now, Naomi was telling me I'd be seeing Sally, Sara, and Gareth today. How could this be? Why was this happening?

As my sobbing began to calm down, Naomi touched me gently on my arm and kept explaining.

"Eusebio, everyone in the Primal Rights group felt you were being forced to sacrifice so much to fight for your race. We couldn't get your agreement in advance. So we wanted to give back to you something more precious to you than anything in the world. It didn't take much neurographic analysis to figure that out.

"We had to come up with a rationale that UNAPS would buy into. Well, that was fairly easy. As you know, Llandovery is a thriving community. We'd already visited Shaktigarh. So we argued it was reasonable to visit Llandovery as an example of a Primal community that worked."

I was trying to absorb this new information. I was literally stunned. For a moment, my thoughts of Sally and Gareth were flooding out the torment of Yusef's jihad within me.

"We'll be meeting the UNAPS district field supervisor for Wales," Naomi continued. "We've set it up as a routine UNAPS headquarters visit. As far as they all know, there are three UNAPS officials from New York who want to interview a successful family in a healthy Primal community, in their own home. Gareth's art has been getting increasingly popular, so it was easy to identify Gareth and Sally as the people we wanted to interview."

Naomi paused, and her face changed. A sternness invaded the warmth in her eyes.

"But there's something very important you need to understand, Eusebio. The UNAPS authorities were afraid that you'd 'lose it' when you saw Sally and do something unauthorized. The only way we could get them to agree was to add a PVA to your virtual reality set-up for this trip."

What the hell was a PVA?

"PVA, Eusebio, stands for Pre-Verbalization Analyzer. It's a special neurographic scanner that's less invasive than the one you've been wearing at the PEPS sessions. It's not analyzing everything you're thinking, only what you're about to say. If it figures you're about to say something that breaks the rules, it would simply cut off the virtual reality connections, and your VRU would go dead. Obviously, you don't want that to happen, so the one thing you must remember, during the visit, is to play by the rules. Don't get carried away emotionally. Just try to make the most of something very special to you. Enjoy the sight of your daughter you love so much. Enjoy the sight of your little granddaughter. And then, everything will go just fine."

These bastards have thought of everything. They get me check-mated before I even know I'm playing a goddam game of chess. But still, Naomi was right. She had hit upon the one thing in the world that still mattered to me. To see my precious Sally. My little granddaughter, Sara. I'd agree to just about anything for that.

* * * *

It's less than an hour later, and I'm getting into my "skin" for the virtual reality trip. My adrenaline is racing. I'm so excited at the thought of seeing Sally. I can hardly stand the anticipation.

As I start zippering up, a dreadful thought tingles the hairs on the back of my spine. I suddenly realize that, in every virtual field trip I've taken since the PEPS session began, someone's died. First it was Subrata. Then it was the Thomson gazelle. Then, it was little Sayyida. Was this some kind of omen? If someone were to die today, please, please, don't let it be Sally. Or Sara. Or Gareth. I pray to all the powers that have ever been. Gradually, the sense of dread passes, and I keep zippering up. It's too late to stop now.

I go through the usual initialization process—I'm a pro at this nowadays—and I begin to make out my new virtual environment. It looks like some kind of service station at the edge of a freeway. There are the VRUs belonging to the usual suspects—Naomi and Harry—and another person, in the flesh. She looks impossibly young and seems like she's bursting with bubbly energy. She's a d3-human. I can see that in a second: it's written all over her. She walks over to me and holds out her hand.

"Hi, I'm Peggy. I'm the UNAPS district field supervisor for Wales, and I'm so *thrilled* to make your acquaintance. I haven't been given your name, so I'm guessing you must be a very, very senior official in New York." She said this with a gurgling noise which seemed to be some version of a giggle. "Peggy Wainthrop," she added, as if belatedly realizing that if I was so senior, she'd better make sure I remembered her full name for future promotions.

We all got into the hoverpod waiting next to us.

"We're only about twenty kilometers away from the Primal community of Llandovery," Peggy told us, every word flush with enthusiasm. "As we get closer, though, you'll see the road is blocked by demonstrators. At that point, we'll take to the air and by-pass the demonstration."

"Demonstration? Who's demonstrating about what?" I asked Peggy. I was troubled to think of demonstrations taking place outside Sally's community.

"Oh, it's just the same old demonstrators from the APF."

She noticed my quizzical look and continued with a more detailed explanation.

"You know, the Anti-Primal Front. They heard there were some senior UNAPS officials visiting Llandovery today, so they organized a demonstration to get their point across."

"There's something called a PEPS proposal going around," Peggy confided in us, "which stands for the Proposal for the Extinction of the Primal Species. Perhaps you know more about it than I do. But from what I can gather, there are some serious discussions taking place about a permanent solution to the Primal problem." She shook her head. "I don't know, it seems a bit drastic to me. Some of the Primals are really very nice people when you get to know them. But the politics of it all . . . that's something out of my bailiwick!" With that, she gave another of her little giggles. She didn't seem to want to spend too much time on anything too unpleasant.

By this time, we were getting close to the demonstrators. As we approached them, our hoverpod raised itself from the road and began to climb into the air above the demonstrators. They saw us and let out a huge roar. Some of them shot out what appeared like fireworks.

"Oh no, it's the sky banners," groaned Peggy.

A moment later, I discovered what sky banners were. The fireworks blazed a path into the sky and then settled into easily readable words and phrases before they began to dissolve into the air.

There emblazoned across the sky, were the poisonous feelings of the APF, for all to see.

"Send the chimps back to Africa where they came from!" exclaimed one sky banner. I could see that Second Lieutenant Russell wasn't the only one who thought that was funny.

"Put the Primitive Primals in the Past!" Impressive alliteration, I thought to myself.

And then, a simple sky banner caught my eye, which sent chills through my body, all the way back in its cubicle in the United Nations building. It was short and clear.

"Support PEPS!" is what it said.

Why did that affect me so much? I guess, until that moment, the whole PEPS proposal was still something more theoretical than real in my mind. I'd gone through days of Harry and Naomi, on the record and off the record, evenings with Yusef placing me in the center of a moral hell. And yet, in spite of it all, it didn't seem to have anything to do with the real world. The world of people, humans, Primals, d-humans, actually living their lives. Now, here in Wales, where my precious daughter, Sally, and her family had their home, here was a demonstrator setting off a sky banner calling on people to "support PEPS."

The Proposal for the Extinction of the Primal Species was for real.

I had no more time for reflection. We were landing in front of the Great Hall of the Ancestors, where everyone would meet together on Ancestor Days. A shiver went through me as I saw it. Many, many years ago, when I was still so young, my love Sarah had spent her Year Away here in Llandovery, and in one of her letters that got through to me, she'd described the building to me. A beautiful, angular building made from the granite of the surrounding area, looking like a natural monolith rearing up out of the earth.

There was a man waiting for us as we got out of the hoverpod. He had graying hair and a neatly trimmed beard. Peggy introduced us. It was Bernard O'Malley, one of the senior councilors of the Llandovery Humanist Community. I'd heard of his name from Sally.

"Very pleased to make your acquaintance. We're privileged to have been chosen by UNAPS officials for your visit."

Bernard shook all of our hands with a calm strength. His voice was polite and serious. I felt that Sally was in good hands with people like Bernard in charge.

"The family you'll be meeting lives less than a kilometer from here. I thought you might enjoy walking to their home. It can give you a little feeling for our community."

And indeed, it did. We walked along neat, well-maintained houses. Everyone was whizzing by on some kind of silently-powered motorcycles I'd never seen before. I was struck by how prosperous and well-managed Llandovery looked, compared with our dilapidated community of Tuckers Corner.

Bernard appeared proud of everything around him, and he was taking the opportunity to share his pride.

"Every one of these houses," he pointed out, "is ninety-eight per cent energy efficient. Even here, in chilly Wales, we use up virtually no energy in our home environment."

As we turned a corner, there was a momentary overpowering smell of manure. Bernard smiled.

"Sorry about the odor," he chuckled. "That's a stage in our process of bio-gas creation from the manure of our farmyard animals and our own human waste. It's completely hygienic, don't worry. We create so much energy that, for decades now, we've supplied energy to the local grid and made some extra money that way."

I was amazed. It struck me that Sally had made a good decision when she left Tuckers Corner for Llandovery. I don't want to be disloyal to my home, but we spend so much of our limited resources buying energy from outside, and here was Llandovery actually selling it.

"In fact, there's so much demand for our farmyard products that we'd be the wealthiest community in the area if we were only allowed to sell them at market."

"Why the demand?" Naomi asked.

"It's part of the counter-culture movement going around Europe right now," Bernard explained. "Our farmyard produce comes from animals whose germlines have never been genetically modified." He smiled. "Primal chickens, pigs, and cows, if you will, just like the Primal humans. Well, there's been a recent upsurge in demand for this kind of 'Primal produce,' as it's known. It's almost impossible for people to find it anywhere, so they would come from hundreds of miles just to get some from us."

"So why aren't you allowed to sell it?" Naomi was clearly interested in understanding this. That empathy gene set never left her alone.

"European Federation regulations. It's against the law to sell any produce that doesn't meet a whole set of genetic health criteria. Ours doesn't even come close, because all the rules are based on modified germlines. Our food is perfectly healthy, but that's not the point for the Federation bureaucrats."

"So, your excess produce just goes to waste?" Naomi was asking with obvious concern.

Bernard chuckled again.

"I'll let you into a little secret, since you're not from the Federation, and I'm sure you don't give a whit for their bureaucratic rules. We have a little trick we use to by-pass their regulations. We allow outsiders to visit us for the day—we charge them an entrance fee and give them vouchers. Then, we give them our eggs, steaks, pork chops, bread—you name it—as gifts, and they give the vouchers back to us. That way, there are no laws being broken. Just a lot of gifts given by us because we're a generous community."

The more I heard, the more impressed I was by Bernard and Llandovery.

"Well, here we are," Bernard announced. "Here's the house of the Lewis family. Gareth and Sally. And little baby Sara. I'll take my leave now. Don't hesitate to get in touch with me if you have any questions later."

Bernard shook our hands again and walked back towards the Hall of the Ancestors. As he started walking, I heard him whistling a tune.

But my mind had no more time for Bernard. My adrenaline started pounding. I was looking at Sally's front door. I didn't need to go one step further to recognize it as belonging to Sally and Gareth. There were a couple of Gareth's kinetic sculptures in the front yard. And there were flowering plants and ivy growing neatly around the front door. I could see Sally's hand in everything around. Everything was pretty. Everything was cared for. Everything exuded love.

This was going to be difficult for me. I hoped I could handle it. I tried to steel myself.

Gareth answered the door. He looked great. Older and more authoritative than the last time I'd seen him. He was polite and courteous. His fame as an artist seemed not to have gone to his head, which had always been my only fear. He led us through to the living room. The house was warm, friendly. It was so filled with love.

And there was Sally. Sitting on the couch, playing with little Sara. My heart skipped more than one beat. I love her so much. I've missed her so much. I couldn't believe I was actually seeing her there. She was so beautiful. The young mother. A look in her face that had never been there before. A mother's love. But I'd seen that look before in someone else's face. In Sarah's. So many years ago. I tried to grab hold of my emotions before they went into complete meltdown.

Thankfully, everyone else was doing the polite introductions. Sally got up from the couch. So natural, so relaxed. Baby Sara hid behind the couch at the sight of the three strange VRU humanoids entering her little haven. When Sally shook my hand, I couldn't speak. I just tried to utter a polite sound and sat down.

Naomi and Harry started talking to Gareth about his sculptures, about his views on the Primal debate within the European Federation, about the Humanist community. As always, Gareth was strong and articulate. Sally was sitting next to him, her hand resting naturally on his leg. That was all I needed to see to know what I'd hoped and prayed for all these years. Yes, Gareth had been a good husband to Sally. He'd given her the love he'd promised. She loved and trusted him back.

It was just like those long evenings, years ago, back in Tuckers Corner when Gareth was at our house, wooing Sally. Only the roles were changed. In those days, I remember how Sally used to watch me talking to Gareth, wondering how I'd react to the news of their intended marriage. Now, I'm watching Sally watching Gareth, as he's talking to the UNAPS officials about his life. I see her pride in Gareth; I see her trust in him.

They're talking away, and gradually little Sara gets brave, just like her mother and her grandmother. She starts toddling towards us.

Suddenly I'm overcome by a desire. I must pick up my little granddaughter. I must feel her in my arms.

I'm remembering Naomi's rules. I can't blow it now. But I've got to feel my granddaughter in my arms.

"Excuse me, Mrs. Lewis, would you mind if I picked up your little daughter? I've got a granddaughter of my own back home, and I was just curious how a Primal toddler might interact with a VRU?"

I did it! Bizarre as my question might have sounded, I got it out without their neurographic PVA blowing my visit.

Sally was surprised. She glanced at Gareth, who gave her a reassuring look back. She looked over at me.

"Well, I guess so, as long as you're careful with her."

Oh Sally, if you only knew. I couldn't be more careful with all the jewels of the world.

I knelt down and talked to little Sara.

"It's OK, Sara," Sally said encouragingly. "Let the funny man made of plastic pick you up. Don't worry, Sara, he's a friend."

That was all Sara needed. She clambered towards me. She seemed just as fascinated by my VRU embodiment as I was by her. I got my way. I picked her up and cradled her in my arms. I felt her smooth, beautiful cheeks. I looked at her sharp, green eyes.

This was a moment I will treasure for eternity. A moment I never thought I would experience.

Pretty soon, Sara had had enough of the funny man made of plastic. She clambered down and ran back to her mommy, jumping on her lap.

"She's named after my mother, Sarah," Sally told everyone and no one in particular. "Only my mother's name had an 'h' at the end. My mother died when I was a little girl. I was raised by my father."

The tension in the room started escalating. Sally was up to something. Harry and Naomi could see that. But what?

Sally braced herself and tightened her body. She was summing up her courage. She looked at all three of us in turn.

"There's something I want to ask from you guys, but I don't know how to do it, so I'll just ask. A short while ago, less than two weeks, my father, Eusebio Franklin, disappeared from his home in Tuckers Corner in upstate New York. No one knows what happened to him. He just disappeared without a trace. We think it's possible that he missed us badly, because he lives alone in Tuckers Corner, and maybe decided to try to visit us here. But there's no way he could make it. He's a Primal, with no security chips, no ID, no passport, no money. Can you help us to try to find him? Everything's so regulated in your country, there's no way he could have gone very far without being picked up."

Sally's face softened and tears started falling down her lovely cheeks.

"I love my father. He's so special to me. We're beside ourselves with fear for what may have happened to him. You people can do something about it for us. Please help us find him. Please."

Naomi sneaked me a look. I was doing everything I could to control myself. Not a word.

"I'm so sorry to hear that this has happened to you," Naomi replied. "It must be terrible for you."

I knew that, however much she was concealing the truth, Naomi really did feel for Sally. She had that empathy gene.

"We'll do what we can," Naomi continued, "but I can't hold out a lot of hope for you. If it's already been this long, then it's possible something may have happened to him, and . . . " Naomi's voice just trailed off.

"He's such a special man, my father," Sally clearly wanted to get her point across. "In some ways, he seems so normal, so regular. And yet, he's really special. He's like nobody else. He's so true to something within him. He taught me how to be who I am."

There was a silence that filled the room to bursting point.

Sally broke the silence. "When we have another baby, it's going to be a boy, and we're going to name him after my father, Eusebio."

Another baby? A boy? I was reeling with shock and delight.

Naomi was intrigued. "How do you know, Sally, that it's going to be a boy? I thought, as Humanists, you don't do any genetic modification whatsoever?"

"Well, that's true, but here in Llandovery, we think it's OK to do gender selection. That's not really genetic modification at all. All it means is you get pregnant working with a clinic and choose your zygote as male. It's expensive for us. Even with Gareth's success with his sculpture. Most of the money he makes goes back to the community."

Sally looked over at Gareth with a warm, loving smile and caressed his leg.

"But we're saving up for it. Another two or three years, and we'll have enough saved to pay the clinic. I just really want to make sure that our next child is a son, so I can name him after my dad. Especially now that he's gone missing."

And that's when it hit me. Another two or three years. The PEPS proposal. Isotope 909. Those bastards are going to make Sally infertile. She's already had one baby. They're going to stop her having a baby boy. They're going to sterilize her eggs. They're going to stop me having a grandson called Eusebio. They're going to take away the dreams and happiness of Sally and Gareth. They're going to ruin a happy home. And they're going to do this to millions—no, billions—of Primals across the world.

I can't let them do this. I can't let them get away with it.

"Sally, have a baby now! Don't wait! Have it now!" I scream out at her.

But Sally never heard my screams. The neurographic PVA kicked in. Everything went black. Sure I screamed. I screamed into a black cubicle in the United Nations building in New York, disconnected from Llandovery. Gone. Disappeared. I screamed and I screamed and I screamed. I tore off my "skin." I pulled their goddam cords as hard as I could out of their circuits. I kicked anything electronic I could find with all my might. I screamed. I beat my hands against the walls of the cubicle. "Sally, have a baby now!" I screamed. "Don't wait!" I screamed. "You d-human bastards, I hate you!" I screamed. And nobody could hear the screams except me.

I sat down in the dark cubicle, and I wept and wept, and sobbed. And wept again. I remembered my fear, when I was putting on the "skin," not so long ago, that somebody would die in this virtual trip, just like every other one. And somebody did die. It was me who died. Something within me. Along with my unborn grandson who will never live. Never be born to suckle on Sally's breast; never gurgle "mama" and "dada." Never be taught little games by his big sister, Sara. Never learn about his grandparents from Tuckers Corner. Never grow up to emulate his father and do something special in the world. Never exist. Never even exist.

I thought of all the vibrant lives, the untrodden paths of generations of human beings, laying out ahead in the future. Paths with nobody on them. Paths that should be filled with joy and life and hopes and fears and love. Empty paths. Paths that will wither away into nothingness. Leaving the world for the d-humans to inherit.

And it was then and there, in the darkness, in the death of something inside my soul, that I made my decision. Yusef would have his way. I would find a way to get that PEPS session to continue until the next day. I would take his trigger. And I would blow Manhattan to smithereens. And give Yusef and the Rejectionists a chance to take our lives back again from the death of these d-humans.

* * * *

Naomi came rushing into my cubicle.

"Eusebio! Eusebio! Are you OK? I'm so sorry. I'm so terribly sorry. We should never have done this. It was a big mistake."

I just kept sobbing, ignoring her. Naomi came closer to me to try to put her arms around me and give me a hug. As she did so, an awful thought came into my mind, and I pushed her away. I was going to murder her tomorrow, along with myself and millions of other d-humans. I couldn't allow myself to be hugged by her. I had to keep a distance.

I was now going on instinct. "I'm not OK, Naomi. I'm sick. This has been too much for me. There's no way I can carry on with any PEPS session right now. I need to go back to the hotel room right away. Please, you've got to get me back there."

"Sure, Eusebio, of course. I'll get you back there right now. We can just hold our concluding session tomorrow. That's no problem. By then, hopefully, you'll be feeling better. I'm just so sorry this happened. Nothing in our neurographic models predicted that Sally would be planning to use IVF to have a baby boy in the future. It came as big a shock to me as it was to you. Oh, I'm so sorry."

I had to get away from Naomi. I couldn't stand her empathy, her caring. I was going to obliterate every trace of her in twenty-four hours. I had to close down all my feelings for her, all feelings from her.

"Naomi, I don't want to talk about it. Just get me back to the hotel room."

And so we went back. Naomi a little nonplussed by my refusal to accept her expressions of warmth and sympathy. Maybe she'll go back and get the programmers to add that to the neurographic model, I thought bitterly to myself.

Back in the hotel, I couldn't stand myself. A mass-murderer to be. I couldn't stay still. I couldn't exist any longer in my own skin. I'd made a decision, and I wasn't going to let the sickening doubts torment me like last night. I kept waiting and waiting for Yusef to show up. I didn't know how I'd make it through the hours. I kept looking at the clock, thinking half an hour must have passed . . . It had been one minute. Time has never moved so slowly for me. It seemed to have come to a complete standstill.

It was torture. Finally, I guess I dozed off for a while, since I'd had no sleep whatsoever the night before.

Out of the silence, I heard a familiar voice.

"Eusebio, are you OK?"

I looked across and there was the image of Yusef. The same warm, friendly face I'd seen the first day I began this torment.

"Yusef, what time is it?"

"It's mid-afternoon your time, Eusebio. I heard you came back early to the hotel, and I re-arranged things so I could visit you as soon as possible. Is everything OK, Eusebio?"

I explained that I'd made my decision and how I'd managed to delay the PEPS session one more day, just so I could carry out what Yusef wanted.

I expected him to be delighted. As always, I was wrong.

"Eusebio, I knew that you would arrive at the right place. I knew you had the strength and wisdom to succeed in your greater jihad. But I'm a little concerned . . . "

"About what?"

"About how you got to this decision. It has to be done for the right reason. I want your soul, Eusebio, to make it to the higher reaches of Heaven. Don't make the decision out of anger. Don't do it to get revenge on the d-humans because they'll be stopping Sally from having another baby. That's not the right basis for something so momentous."

I gained renewed respect for Yusef. I knew how overwhelmingly important this was for him, for the whole human race. And yet, here he was, trying to make sure I was doing it for the right reason! Yes, Yusef was for real.

"I'm doing it for the right reason, Yusef. I saw a path without a little baby Eusebio. And I saw a billion more paths. Paths that should be filled with life and joy. Paths with nobody on them. I'm doing it for all those paths. So they can be filled with human happiness again."

So Yusef told me the plan. Tomorrow morning, I would order my usual automated room service breakfast. On the tray, as always, would be a salt and pepper shaker. I should unscrew the salt shaker and there, inside it, would be the trigger. It would just look like a small, cylindrical piece of metal, the shape of a bullet, with a black surface. One end of the cylinder was curved and smooth. The other end was jagged, like a key. That was the end that needed to make contact with the nuclear device to detonate it.

I was to put the trigger in my pocket and go through the normal security procedures with Naomi when I entered the UN building. Yusef explained to me that the black coating prevented the device from being seen by their metal detectors, making it essentially invisible.

As soon as there was a break in the session, I was to tell Naomi I needed to go for a walk, to get some air. That I wanted to check out the roof garden one final time. Get in the elevator and down to the

133rd floor. There, follow the signs for General Conference Room CK-114. It would be down a hall and on the right. The door would be unlocked. It would just look like an empty conference room, with a table and chairs. I'd go to the side of the table facing the window. Feel under the surface of the table for the tubular steel that formed the table's legs. In the middle of the tubular steel, I'd feel a break in the metal, covered over by a ring. I'd unscrew the ring and slide it out of the way. The device was concealed within that tubular steel. At this point, I'd simply push the trigger into the open socket within the steel tube. I'd feel a click. Turn the trigger clockwise. I'd hear two beeps. Then I'd turn the trigger anti-clockwise. I'd hear two more beeps. And then, five seconds later, I would disintegrate into a massive nuclear explosion, along with everything around me. I would have saved the human race.

"I'm ready," I said with gritted teeth. "I'm more than ready."

Yusef looked at me with his eyes sparkling. Sparkling with what? Anticipation? Hope? Fear? "Eusebio, there's one more thing we have to think through. When you arrive at the PEPS session tomorrow, you have to avoid putting on that neurographic scanner. You won't be able to keep your thoughts concealed from it, no matter how hard you try. It will give you up."

"How do I do that?" I asked.

And once again, Yusef came up with a plan. A plan that involved one more stride of courage from me. One more attempt at subverting the usual PEPS session procedures. And one final chance, I thought to myself but I didn't tell Yusef, one final chance to make sure that what I was going to do was right.

Then it was time for Yusef to go.

"I wish I could hold you, my brother. I will never see you again. Either things will work tomorrow, God willing, or they won't. Either way, this is my last visit to you, Eusebio. May God be with you. May your soul rest for eternity in the special place of Heaven reserved for those great and righteous among us who have fought for the good."

And may I find Sarah on the other side, I added silently.

INTERLUDE 4

HARPER ATLANTIC MAGAZINE

February 2117

[Speech Fragment]
PHOENIX RISING

The following is an excerpt from a speech given last month by Juan José Gonzalez, the newly-appointed Chairman of the United Nations Governing Council. The speech was given to the leaders of the G26 nations, which incorporate over 95 per cent of global economic output, at the beginning of their quarterly meeting. Until last year, Sr. Gonzalez was President of Chile.

So we look around us, ladies and gentlemen, at the devastation wrought by nearly twenty years of war, which led to more deaths than all the previous wars of human history combined. Not to mention the multiple of those deaths from the famine and disease that resulted from the Great Global Wars. It would be easy to fall into despair at the radioactive wastelands that were once thriving cities, at the vast refugee camps, at the millions of Tobo clones now becoming pariahs throughout Africa.

But out of the ashes, a true phoenix arises. When we consider the future of humanity, there is more to be hopeful about than ever before. After other disasters in history, the words *"Never Again"* have been uttered sincerely, and yet every one of those same disasters did occur again. And again. And again.

So why is this time different from all other times? With the decision by nations across the world to give up part of their national sovereignty to the renewed United Nations, we now have a global governing authority with teeth. An authority with economic and military power, which can ensure that the breakdown and fragmentation of last century will not happen again.

But even this advance is just a small step compared with the Global Aggression Limitation Treaty, or GALT. The signing of GALT last year by every nation on this earth may be the most important moment in the history of the human race.

I cannot overstate the importance of GALT, the agreement by all of our world's nations to permit only human genetic modification that subordinates the two gene sets of "aggression" and "doctrinal belief." The Great Global Wars proved something all too clearly: technology had developed far in advance of our spiritual and psychological capabilities to manage it. We were careening out of control, destroying our world, and destroying ourselves.

Now, with GALT, we have finally managed to use humanity's awesome technological prowess to bring our cognitive capabilities to a matching level of responsibility. We have evolved, ladies and gentlemen. We have evolved our own species to a new level, one which is capable of handling the powers that our own scientific advances have given us. As a species, we are no longer like children playing with fire. We have evolved to adulthood, and we have ensured that, as we go forward, we won't burn down the house.

That is the great achievement of GALT. But of course, like all treaties, it is only through comprehensive monitoring and enforcement that we can rely on GALT to work. We must ensure that no nation ever fears that another nation is secretly planning to establish dominance through force, by creating a new generation of "genetic warriors." We can't allow the "genetic arms race" that took place in the late twenty-first century to happen again. It will be another fifty years until the new generation of GALT-compliant humans come into positions of power in our world. Until then, it is critical that GALT Enforcement is given the overriding power to ensure that every nation of the world complies with this all-important treaty. It is no exaggeration to say that the future of our world and of humanity is at stake.

For this reason, I have placed the issue of GALT Enforcement at the top of the agenda for this quarterly G26 meeting. The major powers of the world must all yield the key elements of their military strength to the centralized control of the United Nations. I am encouraged by the dialogue that has taken place so far, and with the shadow of the Great Global Wars behind us, I believe we are not far from succeeding in this supremely critical step.

But as we make these advances, let us not forget the less fortunate among us, those that are now increasingly referred to as "Primals." I am, of course, talking about the billions among us who have not yet had the opportunity to take advantage of any genetic optimization whatsoever, who are still subject to the historical diseases and frailties of our unimproved human condition.

As we focus our global energies on ensuring the evolution of our species to a higher level, it remains incumbent on us to care for and manage those who share our world with us, but who have not participated in any genetic improvements.

The Primals are becoming a global underclass, and we must do everything possible to make sure this does not become a permanent condition. Following the implementation of GALT, the next most important step of our global agenda must be to establish an authority, under the control of the United Nations, to ensure that the quality of life of the Primals does not continue to deteriorate. This is fundamental to the humane, caring approach to global governance that forms the foundation for the new United Nations.

We must encourage the Primals, with education and subsidies, to optimize their offspring, so their next generation can take advantage of the benefits our technology has provided to all of us sitting here today. At the same time, we must manage and police their internal strife, because we cannot permit the aggressive tendencies endemic in Primals to undermine our overriding goal for a safe and prosperous future.

To this end, I am proposing the creation of a new United Nations agency with a truly global reach. It will be called the United Nations Authority for the Primal Species, or UNAPS, and given full enforcement powers.

To emphasize the importance of this issue, I am proposing that the new UNAPS agency will report directly to me as the Chairman of the United Nations Governing Council.

Ladies and gentlemen, to be true to ourselves and our values, we need to make sure that the future can be as bright for the Primal species as it is for the rest of us. The phoenix is arising from the ashes. Let us not leave any of our human cousins behind as we progress towards a better, more highly evolved human race.

Chief Joseph

I've been ten thousand miles in the mouth of a graveyard
I heard ten thousand whisperin' and nobody listenin'

'm in a LAM. The same type that took us to Pannakot where I saw little
Sayyida gunned down. Naomi and Harry are sitting opposite me. Just
like the trip to Pannakot, they're in VRUs, staring blankly ahead.

I hear a friendly voice. It's Subrata Bammarjee. He's sitting next to me.

"And it would be such a wonderful thing if you would all come back to
my house for a taste of Bengali hospitality," he's saying. "Of course, it
would have to be a 'virtual' taste. My beautiful wife, Mumtaz, is known far
and wide for her home-made 'rasmalai.'"

I look over to Subrata. I gasp in shock. He's sitting there in person, but
his head is only partially connected to the rest of his body. So as the LAM is
moving, his head keeps rocking and swiveling off his neck, like a broken
puppet. His disconnected head keeps talking.

"I'm sure my distinguished guests must be enjoying the scenic tour," he
says with the usual cheerful irony to his voice. "Perhaps you can put in a
good word for me with the proper authorities back in New York? But you
should really enjoy the view! I understand that the honorable Mr. Franklin
next to me is going to make a very, very big explosion soon, and then there
won't be anything more to see!"

I look back at Naomi and Harry in fear. But they're still sitting there,
just staring blankly ahead.

At that moment, the cockpit door opens and a man walks out. I recognize
him immediately. It's the old tribesman with the deeply lined face who came
to me in Pannakot, after the huts were demolished in fire. Once again, he

utters his words to me with sorrow and suffering, pointing through the windows of the LAM:

"See! See what has been wrought on us! How do we endure? How do we endure?"

I follow his gesture and look out through the window. We're not far above the ground, and I see immediately where we are. We're in the New Jersey area, close to New York. The skyline of Manhattan is there, not far off, in the horizon. Below us are freeways, bridges, houses, shopping centers, car parks: a scenery of steel, glass and concrete.

Then, I notice movement. But it's not the movement of cars. It's a strange movement. The roads, the sidewalks, the asphalt, begin opening up in countless places, and raw earth starts spewing out of each of the spots. And then the most bizarre sight appears. People start crawling out of these holes that have opened up. They're not just any people. I recognize them from their clothing. They're native Americans from the Iroquois confederacy, which had been living in this region when the white man came. They're dressed in their traditional tribal costumes. Men, women, and even some children.

I turn back to the front of the LAM. To the old Pannakot tribesman. But he's not the tribesman any more. I'm looking at the face of Chief Joseph. It's a face that has seared itself deep in my soul. A face of courage, a face of humanity, but beyond everything else, a face of profound, limitless sorrow. Chief Joseph turns and walks into the cockpit. He closes the door.

And then I hear his words. I know they're his words because I've read and taught them to my students for so many years. But they're not in his voice. They're coming over the loudspeaker in the sterilized, monotone voice of the VRU automated translator that I've come to loathe.

"Brother, we have listened to your talk coming from the father in Washington, and my people have called upon me to reply to you.

"And in the winds which pass through these aged pines we hear the moaning of their departed spirits."

I look back out to the landscape. I realize that all the people climbing out of the earth are the ancient spirits of the Iroquois who died here, hundreds of years ago, fighting to keep their territory from the white settlers.

Chief Joseph's words keep coming through the loudspeaker:

"And if the voices of our people could have been heard, that act would never have been done. But alas, though they stood around, they could neither be seen nor heard."

What act was Chief Joseph talking about? Was he talking about my detonating the nuclear device? Or about the treachery of the white man? What act?

More and more Iroquois keep appearing from their burial spots. I realize they're all looking directly at me in the LAM. They're gesticulating to me, screaming to me, but I can't hear a word they're saying. Their faces are contorted with something. With anger? Desire for revenge? With what? What are they trying to say to me?

Chief Joseph's words keep intoning through the loudspeaker:

"Their tears fell like drops of rain. I hear my voice in the depths of the forest, but no answering voice comes back to me."

I look out again through the window. The Iroquois are trying to tell me something. Something incredibly important. They're all gesticulating, their hands curled up into fists. They're shaking their arms at me. I know they're either telling me to go ahead and detonate the bomb to give them revenge . . . or they're telling me not to detonate it, not to commit such sacrilege on their ancient burial places. What are they telling me?

And still the words of Chief Joseph keep coming:

"All is silent around me. My words must therefore be few. I can say no more."

And then there's silence. Naomi and Harry, in their VRUs, are still just staring blankly ahead. Empty vessels. The Iroquois outside keep trying to give me their message.

Suddenly, the LAM picks up velocity, gains altitude and begins to bank. I can see we're heading northwest, away from Manhattan. Subrata breaks the silence. Subrata, the broken puppet, with his head half-attached to his body.

"I'm sure my esteemed friend, Eusebio Franklin, will be so happy with our next stop. We're going to see his most special place, his friendly oak tree where his most treasured love resides."

A moment later and Subrata's narrative becomes true. There's Tuckers Corner below us. And there, down below is my oak tree in Jerry McHadden's backyard. The same beautiful, calm, peaceful oak tree. And standing by the oak tree . . . there she is. It's Sarah. My love. She's looking right at me. She's *trying to tell me something, just like the Iroquois. She's yelling at me. But I can't hear a word.*

She keeps trying, but she can see it's useless. And then she makes a gesture. She points to the oak tree. She looks back at me. She's trying to explain something to me. She keeps pointing to the oak tree.

"Sarah! Sarah! My love! What is it, Sarah? What?"

My own yelling wakes me up. I'm shaking, terrified, covered in sweat. In a moment, reality floods back into my mind. It's morning. Morning of the last day of my life. And the lives of millions of others. What did the spirits of the Iroquois want to tell me? What did the words of Chief Joseph mean? Why was Sarah pointing to the oak tree? Was she telling me that I would join her there today? Did she mean something else? Something entirely different?

Now I'm wide awake. The day of doom has arrived. I go to order my breakfast, along with the salt shaker that will hold within it the trigger of death.

20 The Trigger

Where black is the color, where none is the number

There it is. I unscrew the salt shaker. A little, black, bullet-shaped device falls out. Just like Yusef said it would. I put it in my pocket. My body lets out an involuntary shudder.

I'm putting on my best face for Naomi. Cheery, calm, but not too much. I tell her I'm looking forward to hearing from her what happens next, after the end of the PEPS session. I've got to keep any suspicion away.

We enter the UN building. The words of Naomi from that very first day, eons away in the past, have been ringing in my ears: *"You've been given a Level 2A clearance, Eusebio, just like me. That's the only way you can enter the UN building."* A Level 2A clearance. That means I just need to get through the metal detector, and Yusef told me that wouldn't be a problem.

We walk through into the lobby. My adrenaline is pulsing. The metal detector doesn't go off. We made it!

At least, that's what I thought. But then, before we get into the elevator, a Roboguard comes out of nowhere and a set of laser bars appear around me. I can't believe it's happening. How can this be? What went wrong?

Naomi is livid with rage.

"What are you guys doing with my Primal?" she's shrieking to the egg-shaped Roboguard. "He's Level 2A clearance. Leave him alone. He's been through enough."

"We apologize, Counsel Aramovich," the Roboguard responds in the same sanitized, automated voice of my dream last night. "Our sensory detectors observed an unusual level of metabolic activity in the Primal organism when he passed through the metal detectors. Therefore, this tripped the Status 7 alert for a routine body check."

"The hell with your Status 7 alert," Naomi retorted. "Let me show you my Veto Authority Level 2A, and then I want you to leave him alone. This Primal has been through more than enough stress already, and I won't allow a body search. Of course he has high metabolic activity when he's entering the UN building. It's ridiculous."

Just like that first day, when Naomi saved me from the Department Agents, she pulled out her PDA and a 3-D image of her certificate appeared, shining in front of us.

"Excuse me, Counsel Aramovich, while I authenticate your certificate," responded the Roboguard.

The egg-shaped robot put out an arm towards the certificate, and again, I heard some beeps.

"Your certificate is authenticated, Counsel Aramovich. The level of your Veto Authority, along with your vocal intensity, overrides the routine nature of the Status 7 alert. The Primal may proceed without a body search."

As if by magic, the laser bars disappeared. The Roboguard turned and rolled away without further ado.

Naomi was effusive in her apologies. "Eusebio, I'm so sorry for what you've undergone. I know you've been through too much already. I feel so bad for what we've done to you. But we had to do it. We had no choice."

Please, Naomi, stop! I was saying to her in my mind. Stop being so caring. You've just ensured that your life and the lives of everyone around us will be over a few short hours from now. Stop damn apologizing to me.

But I said nothing. We just got into the elevator and whizzed up to the 146th floor.

Harry Shields had his usual bored expression, along with his barely concealed disgust for my Primal existence. As he sat down nonchalantly in his prosecutor's chair, I kicked off my plan.

"Harry, I'd like to ask you something, before we begin this session."

"What's that, Eusebio?"

"How come you get to ask all the questions?"

He gave me his usual patronizing smile. Hadn't he learned anything from the previous day?

"Come again, Eusebio?"

"How come you get to ask all the questions?"

"Well, that's what this PEPS hearing is all about, Eusebio. I'm asking you questions as the Primal witness, and we're recording your answers and the ensuing dialogue for further analysis by the UNAPS authorities."

"But in a fair process, wouldn't I, as the Primal witness, have a right to ask you questions about the PEPS proposal? After all, it does affect me and all my fellow Primals." I turned to Naomi. "Isn't that true, Naomi?"

Naomi's brows furrowed.

"Well, to tell you the truth, I hadn't thought about it, but it would be consistent with the basic parameters of due process, as set forth in PEPS session 1-2, wouldn't it, Harry?"

"Well, I guess so, Naomi," Harry drawled back. He chuckled lightly to himself. "Well, what questions do you have, Eusebio?"

"Not so fast," I responded. "I'm talking about questions on the record."

"Sure, whatever you want, Eusebio. Take your seat, and ask away." As usual, Harry was underestimating what his Primal witness might be up to.

"No, you're still not getting it. You take that seat, with the neurographic scanner. I take your seat. There's no point asking you questions if you can just lie when you answer me."

Now, just like yesterday, Harry became concerned about where this was all going. But he was too late.

Harry puffed himself up.

"Now, I think we're getting a little carried away here. It's one thing if you have some questions to ask. But to put me in the neurographic scanner . . . that's getting a little absurd."

Naomi seemed to be enjoying the situation. Even she was guilty of underestimating what was going on. She actually smiled, and her voice had an ironic lightness that was a million miles away from what was going on inside my mind. That's why I couldn't allow myself to go anywhere near that neurographic scanner.

"Come on, Harry, what have you got to hide?" Naomi countered. "Why not let Eusebio ask you questions on the record? It would be good for due process."

So I got my way. That's the beauty of being a Primal in a world of d-humans. They always underestimate you, because to them, you're a lesser species.

With a few embarrassed guffaws and chuckles, Harry got up and sat himself down in the neurographic chair. Naomi showed me how the prosecutor's chair worked; where you turn on the neurographic screen to read the thoughts of the witness. Yes, the tables had indeed turned.

I began with a bunch of easy questions. Questions about his role in UNAPS, his background. Questions about the PEPS process. I was trying to use up enough time that it would be natural to take a break once this part of the session was over. I could see Harry was beginning to relax.

That's when I hit him with it.

"Where do you plan to use Isotope 919, Harry?"

Naomi intervened immediately.

"Eusebio, please! Stop with this 919 nonsense. I told you before, it's just a load of meaningless fear-mongering. We've researched it."

But I was focused on the neurographic screen. And I was watching for the same tell-tale signs that Yusef had taught me so many days ago. And there they were. All of a sudden, Harry started singing a song in his head. The lyrics were there to be seen on the computer screen. Some meaningless popular song. And then there was a barrage of hateful thoughts, about primitive Primals, and how Eusebio Franklin should know his place and stop going through this nonsense. Sure, he was good. He wasn't going to give the game away and let his true thoughts be seen. But it was enough for me. I could see he was hiding something.

"Where do you plan to use Isotope 919, Harry?" I repeated.

Harry was humming his song along while he replied in a thin voice.

"What's 919, Eusebio?"

"You know exactly what it is, Harry. Are you going to use it on the Believers' Belt?"

The intensity of Harry's singing increased on the neurographic screen. His hateful thoughts were speeding through faster than I could read them. And in between those thoughts were occasional fragments of other half-conceived thoughts, half-captured by the scanner: "not answer" flew through the computer screen, in the middle of all the white noise.

Harry turned to Naomi for help.

"Counsel Aramovich, can you please ask the Primal witness to behave himself appropriately. This is highly unorthodox."

"Eusebio," Naomi asked with increasing concern, "where did you come up with the phrase 'Believers' Belt'?"

"I got this message passed underneath my hotel door last night, Naomi." I could lie all I wanted, because I wasn't in the neurographic scanner. "It came in that same paper that disintegrated after I read it. It said: 'Ask about the Believers' Belt.'"

I'd seen everything I needed. I knew now, beyond any doubt, that what Yusef had been telling me was true. Harry was involved in the whole thing, and he was hiding the truth. It couldn't be clearer.

Harry turned again to Naomi.

"I've really had enough of this, Counsel Aramovich. It's an outrage. There's no procedure in any of our PEPS hearings that permits this breach of protocol." He pulled himself out of the neurographic chair. "Now, let's get back to our concluding session."

He was speaking sternly, trying to take back control.

"I do agree, Eusebio," Naomi said to me gently. "I think that's enough now. You've asked your questions, and now it's time to get back to our agenda."

This was my moment of truth. I spoke in a calm, quiet voice. I couldn't let them suspect anything.

"Sure, that's fine, Naomi. Thanks for letting me ask those questions. Now I feel much better. At least I got them off my chest."

I stood up meekly from the prosecutor's chair.

"Can I ask just one favor, Naomi? That was kind of exhausting, going through those questions. Can we take a quick break before we begin the final session? To tell you the truth, I'd love to take another look at the Sky Garden before we conclude the hearing."

"Sure, Eusebio, that's fine," came Naomi's predictable response. She turned to Harry. "That OK with you, Counsel Shields?"

"Yeah, that's just fine," Counsel Shields glowered back.

Yes! It worked! I'd made it through this first session without being in the neurographic chair. I'd confirmed for myself that everything Yusef had told me was true. I was going to save the human race. I was a *mujahid*. A warrior for humankind. I would take revenge for what they had done to Chief Joseph. And to all the millions, the billions of others. And I would keep our human race alive.

I walked out into the corridor. My heart pounding. The blood coursing through my veins so violently, I could hardly hear anything other than the "thud, thud" of my temples beating. These would be the last minutes of my life. And the lives of millions of others.

I got to the elevator bank. Hit the "down" button. Got into the first elevator that opened up. Looked for the button for the 133rd floor. It wasn't there! Shit. The first button was for the 100th floor, called Sky Lobby 2. I fumbled around and found the button to open the elevator back up. Stepped back out into the elevator area. Looked around. A couple of people passed by, looking at me with a patronizing curiosity. I guess they'd all been told about the resident "Primal witness."

"May I help you?" one of them kindly walked up to me and asked me.

"I'm trying to find the button for the 133rd floor," I told him.

"Sure," he smiled warmly, like I was his pet golden retriever. "Over on this side. See, these elevators will take you there." He walked down another corridor.

I hit the button for the right elevator. Thinking to myself, that kind man will be evaporated into atomized particles just minutes from now. No time for those thoughts. I've made my decision. I've got to save the human race.

This time, the elevator has a button for the 133rd floor. It stops there. I walk out. Take your time, I'm telling myself. Don't make any more mistakes. I look at all the signs. There it is. One of the signs says: "Conference Rooms CK 110-CK 120." That's where I gotta go.

I walk down the corridor, following the sign. There they are. General Conference Rooms. On the right hand side of the corridor. CK 120. CK 118. CK 116. There it is: CK 114. I open the door. Just like Yusef said, there's nobody in here. There's a table in the middle of the room and chairs all around it. I walk to the side next to the window. I feel the tubular steel under the surface of the table that forms the table legs. My heart is beating so fast, I fear I may have a heart attack right there and then. I can barely control my body. My hands are trembling. My arms are shaking. "Get control," I say to myself. I try taking some deep breaths. It barely makes a difference.

I can feel the ring that Yusef told me about. I start unscrewing it. It turns easily. Finally, it's fully unscrewed. I slide it out of the way. Yes, there's the space. I can feel the inside of the steel tube. Just like Yusef said. I take the trigger out of my pocket. Thumping, thumping, thumping heart. The end is so near.

I start to slide the trigger into the tube. I realize, for a moment, that what I want more than anything is for somebody to open that conference room door and stop me. For a Roboguard to come and laser beams to rise all around me. But nobody's stopping me. It's just me. Me and a hundred kiloton nuclear device. I keep sliding the trigger in. I feel a click. Now, I'm meant to turn the trigger clockwise, hear two beeps, turn the trigger anti-clockwise, two more beeps. And then, it's all over.

And then, Manhattan will dissolve into a nuclear waste. Millions of people will die instantaneously. Millions more will suffer a slow, tortuous death from radiation poisoning. Millions more will be swept away in a massive tidal wave. I'm saving the human race, I tell myself. I'm stopping Harry Shields and his mob from destroying the last vestige of thousands of generations of humanity. I've got to do it.

But I can't do it. I can't turn the trigger. My fingers won't move it clockwise. Turn it, turn it! I'm ordering my fingers to turn the trigger.

But they won't. My fingers are rebelling against me. My heart keeps pounding. I'm gasping for breath. I'm trying to take control of my own body.

I think about everything Yusef's told me. Everything I've seen. "Do it!" I tell my fingers. Do it for Subrata and Pesh. Do it for little Sayyida gunned down in her innocence. Do it for the humans in the future, so they won't be controlled in reservations by some future Ojimo Nkruma. Do it for my unborn grandson. Do it for Chief Joseph. Do it for the hundreds of millions who have died at the hands of the Western world. For the thousands of cultures that have disappeared. Do it for the billions of future paths that should be filled by humans, living, loving, fearing, caring, being human.

But my fingers wouldn't move.

I couldn't do it.

I couldn't turn the trigger.

No matter how hard I tried to control my fingers, no matter how hard I tried to think of all the reasons why I had to do it, my mind was filled with just one image. It was filled with the image from my dream. Sarah pointing to the oak tree. *My* oak tree. My totem. I knew now what Sarah had meant in my dream. Listen to my totem. Be my totem. My totem draws life from the soil around it; it absorbs sunshine; it remains firmly rooted in its place, until one day it will die from old age. My totem's branches bend with the wind. Its trunk remains solid. My totem doesn't massacre millions upon million of innocent people. Not for anything. Not even to save the human race.

I couldn't turn that trigger.

It slowly dawned on me that this just wasn't going to happen. I was simply not going to turn that trigger. No matter what I believed; no matter what I had decided. I couldn't do it. I stood there, with my fingers holding the trigger in the tubing. For how long—I don't know. Seconds, minutes. I don't know.

Then, on an impulse, I pulled the trigger back out from the tubing. I held it in my hand. I ran back to the elevators. Found the one that went up to the Sky Garden. Got into it. Up to the Sky Garden. I ran over to the edge, where I'd been contemplating the scenery on the first day of the PEPS session. Holding the trigger tightly, with all my force, I hurled it out over the edge of the roof, out into the air, away, away, down into the water below. Gone. Disappeared.

No nuclear detonation. Yusef's confidence in me had been misplaced. The Proposal for the Extinction of the Primal Species would go ahead. I was the wrong man for the job.

I hear a voice from behind me.

"Eusebio?"

It's Naomi's voice. Spoken with her usual gentle, warm tones.

"Eusebio, are you OK?"

The Soul

And it's a hard, it's a hard, it's a hard, and it's a hard
It's a hard rain's a-gonna fall

I turn to look at Naomi. Nothing more to hide. No more deception. I just look at her, straight. She's looking right back at me, the same, untroubled warmth in her eyes. I've got nothing to say. It's all done. It's all past. Now there's just me. Me and Naomi. Tears begin to well up in my eyes.

"It's OK, Eusebio. I think I have an idea of what happened."

I stare silently back at Naomi.

"See, I came up here to the Sky Garden to see how you were doing. But you weren't here. So I hooked into the ISV—the Internal Surveillance Video—with my PDA. It didn't take me very long to find you, making your way into that conference room. I saw you at the table. I saw you put that little piece into the steel tubing. And I saw you take it back out again. I think I've figured it out."

I keep staring back at her silently. How could she be so calm, so tranquil, if she had really figured it out?

"I think," Naomi continued, "that the Rejectionists have been getting to you. I think they were trying to get you to do something for them. I don't know what but something bad. A bomb, maybe. Some kind of terrorist attack."

There was nothing to hide anymore. I told everything to Naomi. Her eyes widened at first in shock at the scale of the plan. She obviously hadn't realized quite how close we'd been to total devastation. But as I finished, her face took on the kind, gentle look that I'd gotten accustomed to.

"Don't feel bad about it, Eusebio," her voice was surprisingly calm. "You didn't do it. You couldn't do it. I mean, you *really* couldn't do it. You don't think we'd have brought a Primal into the middle of Manhattan, into the UN building, who could have been capable of doing something like that, do you? Remember, Eusebio, I told you at the beginning. We ran all kinds of neurographic models on you before you were chosen. You were quite literally incapable of setting off that nuclear device. Your own gene sets for aggression and doctrinal belief are naturally subordinated in your CONDUCTER, in your neurogenetic structure. As well as a whole lot more complicated neurographic factors I can't even recite myself.

"Don't you see, Eusebio? That's why we chose you in the first place. Because you're a good person. You're a naturally good person."

But then something changed in Naomi's face. The kind, gentle eyes clouded over. She looked troubled herself.

"But, Eusebio, there is something I need to tell you. I can't leave it any longer. It's something that may cause you to hate me forever. I hope not. But it's important that I explain it to you."

Naomi pointed to a bench underneath some giant bamboo, whispering in the breeze.

"Let's sit down there, Eusebio, and I'll tell you what's really going on."

What was this about? I thought I'd finally gotten to the bottom of what was really going on. How could there be something more?

We sat down on the bench. Naomi took a deep breath.

"Eusebio, I'm not very good at lying or concealing things. So I'm not used to telling people something I've kept from them. Forgive me if I say it all wrong. But I'll just tell you, and that's that."

She looked at me intensely.

"Eusebio, that neurographic chair you've been sitting in from the first day of the PEPS session. It's a special kind of chair. It's actually unique. It wasn't just monitoring your thoughts on the screen, like most neurographic chairs. It was doing something much more important, much more profound."

I looked back at her, my eyes filled with questions.

"Eusebio, that neurographic chair was recording your soul."

"It was doing what?"

"It was recording your soul. You know 'Schumacher's smudge,' the original discovery made by Dr. Schumacher over a hundred years ago?"

"Of course I do."

"Well, Schumacher was right about that smudge. Right, but not completely. I'll explain in a minute. But he called it correctly. That smudge that he saw . . . it's the image of a human soul. And he was right about something else. A neurographically optimized d-human has no smudge. The neurographic picture is completely clear."

She was looking at me with these intense, quivering eyes.

"I don't have a soul, Eusebio, in the same way that you do. And the Rejectionists are right about one thing. We're fighting a losing battle. The PEPS proposal is going to happen, whether we like it or not. We've been playing for time, but we're not going to stop it. Nothing is going to stop it.

"Our Primal Rights group realized this a number of years ago. We felt like the environmentalists from the Age of Denial, who saw that nothing they could do would prevent the extinction of thousands of species from our world. So what did those people do, Eusebio? What did Alison, Dr. Schumacher's wife, do?"

"They collected genetic samples so they could be re-created some day in the future."

"That's right, and they were re-created," Naomi responded, "as you saw in the Kelly Hendrick Game Reserve."

"So," she continued, "we teamed up with some of the leading neurographic researchers at the top universities in Europe, China, and the United States. These researchers have been spending decades analyzing those 'Schumacher smudges.'" And they've made great progress. They're the ones who developed the neurographic chair you've been sitting in. They created the first ever machine capable of recording the Primal soul.

"And that's what we've been doing with you, Eusebio. We had to record your soul through a wide range of different emotions, different states of consciousness, to do it properly. We had to get you to talk about the American Indians, the Aboriginals, all that's special to you, to record your love of those things. We had to get you to talk about the destruction, the devastation caused by the rise of the prefrontal cortex, to capture your anger. We had to capture your fear, your sense of victory, your fatigue, your courage, your sense of right and wrong. Each of those elements of consciousness had to be mapped out in order to get a full recording of your soul."

My anger would have been so much greater if I hadn't already been emotionally exhausted by my abortive attempt at the nuclear detonation. Even so, with whatever remnants of emotion left in my being, I felt angry. Deceived, betrayed. How could they do this to me? How could they try to capture my soul? It occurred to me that I now understood that beatific look I'd seen on Naomi's face when I'd be talking about things that meant everything to me. She was so happy, because she was getting her damn recording done. Recording my soul. Capturing my soul.

"So you've recorded my soul?" I couldn't think of anything else to say.

"Yes, the machine worked. The researchers are delighted at how well it worked."

I felt such a bitter resentment. Such betrayal. Yes, perhaps Naomi was right. How could I not hate her after this?

"What are you going to do with this recording?" I asked bitterly.

"That's what I'm going to explain to you, Eusebio. Researchers have studied the Primal soul for decades, and we now have some understanding of it. Dr. Schumacher was right. Out of the primordial life that first evolved billions of years ago on this Earth, relationships existed between different strands of DNA, which have increased in sophistication but maintained the same essential form ever since. Like the notes of the orchestra, as Schumacher described them. Since Schumacher's time, we've developed the technology to map out the relationships, identify which of the billions of strands of non-functional DNA lead to the overall creation of the Earthly soul. And just like Schumacher predicted, when you manipulate the

DNA for genetic optimization, these relationships get altered; the music stops; the Earthly soul disappears.

"What do you mean—the Earthly soul?"

"Well, Eusebio, what Dr. Schumacher missed, because he was so focused on the tyranny of the prefrontal cortex, was that there's another soul, the Infinite soul, which comes directly from there, from the prefrontal cortex.

"It's called the Duality of the Soul, Eusebio. Basically, you have two souls. In layman terms, you can think of them as the Earthly soul and the Infinite soul. Or even more simply, you can think of one as the "spirit" and the other as the "soul." It's the same thing. Schumacher's smudgy-looking image represents the Earthly soul. But there's another image Schumacher never saw, because his equipment was too primitive. It's a squiggly, wavy line, and it represents the Infinite soul. A chimpanzee, or any other animal for that matter, has the Earthly soul, but not the Infinite soul. I have the Infinite soul but not the Earthly soul. And you, a Primal, you have both."

"The truth is, Eusebio, that Julius Schumacher was right about the prefrontal cortex. It's unstoppable. It's the vehicle that pulls us to the infinite, and it's going to keep going until we reach there. It's the pull of our life force to get back in touch with abstraction, with infinity, with the original source of the universe."

I'd had enough.

"Naomi," I said, "why should I care about any of this?"

"I'm explaining to you, Eusebio, why we had to record your soul, your Earthly soul. Because the drive of the prefrontal cortex to reach the infinite is inexorable, and it's rapidly accelerating. I'm a d3-human, but already they're coming up with d4-humans. By the time the Primals are extinct, two hundred years from now, the very form of what we think of as human will have disappeared. Our very existence will become a gigantically optimized algorithm, perpetuating the Infinite soul in a form we wouldn't even think of as human. That's Dr. Schumacher's tyranny of the prefrontal cortex, carried to its ultimate degree."

Naomi stopped and took a deep breath.

"Our Primal Rights group realized, Eusebio, that unless something was done now, the Earthly soul, the spirit, the form of human existence from time immemorial, was going to become extinct. All that would be left would be the Infinite soul.

"We felt, Eusebio, that would be a terrible tragedy of cosmic proportions. Four billion years of life on this earth would be left behind for something else, something infinite and universal, but which has nothing to do with this Earth. We had to stop it. But stopping it, Eusebio, was something we couldn't do. It was like throwing ourselves in front of a bus. There's an inexorability to this that is out of all of our hands.

"So we came up with a different approach. Instead of throwing ourselves in front of the bus, we decided to hitch a ride on the bus. We spoke with the leading neurographic researchers and came to the conclusion that the only way to save the Earthly soul was to record it. And once it was recorded, it could be incorporated into the algorithms for future neurographic optimization, so that wherever the prefrontal cortex takes us, the Earthly soul will be there, along for the ride.

"But we didn't want to record just any soul. This was a momentous step we were taking. It would affect the very nature of what we now think of as human existence all the way out into the infinite future. We had to choose that soul very carefully. And given the speed of the PEPS proposal, we had very little time. That's how we came up with the idea of these PEPS hearings, Eusebio. And that's how we found you."

My head was reeling. I couldn't digest what I was hearing.

"So Harry Shields, that bastard Harry Shields . . . " I paused in confusion.

" . . . wasn't prosecuting anything," Naomi finished my sentence for me. "He's trying just as hard to save the human soul as I am."

I was shocked into silence. My mind spinning round and round.

"You should be very proud, Eusebio. I know, it's not in your nature to be proud, and that's one of the many reasons you were chosen. But you have every reason to be. Your Earthly soul will achieve an immortality that has never happened before in history. All the great Primals of the world, from Alexander the Great to Julius Caesar to Napoleon, you name it, all of them spent their lives seeking immortality. And now you, seeking nothing at all other than to be back with your love, Sarah, you are the one whose soul will achieve an immortality that goes beyond our imagining. It will be digitized and incorporated in the next version of d4 neurographic optimization and then all versions beyond that. Your soul will be imprinted on every part of our future, wherever that future takes us."

"I just don't know. I really don't know." I was shaking my head. "Why my soul? It makes no sense."

"Because, Eusebio, it's not just your soul in isolation. What's special about you, Eusebio, is the way you've absorbed and harmonized the patterns of so many other souls from the past. Just like Dr. Schumacher explained, each person's soul is ultimately the result of billions upon billions of other souls, human and animal, that have existed through the millennia. Your soul contains these other patterns within it. It contains part of Chief Joseph, part of Sarah, part of little Sayyida. It contains the wise Aboriginal you quoted the other day, saying 'White men just came up blind, bumping into everything, putting up a flag.' It contains orchestral notes from millions upon millions of Primals over the generations, who have loved and suffered and fought for what they cared about. It contains the song of the birds, the fearful courage of the cheetah, the wisdom of the elephant, the loyalty of the wolf, the serenity of the sea turtle. Your soul is the orchestra that Dr. Schumacher described. It's harmonized every note it absorbed from somewhere in your earthly heritage. And that, Eusebio, that soul, is what we've recorded, so it will never be lost, even after the extinction of every Primal being from this earth."

Well, Naomi accomplished one thing. I didn't hate her after all.

22 The Requiem

And what'll you do now, my blue-eyed son?
And what'll you do now, my darling young one?

So what do you do when you had the chance to save your own race and you threw it away? What do you do when you'll never see those you love again? When there's no going back to the home where you've spent every day of your life? What do you do when you're a lone Primal in a society of d-humans? What do you do when your soul's been recorded?

I guess you just fade away.

It wasn't like that at first, though. After my failure to detonate the nuclear bomb, it seemed like every division within the Department of Homeland Security wanted a piece of me. A piece of my brain, that is. I spent endless hours with an MNI strapped around my head while they retrieved from my brain pictures of Yusef, the names of his family, all the details of our conversations. There was nothing, no matter how small, they didn't dig out of the recesses of my neurons.

Finally, Naomi got me away from the clutches of the Department. She told me that the trail on Yusef had gone completely cold. There was no one called Yusef, no one who even looked remotely like him, teaching at the University of Peshawar. There wasn't even a department of comparative linguistics there. They'd checked out every family in the area with a wife called Yasmina, every undergraduate student in Nanogenetics at the University of Peshawar, every daughter called Ishmalia, and every twelve-year-old called Ibrahim. And they'd come up with nothing. I was secretly, profoundly grateful that, having failed Yusef in the ultimate jihad, at least I hadn't betrayed him, and he still had the chance to keep fighting for the human race. Unlike me.

And Naomi, with her good grace, has done everything in her power to make life bearable for me. I'm given a stipend that allows me to live a comfortable life in the d-human world. She even took me on house-hunting expeditions across the United States. We flew on her sky-car to California, Florida, Arizona. In the end, I chose a place in Westchester County outside New York, just so I could be closer to my real home in Tuckers Corner.

As the months have dragged on, I've gotten used to the curious, half-concealed looks from all the d-humans as I walk around in their shopping centers. Yes, that's right, I'm a freak. A Primal living in d-human society. At first, I'd feel aggressive with them. Now, I barely even notice.

Just like every other member of modern society, I've become addicted to the wonders of virtual reality. I spend hours going virtual scuba diving deep beneath the waves in tropical coral reefs. I go on virtual mountain climbing expeditions that I would have never imagined possible. I make virtual visits to the great, restored national parks and nature reserves around the world, all the while thinking about Ojimo Nkruma and his algorithm.

And, yes, I once tried their virtual sex, too. It was an experience beyond my wildest dreams, where they discover fantasies in your mind you don't even know you have, and they sweep you along in a wave of ecstasy.

Just once. Because, after all that ecstasy, when I pulled off my virtual "skin" and came out of the cubicle, I found myself alone in my Westchester County house, and I kept looking around for Sarah, but I couldn't find her. I have never felt so alone as I did in that moment. I wanted to caress her cheeks, to feel her hair on my lips, to look deeply into her eyes. I wanted to feel the warmth of her body and her heart beating next to mine. I wanted to touch her thigh, and whisper to her how much I loved her. But there was no Sarah. Just an empty, automated, suburban d-human house with nobody in it other than the Robomaid and me. And I missed Sarah so much at that moment that my heart ached like it had never ached before. I sat down on a step while my sobs shook my body. "Where are you, Sarah?" I called out, but there was no answer. Just the Robomaid turning up and asking if she could help with anything.

No, there was nothing the Robomaid could help me with.

One day, last month, a couple of slick-looking types turned up at my door.

"Are you Eusebio Franklin?"

"Yes."

"There's something important we'd like to discuss with you."

So I let them in, and we sat in my living room. Karl Schoenfeld and David Kroll, I was told. Those were there names.

"You see, Mr. Franklin," Karl started telling me, "we're from Vireon Incorporated. The NVRX division of Vireon . . . "

NVRX. Memories of the PEPS session, of Reflecting Water, of Warrigal Killara, came flooding back into my mind.

"So what do you want with me?" I was already annoyed by this slick team.

"Well," Karl continued, "we're here because we have a proposition for you. See, the R&D people, they do advance research to find really cool neurographic experiences already recorded, with the idea of turning them into a new NVRX. We patent the NVRX and the person who had the original experience gets the royalties. A really good NVRX pack can sell hundreds of millions nowadays."

"Now," David Kroll took his turn, "the R&D team came across in the UNAPS archives the neurographic recording of your PEPS hearings a while back. It's really something else. It's out of this world. It's an experience we think millions of people are going to want to re-live virtually. Such an exciting story. Saving the Primal race. Standing up to the UNAPS prosecutor. And then, the real slam-dinger is this attempt at blowing up Manhattan with a nuclear bomb. It's a real winner."

Karl nodded emphatically. "Yeah, it's gonna make it big. It's an NVRX that everyone's gonna want to have."

"So we talked with UNAPS," David Kroll continued, "and they put us in touch with someone called Naomi Aramovich. Now, she told us that, even though you're a Primal, you've got the same rights to privacy as the rest of us. So, that's great news for you, Mr. Franklin. There's big bucks on the way to you, because the royalties for this thing could be out of this world."

"Wait a minute," I blurted out. I thought I was beginning to get the hang of what they were saying. "You're trying to tell me that you want to take my recorded neurographic experiences and patent them, and market them across the world so every Tom, Dick, and Harry can get a cheap thrill and experience what I went through during those PEPS sessions? Is that what you're trying to tell me?"

"Sure thing, Mr. Franklin," Karl responded with a big smile on his face.

"Get the hell out of my house! Get the hell out of here! I never want to see you again."

I hadn't been so angry since the PEPS hearings. I started to shoo them towards the door. As I was opening the front door to get this filth away from me, David Kroll spoke up.

"We're so sorry about how your wife died, Mr. Franklin."

I was taken aback.

"You're what?"

"It's such a tragic thing," Karl added. "That your wonderful wife could have lived a long life, that she could be here with you right now, but your little community just didn't have the funds to pay for her cure." He shook his head in a sickeningly insincere expression of regret.

I was ready to punch them both in their faces. But I wanted to understand what the hell they were getting at.

"What are you talking about? What does my wife have to do with any of this?"

"Well, Mr. Franklin, we understand that you're not interested in the money. It just seems like such a shame, though, for your community. See, right here we've got a document that would take all your royalties and put them into a trust fund for Tuckers Corner, and all the other Humanist communities around the world. For special needs, like when someone gets sick and they can't afford to be cured.

Things like that. Things that could save their lives, make them happier, give them what they need to keep their communities going."

David Kroll shook his head. "It's such a shame that all your Humanist friends, your family, all those people you care about, that they'll never get the funds you could have provided to them."

Those bastards had me wrapped around their little fingers. We went back into the living room. I'd already managed to throw away my chance of saving the human race. I wasn't going to give up the chance of saving my own community from bankruptcy, of saving the lives of other people like Sarah who needed money for d-human technology to cure their cancers. I couldn't do that to my own people. For what? For a principle? For my privacy? I was already gutted and opened to the world. My very soul had been recorded. What the hell did my privacy mean anymore, anyway?

I had Naomi check over the contract to make sure I wasn't getting ripped off. All royalties would go into a trust available for Tuckers Corner and the other Humanist communities. Naomi volunteered to visit Tuckers Corner in her role as a Primal Rights activist to tell them that an anonymous benefactor had created this trust for them. I got a brief but profound moment of pleasure when I thought of what that would mean for the only people I cared about in this world. But what a price to pay. It sickened me to think of the suburban adolescents I saw around me in the shopping centers telling each other:

"Have you checked out the new NVRX? There's this chimp who's working for the Rejos, and he's about to nuke the whole of Manhattan. Then he finally chickens out. It's really cool."

But if this final humiliation can save the lives of those I care about, and their future generations, then so be it. Let it roll. I think of the great warrior, Sitting Bull, who finally surrendered to the U.S. Army at Fort Buford in 1881. Four years later, Sitting Bull left the reservation to join Buffalo Bill's Wild West show, earning $50 a week for riding around the arena, plus whatever he could make from his autograph and picture. Well, I guess if a great chief like Sitting Bull could do that, then so could I.

But it's Chief Joseph that I feel closest to. Chief Joseph, who never gave up the desire to return to the land of his ancestors. Chief Joseph, who said: *"It makes my heart sick when I remember all the good words and all the broken promises."* Chief Joseph, exiled from his land until his dying day, and when he died, his doctor said that he died of a broken heart.

So where does that leave me? My song is over. I'm ready for the end. Even if I have to finish it myself. Now I've written this book, there's nothing further for me to do. I've received a solemn promise from Naomi that, when I die, she will personally ensure my ashes are poured on a rainy day around the roots of my totem, my oak tree, so they can merge as closely with those of Sarah as is materially possible in this world that I know.

And now I'm preparing for the end. It will be soon. I feel it.

Chief Joseph visited me in a dream last night. He was up in the sky, looking down at me, his fierce face showing the courage and pain of one who looks directly at the loss of everything that has ever held meaning for him and his people. Then, tears started falling from those courageous eyes. And the tears turned into rain. Gentle rain that fell on to my oak tree, just like the afternoon of my Vision Day.

I think it's a sign that my time has arrived. And now, my mind glides towards the reality of death. My consciousness glimpses it for a split second and then shies away. I think of Dr. Schumacher's description of the symphony of the soul, of the billions of notes that hover in the spaces between our DNA, the music of hundreds of millions of years of evolution. The billions of notes that dissipate at the end of a life's symphony and re-form with billions of others to create new souls, to regenerate life in countless forms. So, I ask myself, what is death other than just a change in form, a change in the music of the soul?

And then I think of the digitized future that Naomi described to me that day in the Sky Garden. The extinction of the human race. The end of those fuzzy images, those Schumacher's smudges. An extinction that I permitted because I couldn't turn Yusef's trigger, and wreak death and suffering on millions upon millions of people. And I think of the decision of her Primal Rights group, not to throw themselves in front of the bus, but to hitch a ride on it. To record my Earthly soul and, thereby, to infuse the abstraction of the Infinite soul with the earthly music of the Yanomami, the Aboriginals, the Bushmen, the billions of humans who have tried to make some sense of their lives on this earth, the untold numbers of other creatures who have all played their parts in the gigantic symphony of this world. A symphony to be digitized and re-mastered in the future forms of human existence.

And I realize that, if Naomi's plan works, then in the end, it's a never end, it's an ever after, it's an immortalization of all the meaning that has ever existed on this earth, even after we humans are finally extinct. It's the eternal requiem of the human soul.

But for myself, I think I have lesser needs. I don't really care about the immortalization of the soul. Just like I didn't really care about being in Yusef's eternal Heaven among the most righteous. No, what I care about is that when I die, some of the notes of my soul meet up with those of Sarah's soul, with the notes of Chief Joseph's soul. And that in some future, living being somewhere in our Earth, in an eagle, an oak tree, a rat, or a beetle, that our souls will make music together. If that were to happen, that's more than enough for me.